Stol

Note from the Author

This book is set in the town of Hereford in the United Kingdom. It is a town of about 60,000 people and is in the West Midlands. It borders Monmouthshire, which is in Wales.

Hereford is famous for its being the home of Strongbow cider and the Hereford Bull.

It is also the base for the SAS. The SAS are the elite Special Forces unit of the British Armed Forces. The unit undertakes a number of roles including covert reconnaissance, counter-terrorism, direct action and hostage rescue.

Hereford Cathedral dates from 1079 and houses the largest Mappa Mundi in existence, which dates from 1300.

It is a market town and has a large mix of Tudor, Victorian and new buildings.

I hope you have enjoyed this brief history.

Fortis Security, Book Two

Maddie Wade

Published by Maddie Wade, September 2016

This is a work of fiction.
Any similarities to real events, people, or places are entirely coincidental.

First edition, September 2016
Copyright © 2016 Maddie Wade

Written by Maddie Wade

Acknowledgments

I would like to thank Crystal Cuffley of *Rockin' Redhead Promotions* for the wonderful cover and editing.

I would also like to thank Matthew Parsons for the technical help.

My wonderful beta readers who have picked up the blips and told me when things suck!

Greta Branas for helping with a name for Nate's Mum.

Dedication

This book is dedicated to my wonderful family, who put up with sandwiches for tea, when I am busy writing. Also my lovely mum who has always supported me.

I love you all so much.

Stolen Dreams

Glossary

The Divine Watchers: A rich, evil cult who believe that people with special abilities will save the world. They wish to control gifted people and cause Armageddon to cleanse the world so they and the gifted can rule.

NHS: The National Health Service is the publicly funded healthcare system for England. It is the largest and the oldest single-payer healthcare system in the world.

Boot: Trunk

Parachute Regiment: The Parachute Regiment, colloquially known as the Paras, is an elite airborne infantry regiment of the British Army.

S.A.S: The Special Air Service (SAS) is a Special Forces unit of the British Army. The SAS was founded in 1941 as a regiment, and later reconstituted as a corps in 1950. The unit undertakes a number of roles including covert reconnaissance, counter-terrorism, direct action and hostage rescue

Cockney wide boy: Wide boy usually refers to a working class male who lives in London, and who lives by their wits and wheeler dealings

Mi cielo: Spanish term of endearment meaning my sky/heaven

Carazon: Spanish term of endearment meaning *heart*.

Cwmbran: Cwmbran is a town in South Wales and is in the County borough of Monmouthshire.

Mucka: Urban Slang for friend.

Mulyutka: Russian for *little one, babe, baby*

Toff: A rich or upper class person.

Charlie: Cocaine

Tidy: Slang, Okay, good, I agree

The Shard: The Shard, also referred to as the Shard of Glass, Shard London Bridge and formerly London Bridge Tower, is a 95-storey skyscraper in Southwark, London, that forms part of the London Bridge Quarter development. Standing 309.6 metres (1,016 ft) high, the Shard is the tallest building in the United Kingdom

Plaster: Bandaid

Slag: An individual who cares not for relationships beyond the realm of the sexual, these people sleep with many partners not caring about anything save for the moment of climax

Table of Contents

Note from the Author

Title

Disclaimer

Acknowledgments

Dedication

Glossary

Table of contents

Prologue

Chapter One

Chapter Two

Chapter Three

Chapter Four

Chapter Five

Chapter Six

Chapter Seven

Chapter Eight

Chapter Nine

Chapter Ten

Chapter Eleven

Chapter Twelve

Chapter Thirteen

Chapter Fourteen

Chapter Fifteen

Chapter Sixteen

Chapter Seventeen

Chapter Eighteen

Chapter Nineteen

Chapter Twenty

Chapter Twenty-One

Chapter Twenty-Two

Chapter Twenty-Three

Chapter Twenty-Four

Chapter Twenty-Five

Chapter Twenty-Six

Chapter Twenty-Seven

Chapter Twenty-Eight

Chapter Twenty-Nine

Chapter Thirty

Chapter Thirty-One

Epilogue

Sneak peek

Thanks

Social Media links

Stolen Dreams

Fortis Security

Prologue

Nate Jones walked past the football stadium on his way to see his fiancée. It was early autumn and he could smell the sweet scent of apples from the cider factory across town. Every year that smell of apple pie signified the start of autumn.

He loved this time of year; it was cooler, and everything seemed calmer. The hot summer nights had cooled, the kids were all back to school, and life quieter as if everyone was taking a breath before the madness of Christmas began.

He wasn't thinking about any of that right now, though. Nate was wondering how he was going to break the life-altering news of his diagnosis to his fiancée, Nikki.

He hadn't worn a jacket as the air had been relatively warm earlier, but now the wind was picking up. He tucked his hands in his pockets as he crossed the busy road by the football ground.

You couldn't really call it a stadium. He was more of a rugby man himself, but he had admired the way the fans had stepped up to keep the football club going after the last owners had run it into the ground. He and Nikki had even gone to a few games. She was big fan.

He knew what he had to tell her would upset Nikki. She wanted everything in life to be perfect ... and now he wasn't. He had been pretty upset, too, but he was sure they could get through this together. They just had to figure out a way to move forward. Maybe they could look at some different treatments? That was what commitment was about, he thought. Figuring out the tough stuff together.

So why was he feeling so unsure of the future? Why was his heart pounding so hard? It was just shock, he reassured himself, it, would be fine. His parents had gone through some really tough times and they were like newlyweds half the time.

His mum was a force of nature. She was the kindest, strongest person he knew. Always there with a wise word or a tongue-lashing if you needed it. Even now, at 32yrs old, he wouldn't dream of swearing in her presence and neither did anyone else.

She was from a province in Castile-La Mancha, in Spain, called Cuenca. She was a practicing Catholic and had raised her children that way, although Nate was very much lapsed. His parents had met when his father had gone out there for work. From all accounts, it was a whirlwind romance. They had married and moved back to his father's native Wales soon after.

Nate had been brought up speaking English and Spanish in equal measure, so he was fluent in both. His mother had felt it was important for her children to know and embrace their Spanish roots and had often spoken only Spanish to them.

His parents were the best and had always had his back. He wasn't sure if he was going to tell them this latest news, yet. He didn't want to worry them.

As Nate crossed behind the Courtyard Theatre and walked around the back of the garages, he thought about Nikki. She had seemed off lately and he couldn't put his finger on why. He wondered, not for the first time, if maybe he was making a mistake by ignoring his mum's cautious words about her commitment to him.

Mimi Jones possessed an innate sense for spotting a person's true nature and he had followed in her footsteps It was very rare for him to be wrong about someone. Nobody was infallible, though.

No, he was being paranoid. Nikki would support him and they would be fine, he knew it.

~~~

Nate used the key Nikki had given him to quietly let himself in so he didn't wake her. She'd worked a night shift at the hospital and knew she would be tired. She had one more night shift then they had a few days off together.

He would wait until she woke up to talk to her, maybe surprise her with breakfast in bed. Although, it would be dinner for him by then.

He wasn't supposed to see her today. He was working a VIP close protection job, but Daniel had agreed to swap with him and he didn't mind owing him a favour. He could have waited until the weekend, but he hadn't wanted to let this news fester.

Easing open the new front door that he'd fitted in the summer, Nate entered the two-bedroom, mid-terrace house Nikki called home. It was a quaint little house on a street filled with 1920s terraced houses. It backed onto the new theatre and the noise from the football stadium across the road was deafening on match day. She liked it though and had decorated it herself.

He found the large amount of black and purple she painted on the walls a bit harsh, it wasn't to his taste at all, but she liked it and that's all that mattered. She'd agreed that once she finished her nursing degree, she would move in with him. She was waiting to move in together since they were going to be married and he hadn't pushed it.

Cocking his ear towards the stairs, Nate thought he heard a noise. It sounded like a giggle. Maybe she was awake? He quickly bounded up the short flight of stairs and froze when he heard the unmistakable sound of people having sex. His stomach flipped as he listened to Nikki moaning and mewling.

His mind went blank, his fists clenched as he listened. Anger made his hand tighten on the bannister and he realised he was pulling it off the wall.

Nate pushed open the door of her bedroom and stopped short. In the middle of the bed was his fiancé. She was so intent on riding whoever was underneath her, she didn't see him. His vision turned red, all he could hear was the roaring in his ears. The room reeked of sex and perfume and almost made him gag.

He stepped forward, intent on seeing the motherfucker that Nikki was going all cowgirl on. She turned, sensing his movement, and gasped. Jumping up from the man, she tried to cover nakedness, to deny what she had been doing.

Nate wasn't looking at her, though, he was looking at the arrogant, self-satisfied smile of his childhood nemesis.

"Nate, it's not what you think," Nikki whimpered as big tears fell from her lying eyes.

"Oh, of course it is sweet Nikki. You and I have been fucking like rabbits for months behind poor old Nate's back," said the arrogant twat who ruined his teenage life. He looked so pleased with himself, Nate wanted to smash the smile right off the bastard's face. Nate knew that was what he wanted. Using every ounce of restraint he could manage, he turned his gaze to Nikki.

"It's you I love, Nate! Please!" She had mascara streaking down her face, her nails gripping the sheet trying to hide her fake breasts, and he realised his mum had been right. Nikki was a scheming bitch. How had he been so blind?

Love. Ha! What a joke; she had never loved him. She simply liked the idea of a tough-guy boyfriend. She'd always bragged to her friends about him being an ex-para. He thought it cute that she was proud of him, but she wasn't. He was just a trophy boyfriend.

Nate started to smile at the irony. How many times had he warned his sister about dating men who only saw her for her looks? And here he was, a victim of his own lecture.

He turned back to look at the man that had plagued his teenage years. The snide comments and sexual innuendo had crippled Nate's shy teenage self. He'd spent years trying to ignore the teasing and jibes, the casual touches, and overall intimidation from this man and his friends.

Nate thought it would end after he came back from the Army, but it gotten worse. This asshole always wanted any and everything Nate had and he'd made it his mission to take things from him including girlfriends and friends. He didn't understand it. This guy could literally have anything he wanted. Women fell for his charm and looks and still it wasn't enough. He had to torture Nate.

He put in words why, but had a feeling it was a power thing. During his school years, Nate was always the quiet, scrawny kid. It wasn't until college that he started to develop into the man everyone saw today.

He hadn't seen the asshole for years, not since he'd joined the Army and then the Parachute regiment. Bloody typical. Now a shit day had turned into an even shittier day. And he was back on this prick's radar.

Well, no more. He was sick and tired of this sick, evil bastard taking from him.

"You can have her," Nate sneered at the man, causing Nikki to cry harder. "I'm done with her, she's all yours. You and your games? Won't work. Get this through your thick head asshole. You cannot bully or manipulate me for your own sick reasons anymore. You're a sociopathic motherfucker who relishes in other people's pain. You make me want to vomit. Just looking at you makes my skin crawl. Stay the fuck away from me and my family, or you won't like what happens next." Nate glowered at the man with so much disgust and fury it was almost tangible.

He turned then and walked away. His news didn't matter now.

~~~

Calmly picking his clothes up off the floor, the man contemplated what just transpired. He'd wanted Nate to catch them. It had taken months of fucking this pathetic bitch until Nate caught them. He had pictured what the expression on his face would be and it had not disappointed.

He'd wanted him for years and had done everything he could to manipulate him into bed, but Nate wouldn't take the bait. He didn't know what it was about Nate Jones that made him want to consume him physically and mentally. Perhaps it was because Nate had always evaded his charms?

He shook his head as he looked at Nikki crying in a corner of the bed. She hadn't been a bad fuck, but she chose to betray her boyfriend so it was her own fault she was now left alone. Walking over to her, he leaned down and roughly grabbed her hair, twisted her face up to his and kissed her viciously, biting her lip hard as he did. She liked a bit of rough and knew her whimper wasn't one of pain.

"Come on, Nikki, you knew it was going to end badly. Stop your crying and pull yourself together." She looked at him with hate then, and it made him smile.

"I fucking hate you." She spat which made him laugh.

"You might hate me, Nikki, but you sure did love my cock when it was pounding into you, making you scream." He pushed her roughly onto the bed and turned to gather his things, as she curled into herself and cried.

When would people learn not to do stupid things if they didn't want to get caught? He whistled as he turned and walked out of her tiny townhouse. Time to up his game with Nate. It would take time and careful planning. Luckily, he had lots of time and loved to make plans and strategize. It was time for Nate to see that he always got his way. People didn't say no to him … ever!

Chapter One

Present Day

Nate and Skye had left the engagement party shortly after Dane and Lauren. The happy couple had decided to have their own party and he thought that was a good idea. He'd decided to hell with good intentions, Skye was his and he was going to show her tonight just how much he felt for her.

Nate thought back over the over the last five months and how Skye and Noah had changed his life. He'd known when he saw them the very first time that they would, but he'd had no idea quite how profound it would be.

He and Skye had gone from those first, tentative phone calls to spending every minute together. She had become his everything. She was the first person he thought of when he woke and the last person he thought of when he fell asleep. Not a night, or morning, went by in the last four months when they hadn't sent a good morning or good night text to each other.

In fact, they had taken to texting each other funny jokes or pictures. He looked forward to it and had become like a fifteen-year-old girl, carrying his phone everywhere with him. Her sense of humour was one of the things he loved about her the most. That and the fact she was such an amazing mum to Noah. Of course, he also loved how easy she was to be around. There was no drama if he did or didn't call or if he had to cancel plans because of work. She didn't take everything he did and examine it to decide if it was a slight on her.

He spent every spare minute he could with them both–be that at the hospital keeping them company with DVD's and games, or at her place doing much the same. He couldn't remember how many meals she'd cooked for him or how many nights they spent eating take-out and just chatting.

He wished he could have wined and dined her, but circumstances as they were with Noah didn't allow it and she didn't seem to want all the fuss. They cuddled on the sofa and he knew she wanted more, and so did he. He realised they had fallen into comfortable friendship, but the sexual fizzle and excitement when he saw or thought of her was there in spades.

Many a night he'd had to take care of things himself when he thought blue balls would actually kill him. He refused to rush this, though. It was too important and if he had his way, they would have years of using up all that sexual chemistry they shared.

He'd held back because he didn't want her to feel like she owed him for the transplant. When he took their relationship to its natural conclusion, he wanted there no doubt it was about the two of them.

However, earlier tonight when she had walked in, his brain had headed south and he'd decided he was an idiot for holding back and Skye would only move their relationship on if that was what she wanted to do. If the signals he was getting from her tonight were correct and he would bet his house that he was then she wanted him, in a big way.

They walked hand in hand to the car. He could feel the pulse in her wrist jumping around and knew his own heartbeat was going wild. He'd never felt like this about sex. Maybe that was the problem it had been just sex with others. Even his ex-fiancé hadn't moved him like Skye did. He felt more for her than he'd ever felt for anyone. Wanted to protect her and consume her in equal measure.

They stepped out into the cool clear night and he looked up at the thousands of stars. This was one of the things he loved about this part of the country–you could see the stars. When they reached his car, she turned to him, her eyes filled with lust. He held out his arms, their bodies came together as if it was the most natural thing in the world.

Their mouths met in an explosive kiss. It was as if all bets were off tonight, something had changed, and neither one was holding back. He slid his hands into her hair and gripped the back of her head, tilting it slightly, taking control the kiss. He could feel the soft heat of her as she pressed into him. He needed to slow this down or he was going to end up taking her up against the car, and he didn't want that … this time. This first time together, he wanted to go slow and get to know every inch of her. In a bed.

Nate stepped back, slowing things down, but she didn't want to be slowed down.

"Do you know how beautiful you are?" he asked her as he looked into her flushed face. Skye blushed and looked away. He took her chin and making her look up.

"Hey you have nothing to be embarrassed about." She looked up, then, and the desire he saw in her eyes made Nate feel like the only man in the world. He knew she was nervous earlier, so out of character for her to be forward in any way. She always referred to herself as just a mother and cake maker. That was her life and she loved it. But Nate wanted to make her feel cherished and beautiful and sensual, like a woman should feel. No man in the past seemed to look out for her and treat her like the gift she was. He wanted to be the man that brought out the sensual woman he knew was inside her.

"Let's get you home," he said and reached for her soft hand.

The loud ringing of her phone broke them out of their moment. He wished she could ignore it but knew she couldn't, it might be her young son Noah who was home with a babysitter. Nate knew, Skye was always slightly anxious when she left Noah because of all his health issues. Being the parent of a child with Leukaemia meant that things could change from hour to hour sometimes. Nate respected the hell out of her for the way she coped.

Nate stepped back and handed her her bag, which she had dropped during their fevered kiss. Her phone display said it was home calling and his heart sank. Had Noah taken a turn for the worse?

"Hello."

"Skye! Oh thank God."

"Joanne, what's wrong? Is Noah all right?"

"He's ... he's gone."

Skye started to shake, "What do you mean gone?" she asked tremulously. Her hand tightening on the phone in fear.

"Someone took him. He was in bed, asleep, when I checked on him at ten o'clock, but when I went to check him a minute ago he was gone. There was a little card by the bed, though, with a phone number on it." As Skye felt the world tilt and her vision started to go spotty, she heard Nate shout her name before her entire world went black.

~~~

Nate caught Skye as she fainted to the ground. Gathering her up in his arms, he grabbed the phone she had dropped and raced back inside. He ran to the room where his friends were still partying to celebrate the engagement of their team leader. He placed Skye on one of the cream couches that were set up along the sidewalls of the room, and looked at her ashen face. Her pulse was strong, but she looked so pale. Lucy, Zack, and Lizzie came rushing over followed by the rest of the team, including Colin, Dane, Lucy, and Lizzie's dad.

"What happened?" said Lizzie, bending down to check on Skye. The two women had become close over the last few months. She looked as worried as he felt.

"She had a call from the babysitter, and the next thing I know, she fainted." He'd known as soon as she took the call that it was bad news and his gut was screaming that something really bad happened, but she fainted before he could ask her.

He watched her intently, willing her to come round. His pulse started to calm as her eyes started to flutter open. She looked confused for a second to see everyone standing round her. Tears filled her eyes as reality returned and she started to shake. Not knowing what to do, Nate lifted her into his arms and held her small body on his lap as she shook.

"Skye. What's the matter, what happened?" That made her cry more. He felt her take a deep breath and tried to explain.

"Someone's taken Noah! It was the babysitter on the phone. She said she went to check on him and he was gone, someone took him!" She sobbed out the last bit. Nate gathered her closer, trying to offer comfort.

"We'll find him Skye," he said and looked to Zack, who nodded.

"Yes, we will," Zack said, instantly taking charge of the situation. Nate was relieved and felt more confident about getting Noah back quickly now that Zack and Fortis were involved.

"Daniel, I know you're on leave, but can you get every team member back to Fortis now? I want a briefing in 20 minutes. Start looking at CCTV around the area of Skye's house and start running plates of any vehicles in the area," Zack checked his watch, "from anywhere from 8pm until just after Skye got the call." Zack took charge so quickly and proficiently that Nate almost breathed a sigh of relief.

"Yes of course, anything I can do to help." Daniel knelt down to Skye and Nate. "Nate's right, Skye we'll get him back." She offered him a wobbly nod of her head, and Nate tipped his head in thanks.

"Lucy, put a call into the local police and let them know what's happened," Zack ordered.

"What about Dane and Lauren? They'll want to help." Lucy said. She looked a bit pale, too thought Nate absently, and he remembered her family had suffered something similar many years before. He would have a word with Zack and make sure that she and Dane would be okay to handle this situation. He was confident they would be, but he hated to see his friends suffer on his account.

"Yes, call and let them know," Zack said quietly, "It might be good for Skye to have friends around."

"Skye, I'm going to need you to tell me everything that was said," Zack stated kindly.

Skye explained haltingly what Joanne had said on the phone. Using the back of her hand to swipe at the tears that wouldn't stop flowing from red rimmed eyes. She clasped onto Nate with her other hand is if he was her only life line.

"Okay, Zin and Drew," who had now joined the group from the public bar after hearing the commotion, "you come with me to the house so we can get a look round to get a feel for what happened. Nate, I think you and Skye should come, too. It will be easier for you to notice if something is out of place."

"Sure," Nate replied, feeling anything but. He felt helpless, he knew what he should be doing from a hostage rescue situation but his priorities were divided. Did he do his job or support Skye or try and do both. He'd been relieved when Zack had taken over, it meant he could concentrate on Skye right now and be ready when the time came for him to do his part. She looked so fragile. Noah was her world, and if anything happened to him, he couldn't imagine how she'd cope.

He felt sick at the thought of someone harming him and he wasn't even his blood. No. He had to have faith that Fortis would get Noah back–after all they were the best of the best, and he wouldn't trust anyone more than he trusted these guys.

Nate decided, as they piled into vehicles, he would play it by ear and see how Skye was holding up before deciding his next move. Colin and Lizzie had insisted on coming, but Zack vetoed that idea– he didn't want civilians walking all over the crime scene and ruining any evidence. Instead, he sent them to Fortis with Daniel and Lucy, they could help from there. This was going to be an all-hands-on-deck case and everyone was determined they would not fail.

~~~

Kanan felt like the dirtiest scum on earth. He'd done some horrible shit in his time, but this was the lowest point in his life. Taking a sick child from his bed and giving him to strangers, for them to do god knew what, was despicable. He rubbed the back of his neck, the other hand clutched on the steering wheel.

Glancing over at the sleeping child he wondered how it had come to this. He had always been a bit of a rule breaker, but he had a code that he wouldn't break. Innocents and children were not to be harmed, whatever the cause or end result.

That was the one thing he prided himself on, and now he didn't even have that. Kanan wondered, again, if it was all worth it. Maybe he should just jack it all in and go find himself a beach hut and some local woman. A nice cabana in Hawaii. A willing woman ready to bring him drinks and maybe fuck occasionally. That was what he should do. He could get a boat and do some fishing. Nobody to bother him or screw with him. *Yeah, and he'd be bored in a month.*

He knew before he finished the thought that he wouldn't do it, but he definitely needed to get away–take some time and re-evaluate his life.

It was time to get out from under the influence of those rotten, scum bastards at SIS t who insisted he do this. When had the British government become so cold and calculating? Oh yes when the Divine Watchers had got involved with someone at the top of the food chain.

He thought he could do anything, just so he could continue his search for her; the woman who haunted his dreams. But it turned out there were limits and he just reached his. No woman was worth sacrificing his morals for. After this, he would get out and take stock of his life. Maybe it was time to let go of her.

He looked, at the child for what felt like the hundredth time and was surprised to see him awake and calmly watching him. It felt disconcerting to have a child look you in the eye with such confidence and surety. The boy was small for his age, but his eyes held intelligence and wisdom beyond his years.

Somehow the Star Wars pyjamas made him look smaller, more vulnerable. He remembered how he'd loved Star Wars as a kid and had collected every character he could. It was one of the really good memories he had of Zack and Catherine. He forced that thought away though, no sense thinking of those times. They were gone.

"I'm not going to hurt you kid." Kanan said quietly, so as not to frighten him. However, it was him that was shocked when the child smiled and said.

"I know you're not, Kanan, I knew you were coming."

Kanan, who was known as one of the coolest operators ever to grace the halls of SIS, was shaken by the boy's words and his calm demeanour. How the fuck did this kid know his name?

"What do you mean you knew I was coming, and how do you know my name?" He knew his words had come out more clipped than he intended, but this made no sense at all.

"I dreamt it, of course." The child laughed as if *he* was the crazy one. Maybe he was, because this was the strangest conversation he'd ever had.

"I don't want to go and see my daddy," said the boy, "I don't think he is going to be very nice."

So this was–a family dispute. Well, surely that couldn't be bad. They wouldn't want the kid if they were going to hurt him. Why was he taking the kids words at face value all of a sudden? He wouldn't have a clue where he was going.

He thought about it for a second before dismissing it as some sort of coincidence. Would they hurt the kid if it was his family? No, probably not, but Kanan knew better. He was only trying to justify his own fucked up choices.

"It'll be fine, kid. Don't panic. I'm sure he just wants to meet you."

"No, he doesn't. He's only doing it because she made him. She wants to give me that horrible medicine to make me do as I'm told. They're evil," he whispered, as if revealing a secret. "They want to kill the world."

The kid's words, on top of what he knew about the Divine Watchers, gave him pause. The fact that it was them pulling his strings through MI5 or SIS or whoever the fuck you wanted to call it made him nauseous. This was a giant clusterfuck waiting to happen.

He was having serious doubts about leaving the kid with them. Maybe he could keep an eye on the boy until he was satisfied that they meant him no harm. His hands clenched on the steering wheel, and he worked hard to relax his tense jaw as he thought through his options.

He could drop the kid back home and hope he wasn't caught by Fortis, or he could carry on and keep an eye on the boy. He thought of his sister and wondered if she was safe. If he dropped the kid home, would Zack honour his promise to keep Celeste safe or would he come after him?

He could try to keep her safe, but if he fucked over the Watchers, he would have zero back-up and would, in fact, put a bigger target on her back. Plus, there was the fact she had no idea he existed. *Stick with the plan and keep an eye on the kid.*

Yes, that's what he would do–keep an eye on the boy covertly for a few days. Happy with his decision, he said, "Look, kid, it'll be fine."

"Okay Kanan," said the boy quietly, "I trust you."

And wasn't that a kick in the balls?

Chapter Two

Nate pulled into the drive of Skye's rented bungalow at just gone midnight. She lived in a small cul-de-sac in the rural village of Burghill. It was a small, friendly village where everyone seemed to know everyone. It was the perfect place to raise a child.

The school was within walking distance, there was play park and plenty of open space. They even held a yearly event, called the community games, allowing kids to get involved with sports. Nate had gone with Skye and Noah. Although Noah wasn't strong enough to join in, he had loved watching his friends. They had done quite a bit in the four months since they had met. That was another reason to love this town. It was full of villages like this.

The property was ablaze with lights and there were already two police cars on the side of the road. He went round the car to open the car door for Skye and help her out. She'd been silent on the way over, as if she didn't even have the strength to speak. She'd stopped crying, but now her eyes looked vacant. She clutched at her bag like it was life-line.

He'd given her his jacket since she had been shivering in just a thin pashmina thing. He knew it was mostly shock, but he wouldn't risk her getting sick.

Not knowing what to do to help her, Nate felt powerless. He couldn't imagine how she was feeling. His heart was breaking for her. He wished he could just make it all go away, but couldn't, so he vowed to do everything in his power to get Noah back. He just hoped it was enough.

Putting his arm around Skye, he guided her through the front door as Zack, Drew, and Zin pulled in behind them.

A hysterical Joanne and two uniformed officers met them. Joanne threw herself into a shocked Skye's arms, crying, and it seemed to break Skye out of the fog she was in. The two women sat on the couch with Skye comforting Joanne.

That seemed wrong to Nate. Why was Joanne so hysterical? He got that she was upset but shouldn't it be the other way around? Nate walked over and shook hands with the two uniformed officers, both of whom he knew from the Jujitsu club he belonged to.

They were good guys and Nate was glad to see them there. He kept a close eye on Skye in case she needed him, and he noticed her eyes kept seeking him out as if to reassure herself he was there. He liked that, he liked it a fucking lot. Even now, in what had to be the worst time in her life, she wanted him. As he watched her, he couldn't help admiring her class, her serene beauty and strength. She awed him.

Her skin was still pale and her hands, which lay in her lap, were clasped tightly around a tissue. But her posture was still regal and she still held herself with dignity. She looked across at him then and her eyes held a determination, instead of the vacant fog.

This woman, his woman, was so strong and even in the face of all that was going on, Nate recognised that he would never find anyone like her again. He needed to fix this for her.

~~~

Zack came in and walked over to join Nate and the other officers. They both turned as a tall athletic looking man of about 35yrs came from the back room. He must be the lead detective. He had that exhausted look about him. The man was assessing Zack and Nate with his intelligent pale grey gaze, he seemed to understand that Zack was somehow in charge, and Nate could sense him bristle a bit, and stand taller.

The male detective's eyes skated over towards Skye, and Nate did not miss the flare of appreciation he saw there before he shut it down and turned towards him. The detective gave the officers an unmistakeable look of *hit the road* and the officers gave him a chin lift and dispersed into the house.

"I'm Detective English and this is my partner Detective Herbert," he said turning slightly to indicate his partner. "We will be handling the investigation." He indicated the tall stunningly beautiful African-American woman beside him. They all shook hands as Nate introduced them.

"I'm Nate Jones, Skye's man and this is my boss Zack Cunningham and my colleagues Zin Maklakov and Drew Preedy." It was not lost on the detective what Nate meant by Skye's man and Nate knew he understood him by his slightly raised eyebrow. He was letting everyone know that she was his and he didn't care what they made of that.

Zack shook both detective's hands and Zin just nodded and kept his arms folded across his chest, Drew followed Zin's lead and settled for a chin lift.

Nate noticed Zack texting someone on his phone and wondered if the team had an update already, Zack would tell them if he did.

"Can you tell me your connections to Miss Mitchell please?" Detective English asked, oh so politely.

"I'm Skye's boyfriend and as I said these are my colleagues and friends." Nate repeated.

"Can you tell me where you all were tonight?" the Detective asked. Nate started to answer when Detective Herbert's phone rang. She answered it quietly and he could see her expression go serious and her stance stiffen.

"Sir," she interrupted. "It's the Commissioner on the phone for you," she said handing him the phone like it was a rabid rat. Detective English swallowed loudly.

"Hello ... Yes, Commissioner, of course. Yes, yes I will." He passed the phone back to Herbert after ending the call. Nate could see him trying to lock down his anger about whatever he had just been told.

"The Commissioner has vouched for you and your team. We would be grateful," he said through gritted teeth, "if you would offer your assistance in this matter." Zack inclined his head graciously.

"Miss Mitchel is one of ours and so is her son, we will do *anything* to see her son safely returned to her."

"Anything legal, I assume you mean," Detective Herbert stated, giving Zack a challenging stare. She obviously didn't like the idea of being side-lined.

"Indeed, Detective," Zack said charmingly, inclining his head and offering the detective a killer smile. Even hot-shot detectives weren't immune because she blushed and looked at her feet, her challenge clearly not strong enough to handle Zack's brand of charisma. It almost made Nate chuckle.

"My team will take a look around the property and in Noah's bedroom while you interview Miss Mitchell," Zack said, turning his attention back to Detective English. The Detective must have decided to play nice, or at least knew when to pick his battles.

"Fine."

Nate spared a look at Skye, who had some colour coming back. He could see how shaken she was by the way her hands twisted the hem of her dress. He went over and knelt down in front of her, cupping her cheek, putting his other hand over her cold ones. She leaned into his hand, slightly, seeing the comfort he offered.

"I'm going to take a look round, *corazón*. Detective English wants to ask you some questions. Is that okay or would you like me to stay?"

"No, you go I'll be fine. Thank you, Nate, for being here for me." He looked into her eyes and then straightened and kissed the top of her head.

"I wouldn't be anywhere else, *mi cielo*. You and Noah are everything to me." She gave him a watery smile as he stood and followed Zack towards Noah's room.

~~~

Skye felt numb inside–someone had her baby. Someone had taken him out of his bed and out into the cold, dark night. Why? Why would anyone do that? He needed his medication or he'd get sick. Was he scared, had he called for her? Did they know he was prone to picking up infection from all the chemo he'd had?

All these thoughts went round and round in Skye's head as she sat with Joanne, listening to her cry. It was starting to grate on Skye's nerves. She needed to do something, not just sit here. She could barely take it in. If she thought about what might be happening to him she was sure she would fall apart.

Her nerves were hanging on by the thinnest of threads. Her eyes kept following Nate as he moved with Zack towards Noah's room. She was so glad he was here. He and Zack had taken over and she felt reassured. She had more faith in them than the police. She had seen how good they were when Lauren was kidnapped.

"Miss Mitchel?" the male detective asked, "can I ask you some questions, please?" He seemed nice and Skye nodded. "Can you tell me a bit about your daily life?"

"Um, well, it's either hospital visits or school for me and Noah. I work from home as a cake maker so that I can be flexible for Noah. He has Acute lymphoblastic Leukaemia and is due a bone marrow transplant next week." She felt her voice break as tears burned her throat. "I'm sorry."

"It's okay, Skye. Can I call you Skye?" She nodded her assent. "Has anything unusual happened in the last few weeks? A falling out with anyone, any new friendships? Have you seen anyone hanging around that you don't recognise?"

"No, nothing." She shook her head as she tried to think of anything that had seemed off, but there was nothing. She wasn't going to tell them about Noah's dreams, they wouldn't understand. And, he hadn't mentioned anything like this.

"What about Noah's father?"

"Ha, that's a joke. He's never been part of Noah's life." Skye absent-mindedly watched as Joanne suddenly stood and went into the kitchen, she busied herself making a pot of tea. "He only met Noah once, when he was born. He didn't even care when I told him about Noah being sick and needing a bone marrow transplant."

"Can I have his name for our records please?"

"Yes, it's Earl Hugo Lockwood." Skye wasn't shocked by the reaction of the detective. Although he masked it very quickly, she could see he was surprised to find that the infamous playboy Earl Lockwood was the father of her child.

"I'm sure you know where to find him," she said dismissively. She wondered now why she had never mentioned it to Nate, but Hugo wasn't in any part of their lives anymore and she was both mother and father to Noah. Nate hadn't asked either – not that he would care – he was too good a man to care about things like that. In fact, she was sure if Nate ever met Hugo, he would have a few choice words for him about his treatment of Noah.

She watched distractedly as he and the team walked from Noah's room. He was so handsome with his dark, Spanish colouring and his huge, formidable size and strength, and yet, she had never known a man with kinder eyes or a sweeter personality. He epitomised the saying, gentle giant.

He was also very intelligent, with a degree in civil engineering. They could talk for hours about anything from music to politics. They didn't always agree, and that was okay, too, because he respected her opinions.

She really enjoyed getting to know Nate slowly and becoming friends, even if they both felt the undercurrent of desire simmering between them. He made her feel safe, like he could take on the world for her and win.

Skye felt sure that if anyone could get Noah back, Nate and his team could. God, the alternative didn't bear thinking. She wished, not for the first time, that he could have been Noah's father. He would be a wonderful father. Maybe one day, when all this was over, they could talk about a future. The detective disturbed her from her musings.

"Okay, I think we have all we need for now. Forensics is dusting for prints and we're going to get a tap put on the phone in case the kidnapper calls. Mr. Cunningham and his team will be helping with the investigation and have offered to stay here with you. But if you need anything, you just call, okay." He handed her his card and she stood on wobbly legs to thank him.

Skye watched as Zack and Nate they came back over to Detective English. Then slowly walked to the kitchen to help Joanne with the tea.

The men walked further into the hallway to talk. They all knew Skye didn't need all the details.

"Did you find anything?" Detective English asked quietly so as not to upset Skye.

"The security lights have been loosened but not damaged, but other than that, nothing at all. I'd say this is a professional job," Zack answered the detective.

"Okay, forensics is going to start dusting for prints and we have everything we need from Skye." Nate stiffened at the familiar use of her name and looked at the Detective with a warning glare.

Zack saw the detectives out as Nate went to Skye in the kitchen. He had a very bad feeling about this entire situation. It had gone down within a couple of hours of the phone call from Kanan. Zack had a horrible feeling this was the thing he had been talking about when he said he had to do something Zack wouldn't like. He hoped he wasn't to blame, because despite the history between them, if he had taken the boy and put him any danger, Zack would take him down, history or not.

They'd found nothing to suggest anyone had forced entry and there were no footprints or signs of disturbance outside, which suggested to that this person was highly trained. Detective English would cover talking to the neighbours and he and his team would run background checks on everyone in Skye and Noah's lives, starting with the overwrought babysitter.

Zack wanted to get back to Fortis to see where the team was in terms of CCTV and if there was any vehicle movement in the area. Hopefully Zin and Drew had picked up something from their look around outside.

"I'm going to head back to Fortis," Zack said to Nate and Skye as he joined them in the kitchen. "Nate, if you can, stay with Skye. I want someone with her at all times, just as a precaution. You're the best choice given your relationship. If you feel that you are too close to this I trust you to tell me."

Nate nodded, "Of course, and I'll be fine. I'm invested, but my ability to do my job is not affected."

"Fine, stay in touch and if anything happens let me know." Zack motioned with a nod of his head for Zin and Drew to follow him out. Zack was pleased to see Drew keeping his cool and watching Zin's every move. The kid would learn a lot from him.

~~~

It was 3am before the crime scene techs left and Nate had finally persuaded Joanne to leave. She had been hovering over Skye the whole time and he could tell it had started to grate on her nerves

She'd changed from her stunning, black dress into old skinny jeans and a large Arran jumper with thick, woolly socks. She was now sitting on the sofa with her legs tucked underneath her, looking into space.

Nate had also changed into old jeans, a navy blue long sleeve t-shirt, and work boots. He was glad to get out of the dress shirt and trousers. He felt more himself like this. The spare gym bag he left in his boot was a god-send sometimes.

Nate crossed to Skye and sat noiselessly down beside her. She immediately leaned into him and snuggled under his arm. He wrapped his large arm around her and held her.

"I wish I could do something," she stated, "I feel like I'm totally useless just sitting here. Isn't there something I should be doing?"

Nate shook his head as she tilted her head back and looked up at him. "There is nothing you can do. Fortis is running all the background checks and looking at CCTV. The local police have checked for prints and have spoken with the closest neighbours. There really is nothing else we can do until we get a lead or they make contact." He ran his fingers through her soft hair. It had been up earlier but she'd let it down and it cascaded over her shoulders in a thick, shiny wave of silk. "I can't imagine how hard this is for you, *mi cielo*."

"What does that mean?" she asked as she leaned into him.

"It means my sky or heaven," he said softly.

"It's nice, I like it," she said simply.

They sat silently for a while before Nate said, "Why don't you try and get some sleep?"

"I can't. I feel totally wired and, anyway, every time I close my eyes, I see my boy's face." She laid her head on his chest and he loved the feel of holding her in his arms, even if the circumstances were the worst imaginable. She felt so right, despite the anguish he knew she must be feeling. He felt his body stir at the contact. He felt like a douchebag. He turned his mind to the detective.

"What did the detective ask you?"

"Just about our routine and if anything had changed, or if we had had anyone new in our lives. I told him everything I could, which wasn't much. He asked about Noah's father and I told him. I guess they will contact him, not that there's any point. He couldn't give a shit about Noah." She went silent then for a bit and then she sat up quickly almost head butting him.

"OH MY GOD, the card. I forgot the card!"

"What are you talking about?" Nate asked, sensing this was important.

"When Joanne called earlier, she said the person who took Noah had left a card with a number on it. I totally forgot. Maybe that's something?"

"Did she give it to the police?" Nate asked.

"I don't know, not that I saw."

"Okay, I need to call Zack and see if he knows about the card." Nate quickly called Zack's mobile. He kept her in the circle of his arms as he did.

"Yes," said a terse Zack.

"Did the police mention a card to you?" Nate asked, feeling like this was big somehow.

"No, nothing. Why?"

"Skye just remembered that Joanne mentioned a card when she called the first time and doesn't remember it being mentioned after."

"Okay. I'll call Detective English and find out. Hang tight. I'll call you in few."

Nate held Skye close while they waited for Zack to call back.

"Do you think it's important?" Skye asked, looking more animated than she had all night.

"Maybe? It's the only lead we have." He snatched up his phone as it rang.

"Yes." he barked.

"Joanne didn't tell them about a card, and now they are getting their knickers in a twist over it. I've told them we will keep them in the loop if we find it. I'm sending Zin and Drew over to Joanne's now to talk to her. There's also some things in her background check that are making me as nervous a cat in a room full of rocking chairs."

"I want to be there when you question her," Nate said. Zack was silent and then he heard him talking to someone in the background. "Fine I'm sending Dane and Lauren over to stay with Skye. I'll send you the address, meet Zin and Drew there in thirty minutes." Nate and Zack hung up then and he turned to Skye.

"We're going to go and question Joanne about the card. Dane and Lauren are coming over to stay with you."

Skye looked like she might object, but after a few seconds relented and sighed.

"Fine. Will you call me as soon as you know anything, please?"

"Of course, *mi cielo*," he said, pulling her onto his lap and burying his head in her hair. They stayed like that for a few minutes him enjoying the feel of her in his arms and her taking strength from him.

"Try and get some rest while I'm gone. You're no good to Noah if you collapse."

"I'll try," she said unconvincingly.

A few minutes later, there was a knock at the door and Nate got up to answer it. He kept his hand on the ever-present handgun that he carried in a pancake holster at all times since the threat of The Divine Watchers had been identified.

Opening the door, he was relieved to see Dane and Lauren. Nate closed and locked the door behind them and Lauren quickly rushed past him and down the hallway in search of Skye.

"Any updates?" Nate asked, hating being away from the hub of the action but not wanting to be away from Skye, either.

"Only that this Joanne has received lots of calls from a burner phone and has a history of making bad choices with men. A few of her ex-boyfriends have criminal records and she has a warning on her work record about her private life interfering with her job. Also, did you know who Noah's father was?" The way Dane asked that question made Nate pause.

"No, should I?"

"It's Earl Hugo Lockwood," Dane said as if Nate should know the name.

Nate recognised the name but had no idea who the guy was or what he looked like. "Isn't he the one that's a bit of a playboy and was in trouble last year for suspected embezzlement?"

"Yeah, one and the same."

"Shit. Skye said he was a low-life scum but not that he was a titled, posh, low-life piece of scum. He's never had anything to do with Noah, even when Skye told him he was sick. He didn't want to know. Makes me want to rip his face off. Some people don't deserve to be parents," Nate said vehemently. Dane nodded in agreement.

"Well, I'm going to get going. Look after her for me," Nate said as he turned to say goodbye to Skye.

"Of course, man," after everything you did for Lauren and me, I am forever in your debt, and I'll always have your back," Dane said, patting Nate on the shoulder.

Nate walked across the cheery, yellow and white kitchen where Skye was brewing tea for her and Lauren. Nate put his hand on Skye's neck under her hair and ran his thumb across her cheekbone gently.

"I'm off now. Call me if you hear anything and let Lauren and Dane look after you."

"I'm not helpless, Nate, I don't need a babysitter," she said, looking at him tiredly and leaning her face into his hand. It was a token protest. He had a feeling that she really didn't want to be alone right now.

"I know you don't," he said pulling her into his arms, "but we don't know who did this and I'm not taking chances with your safety, and plus, I think Lauren wants to look after you. You have a lot of friends who love you and they want to help, so let them."

"Okay," she whispered and kissed his chest just over his heart. He could feel the fatigue in her body as she leaned into him but also the comfort she was trying to give him in that one, simple kiss. His heart soared at the tender gift she bestowed upon him.

"Good girl," he replied, and kissed her on her head lovingly. "I'm going to get him back Skye, he stated determinedly. Skye didn't reply, but he felt her chin wobble against his chest and held her tighter.

As Nate walked away, he hoped to God he was telling the truth and he could get Noah back safely. If he didn't, he didn't think she would survive it.

Chapter Three

Kanan drove up to the security gates and navigated the long gravel driveway of Lockwood Manor. The Manor was an hour from Hereford and set just outside the town of Cwmbran South Wales.

He'd been surprised to be given instructions to come here and wondered what the connection was between the boy and the Lockwoods. He'd met Hugo Lockwood a few times and found him to be an annoying, self-centred, egotistical sociopath.

He didn't understand why women flocked to him. It was probably the money and his pretty boy looks. All his years of training allowed him to see through the veneer Hugo presented or maybe he was just feeling jaded.

Felicity Lockwood was a hard-faced bitch. Maybe he should feel sorry for Hugo being raised by her, the woman didn't have a maternal bone in her scrawny body. How she had carried a child without her venom poisoning it was beyond him.

She had a ruthless reputation and some very shady history. Her ties with The Divine Watchers certainly made him uneasy about leaving this kid with them.

He parked the SUV round the back of the Manor near the servant's entrance; he scoffed at that, bloody servants' entrance. What was this, the Victorian ages?

Reaching into the back seat, he was greeted with the disappointed gaze of the boy. What was it about this boy that made him feel like the worst of humanity and worse than that, made him want to be better?

"Come on kid, time to meet Daddy."

"Okay, Kanan," the boy said quietly, with only a slight wobble to his voice.

Kanan turned as the back door opened and a man decked out in full butler regalia stood watching them. What the fuck did he think he looked like? The man's posture was so stiff he looked like he would snap. The man ushered them into the utility room that was filled with wellies and outdoor coats, and closed the door behind them.

"If you would like to follow me through the drawing room, Lady Lockwood will see you shortly." Kanan was used to the pompous plumb in the mouth way he was speaking, but the snobbery and formality that surrounded some people still shocked him.

He'd met both Princes, William and Harry and Prince William's wife, the Duchess of Cambridge, and they were the most down to earth people you could meet. Still obviously posh, but otherwise normal. Especially Prince Harry.

Kanan had been assigned to his detail while he served his combat tour of Iraq. There had been specific concerns about his safety, so K as an ex-special forces operative, had been chosen to go undercover and join his unit as a 'specialist consultant'. That security detail had been the most fun Kanan had ever had while on duty. The Prince had been an excellent soldier and K would have been proud to have served with him anytime.

He'd noticed over the years, though, the true blue-blood never tried to be posh, it was just in their blood, and they were generally nice people. The ones that married into it were often the snobbiest and rudest. Thinking about that, he looked at the kid who he held in his arms. God, he hoped this kid was going to be all right.

He was such a skinny little scrap of humanity and his pale face with the shadows under his eyes belied the fragility his bravery hid.

Settling the kid on a plush Louis the XIV chaise lounge by the large roaring open fire, he studied his surroundings. The room was the epitome of opulence. It was elegantly decorated in rich burgundies and gold's. There were several Monet paintings hung on the walls that Kanan suspected were the real deal. Every surface seemed to be covered in priceless vases or crystal decanters.

His eyes caught on the boy who was looking around, taking everything in. He seemed focused on the paintings on the farthest wall. It looked like they were family portraits and he could recognise a young Felicity in one. What struck him, though, was the little boy in the painting. He was the image of this kid.

His stomach twisted again and he got the worst feeling. It was a feeling of such foreboding he could hardly breathe. He took a deep lungful of oxygen and shook off the feeling. He, instead, concentrated on his surroundings.

The security was what really interested him. If he was going to keep an eye on this kid, he needed to know what security protocols they had in place. There was a state of the art alarm system and cameras in every room he'd been in so far, except the servant's kitchen which only had an alarm that linked to the exterior door.

They protected the priceless art, but didn't put as much security into protecting the people or the property. Idiots! The people in charge of security were either idiots or overly confident that there was no threat. In this case, it was good for him, though.

The boy was still quiet, but Kanan hadn't really expected anything else. In fact, he was impressed with the kid's bravery, so far. He hadn't kicked or screamed or cried. He had been stoic and accepting. That made him feel like a bigger heel than ever.

Felicity Lockwood entered the room with her grandson, Hugo, trailing behind her. She was immaculately dressed, even at this late hour. Her silver hair swept up into a tight chignon and her pale pink tweed suit had not so much as a rumple in it.

At first glance, she looked like a normal socialite. Polished, regal, and dignified, but when you looked close, you could see the cold calculation in her eyes.

Those eyes swept the room, landing on Noah, who was curled up in a ball now and watching Felicity closely, as if she was a snake about to strike. K didn't like seeing the wariness in his eyes. He did concede to himself that the kid had excellent instincts, though.

"Is this him?" she asked Kanan sharply.

He really didn't fucking like this woman.

"Yes. This is Noah." It pissed Kanan off that she didn't use his name. Granted, he'd been calling him kid, but that was because he was trying to maintain distance and he knew he meant it that way. She, however, was looking at Noah as if he was a specimen in a lab.

"Hugo, come see the boy you sired." She turned and beckoned a bored looking Hugo Lockwood forward. He came over and gave the boy a cursory glance.

"He looks like his mother," Hugo said disinterestedly. Felicity stepped toward Noah and Kanan saw the boy flinch. He had to fight the urge to step between the two. Noah was genuinely terrified of this woman.

Kanan was a big badass guy dressed in black clothing with a ski mask and had taken him from his bed and Noah had shown him no fear. His internal radar was screaming that this was wrong.

"He's a bit scrawny, but we can fix that. Fine, you may leave now, Mr ... "

"K, it's just K." The less this bitch knew, the better, and he knew she was playing games because the people who set this up knew who he was. "What do you plan for the boy?" Kanan asked.

Felicity assessed him calmly, although she wasn't as relaxed in his presence as she liked to have him believe. A pulse ticked in her neck as she played with the pearls at her throat. Good. At least she was getting the message that maybe she didn't have the upper hand here and should be slightly afraid. She should be too, K could snap her neck like a twig and at this moment in time, he kind of liked that idea.

Hugo watched him from over by the bar as he poured himself a brandy. He looked mildly interested by the exchange but Kanan could tell his interest was piqued because Felicity seemed nervous, than the actual words that were being said.

"He is my great-grandson and he has been kept from me," she said, deciding that maybe painting herself as the victim would be the best approach. "I just want the chance to get to know him. He is the future of the Lockwood name and I want him to know his legacy." She turned on the waterworks a bit now.

Kanan got up close to her and bent down towards her face so he could talk to her quietly. He didn't want to scare the boy and what he had to say was not for his ears.

"If I hear that you have harmed one hair on that child's head, or scared or mistreated him in anyway, I will personally come for you and that pathetic excuse for a sperm donor over there. And believe me, you don't want that. You know who I am and you know what I am capable of and if I think you've hurt him I will not only follow through with my threat I will enjoy it." He saw her swallow and then straighten her shoulders.

"I can assure you there is no need for threats. I just want to get to know him."

Kanan ignored her and walked over to the boy. He'd been silent during this entire exchange. He crouched down so that he could talk to the boy and look him in the eye. He still looked scared, but it was the trust he saw there that slayed him.

"I'm going now but I will be keeping an eye on you and if I think they are not being nice, I will come back for you, okay?"

"O…okay, Kanan." he said sniffed quietly. "Be careful," he whispered, "they are watching you and your sister. Noah paused and looked at Hugo and Felicity, then back to him. "Nate is going to come get me soon and he will be mad with you. Please don't hurt him, he loves us."

Kanan was, once again, floored by this kid's knowledge. Nobody knew about his sister. This kid was an enigma, but somehow in the last few hours he had grown attached to this boy. That, in itself, was unusual because he didn't really like kids much.

He didn't say anything, just stood and laid his hand on Noah's head affectionately. With one last pointed look at Felicity and Hugo, Kanan turned and disappeared into the night.

~~~

Felicity stiffened her spine and shook off the fear that that heinous man made her feel. She was not that hungry, weak little girl anymore and resented him making her feel like that.

Schooling her features, she turned to her grandson. She eyed his thin frame and his face, which was so much like her son's at the same age. She fought off the familiar ache in her stomach that thoughts of him gave her. Hate and love were such a fine line and she still didn't know which side she was on with him. Dismissing the past, she turned to Hugo. "Hugo take the boy to his room and for God's sake, show some interest." Hugo sauntered over to the boy and looked down at him with fascination.

"He has my eyes," he said and the surprise on his face made her want to slap him hard for his idiocy.

"Yes, well, with his ability and our position and money, we will be a power to be reckoned with among the Divine Ones, and then we will be able to join the council." Her drive and determination had gotten her to this position in life and she wasn't about to be thwarted now. She deserved this. She deserved to be on the Divine Council and rule these lesser beings.

She watched as Hugo lifted the boy and carried him to his room. She hoped Hugo would show some interest in the boy and stop his whoring ways. He didn't take his responsibilities and position in society seriously and needed to start. She tried so hard with him but he was such a disappointment.

Pouring herself two fingers of Remy Martin Black Pearl Cognac, she downed it in one swallow. It was a waste of the seventeen-thousand-pound brandy but she needed to calm her nerves. She poured another and sat near the fire.

Maybe having the boy around would help her regain some of the control she had lost of late. She needed to call her contact and have the drug delivered first thing. They needed to start the trials soon to see if they could control gifted ones once the drug took effect.

The fact that the boy was sick bothered her a little, as it might alter the results of the drug. But she knew from that nurse the Hugo had cozied up to that Noah wasn't on any drugs right now. It would have been better to wait until after the bone marrow transplant that had been scheduled but time was of the essence.

The threat from K rattled her a little but there was no way he would be allowed to see the boy again. There was no way he'd know what was going on. Satisfied she made all the right moves, she retired for the night.

Chapter Four

As they approached the ground floor flat on the outskirts of the town centre, Nate was surprised to see that a woman living on her own had no outside security lights on. He knew Hereford had a low crime rate, in no small way due to the fact that you couldn't throw a stone in this town and not hit a member of the SAS. It sometimes made people complacent about their own security.

Still, this seemed wrong. It meant she was either clueless to the dangers around her, or that someone had made it so her lights were out. The feeling of foreboding that assailed him when he saw the light smashed and her front door ajar was justified.

They all slipped comms units into their ears to help them communicate inside. Nate quietly pushed open the door with his weapon drawn. Zin at his other side and Drew to his back. Drew had learned incredibly fast in the short time that Nate had been training him.

His ability with a weapon was almost as good as his skills with a computer. Zack recently started his next phase of training and this included riding along with one of the other operatives. Tonight was Zin's turn. Drew would be hard pushed to get a better operative than Zin to shadow.

Prowling into the room silently, they split up with Zin going to the kitchen at the back of the flat and Drew going left towards the bedrooms. Nate followed Drew soundlessly toward the bedrooms and each went into rooms on either side of the hallway.

Nate swore softly at what he saw; Joanne was lying on her bed at an odd angle. Her legs bent awkwardly underneath her and her arms hung uselessly at her sides.

Nate cleared the room, checking the wardrobes before assessing Joanne. He waited for the all clear to come through his ear from Zin and Drew and then turned on the light and spun as Zin and Drew joined him. Behind him, he heard Drew take in a breath and swear viciously.

Facing the bed, Nate crouched in front of Joanne. She had been beaten–badly. Her face was nearly unrecognisable. Both her eyes were black and swollen shut, and her left cheek was cut and bloody. The single bullet hole in her forehead indicated her cause of death.

Zin muttered something in Russian under his breath as he got closer and Nate knew he felt the same. None of the team could tolerate violence against women. Whatever happened to Joanne was bad and had suffered. No decent man was okay with that, regardless of what she might have done.

"I'll call Zack and give him the news," Drew said, solemnly.

"Okay," Nate said knowing that Drew was struggling with the scene in front of him. "Zin we need to look for this card and see if anything obvious has been taken. I'll start in here. Can you start in the living room?"

"Fine," Zin responded shortly. This was not unusual. Zin was not a chatty Cathy by anyone's standards.

How was Joanne involved in all this and why had she been killed? Was she just a loose end? Nate was thinking this as he looked carefully through her bedside drawers. Just the usual stuff–book, phone, contraceptive pills, condoms. Nothing that looked out of place.

He crossed to the wardrobe and looked inside. Joanne clearly had very expensive taste. Her wardrobe was crammed with designer labels next to her nurse's uniform. Nate went through the pockets and hit the jackpot when he found a card with a single phone number, with no name on it, in her nurse's uniform pocket.

Nate met Drew and Zin back in the living room.

"Zack is going to call Detective English and fill him in. They should be here soon. The pathologist is also on his way." As he was saying this they heard multiple sirens. They stepped outside and holstered their weapons. The last thing they needed was a rookie cop getting excited at the sight of three armed men. Especially ones that looked like they did.

Nate watched as Detective's English and Herbert pulled up and got out of their Vauxhall Insignia. He was walking over to Detectives English and Herbert when his phone rang.

"Yes," he said quickly when he saw Dane calling.

"Hey, Nate. You might want to come home, and by that I mean back to Skye's place." There was humour in Dane's voice and that confused Nate.

"Yeah I got that, *hermano*. Why, what's happened? Is she okay? Have we heard any news?"

"No, nothing's happened, but her uncle just arrived, and, umm well, he is eccentric, to say the least."

This didn't sound too bad, although, Skye hadn't mentioned him–but she hadn't mentioned her family at all really except to say they were estranged.

"Okay, we have a situation here. Joanne is dead and it's not pretty. I'll see if Zin can handle it and I'll be there as soon as I can."

"Fuck. That's not good," Dane said quietly. Nate appreciated him being discrete around Skye. She was not going to take this well.

"See you soon, man, and thanks."

"Yeah, later Nate."

Nate spoke to Zin who assured him he could handle the police and would pass anything they found straight to Zack. He, also, said they would keep the card to themselves for now and get it back to Fortis so that they could try the number and attempt get a GPS lock on the phone. He promised, again, to keep Nate in the loop so he left to see what was going on at home. *At home*, he liked that. He liked the thought of coming home to Skye and Noah every day and he was going to do everything, and more, to make it happen.

Chapter Five

Walking through the front door of Skye's bungalow, Nate was met by an amused Lauren, a baffled Dane, and an exasperated Skye. He didn't get further than the hall before Skye reached him.

"*Mi cielo* what's going on?" he asked as she slipped into his arms. "Dane said your uncle is here."

"Um…yes he is. But the thing is, he is…different. I never mentioned him because, well, I'm not sure how to explain it." Her uncertainty was cute and unsettling at the same time. He smiled at her, encouraging her to continue. "He is gifted and very eccentric and very protective."

"Okay. So what's the problem?"

"Well…he kind of talks to his wife all the time."

Nate was confused, now. What was wrong with that, so he asked.

"Well, she died ten years ago. I know it sounds crazy, and believe me, many people think so, too but he also talks to other dead people," she said, rushing through the sentence as if trying to get it all out before he could react.

Nate was trying to process this latest development when a loud, masculine voice shouted from the living room.

"I told you once, woman, stop bloody nagging me. I will tell her when I'm good and ready. Now pipe down."

Skye just looked at Nate with a resigned look on her face. "That's Uncle Reg, talking to dead Aunt Tilly."

Nate had had enough of this. He needed to meet this Uncle Reg. Taking Skye's hand, gently but firmly, in his, he pulled her towards the living room. What he saw stopped him in his tracks. He cast a disbelieving look to Dane who had Lauren curled in his lap on the sofa. Both just grinned at him.

A man in his early sixties sat in the brown leather armchair in the corner with a shotgun across his lap. He wasn't overly tall, about five-ten, Nate would guess, and had a shock of white hair down to his shoulders. He had a neatly trimmed goatee, that was dyed bright purple, and dressed head-to-foot in biker leathers.

Nate had seen some sights, but this was definitely a first.

Skye had come to a stop right beside him. The man looked up at Nate, intently.

"Uncle Reg, this is Nate."

"I know who he is, girlie," he said affectionately. "Your Aunt Tilly's been on me for weeks about him." Nate stepped forward and offered his hand.

"Pleased to meet you," Nate said, and Reg took his hand in a surprisingly firm grip.

"You too, son. Heard a lot about you from the wife. She goes on a bit, but I just ignore her most of the time." He said this as if telling a secret man-to-man. Nate just nodded and tried to hide a smile.

He was shocked out of his smile when Reg turned abruptly over one shoulder and shouted, "Woman, I told you don't nag me! I'll tell em when the time's right."

Skye was looking completely accepting of his actions, Dane and Lauren looked bemused.

"Uncle Reg has kindly decided to stay and look after me and help with rescuing Noah," Skye said, sounding exhausted. Nate tried not to show his amusement on his face for fear of offending the man.

He looked at Reg, trying to take the measure of him.

"Fine. Reg, I have to ask. Do you know how to use that gun? Because I won't have anyone who is a liability around Skye or this operation. They mean too much to me for that. So, although I respect you coming and appreciate it, you have to know that's where I stand."

Reg looked him over then and stood up causing Nate to take a step back. He looked Nate directly in the eye, and after a minute, seemed to come to a decision.

"Son, I was shooting guns before you were a twinkle in your daddy's eye. But I gotta say, I respect what you're saying and I'm only here to help protect my little girl, here," he said, indicating Skye.

"I don't take orders very well but if it keeps her and that darling boy safe, I will try my damndest."

Hands on his hips, Nate assessed the room, catching Dane's eye. Dane nodded.

"Fine, Reg. You stay. Skye, sweetie, why don't you go and get some blankets for Reg. He can take first watch. You need to get some rest and so do I." He turned to Reg, "That cool with you?"

"Sure, son." Reg puffed out his chest and settled back in the chair for his first watch. Nate turned to Skye as she bustled back in with blankets for Reg.

"Go on, *mi cielo*. Get yourself to bed. I'll see Dane and Lauren out and be in soon." Skye nodded. She looked dead on her feet.

"Okay." They had never slept in the same bed before but there was no way he was leaving her alone tonight.

Nate followed a chuckling Dane and Lauren to the door.

"I can't wait to see Zack's face when you tell him this and he meets Reg." *Fuck*. He hadn't thought of that. Zack was going to blow a gasket, Oh well, he'd deal with that tomorrow. He said goodnight to Dane and Lauren, thanked them, and shut the door.

~~~

Skye lay in bed, curled up on her side. She'd pulled on one of her favourite nighties. A pale pink silky slip with cream lace edging the hem. It wasn't that she was trying to impress Nate, although that would be a bonus. It was just that that was all she had. It was what she always wore. She liked to wear sexy, feminine nighties to sleep in.

She crawled into bed, every bone in her body exhausted, and yet, she didn't think she could sleep. How could she with her baby out there on his own, and who knew where?

As she lay there, all she could think about was Noah. Was he okay? Was he frightened? Did he wonder why she hadn't come for him? She found herself praying to God, for the hundredth time, that he would be safe and unharmed. Reg showing up had been a shock but, at the same time, a welcome distraction from her bleak thoughts.

Even as she huddled under the quilt, not able to get warm. She felt so cold. She snuggled under the quilt more, pulling it up to her ears.

She startled as the bedroom door opened with the light from the hallway, she saw Nate come in and close the door. She stayed silent–she honestly didn't have the energy to speak. Skye heard the rustling of clothing as Nate moved around. Then she felt the covers pull back as Nate, for the first time, slipped into bed behind her.

Nate put his palm to her belly, pulled her back to his naked chest, and tucked his legs up behind her knees. Her heart gave a hiccup and her breath hitched at the contact. She instantly felt warm and safe. He tucked his other arm under her neck, using his arm as a pillow, and snuggled her into his warmth.

"How are you doing, *mi cielo*?"

She didn't say anything, she didn't trust her voice not to break. She just snuggled deeper into him. He didn't ask again but she felt his lips touch just behind her ear as he whispered, "I'm going to get him back, *mi amor* . I swear it. I will get our boy back."

Skye believed him, but that didn't stop the all-encompassing fear that clutched at her heart like a vice.

They hadn't talked about where their relationship was going, but somehow him calling her his love and calling Noah his boy, she knew that this was no fling for either of them. Family. They had somehow become a family. Noah's disappearance just moved things along the natural path quicker. On that thought, she kissed the arm that cradled her head and clutched tight to the one at her waist then she fell into a fitful sleep.

Chapter Six

At Fortis Security the lights were blazing and the place was a hive of activity. Zin and Drew had just arrived back and passed off the card to Lucy so that she could run the number.

Zack switched off the signal jammer that currently shrouded the entire building. It worked similarly to a Faraday cage, but the technology was highly advanced and allowed Zack to turn the shield off and on, thus allowing him to advance or intercept signals at will. It had been developed by his tech guy, Will Granger.

Zack called everyone together. He wanted them there to see if anyone was able to pick something up from the voice or the background noise.

Dane had taken Lauren home, along with Lizzie and Colin. Daniel insisted that he was staying, despite technically still being on leave.

Zack called the number and then put the phone on speaker. It rang twice and was picked up. The whole room became wired as a robotic voice came on the line.

Hannibal, the boy is safe and will remain that way. All measures are being taken to ensure his safety. Murdock out.

The line disconnected abruptly.

"Fucking goddamn bastard!" Zack exclaimed, causing everyone to look at him sharply.

"It's a burner phone, so no trace. I can try tracing the towers, but if this person is any good, the phone will have been dumped," said Lucy, still looking at Zack with question.

"Thanks Lucy, and don't bother. This guy doesn't make mistakes."

"You know who has him?" Zin asked quietly. Zack nodded.

"I believe so and I think he wanted me to know. It's a man from my past named, Kanan Harrison. We were friends a long time ago. He works for SIS. He called me earlier tonight and asked me to look out for his sister because he had some bad shit going down–shit he didn't want to do and he didn't want blow back on her." Zack paced, his agitation evident in every move.

"If Kanan has Noah, he's safe. He might have done some fucked up things but he would never hurt a child, of that I have no doubt. Zin, first thing, I want you to go pick up the sister. I don't want her knowing. She has no idea Kanan exists, and it will be kept that way." He gave a firm look to each person in the room. "This is personal and I am trusting every person in here to keep this secret and that is not something I do with ease so please, do not make me regret it." He received firm nods from all those in the room.

"I'm going to offer Celeste Bourdain, the sister, a job as our receptionist." He looked to Daniel who gave a chin lift as his agreement. "She is a good person. I have been keeping an eye on her for years and she's clean. She won't be treated like a suspect, because she isn't one. I am just repaying a debt. That said, having her around while Kanan has Noah is not bad for us." He levelled a look at each of his team members and it was hard not to see the regret in his face. "I know I'm asking a lot but I need you to trust me on this." There were murmurs of 'no problem' from all around the room. Zack's shoulders visibly relaxed, he nodded and continued.

"Zin–I will give you the address, can you go over tomorrow and offer her the job? Tell her we found her C.V on LinkedIn or something, whatever. Just let me know.

"Everyone, go home get a couple of hour's shut-eye. We'll meet back hear at 8am."

~~~

Zin was leaning against his custom Harley Davidson Sportster 48 with his arms crossed across his massive chest, contemplating everything. He agreed with Zack about keeping the sister close and this was as good a way as any. He would reserve judgement on her guilt, or lack of, until he met her. Zin sensed Zack knew this and was okay with him making up his own mind.

He and Zack had a unique understanding and trust that went far beyond friendship. It was forged from a shared experience of the worst kind. The horrors they had seen and experienced cemented a bond that, although came from the worst, had in fact, been a blessing. Not that either of them would have wanted it that way. He would never regret his decision to go back into that hellhole in the desert and help the men who had saved his sister.

He thought of Celeste Bourdain, again and wondered if she was home. Maybe he should do a little surveillance to see if he could figure anything out before morning.

Years in deep cover made it so that he could read tiny nuisances in people; it had kept him alive countless times. He would bide his time and make his own mind up about Celeste Bourdain. Her name sounded French and Zin wondered if it was. Not that it mattered–she was just another job. The main focus was getting the boy back. Zin had a lot of respect and regard for Nate and could see this boy and his mum meant a lot to him. He would do everything he could to help.

Swinging his powerful jean clad leg over the magnificent bike, he zipped up his leather jacket and pulled on his helmet. Time to see if he could get a few hours kip before he went to meet Miss Bourdain. Maybe he'd drive home that way and just check things out.

~~~

Zack closed the door to his office and walked round the desk to his computer. He received an email from Ava Drake's boss, Duncan Caldwell at the NSA, saying they were happy to loan Agent Drake to them on secondment for the next few months.

Zack had spoken to Ava's father, General Drake, and managed to get him to pull some strings. He was sure that if he'd known what Zack had done to his baby girl, the General would have shot him instead of helping him. In the interest of global security, though, Zack had thought it prudent not to share that he and Ava had done the hot and heavy.

He was relieved she would be arriving on Tuesday to help unravel this code. From what they determined so far, it seemed to be written in some sort of extinct, ancient language. He felt a sense of urgency tugging at him about this entire case. He'd only ever felt it once before, and the results were devastating.

Shaking off thoughts of the past, Zack thought about how Ava would respond to his not-so-subtle manipulation. She was very feisty and had one hell of a temper. Perversely it was this, as much as her undeniable beauty, which had drawn him to her. He knew she would be spitting nails over the fact that he ignored her many attempts to contact him after his return to the UK. It would be interesting to see if she would let him explain or if she'd just shoot him.

Zack's trousers suddenly felt tight at the thought of her fiery temper. She had been wild in bed and wanted to try things that made him harden just thinking about them now. Maybe he could persuade her to have a little fun while she was here? He liked that idea a lot.

First things first, they had to get Noah back. He tried calling Kanan's number again, but it was dead. No matter. If he had to use Celeste as leverage, he would. If there was one line that should never be crossed, it was involving children. K crossed that line and would deal with the full wrath of the Fortis team and its allies.

Chapter Seven

Nate woke to the scent of peaches. He opened his eyes and found himself wrapped around Skye. His face was pressed into her hair and his body was cocooned around her protectively. He wanted this for so long, he took a minute to just enjoy the feel of her, soft in his arms. The smell of her skin invaded his senses and he wanted to turn her over and worship every inch of her, as she deserved. But he knew now wasn't the time; they needed to find Noah.

Thinking of Noah, scared and alone, made him want to rip out the heart of the person that had him. The boy had come to mean so much to Nate that he already thought of Noah as his. He knew people would laugh at that but if he was honest with himself, it had started the minute he walked into the hospital room months ago.

He'd been struck then by the strongest feeling that they were his–his to protect, his to love. He already failed the protect part, but he would rectify that and spend every day for the rest of his life making up for it.

He was taking things slow with Skye and Noah so far, however, Noah being taken put things in perspective. He was taking what was his and to hell with everyone else. He would prove to Skye that he was the one and convince her, if need be, he was not going away.

Nate felt Skye stir in his arms. She pushed back into his front, making his morning erection strain painfully. Instantly, she stilled in his arms. He watched as she turned slowly and looked at him with her big ,brown eyes. She looked so beautiful. He saw the exact second reality hit her and the desolation swept in.

Her eyes teared up as she suddenly wrapped her arms around his middle and pulled herself flush with him. She buried her head in his neck, as if to take strength. Her silent sobs nearly broke his heart.

"Hey, *mi amor*, it's okay. I've got you." He held her while she wept, using the time to think of ways he would make the bastard that made her cry pay.

Skye lifted her head after a few minutes and sniffed back the last of the tears.

"I'm okay now. I just forgot for a second." Her breath hitched a little.

"I know, *mi cielo.* How about I make some coffee and call Zack for an update while you get showered? Then we can go to Fortis."

"Okay, that sounds good, Thank you," she said, hesitantly.

Nate started to get up, but was stopped by a hand hooked on his abdomen. He was trying really hard not to make her aware of his erection, but she wasn't making it easy.

"What is it?" he asked as he sat on the edge of the bed and turned to face her.

Skye looked uncertain and shy and seemed to concentrate on his tattoos. Nate lifted her chin with his finger so that she looked at him.

"Come on, tell me. Whatever it is, I will gladly fix it if I can."

"Will you kiss me good morning?" She blushed the deepest red.

Nate caressed her cheek, threading his fingers into her hair and cupping the back of her neck. He could see her eyes had gone molten with desire.

"That, *mi cielo*, is something I can fix, and will do with pleasure."

He lowered his head and caught her mouth in a gentle, but thorough, kiss. She immediately leaned into him, pushing forward onto her knees. Nate felt the timid brush of her tongue against his and he took over the kiss.

Nate gently tilted her head back so he could control the kiss and taste her. Her small hands on his chest felt so good. He needed to stop this before things got completely out of hand. He wanted nothing more than to push her back onto the bed and make her his in every way. But now was not the time, and he knew she wouldn't want it like this, either.

Pulling away, he looked into her eyes. Eyes clouded with passion.

"Good morning, *mi amor*."

They rested their heads together for a second before Nate pulled her up from the bed.

"Come on, *mi cielo*. Time to face the day." He held her for a minute before gently letting go and got dressed.

~~~

Skye watched Nate go and wondered what he thought of what just transpired. She hadn't meant for it to happen, but when she woke up, she hadn't remembered the horror of the previous night for a second. She had stretched and felt him behind her, and only when she saw his cautious expression had it hit her. Her baby was missing.

She'd felt so safe as he held her and let her cry. When he pulled away, she hadn't wanted to let go. She felt shy asking for a kiss, but as they had spent the night together, she felt it was natural. And what a kiss it was. Nate had the body of a God, and could kiss like the devil. She'd known before he was the one for her and now she was certain. The way he was with her, his love for Noah, and she knew the sex would be off the charts hot.

Feeling energised and determined to get her son back, she headed for the shower.

~~~

Entering the living room, Nate could smell coffee and bacon coming from the kitchen. He looked up as he went through the kitchen door to see Reg at the hob, cooking bacon and eggs.

"Morning Reg," he greeted. Reg looked back at him while flipping the bacon.

"Morning, son. Thought I'd make some breakfast for us all. We can't go hunting on an empty stomach."

"Thanks Reg. That's much appreciated."

"Known that girl all her life, and she is the closest thing I have to a child of my own. Ain't nothing I wouldn't do for her or her boy. She means everything to me."

"They are everything to me," Nate said, solemnly, hoping that he conveyed everything in that one sentence.

"I know they are, son," Reg said softly. They were both quiet while Nate made moved to the nearly empty coffee pot to make some fresh java for him and Skye. He was startled when Reg boomed, "Don't tell me how to cook bacon, woman. I've been cooking it for years and don't need your input now." Nate looked around for a second before remembering the events of yesterday and Reg's habit of communing with his dead wife. He smiled slightly at the absurdity of the situation. Reg carried on his mini tirade with his dead wife for a few minutes before Skye came in.

She hugged Reg and then went up on tiptoe to kiss his bristly cheek.

"Morning, Uncle Reg."

"Morning, sweetheart. I made some breakfast for us all. Sit down and I'll bring it over."

Skye nodded and took her coffee from Nate as she went to the breakfast bar to sit down. She smiled when Nate sat next to her and automatically leaned her head on his shoulder. He raised his arm so that she could scoot in closer and he wrapped his arm around her so he could hold her properly. He dropped a kiss on her head then took a sip of coffee.

Reg brought over their food and he and Nate tucked in. Nate ate one-handed so he could continue to hold Skye.

Skye picked at her food, taking a few bites before pushing it away. Nate could see she was anxious to get to Fortis so that she could find her son.

"Have you spoken to Zack, yet?" she asked Nate.

"Not since last night. He texted to say they are all meeting back at Fortis at 8 am, so we will find out any info then. I do have some news, though." He paused. This was going to be hard and knew this would frighten and upset her.

"You know we went to Joanne's last night…"

"Oh my god, I completely forgot! What did she say?"

"She didn't say anything, *mi cielo*…she's dead. Someone got there before us and she was didn't make it." He turned to face her and gently held her by her biceps. He could feel her tremble for moment before she sucked in a breath, and watched her face transform, as she pulled herself together. She was the most magnificent woman he had ever met.

"Did you find the card?"

"Yes, we did. Zack has it at Fortis. He will run the number and check for any evidence that might have been left."

She stood, pushing her plate away.

"Come on, we need to go." She was bouncing on her feet in her need to get going and do something.

"Okay, grab your coat and we'll go. Reg are you coming?" Reg had been quiet as he watched the exchange.

"Bet your ass I am," he said, pulling on his old, scuffed leather jacket. They headed out to Nate's Porsche Cayenne.

~~~

Reg opted to go with Nate and Skye in the Porsche rather than use his beloved Triumph Bont T120. Whilst he'd travelled from

Ewyas Harold on it, he didn't want to ride it in this cold weather more than necessary. Besides, Ewyas Harold was only thirteen miles southwest of town.

He loved that bike, but he wasn't stupid and didn't ride it in winter. He wasn't getting any younger, and he wanted his years on this earth to last a bit longer. Black ice had killed too many of his grip-twisting friends, so now he chose to respect that two wheels and winter didn't mix.

Anyway, he had a great-nephew to help save. He loved his niece dearly. She had been the only family he'd had since Tilly died. When Noah came along, he healed a little of the pain he had still felt from losing Tilly and their son.

He knew it had cost Skye immensely when she chose to stick by his side when her parents had demanded she cut all ties with him. It saddened him that his own brother could hate him so much. But his ignorance and prejudice about Reg's abilities were too fundamentally ingrained. They were close once, but the pressure of being the heir apparent to the family fortune had changed William a great deal. He hardly recognised his own brother in the end.

When Skye's parents, William and Margaret, turned their backs on her for getting pregnant outside of marriage, they further ostracized her for not cutting ties with Reg, He'd vowed to watch over her, as if she were his own.

He was so deep in thought, he hadn't noticed them turning into the old industrial estate at Rotherwas. This had previously been the site of the old Second World War munitions factory. It was long since derelict, and most of the buildings were either empty or crumbling or were knocked down.

Driving towards the right, to the far end, he was surprised to see two large warehouses had been made into one large building. It had to span at least two-hundred thousand square feet. It looked nondescript from the front, the corrugated metal the same as every other unit on the estate and just a sign that read *Fortis Security* on the wall. But, the building obviously had work done to it because, compared to the rest, it was like a palace.

There were eight, black SUV's parked on the right, and a couple other fancy-assed cars to the left, including the bright yellow Mazda. But it was the Harley 48 that caught his eye. The attention to detail was breath-taking and it looked to be in immaculate condition. Reg had previously thought these people might be knuckle-headed macho men but it looked like at least one had some good sense.

They exited the car and as he walked by the bike, barely resisted the urge to stop and admire it. The warehouse backed onto the open-countryside. Reg idly wondered how much land was attached to this operation, and if, indeed, it was *just a security firm*, as Skye had told him. He served his time in the military as a young man, and lived through several tours of Northern Ireland. He'd seen some things that still haunted him today. Although, not in the sense that his wife did.

She chose that moment to give him an ear-bashing about his mind wandering from the job at hand. He rolled his eyes at her tirade and ignored her.

Chapter Eight

Skye walked into Fortis beside Nate–her hand clutched tightly in his. A knot the size of a watermelon was currently lodged in her stomach, making her feel nauseous. The anxiety and nerves hearing about what they learned overnight, if anything, was making her feel slightly woozy.

Right now, she should be giving Noah his breakfast and making sure he brushed his teeth properly. Mundane responsibilities, but every one she cherished for the gift they were. She prayed that whoever had him hadn't hurt him. She felt the few bites of breakfast she had eaten churn in her stomach.

Nate must have sensed her discomfort because he let go of her hand and draped his arm around her shoulders, pulling her flush with his side. She looked up into his beautiful, chocolate brown eyes and took strength from him as she wrapped her arms around his waist.

They walked past the small kitchen and the overnight facilities and into the conference room. It was large with room, big enough for a twenty-person conference table and chairs in the middle. The walls were a pale green–almost white–colour. The florescent lighting was bright and harsh after the dank greyness of the morning light.

A coffee station and fridge with drinks was along the back wall. A large white board and screen to the left of the door and front of the room. The screen was hooked up to two laptops with other technical equipment Skye couldn't make head-nor-tail of. There were no windows and it gave the room a cave-like feel that for some bizarre reason, made Skye feel safe.

She felt Uncle Reg at her side and turned to see what he made of it all. She was not surprised to see he seemed to be taking it all in his stride. Nothing seemed to faze him, but she guessed when you spoke to the dead, nothing would. She wondered if she should have mentioned her uncles special gift to Nate and her new friends here when news about Lauren and Claire's abilities had come out. But it hadn't seemed like the right time and then the opportunity never really arose afterwards.

She startled as the door opened behind her as Zack, Zin, Daniel, Drew, Dane, and Lucy walked in. She got chin lifts from Daniel and Zin, but Dane surprised her when he walked past her and gently squeezed her shoulder as he did. It seemed to impart everything he needed her to know because he didn't say anything. He was a good guy and will make an excellent dad.

Nate guided her to a chair near the head of the long conference table next to Zack's chair at the top and sat beside her. They both faced the door so saw when anyone came through. He placed her hand on his thigh and threaded his fingers through hers. She was grateful for the connection and offered him a tentative smile. Lucy, who was wearing black, leather, skin-tight trousers, black heeled knee-high boots, and a black long sleeved tee shirt with a silver skull and purple butterflies on it, came and sat next to them and lent across Nate towards her.

"How you doing hun?" Lucy asked kindly–compassion and determination in her eyes.

"I'm hanging in there," Skye replied.

"Good. Don't worry, we'll get Noah back, and then I'm personally going to kick the ass of the person or people who took him." From the look on her face, Skye believed she would not hesitate to kick some ass. She wished she were more like Lucy–confident, sexy, capable of looking out for herself and those around her.

She felt eyes on her and turned to see Zack watching her from the head of the table.

"Morning, Skye. How you holding up?" he asked gently.

"All right. I just want to know what's going on and help in any way I can."

Zack nodded, "We have a few updates and some progress." Just then, Reg started to shout at his Wife.

"Goddamnit, Tilly, give me a break woman. …… fine, I'll tell them."

Skye looked around hesitantly at all the faces staring at Uncle Reg. Most were bemused. Dane was openly smiling and Zack looked pissed off at having his meeting hi-jacked.

"Would someone like to introduce us?" Zack asked, openly glaring at Nate.

"This is Skye's uncle, Reg. He's offered to help us keep an eye on Skye and help get Noah back." Nate said calmly holding Zack's gaze.

Skye held her breath, waiting for Zack's reaction. She let out an audible breath when Zack looked down and blew out a sigh as if trying to control his temper.

Skye decided she needed to step up and tell everyone about Uncle Reg's quirk. He wouldn't mind, he never did and he never tried to hide it–hence the loud conversations with Tilly.

"Umm, I feel I need to explain a few things to you all." Dane openly started to chuckle now, but tried to shut it down when Zack cut him a look that would freeze the balls off an Eskimo. "Uncle Reg has some quirky abilities…" she paused to let that sink in.

"Go on, Skye," Nate said gently, squeezing her hand.

"Uncle Reg can talk to the dead. It's not some weird, dark thing," she said quickly, "but he does talk to his dead wife, Tilly, a lot."

"That is the shit," stated Lucy excitedly, leaning back in her chair and towards Reg.

Reg smiled widely, his eyes crinkled at the corners, showing the handsome man he still was despite his funky purple beard.

"Up top, babe," he said to Lucy, holding his hand up for a high-five. Lucy happily obliged. Skye watched this and then cast her eyes around the silent table. Well, silent except for a still chuckling Dane. Lauren was good for him, she thought. He had really loosened up.

Her gaze skittered to Zin, whose intelligent eyes were smiling. She then caught Zack's eyes. He looked pissed and resigned at the same time. But, not one of them looked like they didn't believe him or thought he was crazy.

"Nate, can I have a word *outside*?" Zack said as he stood and walked to the hall.

"Sure," Nate replied, before turning to drop a light kiss on her head before following him out.

~~~

Nate walked out, knowing that he was going to have to stand up to his boss to defend his woman. He didn't like it, but there was no way he was allowing Zack to sideline Reg and make this any harder on Skye. Zack turned to Nate, hands on hips.

"Care to elaborate?" Zack asked.

"Look, boss, he turned up at Skye's last night while I was at Joanne's place. He was sitting with a shotgun across his lap, having an argument with his dead wife. I talked to him about what's expected and he agreed. I know this is not how we operate, but this is not a normal case for us, either." Nate huffed out a breath and shook his head. He could totally see why Zack would have reservations, but he had also seen Reg`s genuine love for Skye and would not allow that support to be taken away from her. "Look, despite his strange ability, he seems like a good guy and he loves Skye and Noah."

"Fuck," Zack said, shaking his head. "We don't need him fucking anything up, Nate."

"Do you think I don't know that? Fuck, man, that's my woman's son who`s missing. I held her while she cried her eyes out this morning, so don't tell me what's at stake. I know." Nate was annoyed now. He paced, hands on hips, waiting to see what Zack would do.

"Fine. He stays, but you are in charge of making sure he does as he is told, and I want Lucy to run a background check on him."

"Fine. I can do that," Nate said, relieved that he wasn't going to have to go up against Zack. "Can we get things started now? This is not helping to find Noah."

"Sure, come on, lets go," Zack said, and then shocked Nate by slapping him on the shoulder good-naturedly. They turned and walked back into the conference room. Skye looked up at him anxiously. He gave her a wink and smiled to reassure her. He slipped into the seat beside her and grabbed her hand.

"It's all good, *mi cielo*." He ran the backs of his fingers along her upper arm, and despite everything that was going on, he felt her react to his touch with a tremor. He liked how responsive she was to him—he liked it a lot.

Nate and Skye focused on Zack as he began to bring everyone up to speed on developments.

"So, first things first. We think we know who took Noah," Zack said, addressing the room, but zeroing in on Skye. "It's a man named Kanan Harrison who works for SIS. He and I have a chequered history that I won't go into, but I will say this…he would not hurt a child. Whatever his reasons for doing this, hurting Noah is not one of them." Nate felt Skye tremble beside him and ignored his own need to go tearing out of the room after this Kanan guy, and concentrated on Skye.

"He called me last night out of the blue and called in a favour. He asked that I look out for his sister, who incidentally, knows nothing of his existence. I agreed and Zin is going to talk to her in a bit. We'll be offering her the receptionist job. I ran checks on her, myself, and she is as clean as a whistle." Zack looked everyone in the eye as he spoke–his calm authority reassured Skye that they were the right people to handle this.

"I'm using other channels to try and get a lock on Kanan. Other than that, we also have the Joanne lead to run down, which Dane and Drew are going to do. Lucy, I want you to check for any chatter about her murder, and lets not rule out this being connected The Divine Watchers. Look into Redcast and any other connections that lead back to Skye or Noah. Nate and I are going to talk Noah's father. I have dealt with him and his family in the past." Nate nodded his assent. "Daniel, we have the five new recruits coming in tomorrow for induction. I know you've met them, but I want you to spend tomorrow getting to know them and showing them the facility. The new training course is set up but can you spend today checking the outdoor range is ready to go?"

"Sure, no problem," Daniel said amenably.

"What can I do? I need to do something," Skye said.

"Yeah, we can help," Reg said gruffly.

Zack nodded, "Okay, I need you to watch the house, Reg. And Skye, I need you to stay by the phone." He held up his hand before she could speak. "I know you want to be more hands-on, but they might try to get in touch and I need them to be able to get hold of you. While you are home, make a list of anything that has seemed off in the last six months."

"Fine, I'll do it." She turned to Nate, "Will you keep in touch, please?"

He reached for her and cupped the back of her neck, not caring what anyone thought. "*Mi cielo*, I will keep you in the loop at every turn, I promise. You just need to keep safe."

Skye nodded. "Okay," she whispered, reaching out to grip his forearm tightly.

"Lucy," Zack said, breaking them out of their moment, "go with Skye and set up trace equipment on her home phone. And do her mobile before she leaves."

"Yes, Sir, boss man, Sir." Lucy answered with a salute, causing Zack to roll his eyes as if he was dealing with an errant child.

"Right, that's it. You all have your missions. Keep checking in with me regularly, and I don't have to tell you to stay frosty–we don't know exactly who we're up against, and this is personal. Briefing at eight o'clock tomorrow morning."

Everyone started to get up, ready to go about their jobs. They looked focused and determined, and Nate was proud to call them all friends.

"Umm, before you go, I just wanted to pass on a message from the missus," Reg said, getting everyone's attention. "Now, I don't know any more about this than you, but she said, and I quote, 'Watch for the people from your past.' I don't know more than that, but she thinks it's connected to Noah.

"I know you are all probably sceptical and think I'm a flake, and you might be half-right, but do not ignore this. It may not make sense, but keep it in the back of your mind. You have nothing to lose." He shuffled his feet as he stood and put his arm around Skye. "This little girl and her boy are all the family I have, and I will do everything to protect them," he said the last turning to Nate. "I won't let any of you down."

Nate looked at him and dipped his head, "I believe you, Reg, and we're glad for the help." Reg's chest puffed up with pride and nodded his head. "Thank you, son." He then spoilt his cool demeanour by turning and yelling at his wife again. "Tilly, will you please stop yammering in my ear. Now pipe down about cakes. I don't do no cake making…I don't care about bloody icing, for Christ sake. Stick a sock in it woman." He turned back to the openly bemused and amused gazes of the room.

"Right, everyone go," said Zack, shaking his head. Everyone filed out with a grin on their faces. Nate grabbed Skye's hand to stop her from following.

"Go on, Reg. I'll meet you out front," Skye called to him.

"Come on, Reg. I'll show you the tech room while I grab what I need," said Lucy, sliding her arm through his and guiding him out of the room.

~~~

Nate pulled Skye gently into his arms and held her tight. He didn't like the idea of leaving her. He knew Reg would look after her, but he still didn't like it. "You okay, *mi cielo*?" He felt her nod into his chest and touched his lips to her head. "Do you want me to call anyone to come sit with you?" Skye eased her head back. "No. You get going. I'll call Lizzie when I get home. I still have some cake orders to get done, so maybe she can keep me company while I do it."

"Why don't you cancel? Everyone would understand." Nate said softly.

"I know, but I want to keep busy. If I stop to think…" her voice broke then, but she rallied. "I just need to keep busy," she said, again.

"Okay, *mi cielo*."

Letting her go, he grasped her hand and went to find Lucy and Reg.

Chapter Nine

Cocking his leg over his bike and pulling on his helmet, Zin contemplated what he was going to say to this Celeste woman. He wondered, for the first time ever, if perhaps Zack was being too emotional over this. He seemed almost protective of her. He never thought he would call Zack emotional. Hell must have frozen over. The drive-by he did last night had yielded exactly nothing and left him feeling off, somehow.

Riding his bike past the Honda garage and the chip shop, he turned onto the street where Celeste lived on. It was on a steep incline and she lived at the top. He manoeuvred his bike past all the parked cars on the street and found a space a few doors down from her place.

Her home was a semi-detached Victorian house with big bay windows on the top and bottom, which was typical of the period house. The area was middle class family income, and all the front steps and houses, in general, were well maintained. He was glad to see they hadn't gone the way of most large, old houses in the area and been made into flats or bedsits. It depressed him to see old houses turned into money making properties rather than family homes.

Zin was surprised that she could afford this house on a tattoo receptionist's wage. The front door was painted red and the brass letterbox shone. He climbed the three steps to her door, rang the bell, and waited. It was after 9 am, so she should be up. He saw movement in an upstairs window and waited. He waited some more, but nothing, so he rang the bell again. He was starting to get impatient, then the door opened.

What he saw shocked him to his biker boots. Standing in front of him was a tiny pixie. That was the only explanation. She was about 5ft 2in and very petite. She had short black hair that framed her face in little wisps and the most shocking green eyes he had ever seen.

She was dressed in black leggings and slouchy purple jumper that hung of one-shoulder and pink pig slippers. Her skin was a warm rosy colour and looked so soft that he itched to reach out and touch it. Her cheekbones were high, her lips lush and pink. It made him wonder if the rest of her was that rosy colour. She was the most stunning woman he had ever seen and he didn't trust her as far as he could throw her.

It was the most intense, vivid reaction he had ever had to a woman, and he had to fight to keep his face impassive. Zin swallowed his extreme thoughts and zeroed in on the beast beside her.

Lounging at side was an enormous German Shepard dog. It was completely black and had big black eyes. He looked at Zin with an alertness that made him aware that if he put a foot wrong with this woman, he would likely lose an arm, and hopefully just an arm if he was lucky.

Zin snapped out of his exploration of her and her dog when she asked in a soft voice, "Can I help you?" She held herself in a protective way–slightly behind the door, as if ready to shut it in his face.

Putting his hand out cautiously for her to shake, he said, "Yes, my name is Zin." She looked at it as if it was a snake, and then so quickly he might have missed it, grasped his hand, shook it, and dropped it before he ever registered her touch.

He shifted his eyes to her face and was surprised to see that she had gone pale and looked like she might faint. She reached out her hand and started to pet the dog's head as if that one action would make her feel better. The beast looked up at her with total adoration then returned his gaze to Zin.

"Are you okay, Miss?" he asked, his accent becoming more pronounced as he spoke to her. He noticed her hands shook, she put it behind her back.

"Umm, yes. Yes, I'm fine. What can I do for you Mr. Zin?"

"It is just Zin. Zin Maklakov," he corrected. "I saw your profile on LinkedIn and came to offer you a job. I work for Fortis Security and we are looking for a receptionist. I could see by your profile that you have experience as a receptionist." Zin could tell by her face that she seemed dubious and he didn't blame her. This was lame.

"Look, Miss Bourdain, I can see that you don't trust what I am saying, so I will leave a card and you can check it out yourself. But I will say this, we need this position filled immediately. So if we don't hear from you by lunch time we will offer it to the second person on the list." Zin knew this might backfire. She could walk away, but he also knew she needed the job if her bank account was anything to go by. "Think about it and call us. The salary is good and there is a benefits package."

She snatched the card from him, careful not to let their hands touch.

"Okay. I'll give it some thought and call by one if I'm interested. Thank you."

Before Zin could reply, she had closed the door in his face. Well that went well…not. Not only did he not convince her, he likely scared her silly. He was loath to explore his reaction to her. She was not his type. He liked his women tall, blonde, curvy, and convenient. He didn't have time to be tied to anyone and had no wish to be, either. He liked when a woman knew what she was doing and understood what he wanted–and Celeste looked like a scared virgin.

So why had he felt his body start to react to her like it did? Must be the dry spell, she was not his type at all–she looked far too innocent for his tastes. He needed to get laid. Scrolling through his phone, he sent a quick text to Tara. She was always up for some uncomplicated fun. Still, he couldn't get that little pixie's face out of his head, and that was bad news. Therefore, he was going to give Miss Bourdain and her scary assed dog a very wide berth.

Turning from the door, he went back to his bike and swung his leg over. He could see the curtain twitch and knew she was watching him. Maybe she would call. He hoped so–she needed the money and Zack was very keen to uphold his end of this crazy bargain. Zin didn't want to let Zack down. It had nothing at all to do with wanting to see her again. Nothing at all, he told himself.

Starting the engine on his beautiful bike, he smiled as she purred and turned her back towards Fortis.

Chapter Ten

Skye entered her home and it immediately felt wrong. It was so quiet and somehow different from the other times when Noah wasn't home, for whatever reason. She'd let Uncle Reg enter in front of her and appreciated him being here. Lucy followed behind her.

"I'm going to get set up," Lucy said, lugging her equipment into the living room to the main telephone line.

"Okay. I'm going to get started on some cakes, but I'm going to phone Lizzie first."

"No need, she texted me that she's already on her way."

She and Lizzie had met this summer through Lauren. Lizzie was Dane and Lucy's older sister who had a son of her own. They'd become close and just clicked. Lizzie had been at the party last night, when she had got the awful call, but Skye couldn't remember a lot about it. It all seemed blurry already. It was just like Lizzie to drop everything and come to her aide, though.

She had two birthday cakes to get started on. One a second birthday cake for a little girl named Alice–who was Peppa Pig mad– and the other an anniversary cake for a golden wedding anniversary. She had the ideas all sketched and the customers had approved everything. She needed to start on the fondant flowers for the anniversary cake so that they could dry out. She loved this part the most and found it relaxing and soothing.

Skye wandered into the kitchen and began getting everything she would need together. She could hear Lucy and Reg talking in the living room, and it soothed her. She didn't think she could take the silence right now.

Soon she found herself rolling and manipulating the fondant into beautiful yellow roses and cream calla lilies. She'd leave them to set in the cool, dry air of the office. Well, less of an office, more of an art room, really. It was, actually, just a large summer house that had been converted into extra work space for her. Reg had built it for her and she loved the way the windows at the front of the wooden construction let in loads of evening sun

She had just started to roll the fondant for the Peppa Pig cake for Alice when Lizzie came rushing through the door. She ran to Skye and enfolded her in a hug–pink icing and all.

"Oh, sweetie. What can I do?" She stepped back, but kept hold of Skye's arms, looking at her closely, assessing to see how she was holding up.

"I'm not sure we can do anything. The guys seem to have it all covered. I just have to sit, wait, and drive myself crazy. I could do with some help with this order, though. I have twenty-four tiny Peppa Pigs to make for the top of the cupcakes, and I'm behind. I've had about three hours of sleep and I can't seem to focus properly, so everything is taking twice as long.

Lucy entered the kitchen then.

"Hey, sis," she said, threading her arm through Lizzie's, who just let go of Skye.

"Hey, baby girl. You done with your super geek thing?"

"Yeah, I'm going to head off now and conference call Will. He has a few shortcuts he thinks will speed up the investigation. Just wanted to check on Skye before I go."

"I'm fine, Lucy, thank you. You get back, but keep me in the loop, please. I feel so out of it here."

"Of course, chickadee. Look after my girls, Reg," Lucy shouted as she hauled her stuff out the door.

"No problem, Lucy Lou," Reg replied from the living room.

"So, do I get to meet Uncle Reg? Lauren has told me all about him. He sounds like a scream."

"Yeah. Come on I'll introduce you."

Skye and Lizzie didn't finish the Peppa Pig decorations until two in the afternoon. Lizzie had forced Skye to sit down on the couch and pushed a sandwich and a cup of tea on her.

"You have to eat something, Skye. I know it probably feels like lead, but you need to keep your strength up. Noah is going to need his mummy healthy when he gets home."

Skye was sitting on the sofa, her legs tucked underneath her, looking at the sandwich distastefully.

"I know, I'll eat it. Do you think anyone has heard anything yet?" Skye asked as she picked at the crust of the sandwich. She hated crusts, she thought and couldn't remember why. She focused on the bread to try and stop her mind from wandering to what might be happening to Noah and failed.

"I'm sure they will call as soon as they can, honey," Lizzie said gently, sitting down next to Skye.

"Come on, girlie. You got more grit than this. Eat your food then phone that man of yours and ask him for an update," Reg said sternly. Her head came up at his words and the way in which he said them. She looked at Reg with a pained and slightly annoyed expression.

"Listen, baby girl," he said more softly, "I've known you all your life and you are the strongest person I know. When your father and mother disowned me, you stood by me. When that idiot left you alone and pregnant, you got up, got yourself a home, and started baking cakes to keep you and the boy fed.

"When beautiful Noah was diagnosed with that awful, soul-destroying illness, you didn't let it stop you. You carried on making your cakes, making a home for him, and you did it with guts and determination. Now, I know you had a lot of blows, but now is not the time to sit quietly back and wilt. You need to eat and stay strong and ready for anything. I'm getting me some heeby jeebie vibes right now, Skye, and they are telling me you are the key. So you need to buckle up, butter cup."

Reg relaxed back in his chair, hands laid across his middle, shotgun at his side. His speech obviously finished.

For a second, Skye was stunned, but then she realised he was right. She was a scrapper. Not in the sense that she went out on a Saturday night and got into scraps with people–she never hit anyone in her life–but she didn't let life get her down, ever. She just got up and kept going, and that was what she going to do now. She picked up her sandwich and finished her tea quietly. She saw Lizzie let out a relieved breath and go back into the kitchen.

Skye needed to think. She got up and crossed to Reg. Leaning down, she kissed his grizzly cheek.

"Love you, Uncle Reg."

"Love you, too, girl," He said gruffly.

"I'm going to catch an hour on the bed. Will you wake me if you hear any news?"

"Course I will. You go straighten your head out. I got this."

Skye walked down the hall to Noah's bedroom. She looked around at the Lego models he had spent hours building, and all of the boy paraphernalia–posters, books, lightsabre's, and costumes. He loved all things Star Wars and superheroes. He wanted to be like Luke Skywalker or Captain America one day. She teased him constantly that Han Solo was the best.

She climbed onto his bed and picked up his cuddly Bruno dog. It was ratty and faded, but he loved that dog, had since he was a baby and never slept without it. Even in hospital. She laid down and hugged the teddy to her face. Silent tears tracked down her cheeks as she prayed to God he was safe and he would be home soon.

~~~

Nate was surprised at the size and beauty of Lockwood Manor. He'd never been there before, but he'd heard about it. It was set on four-hundred acres of land, including a large forest that wrapped round the back of the property like a cloak. It had to be 100 acres of

Ash, Beech, Oak, and Elm trees that were at least two hundred years old.

The house itself was more of a castle in style. The research Nate managed to do on the drive over told him that it was thirteenth-century with 24 bedrooms. The grounds included a large natural pond with koi carp and large decorative water lilies. The gardens were a tourist attraction with privet hedges shaped into swans and lions.

There were special rose gardens, that history told, were a favourite with Mary Queen of Scots, or so the website said. The ten acre maze had to be one of the biggest draws, though. Every year they held an Easter egg hunt for all the local schools. Apparently, it was very popular.

There was a small chapel on the grounds where all of the Lockwood family were buried, and historically, the Manor had belonged to Henry Tudor who gifted it to the Lockwood's after they'd shown loyalty to him during the War of the Roses.

It struck Nate that this was Noah's birthright. Did Skye have any idea? He hated Hugo Lockwood on principal for leaving them in the lurch as he did. He was overjoyed for himself, because now, he had the privilege of making Skye and Noah his.

As Zack pulled the car into the large circular driveway with the golden gravel paths, and the water fountain making the centrepiece of the drive, Nate was shocked, again, at the size and magnificence of this place. Wisteria hung like a beautiful blanket over a majority of the front giving the manor a romantic feel.

He and Zack had talked on the drive over about the likelihood of the Lockwoods being involved. Zack had had some dealings with them through his family and Nate was shocked to hear that the Cunningham family had some blue blood. But this shouldn't have surprised him.

You only had to see how Zack dressed to see he was used to the finer things in life–every shirt he owned was designer. Nate had no problem with that. Zack more than gave back and earned every penny he had. In this instance, it would help that his boss was familiar with these people.

Striding up to the enormous double front door, Nate was hoping Hugo would be here. They didn't know he and Zack were coming, and Nate really wanted to meet the guy that abandoned Noah. He would try to curb the desire to hit him in the face. Apparently, it was classed as bad form. His jaw hardened as he thought of Skye's pale face when he left her earlier. Maybe a small punch to the face wouldn't hurt?

He wasn't normally prone to random acts of violence, but he felt so protective of Skye and Noah, and the thought that anyone could abandon his own child, and leave the mother of that child swinging in the wind, was abhorrent. Especially as the Lockwoods obviously had tons of money. And yet, he had still left her to struggle to keep a roof over her and Noah's heads. He shook his head at that thought– Hugo was a fucking scumbag, even if he did wear designer suits and monogrammed cufflinks.

Zack rang the doorbell and after a short wait a tall, thin, severe looking man, in full butler regalia, opened the door. He glanced at Nate dismissively, but when his eyes cut to Zack, he was more respectful and dipped his head, slightly, in acknowledgment. Fuck, was this real? Did people actually behave like this? Where the hell was this man's common decency that he would feel deferential towards one person because of their social status and the next minute look down his nose at Nate? *Dick*.

Zack took charge and Nate let him.

"Is Hugo Lockwood in?" he asked, stepping forward, forcing the man to step back.

"He is indisposed at this time, Sir," the butler answered pompously.

"Tell him Zack Cunningham is here to see him, and I won't be leaving until I do." Zack's tone brooked no argument and the butler obviously realised that.

The butler tipped his head again, "Of course, Sir."

Nate looked at Zack, who seemed used to all this.

"How the fuck do you put up with this shit, *hermano*?"

Zack laughed humourlessly, "I grew up with this shit, so, this shit is normal. Thank god, my mum was not born to it and she brought me up to be normal. Well, normalish," he conceded on a smile.

"Yeah, thank god," Nate smiled back.

They were brought out of their discussion by shouting coming from upstairs. They stepped forward as one towards the magnificent staircase made of hand carved oak.

"Time to make our presence known, I think," said Zack determinedly, starting up the stairs quickly, Nate onestep behind him. They followed the sound of the escalating shouting down a long, elegant hallway. Stopping as, what appeared to be a glass, came sailing out from the door on the far left, and hitting the wall and shattering into hundreds of tiny pieces. Nate stopped, his hand moving to his weapon at the back of his waistband–he saw Zack doing the same.

The next minute a very pale butler came running out. He stopped short when he saw them and tried to regain his composure.

"You can't be up here," he said pretentiously

"Yeah, well I am. What you going to do?" said Nate, feeling pissed off beyond belief. This shit was going down and all he wanted was to find a, most likely, terrified out of his mind little boy.

"Out of the fucking way," he said as he pushed past the butler into the room.

What he saw when he entered made his spine stiffen and his hand on his drawn gun tense. He couldn't believe it–surely nobody's bad luck was that bad. He stalked towards the bed and at the grinning, self-satisfied, smug face of his childhood nemesis.

The man who had tormented him, who had pursued him and had fucked his fiancée just to fuck with him, was lying in bed in all his naked glory.

"Tell me you are *not* Hugo Lockwood…" Nate growled, dangerously. He'd honestly never felt so close to losing his shit. His hand tightened again on his gun and his stance was rigid as he stood by the bed.

"Nate, what's going on? Do you know Lockwood?" Zack asked from beside him, close enough to lock him down if needed.

"This is Lockwood?" Nate asked instead.

"Yes, this is Hugo Lockwood."

"This is the Hugo Lockwood who left my woman alone and pregnant and abandoned his son?" he ground out.

"Yes, unfortunately. Now, Lockwood will you tell me why Nate looks ready to commit murder?"

Hugo Lockwood started to chuckle and both men's eyes swung back to him.

"Shut the fuck up," Zack commanded in a frigid voice, causing the smile to die on Lockwood's smug mouth.

"When I knew him from my time at scout camps, he was known as Sam Reeves. He and his posse made my life a misery as a kid at those camps. And it got worse when 'Sam' decided he liked me and wanted a bit of this," Nate said pointing to himself and indicating exactly what way he meant. "Then, when he couldn't get his own way, he fucked my fiancé and made sure I would walk in and find them, and now you are telling me he is the father of my woman's son?"

"*Fuck*. That is fucked up," Zack said, shaking his head. "Sorry, man. I had no idea. Knew he was a prick, but not that he was that much of one. Shouldn't be surprised, though. His dad was a prize prick, too."

"Umm, I am right fucking here, you know, and this is my house," Hugo said, recovering some of his arrogance. "You can't just burst in here and insult and wave guns at me."

"Think I just did," replied Nate.

"Put some clothes on and get downstairs. We have some questions you are going to answer, and I don't want to look at you naked while I do it," Nate said disgustedly, waving his hand at Hugo and his nakedness. He was finished with the reunion. "We'll wait outside, and *please* do something stupid to give me a reason to put a bullet in you." Hugo must have known not to push his luck, because he just nodded.

Out on the landing, Zack looked at Nate, "You going to be cool" he asked?

"Trying, man, but what I know of this guy, he won't make it easy."

Zack nodded, "Yeah, I can see that. But we need to stay focused on Noah." Nate cut his eyes to Zack, "I know that," he said through gritted teeth.

Lockwood came out a few minutes later, dressed in dark slacks and a hunter green shirt, his hair still messy but his clothes immaculate. They started down the stairs–Hugo in front of them. He'd regained some of his swagger and decided to try to push Nate's buttons.

"So, we both fucked the lovely Skye. She is rather beautiful and classy in a common sort of way." Clearly, the look on Nate's face and the muscle twitching in his jaw was not enough of a warning for

Hugo to shut up. "Did she do that thing with her tongue? You know, the one that makes you feel like you are gonna blow any second if she doesn't stop?" he asked smugly, and then, as if he had a death wish said, "Ha! You haven't fucked her have you? Oh, man, are you in for a treat."

Hugo tripped suddenly, after Zack pushed him the last few steps down the stairs, causing him to fall. Before he could get up, Zack had him up by the collar and punched him in the face.

"What the fuck!" Hugo whined, "You split my lip!"

"Well, shut that fucking mouth of yours and I won't do it again. Be warned, dipshit. I was in control when I hit you. If I let him have a go at you, he's not going to stop until Granny has to have you cleaned off the marble flooring." Hugo cut them a scathing look, but shut up.

"Why'd you do that? You said I couldn't." Nate asked, slightly pissed that he hadn't got his go at Hugo-Dickhead-Lockwood.

"Three reasons–one, I'm the boss, two, he was annoying me, and three, I'm not sure you would have stopped." Nate huffed. He was probably right. When he'd start pounding that bastard, he probably wouldn't stop.

Grabbing Hugo by the shoulder, Nate shoved him towards the first door they came to on the ground door. It was a large library; Nate was astounded by the opulence of it. The walls that were not covered in ancient books were a deep, dark red.

Ancient tapestries hung from the ceiling, and down the walls, there were even swords and shields displayed. A chaise lounge was in front of an open fireplace that was lit and roaring. Beside the lounge were an antique sofa and chairs set in a semi-circle round the fire. Behind the chaise was an antique, dark wood drinks cabinet with a cut glass crystal decanter filled with a dark, amber liquid. As if that wasn't enough, two of the windows on the front were stained glass and depicted some sort of family crest with roses in it.

Hugo walked over to the crystal decanter, grabbed a glass and poured himself a healthy dose of whatever was in it. He knocked it back and glared at them.

"So, what do you want?" he asked, acid in his voice.

"Where were you on Saturday night between 10 pm and 1 am" Zack asked as he circled to the left, leaving Nate to stand near the door and only exit. Nate watched Hugo intently, looking for any tells he was lying as he spoke. And there it was. Hugo looked to his feet, then swallowed before answering. He was going to lie.

"I was here with grandmother." Zack looked at Nate, who shook his head.

"Wrong answer. Come on, Hugo, don't fuck with me. Now, try again or I'm going to let Nate have a go at using your face as a punching bag." Nate stepped forward, playing his part, although, it wasn't a part. He would happily pummel Lockwood's smug face.

"Oh, *please*, lie again, dickhead. I just need one excuse to rip your head off." Hugo didn't look quite so cocky, now.

"I was, umm, I was with friends at a private party," he hedged, looking uncomfortable, now. "Why are you asking me all this?"

"Because someone has kidnapped your son, you piece of shit and we *are* going to get him back. If I have to shoot every person I meet between now and when I find him to do that, I will. Because, you see, I love that boy and his mother, and I will stop at nothing to get him back to her. Now do you get it?" Nate had walked closer to Hugo as he spoke, his face barely containing his anger, his body tight, trying to control the desire to hit Hugo.

"Well, I didn't take him," he denied vehemently. "I was nowhere near Skye's house on Saturday night."

"Who said anything about Skye's house?" Nate growled.

"Well," Lockwood lounged back against the back of the sofa and rubbed at the back of his neck as if he didn't have a care in the world, "I just assumed that he was, at home when it happened," he defended cockily, not once looking them in the eye.

Nate lost it, then. This dickwad knew something, and he was going to tell him. Stalking up to Hugo, he grabbed him by the throat and pushed him nearly double against the back of the sofa, putting his gun muzzle to Lockwood's temple. "Start talking," he snarled.

Lockwood pulled at the hand locked tight around his throat, desperate for air.

"Let him breathe, Nate," Zack said nonchalantly from beside him. He'd materialised there when Nate lost his patience. Loosening his grip a bit, Lockwood sucked back air.

"Fuck, you're nuts man," he wheezed.

"'Yeah, I am, so start talking before I shoot you."

Hugo was just about to start talking when they all heard a screech from the door, "What is the meaning of this?"

They all turned to see a coiffed and demure Lady Lockwood standing at the door, with the smug butler behind her. She quickly, but elegantly, crossed to her grandsons side. Nate held fast to Hugo's neck until Zack indicated to let go. He dropped his gun to his side and released his hold on his throat. Hugo stepped sideways, rubbing his neck and sucking back more air.

"Zack, what are you doing here? Why have you come into my home with your thugs and brutalised my grandson?"

Zack laughed. "Oh, please, Felicity. Let's not pretend you don't think that Hugo is the weak embarrassment to the Lockwood name. As to why I'm here, Hugo was just answering some questions about his son for us."

Nate saw Felicity go stiff at those words and wondered what she knew. Was she in on this? Nate was certain Lockwood knew something about Noah, but did the old lady know, too?

"What about the boy?" She asked, cautiously.

"He was kidnapped on Saturday night, and as you can imagine, we had questions for the next of kin. Unfortunately for Noah, that means Hugo."

"But, why are you and your mercenaries handling this and not the local police?"

Zack didn't bother to explain the difference between what he did and what mercenaries did.

"Because Noah's mum, Skye, is one of our friends and Nate here's girlfriend" he said, pointing at Nate. "So, that makes it our business." Felicity Lockwood turned her cold, imperious gaze to Nate. She gave him the once over, clearly finding him wanting.

"Well, we know nothing about it. And, it would seem to me, that if the boy is not safe with his mother, maybe it is time for Hugo fight go for custody."

Nate felt the like his head was going to explode. Never in his life had he wanted to lay his hands on a woman in anger, but right then, he wanted to ring her scrawny neck. Zack must have sensed this, because he stepped in front of a growling Nate and got up in Felicity's face.

"Saying that right now is very unwise, Felicity. And in light of your grandsons proclivities, I would think you ever gaining custody of Noah is unlikely wouldn't you. If you gave a shit about your family, you would want to help, not grind his mother down further by saying fucked up shit like that. Also, if you cared so much, why is Nate the one giving your great-grandson the bone marrow transplant he needs instead of his father, who refused to be tested?"

Felicity looked at Hugo, "Is this true that you refused to give the boy bone marrow?" She asked with an ice-cold tone in her voice.

"Umm…well, I…"

"Spit it out, you stupid boy," she said, losing her cool and cuffing the six foot Hugo behind the head. Nate saw him go red, and his nostrils flare angrily. "Well, did you? Oh, forget it, of course you did. Always out for yourself," she said furiously.

Nate was surprised she had let her mask slip. God, what an utter bitch. No wonder Hugo was the way he was, being raised by that. He might not have had been rich growing up, but he never doubted he was loved by his family. This woman was as cold as a witch's tit. In fact, witch felt like a good description, even if she was a well-dressed one.

"As fun as this is, we do have things to do. So if you wouldn't mind answering the question we will be going," Zack said, in a bored tone, contradicting the frustration Nate knew he was feeling.

"Well, go on then. Tell them what they want to know, Hugo," she said, patting Hugo's arm, almost kindly, as if the last few minutes hadn't happened. She had gotten a grip on herself now and was back to showing her caring grandmother side.

Nate could see something flit through Hugo's expression. The man hated this old lady, and if Nate wasn't mistaken, he was close to snapping. But he wasn't quite there, so he answered, "I was with some friends and we went to a private party. I had a few drinks, smoked a bit of weed, then came home. You can check with Delilah and Henrietta Ibbotson-Smythe and Ashby Clements–they were there, too."

He looked like a child who was acting out and being told off by the head teacher. It made Nate wonder how this dipshit had ever managed to pull someone as clued in and wonderful as Skye. The thought of her with Lockwood soured his stomach.

It made him want to lay claim to her in the most intimate way possible. To eradicate Lockwood from her mind and body. If he could wipe any memory of this man from her, so that she was his for all time, he realised he would.

Concentrating on what Hugo said, not on his history with Skye, he thought about his answer. Although he felt Hugo was telling the truth just now, he was sure he knew something about what happened with Noah, and he would bet his house that Witch Lockwood did, too.

"Fine. We will check that out, we have all we need for now," Zack said, watching Lady Lockwood intently, and making Nate wonder what he was thinking.

"We'll show ourselves out." Zack spun on his heel, ready to leave. But Nate stopped and got up into Hugo's face, "Don't forget, dipshit, you come near my woman or her boy again, this is not going to end with granny holding your hand. You get me? From now on, they cease to exist for you. If I find out differently, you're going to be the one who ceases to exist, are we clear?" Nate watched Hugo swallow and fight not to take a step back. "Yes, we're clear," Hugo answered through pinched lips.

Nate turned his glare on Lady Lockwood, then, just to make sure she got it too. She had more backbone than her grandson, but she also had some sense, so she just glared back–lips pursed as if she was sucking a lemon. He strode to the door, then, and followed Zack out.

They climbed in the car and Zack turned to him, "You love her," he accused.

"Yep," he said, no more and Zack chuckled. "What is in the water–my men are dropping like flies." He sobered then, though, "Sorry you had to deal with Hugo. I had no idea you had history."

"Don't sweat it. It's done, it's over. Skye and Noah are mine to protect, now, and I think I made that clear."

"That you did, brother that you did."

"So, he knows something. I think we can agree on that," Zack said. "I'm going to get Lucy to concentrate on Hugo and Felicity Lockwood and keep Drew on general backgrounds. I'm also thinking I'll bring Jack and his team in on this. See if they can get surveillance on this place and on Hugo and Felicity."

"I think that's a good plan. I have a very bad feeling about this. I know he is your friend, but if I get hold of this Kanan guy, I 'm going to rip his head off. What he's putting Skye and Noah through can't be justified, no matter what he says." Zack nodded his understanding, "I get that, and I wouldn't call us friends, now. More like acquaintances." A look of regret crossed Zack's face before he could stop iy, but Nate said nothing. Whatever that was about was his business.

Zack put the call in to Lucy as he drove. He also called Jack Granger and got him to put a team on surveillance. They were just driving back into Hereford when Zin called.

"Zin, talk to me," Zack answered.

"Just had a call come into Fortis, Celeste Bourdain wants to come in and see about the job. I told her we would call with a time."

"Okay. Daniel is there checking out the outdoor training facility in the woods. Call him and ask to meet with her ASAP. I want her there today."

"Done," Zin replied and disconnected. This did not surprise Nate; Zin was not one for words if a chin lift or glare could accomplish the same thing.

He should call Skye and give her an update, but he wanted to be very careful with what he told her. They didn't know for a fact the Lockwood`s were involved and he didn't want to upset her or her get her hopes up in case they were wrong–not that he thought they were–but he would rather gauge her reaction and talk to her face to face.

He shot of a quick text, telling her he'd be home in half an hour.

Chapter Eleven

Nate let himself into Skye's bungalow using the key she'd given him a few months ago. He was a little concerned she hadn't texted him back. He walked down the hallway, feet quiet on the dark laminate flooring. Entering the kitchen, he saw Lizzie was washing the dishes from what looked like lunch.

She was, as usual, dressed in smart, cigarette leg trousers and a classy wine coloured jumper. She looked like the epitome of elegance. Lizzie always dressed like this. Nate couldn't ever remember her in jeans, even as young girl. She was class from head to toe. Running her own successful antiques shop, he guessed she had to portray a certain look, and she pulled it with aplomb.

Her dark hair was pulled back into a chignon at the nape of her neck. He liked Lizzie, because despite her elegant look and her put together appearance, when you got to know her, she was just like Lucy. And she could put away jaeger bombs with the best of them. He was pleased she was here with Skye. He liked Reg, but he trusted Lizzie.

"Hey, Liz." Lizzie jumped and held a hand to her chest as she spun to face him.

"Nate. I didn't hear you come in." Nate put his hand out to steady her.

"Sorry, didn't mean to scare you. Where's Skye?"

"She went for a lie down about an hour ago," she hesitated. "Is there any news?" she asked, hopefully.

"We have some leads, but nothing concrete. It's a start, though. I'm going up to her," he said, anxious to get to Skye and hold her in his arms.

"Okay. I'm going to head off if you're going to be with Skye. I need to see Mateo."

"Okay, Liz. Thanks for staying with her," Nate said.

"She'd do it for me. Honestly, I can't imagine how she is feeling." Lizzie dried her hands and grabbed her bag. "Tell her I'll call her later," she said, going on tiptoes, kissing Nate's cheek.

"I will, Liz," Nate said, walking her to the door.

Nate walked back into the kitchen and through to the living room. Reg was sitting in the armchair, with his gun by his side, watching football. Somehow, Nate hadn't pegged him as a football fan.

"Hey, Reg. How has she been?" Nate asked, sitting on the arm of the sofa across from Reg.

"She had a bit of a wobble earlier, but I gave her some gentle truths and she seemed to rally. She had some food Lizzie made and then went to her room for some quiet time. She'll be okay. My girl's a fighter." He turned his head as if listening to someone else and Nate assumed he was listening to Tilly. He turned his attention back to Nate after a second, "Is there any news?"

"We have a lead. We think her ex might be involved, somehow so we're going to put some surveillance on him and his home."

"No good, piece of shit, bastard. I knew he would be trouble the moment I met him. Got to my girl when she was young and vulnerable." Nate nodded knowing that that was exactly Hugo's MO.

"Yeah, I had some dealing with him in the past," he said, not elaborating. "He is a narcissistic asshole, and that grandmother of his is even worse."

"I can agree on the first, but haven't met the granny, so can't comment on her," Reg said softly. Nate was about to reply, but Tilly beat him to it.

"Woman, I never met her...I don't remember no garden party! Oh, that pinched faced old biddy, I remember."

He turned back to Nate, "I remember her, now. Met her about twenty years ago at some swanky party my brother had. Tight-faced old cow. All rigid and looking down her nose at everyone. Her husband seemed okay, though. A bit beaten and hen pecked, but okay. He's dead. Died about eight years ago, probably put himself out of his misery from that nagging, old cow."

Nate filed all this information to give to Lucy and Drew.

"Well, I'm going to check on Skye. You good here?"

"Boy, got food and football. I'm all good."

"Cool." Nate patted Reg on the shoulder and left to find Skye.

He looked for Skye in her bedroom, but she wasn't there and didn't hear her in the bathroom. He left her room and crossed to Noah's. Pushing open the door, he saw her lying on her side on Noah's bed, his brown teddy held tight to her chest. She was sleeping so peacefully. He was loath to wake her, but knew she would want him to.

He sat down on the bed in the gap between her knees and her chest. He studied her face, relaxed in sleep. The soft skin pale and marred only by the dark circles under her eyes. He reached out a hand and gently brushed a lock of silky hair from her face, tucking it behind the delicate shell of her ear.

Running the backs of his fingers down her cheek, he whispered softly, "Skye, baby. Wake up." She started to shift slowly, and her eyelids fluttered open.

"Nate."

"Yeah, *mi cielo*. I'm right here."

"Have you found anything?" she asked, sitting up and pushing her hair from her face.

"We have some leads. Why don't I get you some coffee while you wash your face and wake yourself up?"

Skye nodded, "Okay." She still looked a little foggy from sleep. Nate couldn't resist, he pushed his hand into her hair and cupped the back of her neck. Leaning in, he brushed his lips over hers, lightly touching his tongue to her lips for a taste of her sweetness. She surrendered instantly, softening under his kiss. Nate pulled back and touched his forehead to hers.

"Get yourself sorted. I'll make coffee. Okay, baby?"

"Okay, Nate."

~~~

Skye quickly washed her face, trying to wash some of the grogginess from her brain. Nate had looked at her with so much love and compassion, it had almost made her cry. She prayed there was some news. She needed her baby home. She clutched the edge of the sink tightly as she thought of her boy. Legs almost buckling with emotion as she thought of what he's going through–frightened and wanting her.

Taking a deep breath, she locked her knees–she was stronger than this. Reg was right. Everything she'd been through with Noah and her parents, she had never let any of it beat her. She owed it to Noah not to start wimping out now. She needed to take control and help Nate and the team find her boy. Not wallow in pity and pain.

Feeling marginally better, she left the bathroom and headed for the kitchen and the smell of coffee.
Nate was pouring her a cup and she went to him and took it, leaning into his strength as he opened his arms for her. She felt Nate kiss her hair and wished this was all under different circumstances. Reg was standing against the counter, a mug of tea in his hand.

"You okay, sweetheart?" he asked, holding an arm out to her. She snuggled into his side, accepting his silent invitation. She adored her Uncle Reg–always had, always would.

"I'm holding up better, thanks, Uncle Reg." He kissed the top of her head.

"Good, sweetheart."

"Skye," Nate said, snagging her attention. He was leaning against the counter, arms braced behind him. The material of his top pulled tight over his powerful chest and arms. His denim clad legs crossed at the ankles in front of him.

"Zack and I went to visit Hugo and Felicity Lockwood," he said, breaking her out of her perusal. "We think they might be involved," he stated calmly. Skye pulled away from Reg and went to Nate. Looking up at him, she grasped his upper arms.

"Tell me," she demanded, urgency in her tone.

"Hugo seemed to know that Noah had been taken from here. He unconsciously gave that away, though. He has an alibi for the time Noah was taken, but that is not a surprise, as we're sure Kanan took Noah. We have Eidolon providing surveillance on both Hugo and the property.

"Fortis will put an operation together to search the property as soon as we get the information we need on the security. We don't have the men to do a full breach, so it wouldn't be wise. If Noah is there, he could be hurt in the chaos, so we need the info first so we can go in quiet." Nate reached for her, pulling her into him. Resting his hands on her hips, she went willingly.

"We still have Drew and Lucy looking for other leads and Detective English and his team are following other avenues. This is by no means concrete, Skye. I don't want you getting your hopes up."

"But it's the best lead you have, right?" Nate nodded and pulled her head to his chest, cradling her gently against his body. He put his arms around her waist as she raised her hands to rest them on his chest.

"Yes, I believe so." He didn't tell her about what Felicity had said or his history with Hugo.

"Well, what can we do to help? Maybe I could go and talk to Hugo find out if he knows anything."

"No. You are not to contact him or anyone else. Do you hear me Skye? I'm serious on this," he said sharply.

"God, okay. No need to be mean about it."

"I'm not, but I just need to know that you get me," he softened his voice this time.

"Fine. I won't contact him," she said, slightly testily. She put her head down and crossed her arms across her chest, but stayed in the circle of his arms.

"Skye. *Mi cielo*, look at me," his voice gentle. She raised her eyes to his.

"What," she snapped. Seeing Nate's lip's twitch, she smothered the desire to hit him in the gut. He let go of her waist and wrapped his hands around the back of her head, he tunnelled his fingers into her hair, running his thumbs across her cheekbones.

"I won't risk you, too. I can't concentrate on getting Noah back if I have to worry about you. I need you to stay safe. Please, do this for me." The genuine emotion in his voice was disarming.

What could she say to that–how could she stay angry? He was the first man in her life to protect her and want to protect Noah. Yes she had Reg who protected her and looked out for her, but emotionally she always felt like she was the one protecting him. First from her parents hateful attitude and then from the pain of losing

Tilly. With Nate she felt she could lean on him and not be strong for every waking moment. Nate would lay down his life for them both. That was just the kind of man he was and she was lucky enough to have him care about her and her son.

Her body softened and relaxed into his. He kept his hands where they were for a minute, and then stroked his fingers through her hair and down her back, coming to rest at the top of her ass. Despite the situation and the fact that Reg was in the room, she felt her heart beat faster at the feel of Nate touching her like that.

She wanted to drag him into her room and get lost in him. The feel, the smell, the taste. She knew it would be amazing between them and she knew it was wrong feeling like this when her son was missing, and yet, she couldn't turn it off.

"Okay, Nate. No contact with Hugo or anyone else." She felt him shift and bury his face in her neck, touching his lips to the pulse that was pounding there.

"Thank you, baby.

They stayed like that for a while, and when Skye raised her head, she noticed Reg had left the room.

"Have you eaten?" she asked him, looking into is handsome face.

"Not since breakfast," Nate replied.

"I'll make you something. Is a sandwich okay?"

"Yeah, *mi cielo*, that is perfect. Thank you."

Skye eased out of his arms and set about making him a beef and horseradish sandwich–with lots of beef, just how he liked it. She had started buying it in since they had become close and started seeing each other. Noah liked it too, even though he said the horseradish made his nose tingle.

This thought made her heart heavy, that sick feeling coming back into her throat. Tears pricked her eyes and she quickly blinked them back. Knowing that if she let them go again, she would quickly fall apart.

Skye turned her head to the side when she felt Nate gently touch her hip. She felt him lean his front to her back, sliding his arms around her waist and resting his chin lightly on her head. His strong, warm body offering comfort and safety. He seemed to know intuitively what she needed and when she needed it. She leaned back slightly after she finished making his sandwich, taking his support.

Turning back to the counter she reached a plate from the cupboard in front of her head and got some crisps from the one beside it. Adding some fruit from the bowl in front of her she turned and handed it to him. He stepped back and took it from her. He grabbed her hand with his free one, pulling her with him to the living room. Settling down together on the couch opposite Reg, she silently watched Nate talk with Reg. He seemed comfortable with him.

She let the mundane chatter lull her as she thought about how Hugo might be involved with her son's abduction. It was troubling her, because in the beginning, she had encouraged him to be part of Noah's life. Yes, he'd left her and she had quickly seen him for what he was–but she had still wanted him to be part of his son's life.

He'd shown no interest, whatsoever, despite her countless attempts. She had even sent baby pictures for the first year. Every milestone photographed and recorded. Eventually she came to realise he didn't want to know and if he didn't, she didn't want to force it. It was a privilege to be a parent and if he couldn't see it, that was his loss.

So, why after all this time had he just kidnapped him? Why not come to her and ask about visitation? She had never been unreasonable, and if he did want to see Noah, she would have expected a solicitor's letter, asking for visitation. But this seemed off assuming of course that he was involved. She hated not knowing for sure.

She trusted Nate and Zack, and how they read the situation, but her gut said something else was going on.

Deep in thought, she didn't realise Nate had been talking to her.

"What? Sorry…"

"I said, do you want to get some fresh air? Take a walk now that the rain has let up. Reg can stay here by the phone and we'll have our phones with us."

"Yeah, sure, that would be good. Let me grab my boots and a coat."

She and Nate left a few minutes later after Nate had given instructions to Reg and told him where they were going.

Chapter Twelve

They drove into town and parked on the road by the duck pond. Grabbing Skye's hand, Nate pulled her close, and slung his arm round her shoulder. They didn't talk as they walked towards the Victoria Bridge and crossed the river. Following the river footpath, they walked around the St Georges playing fields.

Skye was, once again, lost in thoughts of her son. She was trying hard not to let the overwhelming feeling of fear and hopelessness suffocate her. After a few minutes, Nate stopped and turned to face her.

"I know Hugo from my childhood," he said, watching her intently.

"You do? How?" He took her hand and they carried on walking.

"When I was a kid, I was in the scouts. Every summer we would do camps and stuff. There was this boy, Sam Reeves. Everyone knew he was a rich spoilt brat, but every year he came and made everyone's lives a misery. He bullied everyone, but when I was about eleven, I found him and a few of his friends beating up this other kid. He was only nine and I stepped in. I knew they would probably kick the shit out of me, but I couldn't stand by and watch." Nate paused. She squeezed his hand to let him know to go on. "I was lucky, one of the scout leaders came just as they turned their attention to me, and I got away.

"But, after that, Sam and his friends made it their mission to make my life hell. Every summer I had to constantly dodge being alone with them. Sometimes it worked, other times, not so much. When I was about thirteen, I discovered martial arts and started karate lessons. The next summer when they started hitting on me, they came off worse than I did.

"It never stopped for Sam, though. He just started the mind games, then. He started making sexual advances at me the next year, and let me tell you, as a fourteen-year-old boy, that freaked me the fuck out. I would much rather have had the kicking. When that didn't work, he seduced my sister. She was sixteen and he told everyone about it. I could take whatever he dishes out but, to see him mess with my baby sister just to fuck with me? I lost it and went looking for him."

"What happened?" Skye asked, almost dreading the answer.

"I gave him a hiding he wouldn't soon forget. I went home and sat, waiting for the police to come and arrest me, but they didn't. It seemed Sam had my attention and he loved it. He loved that he had gotten to me. I had stopped going to camp by then. I would see him around town in the summer. He would watch me, but he didn't approach me again. He always seemed to be there, though, wherever I went."

"I went into the army when I was eighteen, and obviously filled out a bit and kept on with the martial arts. Anyway, when I left the para's, I met a girl named Nikki. I thought she was the one. We got engaged and it was going well, until one day I went to her place and caught her in bed with Sam Reeves. He'd known all along she was my fiancé and had deliberately set it up so that I caught them." He stopped their walking and looked at her. "The thing is, Sam Reeves is actually Hugo Lockwood. I didn't know until today."

Skye was shocked speechless. She felt her hands start to tremble and her stomach churned.

"Oh my God, Nate. I'm so sorry. Why would he do all those things?"

'Don't be sorry, you aren't responsible for it. And to be honest, he did me a favour with the whole Nikki thing, and he does it because he is a narcissistic sociopath."

"How did I not see this when I dated him?"

"That's the thing with people like him. They can be extremely charming and you only see what they want you to see."

"Do you think he knew about you and me?" she asked quietly.

"No. He seemed genuinely shocked today. That is another reason I think he knows about Noah. I can read people really well, and I have known him a long time. He knows something, Skye."

"Does Zack know about your past with him?"

"He does now."

"I'm so sorry I brought him back into your life, Nate. If you don't want to carry on with this," she waved her hand between them, "I will understand."

Nate lowered his head so that he was looking into her eyes. He cupped her jaw in his big hands, "I don't care about him being Noah's father. I want this, I want you and Noah in my life. I know now is not the time for these kinds of discussions, but I will say this, I like what we're building, and I want us to continue that. I plan to be in your life for a long time and not as your friend, but as your man. Do you get me?" The intensity and feeling shone in his eyes, making Skye feel warm all over.

"Yeah, I get you and I want that, too," she whispered. He rested his forehead against hers and then tilted her head so he could kiss her.

He was gentle and it was feather light as his lips brushed hers. He deepened it when she touched her tongue to his lips. Skye gripped onto the material of his coat when he took the kiss deeper, forcing all thought from her head except him and this moment. It felt wild and hot and full of promise. Feeling him pull back, she opened her eyes, but kept his lips lightly touching hers. He smiled then, "Come on. Let's go to Fortis and get an update." They walked back to the car, both lost in their own thoughts but feeling more positive.

~~~

Nate parked outside Fortis and noted that Zin's bike was parked near the door, and Lucy's beloved yellow Mazda was in its regular slot, despite Zack asking her to park it round the back. Zack tried to be strict with Lucy, but Nate thought Zack secretly admired her feisty nature, even if it did give him grey hair, or so he said.

Everyone had sort of adopted Lucy as a little sister. That didn't mean they didn't respect her abilities, just that they felt protective of her. Her ability in close combat was second to none. She had been invited to compete in the MMA world championships in Baton Rouge this coming summer, but had turned it down.

Rounding the front of the car, he took Skye's hand. She had been quiet on the drive over, perhaps thinking through everything he said. She had handled the revelation that Hugo was Nate's childhood enemy, well, but he worried she would dwindle on it and get herself in a state. She had already apologised for something that wasn't her fault, and he didn't want her taking that on with all the other things she had to deal with right now.

He would keep a close eye on her and make sure she wasn't bottling things up. A definite lead would really help right now. Going through the front, and past the security door and into the hub of the operation, Nate heard raised voices.

"What the fucking hell is that doing in my conference room?" Zack boomed. Nate looked at Skye, whose eyes had gone wide. He angled her slightly behind him and pushed through the door. Zack, Zin, Daniel, and a petite pixie with a huge, jet-black German Shepard dog, met him. All eyes turned to them. The pixie looked nervous, Zack looked exhausted, and Zin looked pissed off. Daniel was the only one smiling.

The dog, who had been growling at Zack, turned his attention to Nate and growled until the pixie laid her hand on his head, instantly putting a stop to the growling. After a second, the beast took the growl down to a low rumble as he turned his attention back to Zack and Zin. Skye let go of his hand and walked forward slightly.

"Skye, be careful that animal will tear you apart," said Nate. He saw the pixie smirk and glared at her.

"He won't. He is a good boy, aren't you?" she said in a baby voice that Nate had never heard her use.

"Is he friendly?" Skye asked the pixie.

"Yes. He's a big softie, just very protective of me."

"I'm Skye." she said, offering her hand slowly, not to alarm the dog. The pixie seemed to hesitate before shaking Skye's hand. She looked surprised when she did and smiled a beautiful smile, that for some reason, made Zin look even angrier.

"His name is Samson, and I'm Celeste." Nate watched as Skye's features closed down, but instead of saying anything, she knelt down and slowly extended her hand towards the dog to sniff. Nate felt his body go rigid.

So this was the sister of the man who took Noah. Could she really not know anything? She had an innocent look about her, and a vulnerability that screamed yes, she was indeed innocent, but women could be devious creatures–and even Zin, who never showed emotion–seemed pissed off at this woman, and that made Nate wary.

Nate stepped forward, wanting to be able to get between the dog and Skye if he had too. He needn't have worried. The dog, like everyone else took, one look at Skye and loved her. He sniffed her hand, then proceeded to lick and nuzzle it. Sensing that it was okay, he moved forward and licked her face, causing Skye to laugh.

"He is gorgeous. Aren't you boy? Just a big old teddy bear." She ruffled his collar and then straightened.

"So, again, I ask, what that beast is doing in my conference room?"

Nate had forgotten about Zack's question, completely focused on Skye and her interaction with Celeste and Samson.

"Where I go, he goes," Celeste said simply.

"So you're telling me, that if you take the job he comes with you?"

"Yes," she replied unequivocally. Zack went quiet for a minute, studying her, and must have decided that it was okay."

"Fine. Welcome to Fortis, Miss Bourdain." He smiled and went to shake her hand, but Samson growled, so he stepped back, frowning.

"Is he going to growl every time I'm around?"

"No. He'll get used to you, eventually," she smiled, and Nate noticed she had an incredibly pretty smile. For some reason, though, her smiling seemed to further piss Zin off. He muttered something in Russian and pushed past Skye and Nate.

"I'll be in the gym if anyone wants me," Zin said, testily. Nate was trying not to chuckle; he had never seen Zin sulk over anything, but he seemed to be having a moment, now. Celeste and Samson were certainly going to make things interesting.

"Okay, Miss Bourdain. Daniel will go through your job description, hours, and pay. We will see you bright and early tomorrow morning."

Daniel, who stood with his arms crossed over his chest, legs braced, nodded at Zack.

"Come on, Celeste, let's get some coffee from the kitchen and I'll go through it all with you." Daniel walked past Zack, Celeste followed with Samson at her side.

"Nice to meet you, Skye," she said as she passed them. She tipped her head at him and he realised he hadn't introduced himself in the kerfuffle over the dog. He tipped his head, not having decided about her yet.

"You, too, Celeste," Skye replied thoughtfully. Zack followed them out and walked towards the tech room.

Nate watched Celeste leave and turned to look at Skye

"You okay?" he asked her.

"Yeah. It was just a shock to see her. She seemed…I don't know, normal I guess. Do you think she really knows nothing about her brother or Noah?"

Nate wasn't sure but he didn't want to worry her.

"I think that I trust Zack, and if he says she knows nothing, then she doesn't. He's the best man I have ever met at his job, and if he checked her out then you can bet he was thorough."

Skye nodded.

"Come on. Let's go and see Lucy. Maybe she has an update."

They walked to the tech room and Nate, again, punched in the code for the door. Lucy was at her terminal, and Drew was talking to Zack about something, over at the other one. Lucy was talking to somebody on the screen, but Nate couldn't see who it was.

Moving closer, he saw it was Will Granger. Will didn't look like a private security operative, mainly because he wasn't–not in the sense that he, Dane, Zin, and the others were.

Will had been a hacker and had hacked into something he shouldn't have, namely the bank of England. He'd been caught, but because he was only fifteen at the time, he only had an eight month suspended sentence. He cleaned up his act after that, and Jack Granger who was in charge at Eidolon asked Zack to take him on when he set up Fortis. Nate knew Zack was pleased and had said, countless times, that he had been planning to poach him away from Jack anyway. Will was integral to how well the team operated.

Jack and Will were brothers and couldn't be more different if they tried. In looks or personality. Jack was the epitome of badass operative–tall, muscled and broody. Will was a tall, wiry man covered in tattoos and piercings. It seemed to work for him, though, because he was a happy guy and never seemed short of a date.

Nate leaned over Lucy's shoulder and she looked up and smiled. Turning back to the screen Nate said, "Will, when you coming home, bro?"

"Nate, long time no see. I'm wrapping up this project and should be home before Christmas. I hear I have some competition, so gotta get home and protect my turf and make sure this one has been treating my babies right."

Will was the only person Nate knew who would refer to his computers as his babies. He was also the least likely to be intimidated by other people on the job. So, Nate knew he was only kidding around about Drew. From what he could tell, Will had been helping Drew learn the ropes by giving him lessons and tests over Skype.

"Great, man. Be good to have you back. You hear about Sly joining us?"

"Yeah. Had my mum yapping in my ear about it for weeks. I swear her and Aunt Nancy never get off the phone. Its great news and I have more opportunity to give cousin *Sly* some shit about his nickname then. Listen, Lucy was explaining about your girl's son. Sorry about that, man. I'm installing some software I've been playing with that will notify us when the user uses any device that needs Wi-Fi or an online connection. It will, also, be able to trace all their devices including bank accounts that will go back twelve months in the records. It should help find any connections. Lucy has also launched the spider to search the internet for any code or algorithms that lead back to, or mention, the watchers, even if it is not a direct mention."

"How does that work?" he asked.

"So, if you have an internet conversation, say on a dating site, if the spider picks up anything in that conversation that might, in any way, be construed as being linked to the Divine Watchers even if it only used code words or a cypher. It will then run it and determine the link and the statistical viability of it being a lead."

"That's great. Thanks, Will."

"Happy to help, man. Just sorry I'm not there."

"I'll leave you guys to it." Nate squeezed Lucy's shoulder.

"Take care of her, Nate," she said quietly.

"Of course, *corazón*."

He turned and Skye was right behind him. He took her hand and she held his tight. He knew that she was flagging, and as the day wore on and no news came, she was getting despondent. He walked her over to Drew and Zack.

"Hey guys, any news?" Zack and Drew both swivelled in their chairs to look at them. Zack cast Skye a compassionate look. But the look he gave Nate told him the news they had wasn't going to be shared in front of Skye. This did not bode well. He was wondering how to get Skye out of the room when Zin walked in.

Zack stood and started towards the door.

"Nate, Zin my office!" he then strode out past Zin. Zin and Nate looked at each other. Zin shrugged and followed Zack. Nate looked at Skye, the smudges under her eyes were looking more defined by the minute. He needed to get her home.

"Will you be okay with Drew a minute while I find out what this is?"

"Yeah, sure." her eyes told him what her mouth did not. She was terrified that what Zack had to say meant something bad had happened to Noah. Every instinct in him wanted to protect her, and yet, he knew he couldn't protect her from this.

"I won't be long. Why don't you sit down." The fact that she let him guide her into the chair paid testament to how she was feeling. "Look after my girl, Drew," Nate said, and gave Drew a look that told him Nate was worried. Drew nodded and scooted his chair closer to Skye.

Walking through the open door off Zack's office, Nate stopped short. The look on Zack's face was not good and for a second Nate didn't want to go in and hear what he knew was very bad news.

"Nate, come in, close the door." Zack stood behind his desk, which was bare except for a computer and a pen. Zin was leaning against the wall to the left of the door, arms crossed, body stiff.

"We just heard that Hugo Lockwood's finger prints were found at the house of the murder victim." Zack was watching him for reaction. Nate couldn't supress the ripple of relief that coursed through his body. He had been expecting the ultimate in bad news. This was bad, but it was also a good reason to pick Lockwood up and question him.

"Detective English is currently out looking for him. Jack had managed to get a tracker on his vehicle so that shouldn't take long."

"So, why do I get the feeling you haven't finished with the bad news?" Nate asked calmly. Zack looked at Zin. "Just fucking tell me," Nate growled.

"We have reason to believe that Felicity Lockwood is heavily involved with the Divine Watchers. We also found some rather shady things in her past."

"Fuck! If she has him, then we need to get him out, now. There is no telling what she will do. You saw her, the bitch is crazy. And what about her past?"

"Well, going back to before she met Lockwood, she was a high-class call girl. This was very well hidden, and she has changed her identity at least twice, that we can find. The information was buried extremely well, which tells us she has some serious contacts.

"Zin and Drew are looking back further–Drew through searches, Zin through his contacts. But it would seem that each time, just before her identity falls off the map, at least one of the people close to her dies and then she disappears. When she meets Lockwood she is going by Felicity Spencer and working as a PA at a London law firm. That is where she hooked her star to Lockwood. He was a bit older than her and fell head over heels in love."

Zin snorted at this and took over, "Lockwood had no idea what she did at night, but she had some very nasty friends back then, including Brown Bread Fred, or you might know him as Freddie Foreman." Freddie Foreman had been a freelance enforcer for the Kray twins during the 1960s and was a nasty piece of work.

"Fuck! So she has connections to the mob?"

"Yes, and was rumoured to have had an affair with Reggie Kray. She would have been young then, and it is only a rumour."

"How are we only just finding this out? How come nobody ever found out before?"

"No reason to. The Lockwoods stayed on the right side of the law, and although obnoxious, they lived quiet. It's only since old man Lockwood and Hugo's parents died that she has become more visible in public," Zack replied.

Nate stood up and started pacing. Skye was going to flip. "I can't tell her this." He pushed his hand through his hair, making it stand up, and swore again. "Fuck, fuck, fuck!"

"Dane and Daniel are looking into all of her known associates now. We should have intel about Lockwood Manor by tonight, and Zin and Drew are hunting down everything they can on them. I'm going to see if I can speak to Marcus Preedy and see if he is feeling more talkative than last time. You need to tell Skye that we have some good leads and as soon as we have a positive sighting of Noah, we will go in."

"Fine, but I'm in on this. I want to be there when you get him out. He'll be scared enough and he knows me and trusts me." Nate said vehemently.

"Of course," Zack nodded.

"I'm going to take Skye home. Ccall me when you hear anything, and I mean anything, Zack."

Chapter Thirteen

Skye was terrified. Nate had been gone half an hour already. What the hell could they be talking about? She could tell by the looks Nate and Zin had shared that something was going down. She didn't want to know because even though she knew something had happened and it was bad, she didn't know if she could face it. She should have demanded to go in with them and tell them she wanted to know, but she didn't. She didn't want to know if something had happened to her baby.

Her gut felt like it had lead in itm and her hands wouldn't stop shaking. Drew had quit trying to talk to her when she kept zoning out on him. He was such sweetheart. He just scooted his chair closer and continued as if she was listening raptly.

She jumped up from the chair when Nate walked through the door and ran to him. His hair was sticking up as if he had been running his fingers through it. She reached him and grabbed hold off his biceps suddenly desperate to know what she hadn't wanted to a few minutes ago.

"Tell me, tell me what he said." Nate put his arms around her back and pulled her tight to him.

"We have a significant lead on Felicity and Hugo. There is still no sighting of Noah, but we should have eyes in the house tonight. As soon as we get confirmation, we'll go in."

Skye felt her legs buckle and a sob tore through her. She buried her head in Nate's chest and cried. Nate caught her and held on tight. He whispered words of comfort in her ear and held her while she cried it out, right in the middle of the Fortis tech room. After a couple of minutes, she felt controlled enough to look up. Nate didn't let go, though.

"Please, don't let go of me," she said quietly. Nate brought his hand up, and with so much tenderness, wiped her cheeks with his thumbs.

"I won't, *mi amor*, I won't." Nate cuddled her back into his side and she suddenly knew this was where she belonged; forever, with this man, by his side, always–even in the midst of all this, the worst thing to ever happen in her life, she knew.

She held tight to him as he said goodbye to Drew and Lucy. She barely remembered getting to the car or getting home. She just knew everything would be okay as long as Nate held her tight.

When they arrived home, Reg wasn't there. He'd left a note on the kitchen counter saying he was seeing a friend and would call if he wasn't going to be back tonight. Good thing they had had all the calls coming into Skye`s house re-routed to Fortis, thought Nate.

Nate walked her to the couch and lightly pushed her down into it. Skye slipped of her coat, then toed off her boots. Curling her legs up under her, she watched as Nate removed his jacket and put it over the back of the dining chair. Coming to her, he lifted her up and placed her on his lap. She snuggled into him, placing her head in his neck and finding the soft skin and the scent of him calmed her.

"I'm sorry for falling apart," she said.

"You haven't got one thing to be sorry for, Skye. The fact that you even got out of bed is admirable. It'll be okay. Noah's tough. I know he's only a boy, but he has a wisdom beyond his years. Hopefully by this time tomorrow, he will be home."

"Do you think so?"

"Yeah, I do."

"Okay." She stopped talking then, and must have drifted off. The next thing she felt was Nate picking her up and carrying her to bed.

"I can walk," she mumbled.

"I know, *mi amor*," but he didn't put her down. He placed her under the covers and tucked her in. She heard him close the door as he left.

~~~

Nate closed the door to Skye's bedroom but left it open slightly so he could hear in case she woke. He hated to see her so vulnerable. He needed to get Noah home to her now. Opening his contacts on his phone, he shot of a text to Dane, asking for an update. It wasn't long before he got a reply. *Nothing to report. Most associates are dead.* With that a bust, he texted Zin.

Any news on Hugo? He replied quickly, too. *Yes. Cops picked him up, drunk, in Shack Revolution. Going to observe the questioning now. Will report in when I have news.* Nate was surprised, that was quite a long text for Zin.

Nate prowled around Skye's bungalow like a caged lion. He was on the second turn when his stomach started to growl. Realising he hadn't eaten since lunch, and it was now seven in the evening. He went to the kitchen.

Nate lived alone, so he was quite proficient in the kitchen, and Skye being a good mum, had plenty of healthy food in the fridge. He took out a packet of noodles and some stir-fry veggies and quickly cooked it with some packet sauce he found in the cupboard. It wasn't his finest creation, but it filled a hole. He went to the living room and turned Skye's computer on. He googled the Lockwoods and found loads of gossip sites that had stories featuring Hugo. That was as good a place as any to start. He settled in to wait for updates from the team and did some digging.

~~~

At 9 pm, Kanan watched as Felicity Lockwood left the Manor House. By his observations, that meant only the butler and the cook were still on the grounds. He waited fifteen minutes, just to make sure nobody was around, before silently slipping in through the staff entrance. They didn't lock it until the butler left at ten.

Kanan hoped to get in, check on Noah, and then get out before they left. If he didn't, that was okay, the lock would only take him seconds to pick and for some strange reason that he couldn't fathom, it wasn't on the alarm circuit.

Palming his Sig p226 and slipping unseen up the back stairs, he quickly scanned the upstairs bedrooms. They were all empty. Coming back onto the landing, he stopped to listen and think. He crossed to the door he assumed led to the attic. Pulling it open and hoping like Christ it didn't make a noise, he was pleasantly surprised to see it open easily.

Jogging up the steps, he stopped at the top and cautiously looked around, keeping his gun up and ready. It never paid to be arrogant. In the middle of the room was a hospital bed. A small dresser was beside it with a light and a few children's books. In the middle lay Noah.

Coming closer to the bed, Kanan looked down and saw that his colour wasn't good. He seemed pale, but his cheeks had bright red splashes of colour across them. He felt his gut churn. He had done this. His need to find her and his selfishness had brought this little boy here and now he was sick–sicker than he was before.

He hadn't felt guilt in years. Being driven without any conscience had allowed him to be single minded in his job and his personal life, because of that, he was immensely successful as an operative. Less so in his private life though, since he was still alone. He snorted at that. He didn't care at the moment. Right now he needed to fix what he had done to this little boy.

Reaching out, he touched the back of his hand to Noah's forehead. It was burning hot. K brushed the boys sweat soaked hair back from his head.

"Kanan?" Noah croaked.

"Yeah, boy, it's me."

"I don't feel so good," his lip wobbled and he swallowed a sob, "I want my mum!"

"I know, Noah. I'm going to fix this. Can you remember if they gave you anything?"

"They gave me an injection. It hurt a lot, I was brave, though, and didn't cry." Kanan swallowed hard, his throat clogging with guilt and bile.

"I know you were, buddy," he brushed his hand over Noah's head again, as much to reassure himself as to offer comfort.

"I want Nate and mummy. Can you get them for me, *please*." His lip wobbled but K saw him pull in a deep breath and control it. He had seen some bravery in his time in the army, and again since joining SIS, but Noah was the bravest human being he'd ever met.

"I had a dream, K. She wants to hurt people–mummy and Nate and you. I don't want them to hurt you all," he went quiet and then flinched and held his hands to his tummy. "She said it hurts because I'm naughty and I have to have more injections until it stops hurting. I'm scared, K."

Kanan put his big hand over Noah's small one. "I'm going to get you out of here, okay?"

"Okay."

He went as still as marble as he heard voices on the landing. Putting his finger to his lips, indicating to Noah that he should be silent and close his eyes, he slipped back into the shadows and behind a pile of boxes.

He watched as Felicity walked up to Noah, with another man beside her. She pulled back the covers and showed the doctor something on Noah's stomach. Kanan fought the urge to come out of his hiding place and rip the evil bitch away from Noah.

"He is having an adverse reaction to the drugs. He will need to be moved to the Surrey facility so our doctors can keep a closer eye on him. I will arrange transport for first thing tomorrow. For now, give him liquid paracetamol and ibuprofen to control the temperature. That should ease the discomfort, as well," the man said.

"Fine, but I will accompany him to the facility. I will not have your doctors do anything without my knowledge. This child is mine and I won't have anyone taking control over him except me."

"So, if you have him you have power, is that it Felicity?" the man asked.

"Exactly, my friend. Exactly." She replied with a cold smile.

"As is right. I will arrange it and call you later with the details. Give him the medicine and maybe some of this." He handed her a capped syringe

"What is it?"

"It's just a sedative to help him sleep. You don't need to be watching him all night. You need sleep too. I will leave the security detail here over night to protect you and the boy. The police having arrested Hugo has the higher ups nervous."

Kanan watched as Felicity Lockwood placed her hand on the younger man's arm, "You do look after me Fred. You are such a good boy." The man preened under the praise and nodded.

"I must go. I will call soon."

The man left quickly. He watched as Felicity woke a 'sleeping' Noah–none too gently–and forced the medicine on him. She turned then, and left Noah alone.

He stepped out from behind the boxes, cautiously. He looked at Noah, who looked like he was indeed sleeping now and quietly left. He took the back stairs again and managed to just slip out before the security that was left behind saw him.

Pulling back as far as the perimeter hedge, he hunkered down and used his hi-powered binoculars to see what he was up against. He didn't like what he saw. He counted ten men fanned out around the outside of the manor, all dressed in black fatigues, obvious they were all highly trained.

He stayed in position for over two hours. He was about to leave when he became aware of an itch in his neck. Someone else was here. He held his position in the woods and scanned the surrounding area. His night vision goggles that he'd acquired from SIS allowed him to see far more than standard issue goggles.

His eye caught on something to the east of him far out from the house. He wouldn't have seen it if he hadn't undergone intense survive, evade, resist, and extract training with the SAS. A heavily camouflaged operative was belly down in the grass facing the manor. He could tell by the way the operative watched the men patrolling the outside, that he was not one of them.

He wondered if it was a lone wolf or if it was a unit belonging to Zack. Either way, he needed to get gone before he found himself in the middle of this.

Kanan considered his options as he watched, and realised he only had one if he was going to get Noah out safely. Right now, that was all he cared about, he would deal with the consequences of what might happen to Celeste after.

Chapter Fourteen

Nate chucked the mouse onto the desk. Nothing was holding his attention and he was dog-tired. Having waiting for hour`s he still hadn't heard from Zin or Dane. He hated doing nothing. Knowing that he needed to get some sleep, he switched of the PC and made his way towards Skye's bedroom. Reg had texted a couple of times earlier the first to ask for an update and the second to say he was staying out tonight as he had met up with some friends and was going to crash with them. So he had locked up earlier.

Opening the door to the bedroom, he stood for a minute, watching Skye sleep. The light from the hallway cast a shadow over her. She looked serene, even in sleep. Her hair fanned out across the pillow; she slept on her side with her hands tucked up under her face. He couldn't remember ever feeling like this about a woman.

Despite his looks and the attention he got from women, Nate was shy. It never stopped him getting laid though. For some reason, women just assumed he was the strong, silent type, and that seemed to work for him. But the truth was, he didn't know what to say half the time. He couldn't do cheesy chat up lines–it just felt wrong. He was fine when he got to know them though, and was a bit of a joker.

With Skye, though, he never had that shyness. They had developed a friendship first. He had known it was more, but it had happened slowly and developed naturally. Now their relationship seemed to have cemented itself into what it was meant to be. Nate,

Skye, and Noah against the world as one. You didn't get one without the other. He hoped that she would still want him when she found out about his fertility issues. He had studiously blocked it from his mind the last few days. Trying to stay focused on Noah and not how Skye might react.

He wanted nothing more than to give Skye babies and Noah siblings. But an injury that happened on his last tour had made it so his chances, while not nonexistent, were significantly lowered. He'd come to terms with it and had looked into different treatments. There was hope but no guarantee.

"Nate?"

"Yes, *mi amor*, did I wake you?" He went and sat on the bed next to her.

"No. Is there any news?" she asked, sleepily.

"They've picked up Hugo and he's being questioned. No word, yet, on Noah." He saw her nod. She reached for his hands and started playing with his fingers.

"I need a shower," she said, "I feel dirty and icky," but she made no move to get up. Nate raised a hand and tucked her hair behind her ear. She was so beautiful. Skye leaned her face into his palm, her eyes drifted shut.

"I'm going to kiss you, *mi cielo*," He said softly.

"Okay, Nate," she said, opening eyes full of desire. He lowered his head and took her mouth in a soft kiss. It was only meant to be a kiss but soon she was pushing up, trying to take over. Her tongue touched his lips and pushed in. He loved the taste of her. Her hands tunnelled up into his hair and held on tightly. Nate fought to stay in control of himself. He didn't want his need to overwhelm her. He liked to keep control in the bedroom, but he knew she needed this, so he let her lead.

Skye came up on her knees and pushed her body into his front. He fitted her against his chest with one hand in the centre of her back, the other ran up her rib cage, stopping just under her breast. Sliding the hand at her back down, he grabbed onto her ass, squeezing the soft globes, his hand tightening in the soft flesh. His thumb swept across her breast, grazing the nipple and making her shiver. With them plastered hip to hip, it was impossible for Nate to hide his arousal from her.

He thought it might upset her, but she moved and pressed her heat to his hardness, causing him to hiss out a breath.

"*Mi amor*, we need to slow this down or it's going to get out of hand." She pulled back, and the look in her eyes almost took him to his knees. Her eyes were dark and hooded and the need he saw there caused him to growl.

"Shower. Now." He stood and carried her to the bathroom. Once there, he set her on her feet beside the shower and undressed her. He wanted to take care of her and make this about her. This wasn't about sex or anything else. This was him showing her that he cared and cherished her. He reached past her and switched on the shower, allowing the hot water to warm the room.

His eyes never left hers as he stripped his own clothes off. Her eyes shot to his rigid cock and he saw her lick her lips. *Fuck*. He was going to embarrass himself if she didn't stop that.

"If you don't stop looking at me like that, this is going to be over before it starts, babe."

She smiled the sultriest smile he had ever seen and stepped into the shower. He was sure she wiggled her ass as she did.

Nate stepped in behind her and took the shower gel off the shelf. It smelled of watermelon. She must use it a lot because he recognised it. Soaping up his hands, he stood behind her and started to wash her.

His hands roamed all over her slick flesh. Over her ribcage, across her breasts and the blush coloured nipples that hardened under his touch. He palmed her breasts and lifted them, loving the heavy fullness of them in his hands. She moaned and pushed back against him as he pinched the nipples. He let his hands trail down her body and over the silken skin of her ass. Sliding his hand between her legs, he smiled and ran his lips along her neck. She widened her stance, allowing him access to the most intimate part of her. Nate touched her–stroking and retreating, he rubbed his hand against her clit, before pushing two fingers into her. She cried out and pushed back against his hand.

He loved the feel of his cock nestled in her ass cheeks, but Nate wanted this to be about her. She was so responsive and uncontrolled, and he loved that he could give her that. He pushed her higher and higher until her climax crashed through, her making her cry out and her knees sag.

He gathered her round the waist before she fell, and held her while she found her breath. He turned her round and caught her mouth in a gentle kiss.

Nate let her go, but she rested against him, running her hands over his chest, tracing the patterns of his tattoos on his arm and shoulder. He took her shampoo in his hands and started washing her hair as she relaxed against him. It wasn't long before her hands started to wander down towards his straining erection. He pushed her back under the spray before she found her destination, rinsing the shampoo out of her hair.

Before he had time to do anything else, she soaped up her hands and started to trail her hands all over his body. He stood and let her touch, every inch of his body taut with the need to take her and slam into her heat. But, that wasn't what she needed, and he would give this woman anything.

Skye grasped hold of his length and ran her hands up and down. He couldn't control the action as his hips bucked and he strained into her hand.

"Harder, Skye," he ground out. "Hold me tighter." He used his own hand to show her how to work him. He guided her hand as she pumped him harder and faster. His other hand tunnelled into her hair and gripped her tight, kissing her hard and with passion–his tongue mastering hers as she pumped him harder and faster.

He pulled his mouth away and buried his face in her neck as he found his release all over her stomach. He stayed that way while his body came down from one of the most powerful climaxes he'd ever had. The hot water cascading over them, Nate raised his head and kissed Skye gently. She looked relaxed and sated, but her eyes were bright.

"Are you okay?" he asked her softly.

"Yes." But he could tell she was trying not to cry. "I'm sorry. I'm not normally like this, the emotion just got to me."

"It's okay, *mi cielo*. I shouldn't have let things go this far, I just wanted to take care of you." He turned off the water and reached for a towel, berating himself for letting things get out of control when she was so vulnerable.

"No, Nate, look at me," she stayed his hand when he went to wrap her in a towel, forcing him to look at her, "I wanted this, I needed it, I needed *you*. You gave me what I needed. So don't think anything different. Please, don't sully this by thinking it was wrong, because it wasn't."

He touched his mouth to hers. "Okay, babe." He hustled them out of the shower and wrapped her in a warm towel from the heated rail. He watched as she carelessly blow dried her hair and then pulled on a fuchsia coloured nightie with tangerine lace on the edges. He pulled on boxers and climbed into bed. She followed, snuggling into his heat. He reached over and switched of the light.

"Nate?"

"Yes?"

"Thank you."

He was puzzled why was she thanking him. He hadn't found Noah and he hadn't done anything else. "For what?"

"For being so wonderful to me and Noah, and for making me believe there are good men out there." He kissed her head.

"*Mi amor,* you have no idea the pleasure it gives me to be around you and Noah. Watching you with him and everyone you love. You're a very special woman. Skye. It makes me so angry to think that you need to thank me for that. I can promise you this, though. As long as I have you, you will never doubt that you deserve good in your life."

"I think I'm falling for you, Nate." His heart stopped, then continued at a gallop.

"I already did, *mi amor*, I already did. Go to sleep, you need some rest and I'm exhausted."

"Okay, Nate." He could feel her small smile against his right pec.

A few minutes later, Skye's breathing evened out and deepened. She was exhausted. Nate drifted off soon after, but it was a fitful sleep.

~~~

Zack paced the tech room. The visit with Marcus Preedy had been a bust. The guy was closed up tighter than a gnat's chuff. He couldn't figure out if he was a genuine fanatic or if he was scared. He suspected the latter.

He'd gotten back ten minutes ago and was waiting for Lucy to give him an update. She hadn't left Fortis since Noah had been taken. Zin had made her go catch a cat nap in the rest room about two hours ago. He'd woken her and asked for an update. She was just washing up before she came back in and got back on it.

He sat at the terminal Lucy normally used, and loosened his tie. He hadn't gotten any sleep in the last thirty-six hours. He needed caffeine, or sleep, but sleep didn't seem like it was going to happen, so caffeine it was. Draining the last dregs of the strong brew, he went to the conference room and filled up his cup for a second time.

Making his way back to the tech room, he met Lucy and handed her the one he got for her.

"You look like crap, boss." Lucy never failed to amaze him. She hardly slept in two days, and yet, she still had enough energy to give him shit. He wondered if he gave her more leeway because she reminded him of his little sister, but he didn't think so. He thought it was because he seriously admired her grit.

Nobody knew what she had accomplished and overcame–not even her brother. He felt bad keeping that from Dane, but it wasn't his business to discuss, so he didn't.

"Thank you, Lucy. I see lack of sleep hasn't dulled your ability to irritate."

"What can I say? It's a gift," she paused. "Did you have any luck with Preedy?"

Zack shook his head "No. Man wouldn't say a word. Just sat there, silent, no matter what I did," he grimaced, "of course, he is in a government facility right now, so I couldn't use any really good methods for making him talk."

"Did we find out who gave the order to move him to that facility instead of the Eidolon one?" Lucy asked as she pushed open the tech room door and settled herself in her chair.

"No, but it came from high up, and that makes me twitchy," Zack replied. "Okay. Show me what you have," he said, changing the subject. Lucy flicked the mouse, and the screen in front of her came to life. Showing figures and code that made his head hurt.

"So, the things we ran on Hugo Lockwood showed what we expected–no contact with any known Divine Watchers. We did find a few known drug dealers and some establishments known to provide prostitutes. We found he has a massive spending habit. It is not unusual for him to drop 40k on a night out with friends."

Zack whistled, "Guess that's loose change when your richer than god," he snorted disgustedly."

"He does have telephone calls linking him to Joanne over that last six months."

She clicked through some different screens, "He's had access to the hospital, which is worrying. There is footage, which Will helped me find, in the hospital surveillance archives that shows him slipping into the hospital late at night. The footage doesn't show where he goes once he's in, though. He, also, has some very nasty friends– namely Usov Denisovich a member of the Russian Mafia. He settled in the UK fifteen years ago and now resides in Surrey." Zack forced his body to be still and not punch the table like he wanted. He clenched his jaw and forced himself to speak.

"Does Zin know?"

"Not yet. This came in after he left."

"What else?" he ground out."

"Well, when I found this, I started looking into Denisovich. He has some very colourful associates. The rumour that sticks out, though, is the rumour that his brother, Dorokhin Denisovich, is actually the infamous assassin, The Surgeon." Zack nodded. He had heard that rumour, too. He was unsure how Zin was going to take this. With his history with the Denisovich family…he predicted badly.

He'd have to find a way to lock him down so he didn't go off the deep end. That was the last thing they needed was to have to take Zin out of the equation.

"So, what, exactly, is Denisovich involved in?"

"You name it–drugs and weapons, human trafficking, even hints that he provides arms to terrorists. Nobody can ever get any proof, though, and he seems to have protection from the Russian government.

"That's not all, though. What we found on Felicity is worse. She, not only, has links to the Mob, but, Will–and don't ask me how, because I have no idea–has found clips of her meeting with Usov. The footage shows her going into a hotel room and then Usov entering shortly after. Felicity leaves an hour later."

"Show me," Zack demanded. Lucy clicked away on the computer for a minute, then the screen filled. It showed the front of the Corinthian Hotel London. It was in the heart of London, close to the financial and business district. Why would Denisovich be meeting Felicity Lockwood, and why there?

Zack watched as Felicity entered the front of the hotel, and ten minutes later, Usov entered. Usov was a smartly dressed man, never seen in anything but a three-piece suit. He was in his mid-forties, suave and slick in a way that made Zack's skin crawl. He apparently had a tendency towards young girls of barely legal age.

His brother was younger and had been horribly disfigured in a fire when he was a young boy. Intelligence suggested it was the father who had set the fire in retaliation for the mother's infidelity. Instead of dying, though, both brothers had escaped and disappeared. They returned shortly after he died and took over the empire their father had started.

Zack wasn't even going to think of all the conspiracy theories surrounding that–that was for another day. He continued to watch the screen. An hour later Felicity left and got into her chauffeur driven car. It was a good two hours before Usov left.

"Have we got footage inside the hotel?"

"Yes, hang on a sec," Lucy played around with the computer some more, and another screen opened up, "Here you go."

He was looking at the inside of the Corinthian Hotel. He watched as Felicity Lockwood strode down the hallway as if she owned the building, pearls firmly in place around her scrawny throat. She entered the luxury suite on the fifth floor.

Zack had stayed there many times and knew the hotel well. Only those with extremely deep pockets could afford those suites, and they were often reserved well in advance. He kept watching, and ten minutes later, Usov entered. Unlike Felicity, he was not alone. He had two of his goons with him, but they stayed outside while he was inside. The rest of the footage just showed Felicity and then Usov leaving.

"When was this taken?"

"Two weeks ago."

"Okay, I want to know what their connection is, and I want to know why they chose this hotel. Usov has always been known to meet associates at his country home in Woking. Why has he changed things up?"

"Okay, I'll get on that now," said Lucy, perkier than earlier. You could tell just by looking at her. That the thrill of digging into and piecing together things was like a drug to her.

Zack's phone rang, he answered it quickly after seeing Jack Granger's number.

"Yes?"

"We had eyes on a third party at the Lockwood Manor tonight. He was in the woods and seemed to be watching the place, which, incidentally, ten heavily armed men are now guarding. One of ours had eyes on him, but we lost him. He was like a fucking ghost." Granger sounded hacked off. He'd take that personally and he wouldn't want to be the person who lost him.

"*Fuck*. Anything else?"

"No. Felicity Lockwood is in the house, though."

"Okay. Stay where you are and keep me posted," Zack said.

"Copy that," muttered Granger.

He hung up and pocketed his phone. This was a major complication, but it did prove they were on the right track. He'd bet the Cunningham fortune that Noah was in that house.

Zack left and walked back to his office, buzzing from all this new information and how it fit with Noah and the Divine Watchers investigation. He stopped suddenly, the hairs on the back of his neck standing up. Seeing his open office door—which he always kept shut—he withdrew his weapon and proceeded toward his office.

On silent feet, he approached the door and was about to slam it open when a familiar voice from his past called out.

"Come on, Zack. You're not going to shoot me, are you?" Incredulously, Zack pushed open the door. Sitting in his chair was none other than Kanan. He kept his weapon up and trained on the bastard.

"What the fuck are you doing in my office?"

"What, no hug for an old friend?" Kanan said sarcastically.

Zack was surprised to see K had hardly changed. He'd filled out a lot and his hair now had slight greying at the temples, but other than a few wrinkles, he looked the same. He was lounging back in the chair, but Zack knew it was all a charade. His feet were firmly planted and his hands, although, relaxed across the arms of the chair, had a gun held loosely in one of them.

His black jacket was wet and his black BDU's were covered in mud. Guess that was the answer he needed about who was watching the Manor…

"What are you doing here, K? You got a death wish or something, showing up here after taking Noah?" Zack watched as Ks hands clenched around the gun and a nerve in his jaw started to tick. Typical for Kanan, he didn't answer, but posed a question.

"Is my sister safe?"

"Yes, she starts work tomorrow and I have a man watching her house."

"Why did you help me?" Kanan asked, tilting his head to the side as if he really couldn't figure it out.

"Because I owed you," Zack said through gritted teeth.

"Oh, come on, Zack. You must have known it was me that took Noah and yet you still decided to watch out for Celeste?"

"It made good sense."

"Ah! Leverage, good idea. By having her you could use her as leverage to get to me."

"Exactly, and like I said, my debt is now repaid. So, tell me why you would risk walking in here now after what you did."

Kanan straightened up in the chair, suddenly, and Zack tensed.

"Calm the fuck down, Zack. You aren't going to shoot me any more than I'm going to shoot you. Look, I'm putting my weapon away." He said, holstering his weapon.

Zack regarded him for a minute as he holstered his own weapon. He knew this was incidental. Neither man needed a weapon to end the other. They'd both had similar training and were both deadly.

Kanan was wrong, though. He would shoot him if he thought one of his team were in danger, but Kanan didn't need to know that.

"So, what's going on? I assume this isn't a catch up?" he said, sweeping his hand around the room.

"No, its not. We have a problem." Zack did not like the way he said that.

"What problem do *we* have, K?"

Kanan looked uncomfortable and agitated now.

"The boy, Noah, he's sick." Zack crossed his arms over his chest and glared daggers at Kanan.

"We know that."

Kanan leaned his weight on the table and frowned, "No, I mean really sick. The old cow, Lockwood, gave him something, some sort of injection."

"How do you know this?" Zack watched as K came round the desk and started to prowl around the room. Something was really bothering him. Somehow, Noah had gotten to him. He would have laughed if it things weren't so dire.

"It felt wrong leaving him with them, so I went back to check on him. She has him in the attic and he had a fever and was complaining of stomach cramps."

"You do know he is very sick with Leukaemia, don't you?" Zack asked calmly, feeling anything but inside. In fact, in that moment, it took everything he had not to punch Kanan into next week.

"Yeah, I fucking know that, Zack. Listen, I realise this was not the best decision."

"Ya think, K? Ya think taking a sick kid from his bed in the middle of the night and handing him off to strangers might have been the wrong thing?" Zack's voice dripped with scorn and fury.

"Fuck you, Zack. You don't get to judge me, you of all people don't get to judge."

"Wow that was a low blow even for you K," Zack replied, with acid.

"Are you going to help or not?" Kanan asked.

Zack watched him for minute, trying to decide if he could trust him. Of course, he couldn't, but he had little choice in this.

"You do realise that as soon as Nate gets near you, your ass is grass don't you?"

"Whatever. Nate Jones will do what he's going to do, but right now, you need me to help you."

"Fine, but you do as you're told, understand?" Kanan gave him a look that Zack recognised from his childhood and knew he was fucked.

"Fine, give me details," Zack demanded, resignedly, resuming his place behind his desk. Kanan then explained everything about the Lockwoods and what he'd heard and seen.

Chapter Fifteen

It was a little after one in the morning when Skye was woken by a ringing phone. It took her a second to wake up. When she did, it was to see Nate grabbing his phone off the nightstand. It was good timing, as far as she was concerned. She'd been having an awful dream about Noah.

He had been trapped in a well and she couldn't get to him. He was dressed in the pyjamas she had put him to bed in on Saturday night. In the dream, she tried to reach him but had been pulled back by hands clawing at her. She could still feel the hands as they had grabbed and scratched her skin.

She took a big lungful of air and tried to banish the dream. She was no fool, she knew it represented her despair at not being able to help her son. She fought hard not to let it drag her down into a pit of depression, but the fear clung to her.

Skye knew that if she let the feeling take hold, she would not be able to function, let alone help her son. She turned to Nate as he put the phone down and turned to her. The look in his eyes was guarded, and a second later, she understand why.

"We have eyes on Noah."

Skye jumped up onto her knees and grasped Nate by the biceps.

"Is he okay? Who found him? When can we go pick him up?" The questions tumbled out of her mouth with such speed that she failed to take in Nate`s expression.

"The man who took him showed up at Fortis. He had an attack of conscience and broke in to check on Noah at Lockwood Manor," Nate stopped and took her hands from his arms, pulling her to him. "The intel we have suggests that they have injected him with something and it has made him feel very poorly." Skye felt her blood drain from her face and an anguished sob escaped from her before she could stop it.

"*Mi cielo*, all we know is that he was having stomach cramps and had a fever. The good news is, he was lucid and could talk. This is good news, Skye. We now have insider intel, and a plan is being formulated. Zack is calling in the whole team for this and we should have Noah back with us by the morning."

He was right, this was good news. She just needed to get him back to her and everything would be okay.

"Okay, you're right. Let's go." She jumped out of the bed and hurriedly pulled on clothes as Nate did the same. She pulled her hair into a messy bun and followed him out of the room. He quickly grabbed his handgun and keys and they rushed to the car.

The drive to Fortis, thankfully, took half the time than normal since the roads were clear. Skye hopped out before the car completely stopped and ran for the door. Now that she knew where he was, she was anxious to get to him.

Nate grabbed her hand and stopped her, swinging her round to face him.

"Skye, calm down. Getting yourself hurt is not going to help him." This pissed her off. How could she calm down and how could he be so bloody calm?

"I can't calm down!" she shrieked, making herself wince, "My son needs me I have to get to him. How can you be so calm? I thought you cared about him?" Skye watched as Nate's face darkened and his body turned to stone.

"That was a low blow, Skye. You know I think the world of Noah. And I'm calm because this is what we do. It's my job to stay calm."

Before he could finish, she went on, "Oh, so it's just a job now, is that it?"

"No! Goddamnit Skye, stop twisting my words. I have to stay calm to give us the best chance of getting Noah out safely. I can't go off half-cocked or someone could die." He was yelling now and his face hard.

She pushed him too hard and she didn't know why. Maybe it was guilt? She'd been getting hot and heavy with Nate and her son was suffering. What sort of mother did that? She didn't voice this, though, because Nate was tugging her through the door. And even though she knew he was angry with her, he still held the door and ushered her inside as if she was made of glass. What a bitch she was.

He didn't let go of her hand as they walked into the conference room to find Daniel, Dane, Drew, Lucy, and weirdly, Lizzie. The three 'D's gave them head tilts and Lucy and Lizzie came over to them. Nate let go of her hand and carried on to his teammates. She felt the loss instantly and wished she could take back what she had said.

She hadn't meant to be like that it had just popped out. She needed to apologize. She wouldn't get a chance now though and it would be a long time before she did.

Lizzie and Lucy bustled around her hugging her and asking how she was feeling. Lucy seemed positive, as was her usual self, and Lizzie calm and in control. Lizzie got her a cup of coffee and led her to a chair.

"Lucy called me and said it might be good for me to wait with you here while the team goes in." Skye held the warm mug between her cold hands and nodded, "It will, thank you." She couldn't help casting glances at Nate. He seemed to act differently–like he flipped a switch and gone into cool, calm, operator mode. His back was straight and he seemed completely focused on what Daniel and Dane were saying.

The gentle man who had given her so much pleasure earlier was nowhere to be seen. This man was hard, cold, and strong, and despite everything, she felt a little shiver run through her body right to her erogenous zones. Why did she find this side of him so attractive?

She realised Lizzie had been talking to her, "Sorry what did you say?"

Lizzie gave her a funny look.

"Is everything okay with you two?" Lizzie asked, looking to Nate. Skye found herself telling her about what had happened tonight and her subsequent attack on him outside.

"Oh, sweetie. You are a wonderful mum. Nobody would think you are a bad one just because you found comfort in the man you love. It's natural to seek closeness at times like this."

"I just feel so useless. All I have done since they took Noah is cry or sleep. I only wish I were more like Lucy. She would have gone after them herself.

"No, she wouldn't, Skye, because until now they didn't have any knowledge of where he was, for certain, and now we do. You are here, waiting for your son and trusting the man you love to get the job done–and he will. He loves you and that boy to distraction, anyone can see it." They looked over at Nate, who was still deep in conversation with Dane.

Skye watched as Dane put his hand on Nate's shoulder and said something quietly to him. Nate nodded and looked up at his friend. Lizzie was right on all counts. She did love Nate and he showed how much he cared for them in his every action.

Every time he'd stayed at the hospital with her all night–even though he had work the next day–every time he made sure she was eating enough, or he played with Noah so that she could get a cake order done. The fact that he had been so patient about sex and intimacy, not wanting her to think he only wanted her for that. That was what a true father and partner did; put the needs of his family first. She had not set out to look for a partner or father for Noah, but she had found one, anyway, and he was the absolute best. He made her heart beat faster when he walked in a room and made her feel cherished. The fact that he rocked her world in bed was the icing on the cake. She just needed to get Noah back and then tell Nate how she felt. But first, she needed to apologise for earlier. She couldn't let him go off into a dangerous situation to rescue her son thinking she was a bitch.

Skye was about to get up and go to him when the door opened and Zack and another man walked in. The oxygen in the room seemed to go electric. The man was tall and dark haired, handsome in a rugged rough way. He was late thirties and obviously fit if the bulge of his biceps was anything to go on.

He wore a dark jacket, black BDU trousers, and combat boots. It was his eyes that seemed guarded and alert, that told her he was an operator. She had been around the guys on the team a lot and he definitely fit.

He stood off to one side of Zack with his hands loose by his sides, as if ready for anything. What surprised her most was the look he gave her. It was filled with sorrow and regret, making her blanche and reach for Lizzie's hand.

Oh my God. *This* was him. This was the man that took her son. She didn't get a chance to react much after that as she watched in fascinated horror as Nate launched himself forward, landing a solid punch to the man's face. The man took a step back but didn't defend himself.

She'd never seen Nate look like he did now. He looked ready to kill, and his intent seemed to be on killing this guy. The others looked to Zack, who shook his head to stand down.

He swung again, hitting the man in the ribs. Clearly not finished, he grabbed the man by the throat and roughly pushed him against the wall

"You don't get to fucking look at her, you hear me. You took her boy from his fucking bed," Nate snarled. "You have caused pain like you couldn't even imagine, you put Noah at risk you sorry son-of-a-bitch. He's a child–a very sick child. You do not get to look at her and give her your forlorn, I'm sorry, look. Nod if you understand me." Nate was cutting of the man's oxygen and still the man did not defend himself or put up a fight.

Meeting Nate's eye the man nodded and Nate held him for another second then let him go, dropping him to his feet. The man bent over, hands on his knees, sucking in oxygen.

Skye quickly got up and ran to Nate. She inserted herself under his arm, hugging him round the waist tightly. She could feel his heart hammering against her hands. She wanted to punch the man, herself, but knew she wouldn't be allowed to get near him, so she settled for giving him ice-daggers, instead.

Nate held her tight against his side and all around her she could feel waves of hostility coming off every man and woman in the room. Lizzie came up beside her and she'd never felt solidarity, and safety of family, more than she did right now. Her confidence that they would get Noah back grew with every second.

"Right. Now that that is out of the way, shall we get started?" Zack asked sarcastically. They all went to the table and took their seats, Skye tucked firmly between Nate and Dane and Lizzie sat next to her brother. The man who took Noah sat beside Zack and seemed unconcerned that everyone gave him a wide berth.

Zack looked around the table, "Where is Zin?"

"He's on his way. He got held up with something," Lucy said, aware as always.

"Fine. We can start without him. Skye, I am allowing you to be here because this is your son, but if you feel, at any time, you can't listen to this, then feel free to use my office to wait.

Skye nodded, "I would rather stay." She was not about to be kicked out, now.

"Fine," Zack nodded. "Now, I know there is a lot of hostility towards Kanan here," Zack said, indicating the man beside him, "And I understand that–believe me, I do. But we need to put that aside and work together to get Noah out safely." There were some nods and grunts from the men, and a snort from Lucy, which gained a frown from Zack.

"We can deal with the what and why after. Right now, we have a very small window to get in and get Noah out. I understand it is planned that they will be moving Noah tomorrow morning. Kanan's intel suggests he is unwell and needs proper medical attention. K, would you like to tell them what you know?"

Kanan stood and addressed the table calmly. He told them of the guards around the house and the location of Noah. Skye squeezed Nate's hand when she heard how poor his health was, and she fought the urge to throw a glass, or another heavy object, at the man that had taken her son. Nate held her hand tight in his, using his other hand to stroke the back of her neck in a soothing motion. It wasn't working. The more Kanan spoke, the more vengeful she felt.

He finished his brief, and before she could stop herself, she had jumped out of her chair, hurling herself across the table towards Kanan. It happened so fast, Nate only had chance to grab her foot as she sprung, attacking Kanan's face with her nails. Again, he didn't defend himself and just let her take all her anger out on him.

Dane caught hold of her since he was closest and gently restrained her, handing her off to Nate, who held her as her knees buckled and she started to sob.

"Happy now?" Dane snarled at Zack, "we don't fucking need him."

"I say we do," Zack responded in a tone that brooked no argument.

"Fine, whatever, but I want it on record that I disagree. I will do this mission with him, but don't expect me to turn my back on him."

"Please, listen," Kanan said in a quiet voice, every person in the room turned to him–even Skye.

"I know I'm a bastard and you all hate me. I understand, and in your shoes, would feel the same. But quite frankly, I don't give a fuck that you hate me–you won't be the first or the last–but for some reason, Noah trusts me."

He turned and focused on Skye, which caused Nate to growl, "Noah is an extraordinary child. I have learnt more about myself in the last twenty-four hours than I have in the last fifteen years. You can do what you want to me after, I won't fight you, but right now, I just want to help get him reunited with his family and safe from the evil fuckers who have him. So I will say it once, I am sorry, sincerely sorry, from the bottom of my black heart. So, either lock me up now, or let me help. Which is it going to be?"

Everyone was quiet. Daniel and Dane stood still as a statues, arms crossed over their chests, faces filled with distrust. Drew was with them, and had adopted a similar stance to Dane and Daniel obviously in full agreement with his mentors. It was Lucy who stepped up, as usual.

"I'll buy what you said, but if you fuck us over, I'll shoot you myself." Nate stepped up next, surprising everyone. "Fine. I'm in, but only for Noah. Afterwards all bets are off." Zack looked at Dane, Daniel, and Drew. Drew caved first and nodded at Zack, then Daniel and Dane, although, Dane was definitely belligerent about it and threw his hands up as if everyone had lost their minds. "Fine, whatever, but I`m with Lucy. If you cross us I will hunt you down." The scorn on his face evident to everyone.

"I wouldn`t expect anything different," replied Kanan holding everyone`s gaze as he did.

"Right," said Zack as everyone sat back down. "Drew, I want you in the tech room. Will is going to run this with you via satellite. Lucy, you are with Zin on the gate. I want you to take out the two men they have at the gatehouse and then rendezvous with Dane and Daniel, who will be taking out the three men walking the perimeter. Nate, you and I will be going in through the back with Kanan. We'll sweep the floors, I put in a call to Eidolon and their team two they will be assisting us on this. Nate, your primary objective is to get Noah out. Leave any arrests or apprehension to us."

"What about the police?" Daniel asked.

"They are dealing with Hugo, and that's how I want it to stay. They are not equipped to deal with this."

"What about the woods? We have to assume they might have men in the woods," Dane put in.

"Eidolon is handling that."

Just as they were finishing, a very pissed off Zin walked in, followed by an oblivious looking Reg. Reg walked over to Skye and tugged her into his embrace.

"How's my girl doing?" he asked softly.

"I'm okay," she answered, realising she was feeling better, now.

Zin looked at Kanan and pointed, "You!" he said angrily. His posture was relaxed but his face was not. His jaw clenched and his eye twitched, betraying the anger clearly he felt. "Tell me this is not about *her*?" Zin said angrily, flexing his fingers to keep from forming fists.

"Not directly," Kanan replied. The whole room was watching the back and forth conversation.

"Look, Viper…"

"Don't call me that. Don't act like you know me just because we worked for the same team once upon a time." Zin growled furiously, every muscle in his body tensing.

"Fine. Zin," Kanan amended, "I just want to talk to her."

"Because of you I lost the opportunity to see my sister after looking for her for fifteen years." Zin was nose to nose with Kanan. Neither man looked like they were going to back down and the tension was palpable.

Skye was sick of this. She slipped out of Reg's arms and walked to Kanan and Zin, who towered above her. The other men in the room went on alert and Nate stepped towards her. Skye put her hand on each man's chest and shoved them apart as best she could. "Can we save this for later, like when my fucking son is home, please," she said with anger and frustration evident in her voice. Both men looked down at her.

Zin closed his eyes and then nodded, "I'm sorry, *malyutka*. You are correct, we will get Noah back and then I will deal with him," he said, giving Kanan a look filled with hate. Kanan reciprocated the look, but walked away to stand by the door.

"What the fuck is wrong with you all tonight," Zack asked, sounding furious. "You are meant to be seasoned operators. You all know better than this. On a mission, you leave your fucking problems at the door. Now, if you all quit behaving like assholes, let's get moving."

Reg went to follow them, but Nate stopped him.

"Reg, I need you to stay with Skye and Lizzie while we do this. I need to know she is safe." Nate looked at the older man intently.

"No problem, son," replied Reg. "I got my boys coming to help watch the area while you're gone," he said proudly.

"What do you mean?" Nate asked, rubbing his face with his hand in exasperation.

"My MC boys. That's where I've been. I told them what's up and they are going to cruise the area and keep a look out. Funny thing, Zin being a part of the same MC. He didn't look none too pleased when I told them we was working together now, though. I think I gone and broke his cover."

Well, that explained Zin's mood, thought Skye.

"Fine. I'll talk to Zin about this. You just stay inside no matter what, you hear me?"

"Yep, yep, will do. Tilly says you need to watch for the boxes. Not sure what she means, but if you see boxes, watch out for them."

"Fine, Reg. I have to go." Reg nodded and Nate walked out after giving Skye a small smile.

"I'll come see you before we leave," he said, obviously eager to get moving.

Left with Reg and Lizzie in the conference room, Skye felt disjointed and twitchy. She hoped Drew would let her wait in the tech room after everyone left. She paced the room for a few minutes before Lizzie stopped her.

"Come and sit, Skye."

"I can't. I have to do something. I'm going to go see if I can sit in the tech room. At least that way I will hear what's going on."

"I'm not sure that's a good idea, Skye," Lizzie said softly. "You might hear things you wish you hadn't."

"I know, but I have to. I can't just sit here, not knowing anything."

"Fine, but I'm coming with you."

"Yep, me too," said Reg.

As they left the room, they saw Dane and Daniel disappear through a door near the back wall. The door had a retina scan ID and code panel next to it. It must be where they kept weapons, Skye surmised. They were about to go into the tech room when Lucy walked out from the back door.

It was a Lucy none of them had ever seen before. Skye felt Lizzie go stiff beside her and let out a little gasp. Lucy had pulled her hair back into a ponytail and was dressed head to foot in black. She had a shoulder holster on, a leg holster with a small gun, and one on the other leg with a wicked looking knife. But it wasn't that she was carrying a small armoury on her body, it was her whole demeanour.

Lucy was the fun one, the one who was everyone's little sister. The one who brought cakes and always gave Zack shit about her car. This Lucy looked ready to kick ass and take names. Even her face looked different. Gone was the smile, it had been replaced with a severe focus that made her look as much of an operator as the others. She was Lara Croft come to life. God help Sly, thought Skye, absentmindedly.

As if sensing her sister's sudden apprehension, Lucy walked straight up to Lizzie and hugged her. Skye was worried Lizzie was going to pass out if she held her breath much longer. Lizzie finally let out a whoosh of air and Skye relaxed.

"I hardly recognised you, Luce. You look so different," said Lizzie. Her voice only betraying her anxiety a little. In every other way, Lizzie was poised and elegant as always. Her hair was even tucked into its neat chignon, despite it being the middle of the night.

"No, still me. Still annoying," Lucy teased her sister.

"I had no idea you did this. I thought you just ran the office and did computer stuff."

"Don't panic, Liz, I can handle this. This isn't my first mission. Anyway, do you think Dane would let me go if he thought I couldn't handle it? Truth be told, I am totally better than him at this."

"I heard that, Bratfink," shouted Dane, coming up behind her, tugging her ponytail.

"Don't worry, Liz," Dane said, wrapping an arm around Lizzie's shoulder, "she's good at what she does. Not as good as me, obviously, but good enough." He laughed when Lucy went to punch him in the ribs, "Hey! Stop or I'll tell Lauren you hurt me. She likes all this just like it is," he said, referring to himself.

"Eww. Please spare me the gross before I vomit on myself," joked Lucy.

"Children. I think your boss is waiting," said Lizzie in her best mum voice, indicating a glaring Zack with his arm on the door to weapons room.

"Zack, can we wait in the tech room while this goes down? Please?" Skye called. Zack nodded, "Yes, but under no circumstance do you interfere." Skye nodded and pushed through the door before he could change his mind.

Nate could feel the hostility in the room as they all geared up. The men were all silent, each locked in their own private thoughts. Zack was next to Kanan, making sure he was kitted out like the rest of them.

Each had their own locker with their favoured tactical clothing, provided by Fortis, including bulletproof vests, as well as all the other normal things like lightweight under armour vests and BDU trousers.

He put his two p226 sigs in his shoulder holster, in his thigh holster on his left leg held two flash bangs. Around his waist was a belt with extra ammo, and on his right thigh was a deadly sharp tactical knife. He was taking his C8 carbine instead of his beloved L96A1 sniper rifle. Eidolon was providing long-range cover and the C8 would be more effective in this situation. Slipping a small dagger into his ankle holster he grabbed his tac vest. He felt ready for anything.

He just needed to see Skye before he left. He wanted to reassure her that Noah would be okay. He'd been a bit miffed by her outburst earlier and wondered if maybe she regretted what had happened between them. He hoped not. It had been the single best experience of his life and he thought they had shared something that was once in a lifetime.

It wouldn't be the first time he had been wrong, though. But he didn't think so–it was probably the stress of the situation. He would just carry on as if it hadn't happened and hope that was the right thing to do.

He left the room and headed to find Skye. He'd been so deep in thought, he hadn't realised the guys had all left already. He found them in the tech room, including Skye. He walked up behind her and slipped his hand under her hair at the back of her neck.

She was seated at a terminal next to Drew, watching as he and Zack talked with Will. She raised her head to him and smiled. Lifting her hand, she gripped his arm and squeezed. Nate felt the knot in his stomach ease. He hadn't realised he was tense until she did that, and his shoulders relaxed.

He could handle most missions as if they were a trip to the park, but this was personal, and he needed to be fully compos mentis. Now he would be. He felt everything settle again. He smiled back and dropped a light kiss on her forehead as he did. She leaned into him and he dropped to his haunches so that he could look at her.

"How you doing, *mi cielo*?"

"I'm holding up. I just want it done, now. I need my boy and my man back safe where they belong."

Nate palmed her face with his large hand. "I'll bring him home, Skye, if it's the last thing I do." His voice held all the sincerity that he felt. He would do it, too. He saw her eyes go wide with understanding.

"I said my boy and my man, Nate. I want you home safe as much as Noah. So don't go getting hurt, okay?" her voice wobbled, but she shut it down quickly.

"Okay, *mi amor*, I won't." He kissed her gently, then, but with no less passion. He felt her open for him and knew that she was scared and trying to tell him everything she felt in that kiss. Pulling away slowly, he stood, still cupping her cheek.

"Stay inside, Skye. I don't want you going out on your own until we have this sorted out. Zin and Zack have cleared Reg and his cohorts to provide protection for the outside of the building."

"Don't worry about us, we'll be fine you just get you and Noah home safe." Skye answered. He dropped one more kiss on her lush mouth and left.

He met with Zack and the team out the front. They piled into two bullet proof SUV's and rolled out. As soon as he had his comms up and working, the first thing he did was tell Drew that if things went south, then Reg was to get Skye out of the tech room. The helmets they were wearing had cameras in them, that way, any information was fed back to Fortis and recorded. It would help with evidence and the feed would allow Drew or Will to do an instant facial recognition.

Unfortunately, it meant they would see what the helmet cams saw. He didn't want her hearing or seeing any of that shit. It was bad enough that she would hear the rest, but if he or Noah got hurt, he didn't want her listening in, or worse, watching.

He was in the front with Zack driving, and Kanan behind him. Dane and Daniel were in the other vehicle with Zin and Lucy. Kanan had said very little as they geared up. Nate was still trying to control the desire to punch him into next week, but he had enough control to wait until after this was over before he did that.

He was interested to know what the history was with him and Zack. They had a relaxed, yet familiar, body language around each other that belied the obvious animosity. Zack had obviously known him a long time if the fact that Zack, who trusted no one, was willing to trust this man and care for his sister.

It was an odd dynamic, and one Nate fervently hoped would work. Zack had promised to explain the details of Kanan's involvement after the op was successful. Nate agreed that he didn't need the man's history to know he was highly trained, probably with a special forces background. He could work with that; he just didn't plan on being his new best buddy.

It was nearly four in the morning when they made the approach to Lockwood Manor. Jack Granger had checked in and said everything was quiet and were in position. They had eye-balled eight more men spread out in the woods, and their best sniper was in position to take them out, at will.

Eidolon had even more impressive contacts than Zack, and his went to the top. So the fact that Eidolon had been given authorisation for all of them to use kill shots did not surprise Nate. The order had come down from up high that they would preferred it if the men could be detained for questioning, though.

Luckily for them, Will was Jack's brother and Sly's cousin, so, the Eidolon guys were always more than willing and able to help in sticky situations. Zack had also served with Jack at some point, although, Nate didn't know the details of that. He wasn't sure who gave Eidolon the authorisation, but it wasn't the government or SIS, because they had been compromised.

Nate could feel his pulse pick up in the familiar rush he got before a mission. Everything was riding on this one and that made the rush feel different. More intense somehow–like his whole future was riding on this one mission.

He thought of Noah for the first time since they had planned the rescue. He hadn't allowed himself to think of him before for fear of it interfering with his objectivity. Now, he thought of him and wondered what state he was in. Kanan had indicated that he was very sick, and Nate was scared they would be too late. No, he couldn't go there. Noah was a fighter and he would hold on until Nate came for him.

He was Noah's superhero after all.

They parked a mile from the Manor, hiding the vehicles in the woods. Zin and Lucy hoofed it to the front gate to wait for the go-signal from Zack. Dane and Daniel disappeared into the night like apparitions. The way those two worked together never ceased to amaze Nate. It was as if they were of one mind.

This was Daniel's first mission since losing Claire. He had said he wouldn't do any more missions like this, but when it had come down to it, he had insisted that he be in on this one. Nate was relieved. Daniel was one of the finest and calmest operators Nate knew, and he knew many fine men. The fact that he was the team medic was a big plus in case Noah needed him.

Trudging through the sodden undergrowth, at a fast clip, was tough, but they made it to the back edge of the Lockwood Manor estate in record time. Hunching down in position, he waited for Zack to give the green light. His body was thrumming with adrenalin, and the need to get in there was strong.

Zack hunkered beside him, with Kanan to Zack's left.

"When we have confirmation that the perimeter and gate are down, we need to move fast. Eidolon will do the breach and we'll go in behind. You and K will head for the upstairs, and I'll cover your six."

"Copy," Nate and Kanan both whispered.

Nate listened as Zack gave the order to go. A minute later, he could hear the pops of gunfire as Dane and Daniel took out the perimeter guards. They were too far away to hear what was happening at the gate, but it soon became apparent that Zin and Lucy had things under control. Through the comms came confirmation, from Lucy, that the gate was secure.

"Go," said Zack, and they ran for the door, just seconds behind a five-man Eidolon team who had breached the door. Weapon up and at his shoulder, night vision goggles in place, Nate was ready when the electricity was cut by Dane.

Following Kanan towards the stairs, he could hear Eidolon exchanging fire with the tangoes downstairs. He caught a flash of light to his left as he reached the top and turned, firing and taking the man out at the leg. He rushed to secure him, but the man reached for his secondary weapon, giving Nate no choice but to go for the kill shot.

Quickly moving behind Kanan, who was taking out two men near the attic door, Nate fired a head shot at a man who was about to come behind Kanan from the opposite door.

"Ground floor secure," came Jack over the comms.

"Copy," confirmed Zack.

Nate moved in front of Kanan and opened the attic door, carefully. He threw in a flash bang and followed. Two men rushed the stairs and Nate took out one as Kanan took out the other. Stepping over the men, Nate ascended the stairs. The room was dark, but Nate could clearly make out the hospital type bed through his NVG's.

He could hear Kanan and Zack behind him as he cautiously approached the bed.

"Tell Dane to get some lights on so I can see properly," Nate yelled. He heard Zack shout to someone.

Nate's eyes were glued to the small lifeless body in the middle of the bed.

Chapter Sixteen

His heart stopped, as he got closer, the lights came on, blinding him for a second, before he tore his NVG's off. As if propelling him out of his fog, he ran for the bed. Noah was pale and listless, his tiny body looking grey against the white sheets. Nate reached out to gently touch his fingers to Noah's neck.

His skin was clammy to touch and Nate fought the fear that threatened to overwhelm him. His hand shook slightly as he searched for a pulse. Please, God, don't let them be too late.

He heard an almighty, animalistic roar as Kanan came to stand beside him. The grief on the other man's face was harrowing. Nate stood there for a second. Noah's face cradled in his big hand and then he felt it.

A very faint thread of a pulse. The relief almost took his legs from under him.

"Daniel! Up here now, I have a pulse," Nate roared at over the comms. He quickly stripped the sheet off Noah and wrapped him in his arms. Cradling the boy's face to his chest as he rocked him and willed him to live, he whispered reassuring words in his ear

Kanan was slumped against the wall and was now sucking in deep breaths. Zack had gone down to the bottom of the stairs and was waiting for Daniel.

"Come on, Noah. Fight, son. We still have to teach you how to play rugby. And you have to give me a chance to redeem myself at

Lego Batman." He kissed Noah's forehead and wiped away the wetness that was forming on his little face, not realising it was coming from him.

So engrossed was he, he never saw the threat that came from behind the boxes at his six. But Kanan had, and he jumped in front of the bullet and shot the tango in the head. Nate watched as Kanan fell to the ground, a bullet taking him down. He saved Nate's life.

Nate gently laid Noah down on the bed and rushed to Kanan.

He was passed out, bullet wound to the left side of his neck. It looked like he also hit his head on the metal bed as he fell. Stupid idiot had taken off his helmet. He applied pressure to the wound and radioed down.

"Zack. K is down–repeat K is down."

"Copy," Zack replied.

Daniel came running up the stairs, Zack on his heels, and went straight to Noah. Kanan was coming round now, starting to talk. The wound looked more superficial than life threatening. Nate left Kanan with Zack and went back to Noah. Daniel was putting a line in his arm, administering some saline.

"We need an air ambulance now," Daniel said. "I'm not sure what they have given him, so all I can give him right now is IV fluids and oxygen. His pulse is weak and he is hypotensive. I need to get his blood pressure up but we can't push the fluids too fast, otherwise, we send him into shock."

"An air ambulance is en-route. Nate, can you carry him down and Daniel will stay with you and carry the IV. Dane and I will help K." said Zack

"I don't need help, for fuck's sake. It's just a scratch, so stop harping on like you're my mother. Just get the kid sorted," grouched a grumpy Kanan.

Nate zoned out the bellyaching going on between Zack and Kanan and concentrated on Noah. He looked so pale–paler than normal. He lifted him gently in his arms and accepted the blanket Daniel was tucking in around Noah as he stood. Starting down the stairs, he was relieved to see the house had been cleared. The Eidolon guys were handling clean up. Fortis was concentrating on Noah.

This little boy had managed to steal everyone's hearts with his bravery and resilience. He was always happy and content. Adults could learn a lot from him, like how to appreciate what you had not what you didn't. Following Zin and Lucy through the door to the massive lawn at the back, he was surprised to see the air ambulance was already there.

Rushing over to the ambulance's door, he held Noah close to shield him from the cold. He was hesitant to hand Noah over to the paramedics, but knew they could do what he couldn't. They quickly transferred him into the helicopter and got him ready for transport. The paramedic had noticed Kanan off to one side and decided his injury was worrying enough to get him aboard the flight, too.

Kanan had put a bit of a fight, but he was looking pretty shitty now. He gave in, quickly, under the pretence that they were wasting time for Noah.

Once aboard, Nate sat next to Noah and held his hand while the paramedic checked Noah's eyes, his reflexes, and his vital signs. His eyes were dilating as they should be and his pulse and blood pressure had improved slightly. His temperature was through the roof, again, though. So the paramedic administered junior paracetamol and ibuprofen.

"Thank you," Nate said suddenly, turning to Kanan, "for saving my life."

"No thanks necessary. You wouldn't have been there if it wasn't for me," Kanan said in a dejected voice. Nate could see by his tight expression, and hear in the man's voice, that he was taking this hard and his anger thaw a little. Maybe this man did have a shred of humanity left in him. Nate didn't say more. What could he say anyway? Kanan was right, but it wasn't Nate's nature to be cruel.

They arrived at the hospital minutes later, touching down on the roof. The paramedics unloaded Noah as the hospital trauma and paediatric team ran towards them with a stretcher. Nate turned to thank the crew and was shocked as shit to see who was flying the aircraft.

His Royal Highness the Duke of Cambridge, gave Nate, and a now smiling Kanan, a jaunty salute and went back to his control panel.

Nate shook his head. Noah would be gutted to have missed that. Kanan insisted on walking himself inside and shrugged off the nurses who tried to get him into a wheelchairl. Following Noah as he was taken straight to the Paediatric ICU unit, he watched as Kanan went the other way towards accident and emergency The nurses patiently told him he had to wait outside while they stabilised Noah and ran some blood tests to determine what he had been given.

He rang Skye, his heart hammering as he waited for her to pick up.

"Nate," he heard the fear in her voice. She sounded terrified. "What's happening? Drew made me leave. Is he okay? Have you got Noah?" Her voice broke then, and he heard Lizzie in the back ground telling her to sit down before she fell down. He would do anything to be able to hold her right now.

He realised, in that moment, what she was feeling earlier had been guilt because right now, he felt the same. He had been enjoying the time with Skye while Noah was fighting for his life. He couldn't tell her over the phone, he couldn't seem to get the words out to tell her how poorly he was.

"Skye, *mi cielo,* It's okay. We have him…" He didn't get any further because she must have dropped the phone. All he could hear was her broken sobs. He heard Reg talking to her and the Lizzie was on the line.

"Nate, it's Liz," she sounded tentative. "What's happened?"

"We have Noah, but Liz, he's really sick. It's going to be touch-and-go. You need to get Skye here, asap. Don't let on how bad it is if you can. Just get her here quickly."

"Is he in Hereford?"

"Yes. They have him in the paediatric ICU."

"Okay, we will get her there. See you soon"

"Thanks, Liz."

Nate went back to pacing the corridor outside the ICU and was still doing it when Dane and Daniel came rushing through the door.

"How is he, man?" Daniel asked, laying a hand on Nate's shoulder. He had a young daughter so he knew how Nate was feeling, come to think of it, so would Dane–his fiancé was expecting twins.

"Don't know. They took him back there and I haven't seen anyone." He was trying everything to control the fear clawing at his gut.

"They are probably just getting him stable and comfortable. They will come and talk when they can," Daniel said.

Nate bent and put his hands on his knees, pulling in some oxygen as his head spun. Daniel and Dane led him to a chair and pushed him into it.

"Put your head between your knees, Nate," said Daniel, "That's it, deep breaths."

"What am I going to tell her?" Nate asked, "How do I tell her? He looked so sick."

"Nate, Skye is strong. Look what she has already been through with Noah. She's still the beautiful, strong woman you know." Daniel said as he sat next to Nate.

"You should've heard her, though. She just collapsed when I told her we had him; Lizzie had to talk to me. All I could hear was her sobbing like her world was ending."

Daniel nodded and was silent for second. Nate instantly felt like a bastard. He was putting all this on Daniel who had lost his wife just five short months ago.

"Man, I'm sorry. I didn't think. I shouldn't be dumping this on you."

"No, it's all right. It feels good to be useful again. You're wrong, though. What you heard was relief. Skye knows that while he's alive and with you, he has a chance. And as a parent…that's good enough for her to work with. Everything else she can deal with, somehow. He's alive and getting the treatment he needs."

Nate nodded his head in affirmation, finally understanding. "I suppose that makes sense. It's tricky, this parenting thing."

Daniel laughed, "Oh, man, is it. I'd rather face a Taliban fighter than Paige when I've cut her toast into squares instead of triangles." Nate laughed then, and he felt some of the tension ease.

"Uncle Dane never makes that mistake," Dane joked.

"But uncles never do. Daddies, however, can and you won't be so smug when you have two screaming at you for cutting the toast the wrong way." Daniel laughed and Dane groaned. The men fell into a comfortable, but anxious, silence while they waited.

What seemed like forever, but was actually only ten minutes later, Skye came running through the doors, closely followed by Lizzie. Nate jumped up and met her. She grabbed his hands tightly and her eyes moved over him quickly, trying to ascertain if he was okay.

"Where is he?" she demanded.

"He is with the doctors; they wouldn't let me in. I will get Dane to let the Doctors know you are here. Skye, come and sit down." Dane got up, having heard and headed for the nurses station. Nate grasped her arm and gently pulled her over to the chairs. She was reluctant and kept looking at the door, as if she could, somehow, see through it to see if he was okay.

"Skye, listen to me," he made her face him before he continued. "It's bad Skye, he is very poorly." His heart broke as her breath hitched and she fought back a sob. "He was unconscious when we found him and has been unresponsive. His vitals did pick up on the way here, but I want you to be prepared. He doesn't look well." Skye nodded her eyes looking glassy with tears.

"It's fine, Nate. I've seen Noah look poorly and I can handle it," she said, and she looked determined and strong and he fell just a little bit more in love with her. "He's here and he is going to be fine. I refuse to believe that, after everything he has been through, that now, when hope is in sight, he would be taken from me." Her posture straightened with every word, and Nate knew that he was done for. He looked into her big brown eyes, shining with strength and love, and knew he was a goner.

His mother had always said he was a sensitive soul and would fall hard when he eventually met *the one* for him. It was just the way he was built. It was that sensitive soul that had gotten him hurt in the past, but he knew with a certainty he had never felt before, that Skye would never hurt him. He'd make it his life's mission to make sure nobody hurt her or Noah ever again.

When he was growing up, he'd been shy and often times would find himself stepping in to defend those weaker than him, or even sometimes those that weren't.

Boys would often see his sensitivity as a sign of weakness and take the piss out of him, but that wasn't the case. He just didn't like injustice and cruelty. He thought their attitudes were probably why he began martial arts, and then later entered the Parachute regiment. Lucky for him, he seemed to excel at both and that soon stopped any questions or derogatory remarks.

He had found that most men, as opposed to boys, were actually very similar to him. He didn't mind showing that side of himself.

He just hoped that Skye could cope with his need for control in other parts of his life. The bedroom was the one place he needed to be in charge. He didn't mind showing his adoration to her to the world, and people thinking she was whipped but behind closed doors, he needed to be in control.

He had a feeling it would all work out, though. They seemed so compatible earlier. *Fuck* Was that only a few hours ago? It felt like a lifetime, and yet when he closed his eyes he could see still see her beautiful face as she came. No. Skye and he fit–they were meant to be together.

Breaking out of his reverie, he looked at Skye. She was watching him closely.

"Are you okay? Did you get hurt? I heard someone got shot."

"No, I'm fine, *mi cielo*," he smiled and tightened his hold on her hand, "Kanan got shot protecting me." Skye sucked in breath.

"Thank, god. I can't lose you, Nate." She burrowed into his arms, placing her head on his chest and slid her arms around his waist. He draped his arms around her and held on tight. He kissing the top of her head.

They were sitting like this when the doctor came out. Everyone in the room stood, including Dane and Daniel, who had remained quiet, allowing Skye and Nate some space. The doctor, a man of Middle Eastern ethnicity, walked towards them. He was short and slim and was about sixty years old. He had kind, twinkly eyes and laugh lines round his eyes that indicated he smiled a lot. He was wearing the *taqiyah* of the Islamic faith on his head. He stopped in front of Skye and Nate, looking between them.

"Skye," the doctor said, obviously very familiar with Skye and Noah.

"Dr Azzabi, how is he? Can I see him?"

"He is stable, for now. He doesn't seem to have an infection, but whatever drug he was injected with seems to have caused some issues. We are running some blood tests and have him on a drip to help rehydrate his body. As a precaution, we have set up an antibiotic drip. His heart rate and blood pressure have stabilised and he is sleeping comfortably."

Skye held tight to Nate's hand as the doctor spoke. Her heart hammering in her chest as she tried to stay calm and focused on what he said. She nodded at the man who had been Noah's primary doctor for the last twelve months.

"This is all good news, Skye, but I won't lie to you not knowing what he has been given is very unsettling. As doctors we like to know what we are dealing with and at this point we don't."

"What about the transplant? Can it still go ahead?" Skye asked worriedly.

"Let us see what the blood results say first. If all is as before, we will start the chemo as soon as he has recovered from this. I will be on for the rest of today and we will monitor him closely."

"Can I sit with him?" Skye asked.

"When have we ever been able to stop you in the past?" the doctor asked with a small, affectionate smile. Nate shook his hand and ignored the doctor's quizzical look. He would soon figure out who Nate was.

"Thank you, Doctor," he said. The doctor nodded and left.

Dane and Daniel heard everything that was said. After kissing Skye on the cheek and slapping him on the shoulder, they left.

He followed Skye closely as she walked toward the paediatric ICU reception. Her movements fluid and graceful, even now. She must be dead on her feet. Nate stayed beside her with his hand on the small of her back, offering whatever he could, in the way, of support.

The nurse quickly showed them to Noah's room and they pushed through together. Skye turned and grasped his hand tightly.

Noah was sleeping but he looked peaceful now–not the heart stopping stillness when Nate found him. He was still incredibly pale, almost translucent, and he had big dark smudges under his eyes. Nate hadn't seen him like this before and it gutted him. He looked to Skye as she approached the bed and lent down to kiss Noah's forehead. She sat down, took his little hand in hers, and held it tight.

He stayed behind her until she told him to grab a chair. He sat opposite her on the other side of the bed, resting his hands on his bent knees, and watched Skye with Noah. She was such an amazing mum, she never seemed to be too tired to do things, and she was always willing to play games with Noah. He'd never seen her lose her temper.

Was he wrong to potentially deprive her of more children? Was he being selfish? The answer he knew was yes. The real question was if he could give her up–he didn't think he could. He needed to tell her. In a few days when things were settled, he would sit her down and tell her.

So deep in his thoughts, he was surprised when she spoke.

"When he was born, I was so frightened. I was all on my own, except for Reg," she stroked Noah's head as she spoke and Nate's gut tightened. "But when I brought him home, we muddled through. The first few months were a blur of sleepless nights and feeding. But after a while, we got a routine and it became me and him against the world.

"I was happy to have him to myself. As he got older, we did so much together. Nature trails, picnics– just kid stuff–but we had fun. It wasn't until he got sick that I felt it–so alone, so lonely. I use to sit by his bed night after night and the staff would tell me to go home, but I couldn't face it. My home became a cold, barren place and I hated it." She looked up at him then, the tears in her eyes made him get up and cross the room to her.

He crouched down and slipped his arms around her waist. "And then you came along, and I knew the minute I laid eyes on you that you were it. You filled a hole in my heart, and in my life, that I didn't know was there. You offered my son a future and tonight you risked everything to save him."

She let the tears slide, unheeded, down her face. He reached up and swiped them away gently.

"Thank you, Nate. You will never know how much you mean to us. I'm so sorry I was awful earlier."

"Hey, no you were under an incredible amount of stress and I knew that. But you're wrong. It's you and Noah that have filled a hole. My whole life I've searched for something and I didn't know what it was until I walked into that hospital room with Lauren. I can't explain how it felt, Skye. It was like I'd found myself," he blushed. He wasn't good with words.

"You are my life, now, and I want to be with you, always. We'll talk in a few days, but know this…if you want me, I'm yours for all time." Skye cupped his cheek and touched her mouth to his. It wasn't a hot scorching kiss, but it was beautiful and held all the promise of the future.

"We want you, Nate," she said softly.

Chapter Seventeen

Celeste was nervous as she approached the entrance to Fortis. It was such a large, formidable building. She had gotten up early and dressed in a beige pencil skirt and a white, long-sleeved blouse with ruffles down the front. She had black Mary-Jane pumps and a small black purse.

Her faithful companion, Samson, walked at her side. She hoped that Zin guy wasn't there. He was a miserable sod and made her uncomfortable–not in the way people usually did, this was something different. He made her feel funny, and he looked at her as if she was about to shoot the Queen and put the blame on him. No. She didn't want another run-in with him.

Celeste had been relieved when she shook his hand and hadn't reacted to his touch. It was such a lottery for her. Some people were like beacons for her gift and others she had no problems with.

Entering the building, she was surprised to find bikers asleep in the reception area. One grizzly-looking biker opened his eye, must have decided that she wasn't a threat, and went back to sleep. She wondered what she should do now. Did she just wait? Looking around for a bell, she could ring. She spied a phone and wondered if it rang to an inside line.

Picking it up, she was about to call when a stunningly beautiful woman walked through the door. She had cherry red hair that cascaded down her back in waves and forest green eyes. She smiled a genuine smile as she walked up to Celeste.

"Hey, I'm Ava Drake. I'm here to see Mr. Cunningham." Celeste was a bit taken aback. She was not expecting such a strong American accent. The woman seemed friendly but Celeste still felt intimidated. The woman wore a fitted charcoal grey suit and burgundy pumps with three-inch heels. Her skin was flawless and milky white–like Snow White. Celeste bit back a nervous giggle.

"Oh, hi. I'm Celeste," she said. The woman smiled but continued to look at Celeste. She realised then that she was standing behind the reception desk, and the woman probably assumed, correctly, that she was the receptionist.

"Oh! Umm, sorry. It's my first day and I just arrived, I was trying to attract someone's attention with the phone." The woman, Ava, grinned. "No problem. This your dog?"

"Yes, that is Samson." Ava put out her hand and let the dog sniff.

"Is he friendly?" Ava asked.

"Yes, very, but he is very protective of me and won't leave my side."

Celeste watched as Ava bent down and petted Samson. The big baby was soon putty in her hands, prone on his back while he had his belly rubbed.

"Who's a gorgeous boy?" Ava said as she rubbed his tummy. She straightened, then, and looked at the four bikers asleep on the various chairs in the reception area.

"So what's this?" she waved her hand around the room. Celeste shrugged, "Maybe you should try ringing through, now?"

"Yes! Sorry," Celeste said, flustered. Lifting the phone, she dialed nine, hoping something would happen. She was relieved when it rang.

"Yes, who's this?" said a gruff voice.

"Uh, it's Celeste, the new receptionist…" She replied. She took her ear away from the phone when the person shouted, "Hey! Boys' new girl's here!" She didn't have time to tell them about Ava before he hung up.

"Sorry. He hung up," she said to Ava.

"Don't worry, girl. I can handle this."

Celeste came round to the front of the desk and the woman shrieked.

"Oh my god, I love those," she said, pointing to Celeste's legs and the lace work tattoo that ran all the way from the back of her ankle all the way to the top, stopping just below her bum cheek. "They look like lace silk stockings like they wore in the war. So sexy."

Celeste had never thought of herself as sexy. Her boobs were small, her hair short–sure, she had nice eyes and a full mouth, her hips were too big, though. She only got the tattoos because she liked them.

"Thanks," she said in a noncommittal way.

"Do you have any more?" Ava asked.

"Yes…." She didn't get to finish as Zack pushed through the door with Zin behind him.

Samson immediately went on alert. He came and sat at heel beside her, growling low, his hackles on his back rising.

"Ava?" Zack said looking shell-shocked.

"Mr. Cunningham," she replied, all warmth gone from her voice. Celeste watched, rapt, as his face hardened in annoyance. Ava's voice had practically dripped coldness and distain.

"If you follow me, I will get you set up. Zin, can you show Celeste through to the kitchen and ask Daniel to show her around? And get these fucking bikers out of my god-damn reception area," he bellowed.

Ava turned to her, "It was a pleasure to meet you Celeste. We will have to go for a drink while I'm in town."

"Yes, you too and I'd love to. I'll get your number from Mr. Cunningham."

"Enough with the Mr. Cunningham, it's Zack, Celeste." But he cast his gaze to include Ava who only glared at him.

Zack turned, then, and Ava followed, giving Zin a small nod. Samson stayed and continued his growl when Zin approached her.

She heard him hiss in a breath as his eyes travelled from the top of her head to her feet. His eyes lingered on her legs, making her squirm and feel funny and achy between her thighs. Then, his eyes slowly travelled back up to her face and went hard. His hands tensed on his hips as he scrutinized her face.

What had she done to earn his displeasure? Miserable sod. Would it hurt him to smile? Oh, well, bugger him–he could go swing. She didn't care, anyway. Shame though. He was sexy as hell, in a hard-assed kind of way.

He spun on his heel, "Follow me." It wasn't a question but a demand. He walked off, never considering that she might not follow him, which, of course, she did.

She placed her hand on Samson's head and whispered, *hier*, the German command for *come*. She'd trained Samson with an ex-army dog handler and those were the commands he taught her to use. He calmed instantly at her touch and did as she asked and followed her.

As her and Samson followed the miserable, bear of man, she, so, did not check out his tight arse in those jeans, or the way his powerful shoulders filled out his leather jacket. No. She absolutely did not. He was a jerk and she did not like him, but she needed this job, so she would deal.

~~~

Zack was tired and pissed off. Kanan had taken flight overnight and disappeared, and his building was filled with bikers. He'd sent everyone home at five in the morning and they were due back at nine for a debrief. He'd promised the commissioner he would meet with him and brief him. He'd, also, not eaten in twelve hours.

He was on his way to the kitchen to try and scrape together some toast and coffee when he heard Reg bellow, Fuck. He needed to see to this, and why Reg was the only one manning the tech room and the cameras, he had no clue. He tucked back in his shirt that had come untucked as he slept on his couch, and brushed his hands through his hair.

Kanan had taken a bullet for Nate last night, and after a brief chat in the hospital, he had been convinced that K was done with his crusade for whoever he was looking for. It had affected him badly seeing Kanan so broken over Noah.

He and K had been like Siamese twins when they were young, and when Catherine joined them, they had become inseparable. His heart ached as he thought of his sister. Not a day went by that he didn't think of her. He rubbed his chest to ease the ache. He'd missed Kanan and regretted the rift. Still, it was done–time to move on.

He didn't think that everything was going to go back to normal, now–that could never happen. There was too much pain and heartbreak between them. It would be nice to be on speaking terms, again, though.

Leaving the kitchen, he almost walked into Zin, who was hurrying towards the front.

"What's the rush?"

"The woman is here." Zack was surprised by this. Zin never got involved in these types of things. He was strictly a *do the job, go home* kind of guy. He occasionally came to team parties or to the Jailhouse for drinks with them but he didn't mix with newbies, ever.

Zack could hear the rain hitting the tin roof of the building, sounding like thunder as he pushed through the door to reception. He stopped dead in his tracks causing Zin to pull up sharply behind him.

Ava in the flesh, and in his reception area, looking more stunningly beautiful than ever. He felt dumbstruck. It had been nearly two years since he'd seen her last, and she had changed a lot, all of it was good. Gone was the beautiful, girl next door look of sexy tight jeans and rock band tee-shirts, shy and fighting not to show it smiles and before him was a siren. Her long hair looked a deeper red than before, her eyes sparkled with secrets he wanted to uncover, and her body seemed curvier and fuller. Her breasts straining the prim and proper suit jacket, and fuck him…those shoes. He wanted to feel those shoes digging into his back as he drove into her soft heat. He stared for a second, hoping his body would not betray him.

"Ava?" He said stupidly.

"Mr. Cunningham," she replied in an ice-cold voice. She was still pissed, then. He had decided to keep things strictly professional between them, but at the sight of her and the challenge in her tone, he decided it was game on.

He addressed Celeste and told Zin to take her to wait for Daniel, and then seeing the state of his immaculate reception looking like the biker bar from hell, told Zin to get them out of here.

He walked to his office and could hear Ava behind him. Her scent was new, something alluring, and seductive that teased his senses. He sat behind his desk and motioned for her to take a seat in the chair in front of his desk. All the blood rushed to his cock as she crossed her long, shapely legs, the material at her thighs pulled tight, revealing the suspender belt underneath.

God, what the fuck was she trying to do, kill him? And then the horrible thought flashed to his mind. It probably wasn't for him. How could a woman who looked like her be single? He quickly cast a glance at her ring finger and found none. He was ridiculously relieved, and that pissed him off.

She could do what she wanted–he didn't have time for relationships–however, if she was single and of a mind, to, he wouldn't mind her in his bed for a while. As long as the team didn't find out. He didn't want to be the cause of office gossip.

Steepling his fingers, he leaned forward on his elbows. "Thank you for coming, Ava."

"I didn't really have much choice, did I, Zack?" she said coldly.

"Well, no, but it is still good to see you."

"Really? You can sit there and say that after ignoring me for nearly two years?" She was breathing fast, her cheeks were flushed, her temper starting to get the better of her. Fucking hell, she was sexy when she was mad. Made him want rile her up just so he could watch her.

"Come on, Ava. We both knew it was just fucking. Nobody declared lifelong love." Her eyes flickered and darkened at his use of the word *fucking*. She had always loved it when he talked dirty–it had gotten her hotter than anything else.

She took a moment to calm herself, getting her breathing under control as he watched her trying to remain outwardly calm.

"You're right, of course, Zack. Fucking. That's what we did–and good fucking, at that."

He was shocked. He'd never heard her swear like that, she had been such a good girl. He was annoyed to feel his erection pressing against his zipper as the words spilled from her mouth. Who was she?

"My, my, haven't we developed a foul mouth," he mocked.

"Well, I thought you liked it dirty, Zack?" she purred, and he struggled not to go round the desk, bend her over, rip her skirt off and slam into her heat. He clenched his fists instead.

Her face was flushed with heat and he could see that she was pleased at his reaction. Then something changed, her face fell and she looked ashamed.

"Look, Zack. I'm sorry, that was inappropriate. Can we just agree to leave the past in the past and work together to get this done so that I can get home to my family?" She looked genuinely upset now, and he could see that she did, indeed, wanted to get home.

"Yes, of course. Let me show you the files we have." Her being upset had been like a dash of cold water on his erection, so at least he didn't have that to contend with as he led her from the room towards the conference room.

Chapter Eighteen

Thursday

Skye was excited; Noah had been moved out of Paediatric ICU and was in a private room on the ward. She'd stayed with him night and day since he'd been back. He had recovered from the effects of the mystery drug and they were going to allow him home for a few days before they started his chemo to prepare for the transplant.

The relief that he was still okay for the transplant was overwhelming and she had shed a few tears on Nate's shoulder. He'd stayed with her every night since Noah had been rescued. They hadn't talked of the future, but she felt confident that, for the first time in forever, she would have one full of contentment and love.

They had spent their nights at the hospital with Noah. She had mostly slept in the chair, curled up on Nate's lap. She knew they couldn't carry on like that. They were both exhausted, but she couldn't leave him. The thought of him being alone with only the hospital staff made her nervous.

Nate was working the case in the day, but spent as much time as he could with her and Noah. Lizzie was a darling, as always, and kept her company while Nate was working and Mateo was at school. She'd brought her proper food from La Madelaine, not the junk the cafeteria served. She'd sat with Noah while she showered and changed and even phoned around to all of Skye's customers, explaining the situation and sorting out alternate cake makers for them.

She was lucky. In the six years she'd been making and decorating cakes, she had built up a good reputation and even had interest from small businesses to supply cakes for their restaurants. That would have be put on hold now, though. As much as the money would come in handy, she needed to be available for her son.

She didn't know what she would have done without her friendship with Lizzie. Lauren was working during the day, as she was a primary school teacher, but made sure Dane brought her to see Noah, and her, every evening. It was amazing to see that even though she was only three months pregnant, she had a tiny bump already. It cheered her to see her friend looking so happy after everything she had been through with her father and that Terry Griffiths.

The last twelve months had been hard, but they also brought friendship and relationships that she could never regret. Lizzie, Lucy, and Lauren. The guys from Fortis, and of course, Nate. Yes, they were her silver lining in a shit year. She just needed to get past this current nightmare and hopefully her bright future was out there.

The whole thing had, predictably, upset Noah–his obsession with Kanan being the worriesome. As soon as he had come round, he'd asked about him. The worry etched his little face–he seemed so sad– that Kanan had been hurt and then disappeared. Every time she tried to soothe him, he got more agitated.

He constantly asked to see him and it had gotten so bad that Nate had agreed to speak to Zack about it to see if he could somehow get in contact with him.

Nate had insisted that he be present when the police questioned Noah. He stood in the corner of the room with his arms folded across his massive chest, like a sentry. Skye was relieved to know that if the detective upset Noah at all, Nate would intervene. The female detective that had been on his case, Detective Herbert, had questioned him and she had been very kind and sweet to Noah, relieving some of the strain for Skye.

He hadn't been able to tell them much. It had seemed that he had not been hurt, except for the drugs. He seemed scared when they mentioned Felicity Lockwood, but not so scared when he spoke of Hugo. He said that Hugo had spoken to him twice.

Once the night he had arrived, and once when Noah had awoken and found him watching him in the night, Hugo had said 'he was sorry and that no kid deserved this.' Noah wasn't sure when that conversation took place, though, as the drugs had messed with his concept of time.

Zack arranged for his friend, Jack Granger and his team, to have access to the blood results. She didn't know who they were, but Nate had explained they were similar to Fortis and they were working with them on this. Whoever they were, they were trying to analyse the drug.

Nobody from the hospital could tell them what the drug was, but it was similar to a drug that caused memory loss, and was also mixed with something else. Noah did say that the old woman kept trying to steal his dreams. It had made him so upset and they had had to sedate him. Skye wondered if that was the drugs purpose.

For some reason, the dreams were the reason he was so anxious to speak to Kanan. He said he needed to tell him before they stole them. Stolen dreams…whoever thought that could be possible.

Skye was at a complete loss. She didn't know who to turn to for help. The doctors didn't understand this sort of special gift, and that's what it was, she realised. And honestly, she was worried they would think he had lost his mind.

Lauren was a healer and that was completely different. Reg, god love him, would probably scare Noah to death if he talked to him. So, that left who? She didn't know.

She lifted her head from the crochet blanket she was making for Lauren and Dane's babies when the door to Noah's private room opened. Her heart lifted when she saw Nate. He looked so handsome in faded jeans and a tight, long-sleeved tee that stretched across his broad chest and arms.

"Hey, *mi cielo*, how's the little guy?" He dropped a kiss on her upturned mouth, lingering just a fraction. Skye inhaled the scent that was all Nate, sweet musk and sandalwood. She loved how just the smell of him could make her stomach flip.

"He seems a little better. His vitals are all strong and there is no sign of infection. All being well, he can come home tomorrow."

"Is he still asking about K?"

"Yes, but he doesn't seem so anxious today."

"That's good. Have you eaten? It's nearly lunch time, I could get you something."

"No, I'm okay. Lizzie will be here soon and she will bring something from the Mouse Trap Deli." Nate nodded, lifting her up, he sat down and settled her onto his lap. He buried his head in her hair and she relaxed into his strength as he wrapped his arms around her.

"Are you okay, Nate?"

He looked up at her. "My parents arrived in town this morning. They want to meet you and Noah. I told them it's too soon. But my Ma is a force of nature." Skye could see that he loved his parents by the loving, but irritated, tone of his voice.

"I don't mind meeting them. If we are going to be family, we should meet. It will be good for Noah." She blushed a little as she said it. Was she being too presumptuous calling them family? She was relieved to see his large smile.

"That's good, *mi amor*, because they are outside."

Skye sat up abruptly. "What? Now?" she squealed, "But I'm…I mean…oh, fine. I look rough and have bags under my eyes, but sure bring them in."

"You look like the most beautiful woman in the world," he said, giving her a proper kiss. She relaxed into him, never seeming to get enough of his kisses. His tongue grazed her lips and she opened her mouth on soft sigh. Her hands tunnelled through the softness of his dark hair. She could feel the way he wanted her as she shifted on his lap and he groaned softly into her mouth.

Nate pulled back. "We need to stop before this moves way past PG and Noah needs therapy." She laughed at him and dropped a quick kiss on his mouth before getting up.

"Go let your parents in."

Nate left a few minutes later, and two minutes after that, returned with an older couple. His father was Nate, only thirty years from now. His hair still dark and thick, but liberally flecked with grey, his body still strong and fit even though it sported a slight paunch at the middle.

It was his mother who surprised her, though. She was small, barely five feet, and had an ample waist and bosom. Her silver hair was styled into a bun at the back of her head, and a large silver cross hung around her neck. She was classically beautiful the most beautiful skin–hardly a wrinkle in sight. She had a tight hold on her husband's hand, but her eyes were fixed on Noah.

"Ma," Nate called, and she looked at her son, "I'd like you to meet Skye." He had crossed to Skye and slipped his arm around her back, pulling her to his side.

"It's a pleasure to meet you, Mrs. Jones, and you, Mr. Jones." Skye thrust out her hand, but was promptly pulled forward out of Nate's arms by Mrs. Jones into a tight hug.

"Family doesn't shake hands, *mi hija*. Families embrace." Skye was a little shocked at first, but it felt so nice to be held in a motherly hug, that she let it be. She couldn't remember the last time she had been held by her mother. Probably never. Her mother wouldn't want to wrinkle her dress.

"And call me Mimi, please."

Mr. Jones stepped forward, then, and gave her a brief hug that was no less filled with warmth. Skye struggled to hold back tears as these people she hardly knew treated her like a long, lost daughter.

"David. Pleased to meet you, Skye. Excuse my wife, she can be a bit over excitable." It was said with humour and so much love as he looked at his wife that Skye's heart almost stopped.

"Nonsense, I just know what I see with my two eyes. Do you not see it, *mi amor*?" she asked her husband.

"Yes, *cariad*, I see it."

Her eyes moved from Skye, then, and landed on Nate.

"*Mi hijo*, my eyes they do not deceive me. She is the one is she not?"

Nate pulled Skye to him and slipped his arms around her waist, with her back to his front, he rested his chin on her shoulder.

"Yes, Ma, she is." He looked at Skye as she twisted to see his eyes. The look in his eyes said so much and she leaned her face into him for a kiss, completely oblivious of everyone else in the room. They kept it brief, though, and broke apart to see Noah watching them from the bed with a big smile on his face.

"Hey, baby," she said as she broke from Nate and went to him, "how you feeling?"

"I feel much better, now, mummy. Who's that?" he asked, pointing behind her to Nate's parents.

"Those are my parents, buddy," said Nate. He motioned his now nervous looking mother forward.

"Ma, Dad, this is Noah." Mimi seemed at a loss for words. She moved forward and when she reached the bed, Skye noticed she had tears in her eyes.

"Hello, *precioso niño*. I am Mimi, but you can call me, *Abuela*." She reached out and touched his cheek reverently.

"What does that mean?" asked Noah, as always full of questions.

"It means grandmother," Nate said smiling. The look on Noah's face almost brought Skye to her knees. It was a mixture of wonder, hope, and happiness that she had never seen. He had never had a grandparent and she hadn't realised he had missed it, but looking back, she realised he must have. She had been so close to her grandparents growing up, and had spent every summer holiday with them while her parents travelled.

"Can I, mummy? Can I call her *Abuela*?" Skye looked at Nate who had a huge smile on his face.

"Yes, baby, you can call her *Abuela*."

"*Abuela*," he said, trying it on for size, "I like it. It sounds nice on my tongue."

"You can call me Pop, young man," said Nate's dad, stepping forward and shaking hands with her boy. Noah seemed to flourish under their attention and Skye was content to sit back and watch as her son charmed Nate's parents.

They visited for a while, then the lunch trolley was brought round and Nate's parents said their goodbyes.

"We are in town for a week. We will come see you every day if that is okay with your mother," Mimi told Noah as she ruffled his hair. They both kissed Skye's cheek and hugged her.

"I'll walk you out," Nate said to his parents. He dropped a kiss to Skye's mouth and followed his parents.

"Mummy," Noah called.

"Yes, sweet pea?"

"Are you going to marry Nate?" Skye wasn't sure how to answer that. Things seemed good, but they hadn't talked of the future and she didn't want lie to her son or give him false hope.

"I don't know what will happen, baby. Nate is my boyfriend," she said hesitantly and smiled when Noah snickered. "I do know that he loves being around you and playing Legos. In fact, he's been itching to have a Lego batman rematch on Xbox."

"Really, he has?" Noah asked.

She nodded, "Yep." Phew! She'd dodged a bullet, there, or so she thought. Noah carried on eating his mashed potatoes and baked beans with grated cheese on top. It was his favourite and the staff always tried to make it for him while he was there.

"If you do marry Nate, can he be my dad then? I really want Nate to be my dad." It was said so innocently that it clogged her throat with emotion for a second.

"Me, too, baby. Me, too."

~~~

Nate walked his parents to their car–his eyes ever watchful for a threat. He kept getting an itchy feeling on the back of his neck when he was out here, and he couldn't shake it. The police had released Hugo on bail earlier that morning after the finger prints that had been found at the scene had somehow been contaminated, and were now inadmissible as evidence.

They had charged him with conspiracy to commit kidnap of a minor, possession of a class A drug, and possession of a lethal weapon. Unfortunately, he seemed to have a good solicitor who was a friend of the family.

Stopping at his parents cherished blue VW Beetle, he hugged his father, "Thanks for coming, Dad."

"She's a goodun, my boyo. You take good care of her."

"I will dad, I will."

He opened his arms for his tiny mother, who walked into them.

"Now, you listen, *mi hijo*," she bossed, "you take good care of them." She cupped his cheeks with her small hands, pulling his face down to hers, "She is the one, *mi hijo*. I see it in your eyes. She is the one who has captured your heart and will keep it. Her little one he needs you. He's crying out for a father, and the way he watches you, as if you are his saviour, fills my heart with joy. Now, I have decided that she is worthy of my boy, so when you are ready, to do the right thing. you come to me first, I have something for you. And don't take too long, I'm not getting any younger." With that, she kissed his cheek and climbed into the car.

"Thanks, Ma." She nodded and blew him as kiss.

"We will call you tomorrow to arrange a visit."

Nate watched them drive away in the thirty-year-old car, which looked better than most new cars, and smiled. He loved that his parents had loved Skye and Noah as much as he had. It wouldn't have made him pull back from Skye, but his parents meant a lot to him and it would have made life difficult.

Now he just needed to get rid the threat of Hugo and Felicity Lockwood, who had disappeared into thin air, from over their heads and get this transplant done so they could move forward as a family.

Nate was smiling as he approached the door. He was about to push through when he heard Noah ask, "If you do marry Nate, can he be my dad then? I really want Nate to be my dad." Nate stopped and listened while he held his breath, waiting to hear what Skye would say.

"Me, too, baby. Me, too."

The air left him in a whoosh and his shoulders sagged. He wanted that, too. He wanted that more than anything. He pushed open the door loudly, pretending he hadn't heard.

"Hey, champ! How's the cheesy-beans and mash?"

"It's good, Nate, real good. Look, it's making me strong," Noah flexed his tiny bicep to show Nate, who good naturedly gave it a squeeze.

"Wow. I need to hit the gym or you are going to be lifting more than me," Nate grinned when Noah giggled.

He felt Skye come up behind him and slip her hands round his middle. She pressed her front to his back, he felt her softness against him. She dropped a kiss to his back and he shifted and pulled her so she was snug at his side.

"Walk me out?" he asked Skye. "Buddy, I hear they are going to spring you later, so no more excuses. The Batman rematch is on."

"Yeah, as if you could beat me," Noah said with a boyish giggle. Nate put his hand out for a high-five. "Later, tater," he laughed as Noah high-fived him.

"Later, Nate."

Skye told Noah she would be back in second and walked him out.

He loved the feel of her against his side, tucked under his arm. He could smell her hair and the watermelon shampoo she used. They stopped at the lift and he turned her to him. He wrapped his arms around her and held her to him. She looked up, then–he could see the exhaustion in her eyes, and she had never been more beautiful.

Running his finger down her cheek, he traced the shadows under her eyes.

"He seems much better today," he said softly.

"Yeah, he does, it's such a relief."

"I want to ask Lucy and Drew to stay with him tonight. You can wait until he goes to sleep. But, *mi cielo*, you're dead on your feet. You need to get some proper rest."

"I don't know. I don't want to leave him."

"I know, but Lucy and Drew said they will stay and we can sleep at my place in town, so we will only be a few minutes away. You haven't slept properly since this started and I'm worried about you."

"Okay, but only if he is okay with it."

"Okay, deal. Now kiss me, so I can get back to work." Skye gave him that secret smile that drove him wild and lifted onto her toes. She ran her fingers up his chest and looped them around his neck, bringing her body into intimate contact with his.

He hissed at the contact of her breasts pressed to his chest. He couldn't wait to taste her again, and this time make her his in every way. He lowered his head to hers and she touched her mouth to his, sliding her tongue into his mouth. The sensation and taste of her made his body go hard. He moved one hand up under her shirt, caressing the soft skin at the bottom of her back–his other hand lifting to caress her ribs just under her breast.

His cock was painfully hard, and if he didn't think he would get arrested, he'd be very tempted to push her back against the wall and drive into her soft heat. This woman made him lose control and he loved it.

He pulled back when he heard the lift's *ding*, resting his forehead against hers. That was when he heard a voice that he'd hoped never to hear again.

"Nate!"

He cursed and his hands flexed on Skye's hips. He looked up to see Nikki, his ex. She was in her nurse's uniform, the material stretched tight across her fake assets. Her eyes went from him to Skye and he saw pain fleetingly cross her face when she noticed their closeness.

Nate turned to face Nikki. He hadn't seen her since he'd cleared all her belongings from his flat and dumped them on her doorstep. He looked at her, now, and found it hard to believe he thought she was *the one* at one point.

She was pretty enough, but it was all made up–she never went anywhere without her full face done. He knew he shouldn't, but he couldn't help comparing her to Skye, and she fell so short it wasn't funny. Despite all that, they had had some good times and it wasn't in his nature to be a bastard.

"Nikki," he said in greeting. She was looking at Skye.

"I'm sorry. I didn't come and see you when you got hurt. I wasn't sure you would want me to," she trailed off as if unsure.

"I wasn't in for long, anyway."

"I'm just on my way up to Obs and Gynae for my shift. How are your parents?" she asked quickly.

"They're fine. This is my girlfriend, Skye," he saw her wince slightly as he indicated Skye.

"Hi!" Skye said, putting out her hand and smiling.

"Hi, nice to meet you," Nikki replied hesitantly as she shook Skye's hand.

"Well, I should get going, it was nice to see you and nice to meet you Skye," she made to move towards him, to do what, Nate wasn't sure, but he pulled back, anyway. Nikki stopped and blushed. Hurt crossed her face.

"Bye, Nate, Skye."

"Yeah, bye." He watched her walk away and felt nothing–no anger, bitterness…nothing. Just apathy. It was as if he had never known her or the pain she had caused him and that was down to Skye, she had healed him in a way that made everything that had ever hurt him seem insignificant. Her strength and kindness, and watching her around Noah, had shown him true strength in the face of pain. He couldn't believe it, but he fell more in love with her every day. Yes, he was a cliché and he didn't care. It was true.

Turning, he looked at her beautiful face.

"You okay, baby?" she asked, palming his face gently and tilted her head while looking at him.

"Yeah, *mi cielo*, why wouldn't I be?" he was confused by her question.

"Well, that was your ex, and I know it ended badly."

God, even now, she was looking out for him, worried about him. Did she ever stop thinking of others?

"I'm fine. She has no hold over me and when I saw her, I felt nothing, not even anger. The only people who have power over me are people I love, and that is my family and friends, and most especially you and Noah." He held her round her waist with his arm and cupped her cheek with his hand. "You are everything to me, Skye."

Nate watched as her eyes went bright.

"Really?" She whispered.

"Yes, really. I love you. You and Noah. You have my heart." He figured it was good when she buried her head in his chest and held on tight. He wrapped his arms around her and hugged her while she cried silent tears. She pulled herself together and looked up at him, giving him a wobbly smile.

"Sorry. I'm sure that wasn't what you expected in response of a declaration of love," she sniffed and wiped at her eyes, "I love you, too, Nate and I'm not just saying that because you did. I've felt it for a while and I know Noah adores you."

"Well, of course, I'm the Lego Batman king," he laughed, lightening the moment. It worked–Skye laughed and replied, "That you are, honey, although, not for long. When Noah gets home, he has plans to kick your butt."

"Can't wait," he said. "Right, I have to go, I'll pick you up from here later after Lucy and Drew arrive."

"Okay, Nate."

He dropped a kiss to her nose and stepped into the lift. He watched her stand there, "Go, baby, get back to Noah." She smiled and turned to leave, "Love you, Nate."

"Love you, too, *mi amor*." He could tell by her smile she liked it when he called her that. He *wasn't* pleased to see Nikki way down the corridor watching them, though. The doors closed and he decided he needed Drew and Lucy to keep an eye out for Nikki and run an in-depth check on her recent activity. After all, she had ties to Hugo Lockwood, too.

Chapter Nineteen

Rushing to his car, Nate made it back to Fortis in record time. He tipped his head at the new receptionist as he went by. She seemed nice–quiet, but pleasant. He was willing to give her the benefit of the doubt. He walked straight to the tech room a a sense of urgency came over him that he couldn't quite pinpoint. Drew was talking to Will over Face time, and Lucy had her head buried in printouts from Will's new piece of software.

"Hey, guys. Have you seen Zack?"

"He's in the conference room with Ava." Lucy said distractedly

"Thanks." He turned on his heel and went to the conference room. As he walked down the hall, he saw Zin coming out of the exercise room. He was covered in sweat from an obviously heavy workout and looked pissed.

"Hey, man," Nate said by way of greeting.

"Hey. How is Noah?" he asked.

"He's okay. Seems a lot better. Not as agitated about Kanan, either, which is good." He watched Zin's face darken at the mention of Kanan. He wondered what the history was, but didn't ask. If Zin felt it was important, he would share, otherwise, it wasn't his business.

"I need to speak to Zack, I'll catch you later."

"Yeah, later, man."

Nate walked into the conference room. You could cut the tension with a knife. Zack stood at the top of the table with his hands on his hips, a scowl on his face. Ava was leaning over the desk pouring over the data they had collected from Marcus Preedy's computer.

"For fuck's sake, Ava, just take a break. You haven't stopped since you got here."

"No, Zack. I want this done so I can get home," she glared right back. Nate was impressed by her backbone.

"Boss, can I have a word?" Nate asked. Zack ignored him and carried on looking at Ava, then seemed to capitulate.

"Fine, I'll get some food sent in for you."

"Whatever," She waved her hand at him as though she didn't care.

Zack walked to him, "What can I do for you, Nate?" Nate explained seeing Nikki and then explained her history with Hugo, leaving out any details that were not important.

"I see you point," Zack replied, "What else is bothering you?"

"I'm not sure, I just have a feeling that I can't shake. I want Lucy and Drew to watch Noah tonight so Skye can get some rest."

"No, I don't want both of them off the computers. Ask Lucy and Zin. It might help his disposition and get him out of the office. I'll also get Will to tap into the hospital CCTV so that we can keep an eye out. I'll get him to monitor that remotely until he gets back. His deal is done in France, now, so he should be home by Friday." Nate watched Zack as he looked back at Ava, "Have you eaten, Nate?"

"Not yet."

"Come on, let's grab a burger from the Wagon of Death, while I grab Miss Drake some food."

"Sure, is there any progress?"

"Yeah, some. I'll tell you on the way." Nate followed Zack to his Landrover. He was starving, he realised, and a full breakfast roll from the Wagon of Death would hit the spot. Of course, it wasn't a Wagon of Death, it was just a mobile fast food van. He wasn't even sure how it had got that nickname, it's just what everyone called it. His mouth watered and his gut rumbled at thought of it.

Zack proceeded to tell him what Ava had confirmed. The language was ancient, was, in fact extinct, and was only studied by a handful of people, of which she was one, thank God. The text spoke of an ancient disease being spread throughout the world and only the gifted and the new batch surviving to take the world in the right direction.

"New batch? What is that, and how will the gifted be safe from the disease?"

"That, we don't know, yet. We need to get someone in to one of the clinics to find out. We, also, have an idea of a timeline, now. The text mentions five rings a lot, so we are thinking something to do with the Olympics."

"Holy shit. That has massive implications."

Zack just nodded "I have Jack in on this, now. It's too massive for us on our own. Jack can get his international teams on it so they can do the groundwork in Europe and the States. But, we will lead from here with Eidolon.

"That's good. Those guys are great, and we know we can trust them, which, at the moment, is most important. So, how we going to do this?" They had arrived at the Wagon of Death and sat in the car to finish their conversation.

"We will concentrate on unravelling the text and the medical facilities. They are the key to this. So, that is where we are at."

"It's funny how the last two things to hit the team are leading back to the Divine Watchers. Do you think we are being targeted?"

"Yes, I was thinking that. I think we need to increase our vigilance as a team and I'm going to speak to everyone later at the team meeting. We need all team members to brief their families, now. Come on, let's eat." Zack exited the vehicle while Nate brought up the rear.

Chapter Twenty

Skye finished reading Julia Donaldson's, *Monkey Puzzle*, to Noah for thousandth time. He loved that book and always asked for it. He'd heard it that many times that he now repeated it with her as she read.

"Baby, how would you feel about Lucy and Zin watching you tonight?" Nate had texted that it would be Lucy and Zin, not Drew.

"I don't mind, mummy. Are you going out with Nate?"

"No, baby. Mummy just wants to catch up on some beauty sleep so I'm going to put you to bed and then go get some rest."

"Okay. You do look a bit sleepy, and girls have to get their beauty sleep or they get all grumpy," he said with in all seriousness. Skye laughed

"Who told you that?"

"Aunty Lizzie," he said in a stage whisper. "She said Mateo has to sleep until seven am so that she can get her beauty sleep or she gets grumpy. Seven o'clock, mummy. Can you believe he sleeps that late?"

"No, baby, I can't," she smiled and brushed his curls from his forehead. "Are you feeling okay about Kanan now, sweetie?" Skye said, changing the subject.

"Yes, mummy, it's all okay, now. You can go and let Lucy and Zin watch me. I'll only be sleeping, anyway, and I have Bruno and my special quilt." Skye always made sure he had his Star Wars quilt cover and pillowcase and his teddy so that he had at least some comforts from home.

"Okay. I'll let Nate know he can pick me up later." Skye walked from the room to phone Nate and let him know it was all okay for later. She could have text but she loved hearing his deep voice. It was four o'clock and the doctor would be doing his rounds, soon. She hoped Noah could go home tomorrow for a few days until he had to come back to start his chemo in readiness for the transplant.

She had her head down, scrolling for Nate's number, so didn't see Nikki walking towards her.

"He doesn't love you, you know." Skye looked up and stopped, sure she had misheard the woman.

"Sorry, what did you say?" she asked in a deceptively calm voice.

"Nate doesn't love you. He just wants kids so he's latched on to you since you already have a readymade one." Skye didn't respond but observed Nikki's screwed-up, malicious pout and the way she had her hand on her hip, her false assets pushed out.

"Well," Skye replied, "that really is nothing for you to concern yourself with, is it?" She went to step round her, but Nikki blocked her path.

"Why don't you and your sickly kid, just disappear and leave Nate to me? We were good together. We were going to get married and everything." She said in a whiny voice.

"Oh, you mean before you cheated on him?" Skye asked coldly, seriously pissed off at this woman. How dare she refer to her son as a sickly kid? And to tell her to go away after the way she treated Nate? If Skye had to go into a verbal smack down in the hospital corridor, so be it.

"We would have gotten over that if his bitch of a mother hadn't gotten involved."

"Mimi didn't like you? I knew I liked that woman."

"Mimi? Who the fuck is that you stuck up bitch?" Nikki sneered.

"Mimi is Nate's mum, you imbecile. Now, I'm going to give you five seconds to get gone before I call security."

"Call them, they love me," Nikki brushed her ponytail back from her shoulder and flicked her head arrogantly. Argh. Skye, so, wanted to punch her–and to think, she had felt sorry for her earlier.

"You know, Nikki, I feel sorry for you. Seeing Nate must have brought it home just how much you fucked up. He is good and kind, he has a good job, earns good money, and well, you have eyes. I don't have to explain the rest. How could you have fucked that up so royally and still have the gall to think he would take you back?" Nikki was glaring death rays at her now.

Just then, the phone went in Skye's hand. Seeing it was Nate, she answered. "Hey, baby."

"Hey, *mi amor*. Can you give the phone to Nikki, please?" Skye was stunned. How the hell did he know? Looking around, she noticed the CCTV.

"Umm, yeah, okay," she held the phone out for Nikki, "It's for you." Nikki took the phone and held it too her ear. She went exceedingly pale and Skye saw her swallow and say "Okay. Yes, I understand." She handed the phone to Skye with a cold glare and walked away.

"Uh…what just happened?" Skye asked as she held the phone to her ear.

"We have access to the CCTV in the hospital, so Drew gave me the heads up. What did she say to you?"

"Oh, just the usual bitter, ex-girlfriend shit. Nothing I couldn't handle. More importantly, what did you say to her? She looked terrified."

"Nothing much. Just threatened her job and told her he would report her to the chief Nursing Officer if she didn't move along and stay away. Not sure it will work, but let me know if it doesn't and I will follow through with the threat."

"Okay. I was going to call you, anyway. I spoke to Noah. He is fine with me leaving him with Lucy and Zin, so you can pick me up later."

"That's great. I can't wait to have you all to myself for a bit. I have to go, see you later."

"See you later, babe." Skye hung up the phone, body breaking out in a shiver. The thought of her and Nate alone for a whole night, with no extra worries and stress, sounded wonderful.

She'd been so worried about Noah, but that didn't mean she hadn't enjoyed being curled up to Nate's body every night. She felt the effect that had on him and she liked it–a lot.

He was the hottest guy she had ever known and the thought of him and her alone tonight sent her hormones into overdrive. Yes, she was tired, but somehow, not as tired as she was a few minutes ago.

She was deep into her delicious thoughts when Lizzie walked up the corridor.

"Hi, sweetie," she said as she kissed Skye's cheek. "How's it been today?"

"You just missed the fun. I just had a run in with Nate's ex."

"Oh, do tell." Lizzie linked arms with her while they walked back to Noah's room, laying out the details of the encounter.

Lizzie visited with Skye and Noah visited for an hour, in which time the doctor made his rounds, and thankfully, decided that as long as Noah had a good night he could go home tomorrow.

Lizzie had left around five-thirty that evening. Skye was concerned about her friend, though. She seemed tired and not quite as bubbly as usual. When Skye had asked her about it, she said work was busy. She didn't think that was it, though. In all the time they had been friends, Lizzie had never introduced Skye to her husband. She made excuses every time there was a get-together, saying he was working or away on business.

Skye was determined—when things settled a little–she would have Lizzie over for a girlie night and not let her leave until she had shared what was on her mind.

Noah was settled in his bed, just finishing their evening routine of a game of chess and three stories. They only did this when he was feeling well enough, though. Luckily the last few months had been better. He really surprised her with chess. His ability to see patterns and strategies, the next move in the game, before she made it was brilliant. Her boy was a natural tactician and he made her proud every single day.

She ran her finger down his cheek as he drifted off to sleep, he turned towards her. His eyes were heavy as he fought to open them and mumble, "Love you to the moon, mummy."

"Love you to the sun, baby," she replied softly and kissed his soft cheek. She stayed next to him, her hand on his as he slept. He was so precious to her and she prayed every day that the transplant would work. The last blood results had been promising, although, he would feel poorly with the chemo. She was anxious to get started so he could get on the road to recovery.

Deep in thought, she startled when the door opened. Lucy poked her head in and Skye could see Zin's head and shoulders behind her.

"Hey," said Lucy as she motioned Skye outside. She followed her back out into the corridor.

"Hey, guys. Thanks for doing this. Are you sure you don't mind?" Lucy grabbed her arm and looped it through hers, "Of course not. This is an easy gig and I adore Noah, we all do." Lucy looked back at Zin who was scanning the hallway, "Right, Zin?" He looked at Lucy and then Skye.

"This is an honour, Skye, that you trust us with his safety. We won't let you down. You go with Nate and get some rest, we will call if he wakes or wants you." That accent was seriously sexy, thought Skye. Although, not as sexy as Nate's.

"See? We got this. I'll be inside with Noah and Zin will be at the door. Go get some sleep, you look knackered."

Skye laughed at Lucy's blunt assessment of her appearance, "Gee. Thanks. Luce. Love you, too."

"Hey, love you, woman, and with your stunning beauty. Tiredness just gives you that sleeping beauty fragility men go mad for." Zin nodded behind Lucy, "Nate is a lucky man," he said, making her blush

"Oh, look, here's the man himself." Skye looked down the hall and Nate was striding toward them. He looked so handsome in his jeans and Superdry jacket, his hair a sexy, windblown mess. He strode toward her with his loose-limbed walk, arms relaxed at his side. His dark, good looks–and the way filled out his clothes–made her mouth water.

Lucy leaned forward and whispered, "Skye, wipe your drool or pass me a cigarette." Skye turned to her and gently shoved her with her elbow, "Behave yourself," she giggled.

"Who, me? You're the one panting like a bitch in heat."

"Lucy, shut up," she growled laughingly. Nate made it to them, then, and immediately hooked Skye around the waist and pulled her to him. His eyes only on her, not seeming to care that Lucy and Zin stood there, and he kissed her. It was hard and quick and packed a serious wallop.

"Hey, *mi amor*, missed you."

"You only saw me a few hours ago," she said softly, still recovering from the kiss.

"Exactly. *Hours* ago. I missed you." Skye's heart skipped a beat at his words.

"I missed you, too, baby," she replied and rested her head against his chest.

Nate turned his attention to Lucy and Zin. Lucy was grinning like a loon and Zin looked, at first glance indifferent, but on closer inspection his lips where turned up slightly at the corners in a smirk.

"Do you want to go get your stuff and say goodnight to Noah?" Nate asked, tipping his head to Skye and letting her go. She pulled away and nodded, "Yes. I'll go now."

She slipped into the room to grab her bag and check if Noah was sleeping soundly. She watched his breathing,–it was deep and even. No signs of distress or bad dreams to plague him in rest. She tucked his covers up around his chin and tucked his bear in beside him. Dropping a kiss on his forehead and running her hand over his cheek, she whispered, "Night baby. Sweet dreams."

Exiting the room, she found Zin standing sentry against the doorframe and Lucy waiting to go in to sit with Noah. She walked straight to Nate, slipping under his arm so she could wind her arms around his waist.

"I've briefed Luce and Zin and they know to call if anything happens, no matter how small."

"Go, get some rest. Get some food and have some hot monkey sex."

"Lucy!" three voices growled.

"What? You're thinking it, I just said it."

"Right, we're out of here. Call if you need me," Nate said and turned, pulling her towards the lift.

They drove to Nate's flat, which was only a few minute away from the hospital, and they could walk it as quick with the traffic like it always was on that section of road. The old Victorian house on Aylestone Hill was huge. Nate explained that the property had been split into four flats when he'd bought it. He'd taken the top two floors as his own, and was slowly turning it back into the beautiful house it once was.

The two flats on the ground floor would be next, but one was still occupied. Nate was putting that off, though. He didn't have the heart to evict Mrs Beatty. She was eighty-eight years old and not a well lady. He'd told her that she could stay as long as she wanted. Unfortunately, he didn't think that would be long.

Walking up the front steps, Skye was not surprised to see state of the art security on the door. The front of the house had two massive bay windows and the large, black front door had a big, brass knocker and letterbox.

Entering the hallway, she looked around. The floor was solid oak parquet flooring, the walls a clean white. She marvelled at the detail on the cornice and mouldings. This was beautiful. She couldn't stop her eyes scanning every inch, trying to take in the detail.

To the left was a sturdy, red with flat A next to it. The handle shone and the paintwork was clean and new looking.

To the front of her was an impressive stair case with wrought iron spindles and a curved oak balustrade. The stairs, themselves, were polished oak wood. On the right was another door with flat B on the front. This door was blue and looked slightly worse for wear. The paint was peeling and the door handle looked dull and unloved.

Skye followed Nate up the stairs, running her hand over the smooth wood as she went. As they reached another security door, she watched him use his thumb to open the door lock and thought it was a great idea–she was always forgetting her keys. Maybe she would ask him about fitting her place with one.

She didn't know what to expect from his space but she was pleasantly surprised. The door led through to a large open hallway. The floor was, again, oak. The walls were a soft dove grey, a large gilt mirror with the Prince of Wales feathers on the frame, hung on the hall wall between two doors.

On the right were two more doors, leading to what looked like an office and small bathroom. She allowed Nate to take her coat and he hung it in a cupboard on the left, which was under a second set of stairs going up to a third floor.

Nate took her hand and she went to him willingly. Putting her arms around his warm, hot body, she rested her head against him. He held her tight and wrapped his hand around her hair, tipping her head back with a gentle tug.

"You okay, *mi cielo?*" he asked, scanning her face.

"Yes, I'm surprisingly fine. I love your house. It's absolutely beautiful."

"Do you want the tour or food first?" he asked as he nuzzled her neck. She she was hungry, but she wanted a tour.

"How about we order food and then you give me the tour while we wait?"

"Good plan. Let's go find the menus." He dragged her by the hand into the kitchen of her dreams.

"Oh my god. This kitchen is divine. Is that a Kitchenaid mixer?"

Nate shrugged, "Not sure, my mum and sister kitted out the kitchen. I just footed the bill and chose the cabinets."

Skye took a closer look, "Nate, how can you have Kitchenaid appliances and not know that they are the caviar of kitchen appliances?" He barked out a deep laugh as he went through what was obviously a junk draw filled with menus.

"Caviar. So I take it you approve?"

"Approve? This is the kitchen of my dreams." Nate abandoned his hunt and came to her. The look in his eyes made her stomach flip and her body go soft. He kept coming until he backed her up against the counter. His hands came up and cupped her face.

"Kitchen of your dreams for the woman of mine."

"Nate…"

"I mean it, Skye. You don't know how much it means to me that you like what I'm doing here. I want you to like this. I hope, one day in the future, you and I will make this our home–and if not here, then somewhere else. I want to see Noah's toys and game console in my living room, and your cake paraphernalia in the kitchen. I want this for us."

"I want that, too," she said quietly, "But until Noah is over the worst, we need to give him stability, not rush into a move."

"I know that," he said as he rubbed his thumbs over her cheeks, "I'm talking down the line. I want a future for us. This is it for me, you are it for me."

"You are it for me, Nate, and I want it, too. So much." His head lowered and he kissed her gently, his lips teasing hers until they opened for him. She felt herself relax into his hard body and her arms went around his shoulders, hands in his soft, thick hair.

He gripped her head, his other hand went down as he palmed her ass through her jeans, causing a flood of heat to her girlie parts. They kissed like that for a few minutes until her stomach rumbled and he pulled away laughing.

"I think we need to order food and then I'll give you the tour."

Skye blushed, "Yeah, good idea."

They settled on Thai and Nate phoned in the order. They had thirty minutes to kill, so Nate showed her the rest of the flat.

The living room was a definite man den. There was a fifty-two-inch, 3D television on the wall with a massive sound bar underneath. All the walls where painted in a very pale lavender colour with accents of grey and black.

The oak flooring was covered by two, thick plush rugs in mauve and grey with swirl patterns on them. The beautiful bay window had wooden blinds and thick charcoal grey curtains, which were drawn back with wrought iron tiebacks.

A seat, which was ideal for reading, had been built into the windowsill, with soft, padded cushions in dove grey. She could imagine herself reading there or just people watching.

Above the open fireplace was a large oak mirror–the fireplace, itself, was original by the looks of it. The mantle–carved with intricate patterns of scrolls, with long curving lines, were a white colour and, somehow, worked against the dark oak of the floor.

She was delighted to see how many of the original features Nate managed to restore. Skye followed him out of the living room, which was the first door as you came up the stairs, into the small office next door. This was definitely functional rather than decorative.

The Victorian writing desk faced the sash window to the back of the house. A computer sat on the desk, a printer off to the side on a shelf set into an alcove. A modern computer chair looked completely out of place against the antique furniture. This room had cream carpet instead of wooden flooring. It worked, though, especially against the cream walls, which someone had covered in family pictures.

She stopped to study them. There were pictures of Nate as kid, Nate and his parents, Nate in a morning suit at his sister's wedding, looking dashing. Nate in his Parachute regiment dress uniform and maroon beret at his passing out parade, looking sexy as fuck and so proud. It was the picture of Nate with his teammates from the para's that really caught her attention.

They were all grinning at the camera, arms slung over each other, dressed in fatigues. It was obviously taken somewhere in the Middle East if the surroundings were anything to go by.

"Who are these guys?" Skye asked. He stepped up behind her and wrapped his arms around her chest, tugging her back to him and resting his chin on her shoulder.

"That's Jake, Dai, and Reece," he said of the men to his left in the picture, "and that's Simon, Stoner, and Ice," he said of the other three.

"Who's that?" she asked, pointing at a handsome man who was sprawled at their feet. He was lying on his side, a big cocky grin on his face. She felt Nate tense.

"That's Tiny," he stopped and she wondered if he was going to continue. "He died a few years back. We went through basic training together; he was one of my best friends." He sounded so sad, it broke Skye's heart.

"What happened?" she asked quietly.

"He had a brain tumour." Skye had not expected that answer. Somehow, she had assumed it had happened on a mission. Nate carried on and she remained silent. "He'd just gotten engaged when he found out. They have a little boy, Ben, who was only two when he died. I try to go and see them when I can. They live in Bristol so it's not as often as I'd like. She has a new guy now. He's nice–a computer programmer. It still hurts seeing him where Tiny should be, though."

She turned in his arms and hugged him tight, listening to his steady heartbeat against her ear. "Thanks for telling me."

"It's not a secret, I just don't talk about him much. None of the guys knew him, so it never comes up."

"What about the others?"

"Jake, Dai, and Reece are still serving. Those guys are fucking nuts, but in the best way. I still see them from time-to-time. Simon went into the SAS and serves with Smithy. Stoner and Ice have their own corporate team building company up north. They are both Manchester boys, so when they left, they decided to use the skills they had to make some money. They do a lot of work with T.V companies."

"You didn't fancy it."

"God, no. I love working with Zack and the team. I've helped out a couple of times with team building gigs, but I'd rather my work actually mean something."

"Come on, let's finish the tour before the food arrives."

Nate was obviously finished sharing, and that was fine. She'd learned more about the intrinsic depths of him in the last few days than she had the last few months.

The upstairs was equally beautiful as the rest. The floors were all oak, the walls in differing shades of cream or dove grey. There were three bedrooms on this floor, all double bedrooms and two with en-suites. Two faced the front and one the garden at the back. All had double beds and were fully furnished with wardrobes and chests of drawers.

A large family bathroom also faced the back garden. The claw foot tub was beautiful. The black and white diamond style tiles on the floor gave the room a clean sharp look.

It was the master suite, which was on the fourth floor, which blew her away. This was obviously Nate's room. A large Velux window was in the middle of the set of windows. Fitted wardrobes were along one whole side in a pale cream. The king sized bed faced the window and had cream bedside cabinets on either side. The walls were a peacock blue and the quilt cover was turquoise and gold. It gave the room a masculine, but luxurious, feel. Two doors on the far side of the room were shut.

"What are those?" she asked, pointing at the doors.

Nate walked to one and pulled it open, "That is the bathroom." The bath was a gorgeous corner bath with Jacuzzi jets. Beige and cream Italian tiles on the walls and floor and beautiful marble his and hers sinks with waterfall taps. The double shower in the opposite corner to the bath had opaque glass sliding doors and a heated towel rail next to it.

"Oh my god, that bath is amazing," she declared, losing his hand going straight to the bath.

"We can try it later if you'd like," he said with a deliciously devilish grin." Skye smiled and blushed slightly at the thought of the things they could get up to in that bath. Nate grabbed her hand and pulled her out of the bathroom.

"Come on, before I forget about food and go straight to dessert." He leaned down and kissed her neck where her shoulder met her collarbone, causing her to shiver.

"Okay," she said, secretly wondering if she needed food.

"So, what about that door?" she noticed it was locked with a keypad?

"That's my weapons room."

"Weapons room," she repeated as if he'd said that was the room he kept virgin brides in.

"Yeah. Sniper rifles, handguns, knives, and other stuff. It's kind of a work thing."

"Okay, then," she said, because, really, what was there to say to that? "Your house is truly amazing, Nate. What will you do when you get the bottom floor back?"

"I will restore it back to a fully functioning family home. The bottom floor will probably be a games room, utility room, den, and maybe a small bedroom annexe for guests."

"Wow. This must have cost a fortune," she regretted it the minute she said it. It was so crass to talk about money, but as a single mum, she was always watching the pennies. But she knew from how she was brought up, how much this would have cost. She recognised luxury and quality when she saw it, and this was top-notch workmanship. "Sorry, I shouldn't have said that." Nate laughed aloud and she bristled.

"Hey don't laugh," she punched his arm to make her point, but he just picked her up and chucked her onto the bed. What the hell? Before she had chance to say anything, he came down on top of her, pinning her to the bed.

"Nate," she breathed as she felt his weight and heat cover her body. Nate took her hands and interlaced their fingers. He pushed them above her head, causing her breasts to push against his chest. She felt her nipples tighten her breath coming quicker.

"Skye, nothing you ask me is off limits. Yes, it cost a lot. Luckily, I had some in the bank. You don't spend a lot of money when you're on deployment and Zack pays really well. I also had a decent inheritance from my grandfather when he died six years ago. So it didn't actually cut into my wages from Fortis. Anyway, it's an investment in my future, and I wanted the best."

"It's the most beautiful home I've ever been in," Skye said sincerely. He seemed pleased with that and showed her by kissing her senseless. He pulled back and released her hands, moving to stand, he held out his hand and pulled her up.

"Time for food," he said, but the promise of what would come after hung in the air between them, causing a delicious anticipation to stir her blood.

Nate encouraged her to call Lucy while he dished up the food that arrived just as they came downstairs. She grabbed her handbag and went to sit at the kitchen table that was set at the far end of the kitchen, forming an open dining space.

She, again, admired the kitchen. She always wanted a kitchen with a centre island, and this one was large and spacey. She fell into a little daydream while she dug around her bag for her phone. Finding it, she quickly called Lucy.

"Hey Skye, what's up?" Lucy said by way of greeting.

"Hi, Luce, I just wanted to check all was quiet."

"All quiet. Nurses keep doing their normal checks and Noah's sleeping soundly. Seriously, how do you get any sleep in here? Its constant interruption and chatter. Honestly, you enjoy your night after days of this. You deserve it."

Skye laughed softly, "You get used to it. Cat naps are just a way of life for me."

"Yeah, I guess they are," Lucy said, sounding thoughtful, "I never had a clue what you went through before, you know. I thought I did, but this must have been so tough on your own."

Skye's throat closed with emotion, "It is tough, but you just do it. Honestly, Luce, you have never known a love like that, then the love of a mother for her child. It transcends everything. Your comfort, your life, and yes, definitely your sleep," she smiled as she said the last, leting it show in her voice. She needed to lighten the moment before she became a blubbering mess.

"I guess it does," Lucy said in almost a whisper. Skye wondered at the crack in her voice. She seemed to rally then, "Anyway, get back to your monkey sex and leave me be. I have a good bodice ripper book that I'm enjoying." Skye laughed aloud, "Yes, boss, and thanks, Luce."

"No problem, sister." Skye hung up and sat silently, thinking about Lucy and Lizzie; they had both seemed quiet this week.

"Skye, food." Nate stood in front of her with two plates in his hands. "Where do you want to eat?"

"I don't mind, wherever makes you happy." Nate put the plates on the table and leaned down to kiss her, "You make me happy, Skye, so where shall we eat?"

"Living room, then. I want to check out your huge-ass telly."

"A woman after my own heart." Skye got up and followed him. "Can you grab the drinks off the counter?" he asked as they passed the centre island that she'd been drooling over.

"Sure." She grabbed the drinks, but her mind was still on Lucy and Lizzie.

They settled down on the sofa. Nate, multi-tasking as he ate, and tried to find something to watch on telly. After flicking through the channels, they settled on the Great British Bake off. Skye was slightly obsessed with this show and had squealed when he went to flick past. He had relented and now sat grinning as he watched her critique the contestants and moon over Paul Hollywood.

"Please don't tell me you think that guy is hot?" Nate said on a groan.

"Any guy that can bake like that is hot," she teased. She giggled as Nate made a dive for her, pinning her beneath him.

"Is that so? So, am I going to need cooking lessons in my future?"

"Well, it might be nice not to have to bake my own birthday cake," she laughed.

"*Mi amor*, you don't really do that do you?"

"Well, yeah. But only because I'm such a tough critic."

"Hmm...well, I guess I'm going to need cooking lessons if I have to beat you and bake your birthday cake to perfection."

"Wow. Competitive much?"

"I'm a guy, it's in my blood. Still, I won't be wearing a flowery apron, though. I'm going to have to get a nice, butch one–maybe camo." Skye liked this side of him. The easy teasing and banter. She could see her spending her nights curled up watching T.V. or messing around with him like this. Noah in bed upstairs or her baking while her two guys played Xbox.

"I'm not sure even a flowery apron could diminish your masculine charms, Nate," she said as she stroked her hand down his handsome face. His eyes went soft and hooded. He gave her a look that was all male.

He didn't say anything, just kissed her, wet and hard, his hands sliding down her sides to the soft skin of her ribs. He let go and pulled back.

"How did I get so lucky?" he asked nobody in particular.

"It was us that got lucky, Nate. You saved my son once, and you're going to do it again, when you give him your bone marrow. The best day of my life was the day Noah was born, but, without a doubt, the next best was when you walked in to his hospital room and tipped my world on its head. We are definitely the lucky ones." He kissed her again, and she could feel his emotion in the tender way he kissed her.

Tucking her so that she was lay in front of him on the couch, he wrapped his arm around her, and he proceeded to introduce her to the world of Luther. This was not a hardship; Idris Elba was one of her favourite actors and so sexy.

She must have drifted off after the first episode, though, because the next thing she knew, Nate was lifting her to carry her to bed.

"What time is it?" she asked sleepily."

"A little after ten-thirty."

"Sorry," she said, rubbing her face, "I can walk. Put me down before you hurt yourself. I weigh a ton."

"You are no more than 60kg wringing wet, Skye, so behave. And anyway, I like having you in my arms." She smiled at him, then, and realised she liked being there. She fit so nicely against his broad, muscled chest. Her hand ran along the muscled ridges of his pecs and up around his neck.

"Skye, if you want to go to sleep you need to stop," Nate's voice sounded strained. She looked into his eyes and could see the desire there. Her body seemed to soften into his even more, and leaned forward to rub her nose along his neck, inhaling his scent. It was a mix of musk and sandalwood which made her want to lick him all over.

"Skye, I'm holding on by a thread here," he cautioned. She felt his muscles twitch with the strain and marvelled that she had such power over this big, strong man. It was a heady feeling.

"Then, don't," she whispered in his ear and gave the lobe a tug with her teeth. With a growl, Nate strode from the room with her still in his arms, practically running up the two flights of stairs to his room.

Nate dumped her on the bed and before she knew it, his body covered hers and his mouth was on her. The kiss was hard and rough and she loved it. Every inch of his hard body was pressed into hers, but Nate, considerate as ever, kept his weight off her.

She ran her hands through his soft hair as he tunnelled one of his hands into her hair, the other went up her top. She shivered as he caressed the underside of her breast with his thumb, grazing the nipple.

Arching her body into him, she tried to convey that she needed more. Nate was very good at reading her and was soon sweeping his hand over her straining nipples, teasing them into peaks, as he continued to kiss her senseless.

Lifting up, Nate reached down and drew her top over her head, leaving her in a hot pink, lace bra. His eyes were dark, almost black, and hooded as he looked at her. She gripped the bottom of his t-shirt and tried to tug it over his head, Nate flicked her breast through her bra as she reached to take the tee over his head, making her suck in a breath at the feeling.

He captured her lips, again. Legs on either side of her thighs, he pulled her to a sitting position, his hands going to the clasp on her bra. He flicked it open with a practiced move and pulled the straps down her arms. Her breasts fell free and he broke the kiss to look at her.

She knew her body was flushed and her lips swollen from his kiss. She looked down, suddenly feeling shy.

"Don't. Don't hide from me, *mi amor* . I want to see your beautiful, expressive eyes as I make you scream my name." Skye shivered and her body went languid at his words. He seemed so in control. She lifted her head to meet his eyes–the look in them giving her confidence.

Nate pushed her gently back on the bed, his eyes never leaving hers, telling her how much he wanted her. Coming down on top of her, his chest rubbed against her and the friction almost drove her over the edge. His chest had light sprinkling of dark hair that led into a trail all the way into the waistband of his jeans. She shuddered with desire. How could he do that to her with only a slight touch?

He kissed his way across her forehead and down across her jaw, never touching her lips. He kissed her neck and nipped at the delicate skin behind her ear, making her squirm.

The delicious torture continued over her breasts–never touching the nipples–delicately kissing down her stomach. He deftly flicked open the button of her jeans with one hand and pulled them down her legs, all the while kissing every inch he bared.

Nate ran his lips over her hipbone and down the inside of her thighs, when he got to the back of her knee, she giggled when he hit a ticklish spot. She felt him chuckle against her leg. The torture didn't stop, though. He went past her knees and placed soft touches of his mouth on her feet. She was so glad she had slipped her boots and socks off earlier while they were watching television. She didn't want anything to get in the way of this.

Eventually, he pulled the jeans off her legs, kissing a path back up. She was drowning in sensations as he worshipped every inch of her. Her hands twisted the quilt, but when he skimmed his mouth over her most sensitive spot, they dove into his hair, her hips bucking involuntarily.

Nate growled, "I love these," he said, indicating her hot pink G-string. He cupped her ass in both hands as he nuzzled at her most intimate place.

"Good," she let out in a whimper.

"How much do you like them?" he asked. She wasn't sure of the question, "Umm…I don't…" but before she could finish her answer, he'd ripped the G-string from her body.

"I'll buy you another one," he groaned as he pulled the scrap off material away, replacing it with his mouth.

It was the single most erotic thing that had ever happened to Skye, and she thought she would spontaneously combust. Heat flooded her body and she felt the pull of his lips on her clit, feeling it all the way to her nipples. She bucked her hips and pulled his hair as he devoured her. He seemed to like it, though, because he increased the tempo and soon she was screaming his name as her climax hit.

"Look at me," Nate rasped, and she opened her eyes to meet his. The emotion she saw there only made her climax harder.

She floated for a minute, her eyes drifting shut as she revelled in the feeling of complete satisfaction. She'd never felt anything like that. Her body was still tingling when she opened her eyes again. She looked down into his gorgeous face.

"You are so beautiful." The emotion in his voice nearly undid her and she had to fight back tears that suddenly overwhelmed her. Nate crawled up her body, kissing her tenderly. She had always thought that she would hate being kissed after what he did, but she found her body starting to thrum again.

Her hands travelled over his back, enjoying the ridges and dips of his hard muscle. She'd never been with someone as physically fit as Nate, and she wondered what he thought about her body. She had a few stretch marks on her tummy from her pregnancy and it was slightly rounded instead of the perfect washboard abs that seemed to be the pinnacle all woman were told to strive for.

She didn't regret it, of course, but maybe she should have put in more effort to get the muscle tone back.

"What's wrong?" Nate asked into her neck. Typical Nate, picking up on her nerves.

"Nothing, really. I just…it's just that you…" she kept stopping because she didn't want to point it out if he hadn't noticed. Nate rolled off her and lay on his side beside her, his head in the crook of his elbow, as he traced his finger up and down between the valley of her breasts.

"Tell me, *mi cielo*." Skye turned her head to him, the sight of him looking at her as if she hung the moon made her realise she was an idiot. Nate was not like other men; he would never judge her like that.

"It's just…well, look at you. You're perfect, your body is like Michelangelo's David, only better. You have amazing tattoos and

I'm...well, I have stretch marks and a wobbly tummy." He leaned in towards her then, but instead of kissing her like she expected, he proceeded to kiss along her tummy and kiss every stretch mark she had.

"You are the most beautiful woman I have ever met. Every mark on you tells of the wonderful, selfless person you are. Nothing is more beautiful than a mother, Skye." He caressed her tummy and hips and she could see he meant very word. If his eyes hadn't been a dead giveaway, the bulge in his jeans certainly was.

Instead of telling him she believed him, she showed him. Rolling onto her side and into him, so they were face to face, she reached for his zipper and slowly slid it down. He hissed out a breath when her hand lightly grazed him. He rolled to his back, bringing her down on top of him. Skye undid the button on his jeans and eased her hand inside. The tip of his ridged cock peeked out the top of his boxers.

She ran her thumb over the end and stroked the pre-cum gathered there. Nate, clearly done with her teasing, wrenched her hand away and broke the kiss. Standing up he shed his jeans and boxers and stood in front of her in all his glory.

Skye watched in desire-induced fascination as he gripped the length and stroked twice, his eyes never leaving hers. He reached into the drawer by his bedside and took out a condom. With his eyes still on her, he opened the packet and was about to roll it on when she reached for it, "Let me." Nate relinquished and she grasped his hard length, loving the feel of his soft skin over the hardness.

Rolling the condom on, she grasped his arms, pulling him down on top of her. She opened her legs and he settled between them, his hard cock pressed close against her, causing her clit to twitch.

He kissed her hard–their tongues duelling, hands roaming everywhere. She felt him nudge the head of his cock against her opening. He was big and she felt slightly apprehensive. Nate stopped moving and kissed her harder, his large hand cupping her breast and rolling the nipple. The other went to her ass cheek and then to her hip, lifting her leg over his hip.

He slid inside in one slow, continuous movement. The feeling of being full, with all the other sensations, took her straight to the edge of another climax. Nate started to move slowly, and with every slow thrust, the feeling built.

"God, you feel so good, Skye," he growled, "Lift your other leg, baby." She complied and wrapped both legs round his waist. Nate powered into her, but she sensed he was holding back.

"More, Nate. Harder. Please," she whimpered, and he seemed to snap. He slammed into her–hard and rough and she loved it. Her hands pulled at his hair, her climax hitting her so hard she screamed, throwing her head back. Nate grasped a nipple in his lips and pulled hard, increasing the feeling she could hardly stand the intensity.

As she started to come down, Nate continued to drive into her heat and she felt his movements become jerky, his length swelling as he spilled his release into her.

He relaxed into her, his breathing heavy.

"I'm sorry, baby. I didn't mean to be so rough." He lifted his weight off her, looking contrite. Skye stroked his face, "You weren't rough. You were perfect and I loved every single second. Only one problem, though," she stopped and watched his face fall. God, she loved this man. "Only problem is, I'm hooked. You aren't ever getting rid of me now." His big smile split his face and he kissed her, rolling onto his back he pulled her with him so she was lay with her head on his chest.

"Good, because I'm never letting you go," he said, wrapping her in his arms, pulling the covers over them both. Skye lay there feeling happier than she ever had. She traced the line of the tattoo on his chest, the tribal design was beautiful. The gunshot scar on his shoulder marred it, but like her stretch marks, they proved his bravery and courage. She closed her eyes as she thought of how close he'd come to losing his life

"What does this mean?" she pointed to the tattoo over his chest.

"It means strength and honour–its Latin. I had it when I was in the army," he continued. His fingers where stroking her shoulder and she was relaxed, but she could sense he was troubled.

"What's the matter?" She waited and wondered if he was going to say anything.

"I have something to tell you." She tensed at his words.

"When I was in the para's, there was an incident. We came under fire from insurgents. It was a completely freak thing, but a round hit some rock next to me and a piece flew off and hit me in the groin. It was so random and never could have been predicted."

Skye was quiet as he talked. "It was the most excruciating pain I've ever felt. I was taken straight to the hospital. I had a testicular torsion. They operated and it was all fine. But it left me with reduced fertility. It's not impossible, but it won't necessarily be easy."

Skye was silent. She didn't know what to say. Obviously, this was big for him and she had a feeling he felt it would affect how she felt towards him. She lent up on her elbow and felt him tense, as if waiting for the ball to drop.

"Thank you for telling me," she placed a kiss on his chest, "It would be amazing to carry your baby one day, Nate, but if, and when, the time comes and it doesn't happen, then there are always other ways. There are so many children looking for families. If we have to go that route, then so be it. A family is made of love, not biology. You have already been more of a father to Noah than he's ever had." Skye watched as his face changed, the look of complete adoration made her chest hurt.

"I don't think I could love you more than I do right now," he said as he stroked his hand down her face and neck. His hand gently held her neck, rubbing the pulse there.

"Good, because I love you, too." She settled back against him, her head on his chest.

She drifted off to sleep, feeling that everything would be okay.

~~~

Nate lay quietly with his whole world in his arms. Never in his life had he shared a physical connection with a woman as he did

Skye. Even now, he could feel himself getting hard as he remembered the way her hot heat had gripped him tight.

The way she had let herself go, surrendering to the moment, made him lse control in a way he never had before. She made him want her in a way that was more than physical–it was almost spiritual. She occupied his thoughts all the time and now that he felt what it was like to be inside her, he didn't think he would ever get enough.

The fact that she had reacted to his fertility issues as if they were theirs, not just his, floored him. It didn't seem to cross her mind to walk away. She was a miracle, and one he would make sure he held onto with every breath in his body.

His thoughts turned to Noah. That boy had grabbed his heart, from the first time he'd called Nate his superhero, and never let go. He didn't think he could love him more if he had been his own blood. The fact that his parents seemed to love them only cemented his decision.

He was going to make Skye and Noah his at the first opportunity. He just wanted to wait until the transplant was done and the threat from Hugo and Felicity Lockwood was over. With that thought, he drifted into a deep sleep, a smile gracing his face.

~~~

Waking at his usual five-thirty in the morning, Nate slipped from the warmth of the bed. His first thought had been to wake Skye by making slow sweet love to her, but she looked so peaceful and she'd been so tired that he decided to let her sleep for a bit.

Going downstairs, he went to the ground floor and the spare flat. He'd set up his home gym in there and it was time to get back into routine. He did an hour on the weights before going back up to the kitchen grab a glass of water. He downed it at the sink and set about making Skye breakfast.

He would take her breakfast and see if he could persuade her to take a shower with him. Mixing the eggs and with the cheese, ham, and mushrooms, he poured it into the pan. Grabbing a coffee for Skye and orange juice for himself, he plated up the omelettes and loaded everything onto a tray.

Climbing the stairs, he pushed open the door and nearly dropped the tray. Skye was lying on her back, the covers pulled down to her waist. Her arms flung behind her head, pushing her luscious breasts up.

He rushed to put the tray down before he dropped it and sat next to her on the bed. She didn't even twitch. Placing an arm over her, he leaned down and he very gently trailed his tongue around her plump nipple then slowly sucked it into his mouth. She moaned and began to writhe.

Her eyes fluttered open and she groaned, "Mmm…can you wake me like that every morning?"

Nate let her nipple pop free from his mouth, "It would be my pleasure," he chuckled. "I made you breakfast sleepy head. He stifled a groan and adjusted his gym shorts as she stretched her delectable body. "You did?" she looked so surprised, it sobered him. No one had been there to look out for her like that. "I did, but if you carry on flaunting all that in front of me, it will get cold."

"Well, that would be a shame," she said, but she leant forward, gripping his cheeks, and planted a soul-searing kiss on him.

"Someone is playful," he growled.

"Yes, but I'm also starving, so hold that thought. I need to try your cooking before we get in too deep," she said jokingly, "I would hate to fall for you anymore than I already have, only to find out your cooking doesn't cut the mustard."

"Well, if I'd known how important it was, I would have put more effort in." he handed her a plate and put the coffee within reach. He watched as she took a bite, her eyes crossed in delight.

"You like?" he asked with a smile.

"I love," she said. "Phew! I don't have to kick you to the curb, because that would have been hard after the wonderful orgasms you gave me last night." They had finished their food and Skye was drinking coffee.

"I need to call and check on Noah," she said over her mug.

"I already called Lucy. He slept well and was eating toast and marmite when I called."

Her face softened, "Thank you."

He took the cup from her hand and placed it to the side. "So, I was thinking we could shower together. You know, to share water and conserve the planet."

"Yeah." She said on a soft sexy smile

"Yeah," he echoed as his hand slid under the covers and stroked her thigh.

"I like how you think." Skye replied. He picked her up in one smooth move and threw her over his shoulder as she screamed and laughed. Walking to the shower door, he caressed her bare ass as he did, making her laughter turn to soft sighs. Opening the shower door, he turned the water on and placed her under the warm water as he shed his shorts and t-shirt.

Joining her, he proceeded to wash every inch of her perfect body until she was panting for more. He pleasured her with his hands and mouth until the water went cold.

Helping her from the shower, he wrapped her in a warm towel from the heated towel rail and put one around his hips, ignoring the raging hard-on he had.

He patted her ass and asked, "What time do you want to be at the hospital?"

"Around nine is fine."

"Okay, *mi cielo*," he dropped a kiss onto her shoulder blade and walked past her into the bedroom. He looked through his wardrobe for clean cargo trousers and a long-sleeve t-shirt. He was dressed and sitting on the bed, putting on his socks, when he caught sight of Skye. She had combed her wet hair out and was leaning into the mirror over the sinks, putting on some make-up.

The towel had ridden up and was only just covering the peach of her ass. He couldn't resist and walked up behind Skye. He caressed her ass with his hand and looked at her face in the mirror. Her eyes were hooded, as if reading his intent. He tugged the towel until it dropped from her body. He watched in the mirror as his hands travelled up over her breasts, pinched the nipples into hard peaks, making Skye dropped her hands to the counter, her head falling forward.

Nate ran his hand up her spine and gripped her hair lightly, forcing her to look up. His other hand went to his fly and he released his painfully hard cock.

"Grab a condom from the draw in front of you." He commanded–and it was definitely a command. And by the way her legs quivered, she liked it. Passing him a condom, he rolled it over his hard cock and rubbed his length against her ass cheeks. His hand moved from her hair and went down her flat stomach and gently gripped her hip, his other hand travelled up over her stomach, over her breast and lightly held her shoulder, his fingers brushing her neck.

With one smooth, hard stroke, he filled her. It was the most erotic thing he had ever seen The sight of her watching them in the mirror, the desire on her face, evident in her flushed face. The tight, wetness of her channel gripping him so hard made him lose it.

He pumped into her hard and fast, his eyes never leaving hers, as he brought them both to a hard, fast climax that left them weak in the knees. He kissed along her spine.

"I love you, Skye." He pulled out as he said it and she hissed at the loss of him.

"I love you, too. I didn't know it could be like that in the real world."

"Me, either." He dealt with the condom then turned her around and kissed the breath out of her.

"Now, stop distracting me and get dressed," he said, and swatted her ass and kissed her nose.

"Me? Distract you? I was innocently putting on my make-up when you ravished me."

He nuzzled her neck, "Yeah I did, didn't I? And I'll do it again if you don't get dressed, so hurry up."

"Okay, Nate." She touched her mouth to his then and walked into the bedroom to grab her clothes.

He stood in the bathroom and wondered how he would ever get anything done when all he could think about was being inside Skye. He'd just had her, and yet, he wanted her again. He shook off the stupid grin and finished getting dressed.

Chapter Twenty-One

They were out of the house thirty minutes later and on their way to the hospital when they got the call. Nate hit the speaker on the car.

"Dane, what's up man?"

"Is Skye with you?" Dane asked, instantly putting Nate on guard.

"Yes, what's going on?"

"There was a fire at Reg's house last night." Skye looked at Nate as she gasped. "He is all right, just a bit of smoke inhalation," Dane continued, "They released him this morning. He was upset about losing the house. It's completely destroyed. He would have been fine except the stupid man went back in to grab a suitcase full of photos and mementos."

"It's all he has of his son." Skye said quietly, trying to explain.

"The problem is, it wasn't an accident. The fire investigator says it was arson."

"Fuck!" Nate exclaimed, "Do we have any leads?"

"Yes, a definite message was sent. You need to come to the office. We had a video sent in to Drew at five this morning. It was the Divine Watchers letting us know that they want us to back off."

"Okay, I'm going to drop Skye at the hospital and then I'll be in."

"Cool. See you soon, and just so you know, Zack has put a permanent guard on Skye and Noah until the Lockwoods have been found." Nate bristled slightly at that. Skye and Noah were his to protect. Putting aside his own issues with the situation, he realized it was the sensible thing to do.

"Okay, see you soon," Nate replied.

Nate disconnected the phone and glanced at Skye as they pulled into the hospital.

"You okay?" he asked, watching her face.

"Yeah, I'm fine. I just want to get to Noah, now."

"All right. I'm not sure who Zack has on you, but I'll walk you up and check things out."

They exited the vehicle and Nate grabbed her hand as they made their way up to the second floor. Walking towards the ward, they saw Zin at the door.

"Hey, man," Nate shook Zin's hand, "thanks for last night."

"No problem. He's a good kid and very good at chess." He smiled and it encompassed his whole face, turning it from stern to stunning.

Skye smiled proudly at his comment.

"Who did Zack send to watch Skye and Noah?" Nate asked Zin.

"A man from Eidolon named Ambrose. He's ex-spec ops and is one huge-ass mother fucker." He looked at Skye, "Sorry." Nate laughed inwardly at the blush that stained Zin's cheeks.

"No problem. Reg is my uncle, remember? Nothing shocks me." Skye replied with a smile. Zin nodded and his lips twitched, again. *That was his Skye, always putting everyone at ease*, thought Nate proudly.

"Let's go meet Ambrose," Nate said to Skye and put his palm to the small of her back. "Do you want me to send Lucy out?" he asked Zin.

"Yes please. We have to get back to Fortis and help with the investigation. It sounds like things are heating up."

"Okay. I won't be far behind you."

Nate pushed through the outer door of the ward and headed for Noah's room. He could hear laughing–one giggly and child-like, the other deeper and belonging to a man.

Lucy was sitting in the chair next to Noah's bed and a tall, muscled black man was, at that very moment, arm wrestling Noah and pretending to lose. He looked up at Skye and Nate as they walked in.

"Mummy look," exclaimed Noah, "I beat him. I beat Ambrose!"

"I see that, baby boy," she said, kissing her son's cheek.

"Hi. You must be Noah's parents pleased to meet you." Ambrose stuck out his hand for Nate and Skye to shake. Nate felt like he'd been punched in the chest. That someone would assume he was Noah's father pleased him more than he could say.

He shook Ambrose's hand, "Pleased to meet you." He was about to correct Ambrose when, Noah beat him to it.

"Nate's not my daddy yet, Ambrose," he said matter-of-factly. "But when he marries mummy, he will be."

"Noah!" Skye shrieked, clearly embarrassed.

"I'll just let myself out. I'll see you back at work, Nate," said Lucy with a huge grin on her face. Nate just nodded before turning his attention to Noah.

"You got that right, buddy," Nate replied with a massive grin of his own. Nate smiled at his mum, "See, I told you." He said to his mother.

"Umm…yes, well…"

"I'm sorry, this is my fault. I just assumed. He looks just like you."

Nate had never noticed it before, but Noah did have features similar to his.

"No problem, man," Nate replied. He turned to Skye and pulled her flush with him, hooking his arm around her waist, "I'm going to have a quick chat with Ambrose and then get going. I'll call you in a bit, but if you need for anything, just call."

"Okay."

He dropped a kiss on her mouth and followed Ambrose out the door.

After talking to Ambrose, he felt better. The man was clearly very good at what he did and was clued up about what was going on, leading Nate to the correct assumption that he was pretty high up the food chain at Eidolon. He would still check with Zack, though.

Leaving the hospital, Nate quickly drove to Fortis, pleased he missed the morning traffic. When he arrived at Fortis, he saw Reg's Triumph Motorbike outside next to Lucy's yellow Mazda. Beside that was Zin's Harley, Zack's Landrover, Dane's 4x4, and Daniel's

Jeep. So, it looked like the whole team was in, unless Drew was out doing something. That meant something big was going down.

Walking into the reception area, he smiled at Celeste and petted Samson, who was lying next to her.

"Hi, Celeste. How you settling in?"

"Good, getting the hang of it." She smiled and Nate wondered if she realised how pretty she was. The resemblance to Kanan was definitely there, but her features were softer. He felt sorry for her. He'd hate to have a sibling he knew nothing about. Although, after what happened with Lauren and Drew finding out they were brother and sister and having never known about each other that seemed to be a new theme around here.

"Good," he nodded, "Catch ya later," he said as he went through the door to the belly of things.

Nate walked straight to the conference room, he could hear Zack's pissed-off voice. *Great. What now*? Pushing through the door, he saw that the whole team was assembled. The big screen had been set up and Zack was casting an exasperated look at Reg.

He didn't look any worse for wear from the fire and was currently conducting an argument with his dead wife. Nate considered himself an open person, but the talking to the dead thing stretched even his beliefs in the unknown.

Nate felt that uneasy feeling creeping up his spine again. He couldn't shake the feeling that something was going to go down. He just wished it would happen so he could deal with it. Limbo sucked, he was more of an action man.

Taking a seat opposite Reg, Nate watched as he continued his conversation with Tilly. He certainly seemed to believe that he was talking to his dead wife. The patient indulgence on his face as she 'nagged him,' told of the deep love he still felt for her despite his harsh words.

Nate turned his attention to Zack at the head of the table, standing with his hands on his hips, waiting for Lucy to finish doing something on the laptop next to him. Zack looked edgy and his eyes kept sliding to Ava Drake, who was seated next to him.

She appeared calm, except for the fact that she kept playing with a locket around her neck. She was perfectly dressed in a navy shift dress and dark burgundy jacket. Nate had only spoken to her once, but she seemed nice–and more importantly–she was finally getting them the answers they needed to move forward with this investigation.

"Right, everyone quiet," Zack bellowed, clearly losing patience. Everyone immediately went quiet and looked to Zack.

"As we know, Reg had a fire at his place last night. Thankfully, he is okay." Zack was interrupted by Reg.

"Only cos my Tilly girl warned me," he said proudly, a smile breaking through his purple beard.

"Yes, and we are all very glad she did," said Zack graciously, and everyone murmured their agreement.

"I'm not happy you went back in, but all is well," Zack continued and again Reg interrupted.

"Yeah, yeah, I'm already getting an earache from the little wifey, don't you lot start. That suitcase is all I have left of my wife and son now. If I didn't have that, I would have nothing." That was the saddest thing Nate had ever heard and he felt for Reg. He was a good guy, and despite his idiosyncrasies, Nate liked him and by the looks of everyone in the room, so did they.

It was Lucy that voiced it, though, "You have us, Reg." She sat across from him and down from Nate.

"Thank you, girlie. That means a lot to me." Reg's eyes looked bright and Nate thought it best to turn the attention away from him to give him a minute to compose himself.

"So, what's this about a video?" he asked Dane.

Dane's jaw went hard as granite and Nate was shocked he couldn't hear bones cracking; he was clenching his fists so tightly. This was bad. Dane was a pretty calm guy, and something had gotten him unusually riled.

"Play the video, Luce," Zack said in answer.

Everyone turned to the screen and Nate was shocked when Marcus Preedy's face filled the screen. *What the fuck!* He wasn't on his own in his shock, he heard inhales of breath from others in the room.

Preedy was Lauren's estranged father and had been behind the Divine Watchers plan to get Lauren to join them because of her special healing abilities. That explained Dane's reaction.

Preedy was seated in a small room in with no windows and white walls. He was sitting in a small folding chair facing the camera. He stared at the screen, the coldness of his eyes making Nate wonder how he could possibly be related to Lauren.

Preedy started to speak, "Tonight was a warning to you all. Leave the Divine Watchers alone. This is bigger than all of you. You cannot stop us from our mission to rid the world of lesser beings. The true and rightful Divine ones will rid the world of weak and narrow minded people. Armageddon is coming–nothing can stop it. Hundreds will die and the world will be righted to its pure and natural state.

"Tonight proves that we can get to anyone who pokes their noses in where it shouldn't belong. Enjoy the time you have left–make peace with your loved ones or join the cause. *Zibuthides Melsambria.*"

The room was silent for second as everyone tried to take it in. Nate was the first to speak.

"So, first things first, how the *fuck* did Preedy make that video from inside a secure prison?"

"That is the burning question. We have spoken to the Governor of the prison, and he assured us that Preedy has been kept in solitary since his arrival," replied Zack.

"So, that means someone on the inside is helping them," said Nate.

"Yes. I've spoken to Jack and he is sending a man to the prison now."

"Reg has admitted that he and a few of his friends from the MC he belongs to have been poking around into Felicity Lockwood.

Obviously, that has garnered him this attention. He has assured me it won't continue," Zack gave Reg a very stern look, causing Reg to grumble under his breath.

"Zin is going to have a word with the guys from the MC and ask them to back off." Zin nodded slightly a frown firmly in place.

"Next question," Lucy said, "What the hell was that he said at the end?"

Ava sat forward then, "I think I can help with that," she said. "I've identified the language as Thracian. Very little is known about it. I can tell you that it originates in Europe in the area of Bulgaria. The phrase he uses means 'Noble Thracians Settlement.' I don't know, exactly, what it tells us, except that the sacred settlement was originally a Thracian settlement, known as *Menebria*. The town became a Greek colony when Dorians settled there from Megara at the beginning of the 6th century, BC. It was later taken over by the Romans. What is interesting is that there was a large belief among the Thracians that paranormal abilities were the way of the righteous."

Wow. Nate was impressed this woman had found out more in two days than the rest had in months of work.

"Thank you, Ava," Zack said sincerely. She nodded graciously.

"Umm, isn't Bulgaria where the Olympics are being hosted next year?" asked Drew.

"Yes," Zack confirmed.

Drew looked around, "Well, doesn't anyone else find this strange?" he asked. "The main settlement is mentioned by them, the

Olympics are being hosted next year, and they are threatening world annihilation."

Nate nodded. That was more than a coincidence. "I agree," he said.

Zack scrubbed his face with his hand, "Okay. Let's take this one step at a time. Drew, I want you to work with Ava and help with any searches she needs. Zin, talk to the MC and secure that end, then I want you chasing the link between Felicity and the Russian mafia.

Dane and Lucy, work with Will to find the money. An operation like this needs an immense amount of money. Look into Redcast and find all the addresses of these medical facilities in Europe. Go speak to people, but be discrete. We may need to send someone in undercover.

"In fact, use the aliases that Will set up for you and make some innocent inquires to get you in the door. I don't care how, just do it. Daniel, we need to increase the training schedule. I want these recruits ready in half the time. If they aren't up to it, cut them from the program and find new ones.

"Nate, you need to spread your time between guarding Skye and Noah, and looking for Hugo. Jack is willing to let Ambrose, and a man named Liam, help out with that. Any questions?" he looked around the room. "No? Good. Let's get going." Everyone got up and left the room. Reg and Nate remained.

"What can I do for you, Nate?" Zack asked.

"What's the score with Ambrose and this Liam guy?"

"They are solid operators. Ambrose is Jack's right-hand man–ex-spec ops– and he also has a degree in virology. He might look like a muscled-up tough guy, but behind that muscle is an extremely clever man. I've worked with Liam a couple times. He is a weapons and demolitions expert and you definitely want him in your corner. They are both south London boys and came through spec-ops together." Nate nodded, he was impressed and if Zack trusted him, that was good enough for him.

"Right, as Ambrose is with Skye and Noah, I'm going to get going chasing down leads on Hugo."

"Liam will be here in a few minutes, if you wait he will go with you," Zack said.

"I'll wait out front."

Zack looked to Reg, "Reg?" he said in question.

"I need a word in private, Zack." Nate wondered what that was about? He should make sure he has somewhere to stay. He could offer him the flat he used as a weight room. Not wanting to hang around, he decided to mention it to Skye and she could call Reg later.

Walking towards reception, he fell in beside Zin. They walked in a comfortable silence. He walked in front of Zin to go through the door, remembering his aversion to people walking behind him. Nate stopped by the reception desk to wait for Liam, taking the time to scratch Samson's belly. He was such a sweet dog. Noah would adore him. Maybe one day in the future he could persuade Skye to get one.

Weirdly, when Zin walked past, he threw a cold look at Celeste. Nate was surprised by this. Zin wasn't an overly communicative man, but he wasn't hostile either. Somehow, his hostility towards Celeste transmitted to the dog and he jumped up and settled beside Celeste, a low growl rumbling in his throat.

Zin took no notice. Just slammed out the door, fired up his Harley, and flew out of the car park. He passed a slick red sports car on his way. Nate waited, wondering if that was Liam in the flash car. His question was answered when a tall man, who looked just like Tom Hardy, walked in.

He was wearing old faded jeans, a blue crew neck jumper, and a leather jacket. He epitomized the vision of a cockney wide boy. The only give away to his lethal ability was the gun in a holster under his arm, and by the way his jeans hung on the ankle, an ankle holster, too. Nobody else would have noticed, but Nate had both, these on, too.

"Hey, me old, mucka. You must be Nate?" he said in a very strong east London accent, thrusting out his hand to Nate. He appeared very friendly and Nate liked him on sigh.

"Pleased to meet you. You must be Liam," Nate replied.

"Yep, so, me old mate, we gonna go looking for this toff in the boozer, or is he off scoring some *Charlie* somewhere." Nate laughed and thanked god for his friends down south. He never would've understood Liam, otherwise.

"Yes, let`s go look for the posh guy in the pub and see if he is off buying some cocaine."

"Tidy, lead the way," said Liam. Nate was about to leave when Liam veered back and walked towards Celeste.

"Hello there, my beauty. What's your name?" Celeste looked like a deer caught in the headlights.

"Umm…Celeste. My name is Celeste."

"Well, my sweet Celeste, are you going to let me take you up the Shard?" The Shard was the tallest building in the UK and shaped like a shard of glass hence the name. Somehow Nate didn't think Liam meant that literally when he asked that double entendre question. He was about to intervene when Samson made his presence known.

Liam had rested his hip on Celeste's desk and was leaning towards her. He hadn't seen Samson at her feet. The dog chose that moment to let out a loud growl. Liam jumped back, "What the fuck!" he yelled, putting some distance between him and Samson.

"That's Samson. Apparently, he has a problem with you taking me up the Shard, sorry," she said prettily, but Celeste didn't look even a tiny bit sorry.

Liam recovered his charm pretty quickly, "No problem, treacle."

"Come on, leave her alone before Samson decides he hates your chat up lines more than the rest of us do and bites you," Nate said, saving Celeste from more corny chat up lines.

"Later, treacle." Liam waved and Celeste smiled and waved back, "Bye, guys."

Walking into the frigid air, Nate noticed the temperature had dropped a lot. The sky was grey and overcast and the promise of rain wasn't far away.

"I'll follow in my car, chief," Liam said, "Don't like getting caught without transport.

"Fine by me. We'll try the Jailhouse first. Do you know it?"

"Yep. Did my spec-ops training in this neck of the woods and part of that training was learning to hold your booze. There ain't a pub for miles I ain't been pissed in."

Okay, then, thought Nate and wondered how this was going to work. He hoped this guy could be serious when shit went down. Having met Jack, he didn't think it would be a problem–he only hired the best.

He guessed time would tell if this guy was a total twat or a good operator with a weird sense of humuor.

After they visited their fifth pub, they decided it was time to grab some food. Nate was relieved when they got to the Jailhouse and Liam proved exactly what kind of operator he was, handling the manager so deftly. The man had been ready to sign over his first born son by the time Liam had finished with him.

Nate had remarked on it, and Liam had shrugged it off, saying it was how he was brought up. His dad had been a hard-ass and he had grown up on a diet of getting your ass kicked or kicking someone else's. He had chosen the second.

Nate went the friendlier route; he knew nearly every doorman in Hereford through the MMA club he trained at. Most of them trained there and were good guys. There was the odd wanker, but most were just doing a job. He put the word out that he was looking for Hugo Lockwood, who was well known for different reasons.

Nate had phoned Skye earlier about Reg. She promised to call him after she had chance to talk to Reg. He told her he would drop by at lunch time, and if they got the okay to leave before then, to let him know.

His body reacted as he thought about her sweet voice. She was like a drug, one taste–okay, two–and now he couldn't go more than three or four hours without hearing her voice. He told her about Liam and told her he would bring him to the hospital to meet her later since he was on her guard team.

They were cruising towards the hospital when his phone went off. Answering using the Bluetooth, he was surprised to hear from Dane, "Hey, Dane. What's up bro?"

"We just heard from Jack. Marcus Preedy was found in his cell this morning with his throat slit."

"Fuck! Do Drew and Lauren know?" he asked. They had been through hell at Preedy's hands, but even so, he *was* their father.

"Drew knows–Zack just told him. I'm going to collect Lauren from school and tell her now. I'm honestly not sure how she will take it. She despises him, but it's her father, so, who knows. I just don't want upset her, what with the pregnancy and all."

"Yeah, I feel ya, man. Let me know if we can do anything."

"We will. Anyway, Zack wants you and Liam back at Fortis, ASAP."

"Okay, we're on our way. I'll let Liam know. Catch ya later." He hung up and called Liam. He quickly explained what had happened and told him to head back to Fortis. Next, he called Skye and explained that something had come up and he would see her tonight. The doctor was releasing Noah after they had taken a last set of blood tests. Ambrose would take them home and wait until he returned.

He didn't like the idea of another man doing the job he should be doing, but he, also, realized now was not the time to be a control freak.

Quickly cutting through, traffic, he headed for Fortis. He pulled into his space and Liam pulled in behind him. They got out of the car, both turning and ducking when they heard, and felt, an explosion. Nate dove behind his car, Liam following right behind him. The air was full of smoke and Nate immediately heard gunfire. Grabbing his weapon from its holster, he poked his head over the side of his car. Out of the corner of his eye, he spied Liam doing the same.

"Can you see anyone?" Liam shouted

"Negative," Nate replied.

A shot hit close to his head and he returned fire, hearing a scream as he hit his target. Liam had his back to Nate as they hunkered down behind the car, he was returning fire and had also hit something. Nate saw the shutters go down on the building and knew Zack would have put the building into lock down, but would be watching on the monitor.

"How many do you see?" Nate asked.

"I make out six, heavily armed men." Liam replied as he returned fire. "No, make that five."

Nate tapped Liam on the shoulder as he heard a chopper. "Fuck. We have some serious company. We need some help," he said, and a sick grin came over Liam's face.

"If you can take care of these five, I have something in my car to help with that," Liam replied.

Nate took aim and took out one more man. *That's four fuckers*, he thought. Opening his car door from where he was hunkered down, he accessed the boot from the back seat and grabbed his semi-automatic. This was why he kept weapons in his car.

He put his head up over the top of the bonnet to lay down suppressive fire, allowing Liam to get to his car. Spraying the remaining four men with bullets, he managed to take out two with kill shots before gunfire from the chopper made him duck down again. His car was being pummeled with bullets and it was only a matter of time before he got hit with one.

His blood was pumping, adrenalin flooding his system. He needed that fucking chopper gone. Just as he thought it, Liam stood up, bold as brass, with a fucking RPG on his shoulder. *That mad fucker*, thought Nate.

Nate had no choice but to trust Liam to deal with that, and got back to dealing with the other two men. He only grazed the one, hitting him in the hand that held his weapon and then putting another on the man's shin immobilizing him and taking out the threat of return fire. Zack would want answers and that way the fucker could still speak.

He heard an explosion behind him and turned in time to see Liam had taken out the chopper. The man was nuts, and Nate, for one, was glad he was. Who knew, there were other men that carried weapons in the boots off their cars like he did and especially RPG's.

The chopper crashed to ground on the other side of the building, towards the woods, with a sickening sound of twisting metal. Daniel came running out the door seconds later with Zack behind him.

"You guys okay?" he asked, checking Nate and Liam over with a quick sweep of his eyes.

"Yeah," they chorused.

"Dan can you and Zin secure the scene and check those fuckers are actually dead." Zack instructed.

"Sure, no problem." Dan walked over to Zin as he came out the door loaded for bear and they both meticulously checked the area. Nate knew Drew would be backing them up by watching the live feed from the camera in the tech room.

Zack turned and walked for the door as Nate and Liam fell in beside him.

"I can't believe you took that chopper out with an RPG," Zack said turning his head to glare at Liam and making Liam grin. "How the fuck am I going to explain that?" Zack asked, shaking his head. "I don't know whether to hire you or punch you. Get yourselves cleaned up. We'll debrief in ten minutes." Zack said as they strode to the front door.

Nate looked back at Dan, who was checking out the dead men.

"We got a live one," Daniel shouted, with delight in his voice. Zack gave a feral smile, it was the scariest grin Nate had ever seen from him–angrier than Nate had ever witnessed. Nate knew he would take this attack personally.

"Take him to the holding room," he shouted to Daniel. Nate went over and helped Dan drag the groaning man, none too gently, into the building. Liam followed behind. They walked past a petrified Celeste, who was being comforted by Ava in the hallway, and went straight to the holding room at the back.

"Zin!" shouted Zack. Zin walked up the hallway were he had stopped to check on Celeste. Nate watched as Zack cast a look at Celeste and Ava. Celeste was calm now, but still looked pale, Ava was as cool as a cucumber as usual. Dismissing them Nate watched Zack bring his eyes back to Zin who had closed down his expression, Zack continued, "I need to sort out this mess at the front and speak to the relevant departments. We don't have time to question this prick, so I need you to get the information out of him quickly." Zack said matter of factly.

Zin smiled a cold nasty smile, "My pleasure." And by the look on his face, it would be a pleasure. He looked downright scary. Nate would not swap places with that guy for all the tea in China.

Liam followed them back as they walked to the holding room. Nate and Daniel tossed the man onto a chair and he groaned as he held his leg, which was bleeding profusely. The man spat at them, and judging by the tone, swore at them in some sort of eastern European language.

Zin just grinned and rolled up his sleeves. The man's eyes went wide when Zin replied in the same language. What was said must have terrified him, because he lost all colour in his face. Zin turned to the rest of them, "Wait outside," he ordered, and it caused Daniel to grin. "Yes, Sir" he replied and left the room, ushering him and Liam out ahead.

"What the fuck is going on, Daniel?" Nate asked.

"Just wait. This guy will be singing like a canary within half an hour." Nate's eyes bugged. "Is he that good? I'd heard he was but have never seen it. We haven't had a lot of call for this in the last two years."

"Better. I've never seen anyone better at interrogation than Zin. He's like some zen master."

"Steady on, Chief. Shouldn't you buy him dinner before you suck his cock," Liam unwisely piped up, causing Daniel to get in his face.

"What did you say, you cockney wanker?" Daniel was nose to nose with him, now.

"Easy, Dan," Nate said, putting a hand on Dan's arm, "He doesn't mean any harm. He just has a bad case of foot and mouth."

"Yeah, well, check it at the door, arsehole. Someone could have been killed tonight and you're making fucking jokes."

"Okay, okay. No harm meant. Just having a laugh, don't get your knickers in a twist."

Daniel stepped back and they walked into the conference room, but continued glaring at Liam. They were still glaring twenty minutes later when Zin came in, rolling down his sleeves, he hadn't even broken a sweat.

"They work for Felicity Lockwood. They're just contractors. The plan was to take down our operation and then go after Noah. Did you find Hugo?"

"No, he's smoke. I need to get to Skye and Noah. If they go after them now, Ambrose won't be able to protect them on his own." A sense of urgency and fear crawled down Nate's back and settled in his bones.

"Yes, go. Take Liam with you," Zin said, "I'll let Zack know." Turning to Liam, he put out his hand, "Thank you for taking care of the chopper." Liam laughed and shook his hand, "No problem. Glad I could help."

Zin turned and walked back towards Zack's office, motioning for Daniel to follow him. Daniel gave Liam a glare, then strode purposefully after Zin.

Nate and Liam quickly walked back outside and Nate told Liam to meet him at the hospital. Luckily, both the cars, although now covered in holes, were drivable. He slipped into the driver's seat and he noticed his hands were covered in dust and smoke from the explosion.

Chapter Twenty-Two

He needed to wash up before he saw Skye and frightened her to death. She knew what he did, but she didn't need it shoved in her face. He quickly parked and raced to the entrance where Liam was waiting.

"I need to wash up. I don't want to scare Skye and Noah."

"Good plan, Batman," Liam replied and followed him inside. Nate found Liam quite amusing and he had certainly proved he could cut it in a crisis.

Pushing through the door of the ward, they were met by Ambrose who was standing at Noah's door. Liam went straight over to Ambrose and Nate went through the door quietly in case Noah was asleep. He immediately saw he was awake and put his finger to his lips to quiet him. He looked at Skye, who had her back to the door, and his world righted. She was fine. Noah was fine. He walked up to her on silent feet and slipped his arms around her waist from behind and dropped a kiss to her neck.

She jumped a mile high and turned, "Nate, you scared me." She laughed and tapped his chest. He grinned and dropped a kiss on her mouth.

"Sorry, *mi cielo*, I couldn't resist."

"Why do you smell of smoke?" she scrunched her nose and it looked adorable. It made him wish they were alone so he could show her just how adorable.

"We had a little incident at Fortis, but I'll explain later when little ears aren't around."

She frowned and nodded, "Okay. Noah has been discharged, haven't you, baby boy?" she turned to Noah who was grinning at them.

"Yep, and I beat Ambrose at chess." His excited little face was beaming.

"Wow, that's great, buddy, well done. I get to take you guys home, then. I need a quick word with your mum outside, okay, pal?"

"Are you going to make kissy faces again?" he asked, giggling.

"You got me, pal," Nate said laughing. He grabbed her hand and pulled her out the door.

Walking past Ambrose and Liam, he went round the corner and sat her in a chair near the ward clerk's office.

"What's the matter, Nate," she asked looking concerned.

"Fortis was attacked," he held her hand tight as she gasped.

"Is everyone okay?"

Yeah, everyone's fine. Zack has a lot of cleaning up to do, and I think Celeste and Ava are a bit shaken, but the point is, we managed to get some information. The men were working for Felicity Lockwood. They still want Noah."

He felt her hand start to shake in his and pulled her out of the chair, into his arms. "It's okay, Skye. I won't let them get him. Either Ambrose, Liam, or I will be with you at all times. But I want you to come stay at my place. It offers much more protection and security," he watched as several different expressions crossed her face.

But she looked up at him and said, "Yes, of course. I'll do whatever it takes to keep him safe."

He let out a breath he hadn't realized he was holding, "Good. I'll sort out whatever Noah needs. If you write a list, I'll get Ambrose to pick it up."

"Well, we're ready now. I was just about to call you."

"Okay. Let's go tell Noah." They broke the news to an ecstatic Noah, who was practically bouncing now. Skye had apparently told Noah about his place and it pleased him to no end that she liked it so much that she had talked about it.

They proceeded to get Noah packed up and all his medication bagged and dispensed from the pharmacy in record time. Even with Noah asking a hundred excited questions per minute.

An hour later, they were driving to his house, with Ambrose and Liam following in separate cars behind them. Nate waited until Liam and Ambrose where in place on either side of Noah and Skye before ushering Noah and Skye up the steps to his front door.

~~~

That was the start of a perfect two weeks in Nate's eyes. Apart from the fact that they had a threat hanging over them, and were having to stay in a lot, he felt happy. They cooked together, with Skye even giving him a baking lesson–which he enjoyed immensely–they played games, did puzzles, he and Noah had many, many re-matches on the Xbox.

He and Skye had decided that it was okay for Noah to see them sharing a bed since Nate had been around for a while now and was used to him. Noah had taken that like everything else, in stride. The first morning he had jumped on them both at 6 am, asking for pancakes for breakfast.

Thankfully, he and Skye got the evenings together, which were mostly spent putting something on the T.V., and then making out until it was time for bed, by which time they were both more than ready to go up in flames. It was insane how much he wanted her.

He loved the fact that she wanted him as much as he wanted her. He went from making slow seductive love to her, driving her crazy with pleasure, to the next day, fucking her hard against the wall. Just thinking about it made him want to drag her to bed.

It was the eighteenth of November, and Skye received a call from Noah's doctor. He wanted to see Skye and Noah, urgently. He made an appointment for two that afternoon. Nate knew she was nervous about what the doctor would say. Noah had seemed better–his colour had improved and he seemed to have more energy than Nate had ever seen. He prayed that his health hadn't started to deteriorate. He loved that boy as if he was his own.

Skye had discussed it with him and she had decided not to tell Noah about the urgency, letting him think it was a routine appointment. They enjoyed a lunch of chicken noodles, but Skye had picked at hers, and hardly eating anything. Her face looked pale, and he realized that the last few weeks had been the most carefree he had ever seen her.

Even the constant presence of Ambrose or Liam downstairs hadn't upset her. In fact, she had charmed them both with her baking frenzy, constantly making Nate take them, treats. Nate didn't mind, it gave him a chance to check on things.

Noah had equally charmed them and had challenged Liam to chess, but Liam had declined and said he was more of monopoly kind of guy. Noah had taken that and run with it making Liam promise to play him as soon as he could.

They were in the car on the way to the hospital at just after 1:15pm. Noah was in the back and seemed fine and Skye was trying really hard not to let her nerves show, but failing. Nate reached over, put his hand on her Knee and squeezed gently.

"It'll be okay, *mi amor*," he tried to reassure her. She smiled a small smile and put her hand over his, holding on tight. He parked and they went to the paediatric outpatient department.

The young, friendly male receptionist told them to wait, and Noah sat and played with the toy farm. Skye had her hands clasped so tight her knuckles were white. Nate stayed silent, but slipped his arm around her shoulders, kissing the side of her head.

Dr. Azzabi walked out, "Skye, Noah would you like to come through?" Skye and Nate stood and Noah jumped up from the toy farm he was playing. Nate watched her look at Noah and felt her stiffen her spine under the hand he placed on the small of her back. She tipped her head to him and offered him a firm nod. She would get through this whatever happened.

Chapter Twenty-Three

He'd been looking for this prick for two weeks and had finally caught up with him, here of all places. He couldn't believe he would be so stupid to come back home. Maybe he had run out of rich friends to sponge off of. Kanan had been watching his bank accounts, as had Fortis, and they hadn't been touched.

Hugo Lockwood had not been home since the police had released him. At first, he thought he might have gone to the Green Dragon hotel, but he hadn't. He'd checked all his usual haunts, almost running into Nate and some cockney guy he didn't know. But Hugo was gone.

He finally caught him going into Lockwood Manor. He didn't want to confront him, but was certain he could lead him to Felicity, that cold hearted evil bitch. Never in his life had he felt such a strong need for vengeance.

He could not explain why, either, except there was something about Noah that called to him. His innocence and bravery had made him ashamed of the man he'd become. The fact that Felicity could so easily endanger him for her own cause, made him want to kill. Yet, he was forced to recognize he had done the same thing.

When he'd seen Noah, lifeless on that bed, it reminded him so much of Catherine, that he'd lost it. The fact that she had died of Leukemia made it so much worse. Every time for the last two weeks that he had closed his eyes, he had dreamt of her, and in every dream, she morphed into Noah, crying and asking why he had killed him.

He rubbed his hands over his face and stretched his aching body. His neck was healing well from the gunshot wound, but he wasn't twenty anymore, and his body ached from exhaustion.

He knew Zack was looking for him, but being around him made him feel worse. Every time he looked at Zack, he saw Catherine–he'd had to get away. Even the need to stick around and check on Celeste wasn't as strong as his desire to make Felicity die a slow, painful death for putting Noah through what she had.

He had caught glimpses of Celeste as she went into Fortis, and was proud of the beautiful woman she had become. He knew Zack and the team at Fortis would protect her, and he'd seen one of Granger's men slip into her house and install cameras and alarms.

He, also, knew Zack would only have told her about the alarm system. He ached to get to know her, but his life was such a mess, and it had been so dangerous, that he hadn't wanted to endanger her, or so he told himself.

It troubled him that she had so few friends and seemed so alone. He hoped being surrounded by a tight knit group, like Fortis, would help bring her out of her shell. She seemed to love that dog, though, and what an amazing and loyal animal he was. He knew if he dropped a puppy at her door she would automatically take it in and was glad he'd done that one, small thing for her.

He would keep his distance and hope she went on to have a normal, happy life–not one marred with grief and distrust like he had. He wasn't feeling sorry for himself, most of his bad luck was down to his own shitty decisions. He just wanted to put this right with Noah, and then that cabana on the beach, the one calling his name, could become a reality.

So, he sat in cold, wet woodland in South Wales with his binoculars, watching Lockwood Manor, and waiting for Hugo to lead the way. He might have failed Catherine, but he wouldn't fail Noah.

~~~

It had taken a huge amount of wrangling for him to talk his way out of the destroyed Russian chopper behind Fortis. The police commissioner had done some major string pulling, and Zack had never been more thankful for that connection.

The investigation was going well and Lucy had made some minor inquiries about the Pure Living clinic. Her alias was good and so was the cover. She was a twenty-eight-year-old woman looking into private fertility options. Her husband was away on business and she would be at the meeting alone.

They hadn't gone in thinking about using the fertility angle, but when they got there and seen it advertised, Lucy went with it. Her original angle had been cosmetic surgery for breast enhancement, which Lucy had found hilarious.

The other reason she had taken the initial meet alone, was Zack wasn't sure about sending Dane in. He'd been really worried about Lauren, who was struggling with losing her father, even though she hadn't really known him. Zack had thought it was probably Dane worrying too much, but he was no good going in and not having his mind fully on the job.

Zin had gone as her back-up, but stayed in the car with an earpiece in case she needed him. Lucy was the consummate professional, though, and had played her part to perfection–even getting the name of a sister company that handled exclusive clients only.

Lucy had an appointment set up for a week after Christmas. Will was now back in the fold, and was setting up some dummy medical records, stating Lucy's fertility issues.

Will had taken over mentoring Drew, whose reaction to his father's death had been to go out and get completely pissed. Zack had asked Will to take him under his wing and keep an eye on the boy. He hated to see his skill and ability go to waste because his lousy excuse for Father had croaked it.

Zin had disappeared for two days, tracking Usov, and had some interesting information for them regarding his links to Bulgaria. All lines kept leading back there. Ava also found more references to five rings in the data she was trying hard to decipher. The whole team agreed this made the Olympics the most likely target of a big attack.

Ava. Zack poured himself a glass of the fifty-year-old scotch from his bottom draw, and thought about the woman who seemed to occupy his every spare thought. She'd been a consummate professional since that first blowout at the beginning. She was polite and succinct in her discussions with him, friendly with the team, and had even gone out for drinks with Celeste, twice.

So why did he feel so angry about it? Was it because she treated him with indifference, or was it because she didn't seem to be as affected as him by the sexual chemistry between them, or was it because he couldn't stop thinking about her every hour of every day?

Was it because he had to fight the urge to storm into the conference room, bend her over the desk, and see if those stockings were as sexy as they seemed, as he thrust into her.

He found himself looking for the smallest excuse to go and talk to her. Never in his life had he been like this over a woman…and he didn't fucking like it.

He decided it was all of the above, and it was driving him crazy. He knew he'd been an idiot when he told her what they had in the past was just fucking. Maybe he should try talking to her and see if they could come to some sort of arrangement? Maybe a fling would get her out of his system…

Chapter Twenty-Four

Skye tensed as she followed Dr. Azzabi to his office. Her hands kept clenching at her sides, the muscles in her neck starting to ache from tensing and grinding her teeth. She felt Nate grip her hand and his thumb rubbed a circle over the top, the soft rhythmic pattern soothing her.

She was further relaxed by Noah's calm, happy countenance. He smiled at Dr. Azzabi and took the doctors outstretched hand.

"Hello, Noah, how have you been?"

"Hi, Dr. Azzabi, I feel great. Nate's going to teach me how to play rugby." The joy and happiness on Noah's face made Skye smile.

"Really?" said the doctor with a huge smile, "well that sounds wonderful. I love rugby."

"He can teach you, too, can't you Nate?" Noah turned his big eyes on Nate, who smiled widely at him

"Sure can, buddy."

"See," Noah grinned.

"Well, now let us take a look at you." Noah climbed up on the examination table and let the doctor check his blood pressure, weight, height, and listen to his heart. Dr. Azzabi smiled and noted everything down on Noah's chart.

"Why don't you go and see if Jeremy, at reception, has a sticker for you while I talk to your mum a minute?" he spoke to Noah, but turned his expressionless face to Skye. Her heart beat faster as she nodded to Noah. Her hand gripped Nate's in a death grip and she smiled until the door shut behind Noah. She was happy to let Noah go because she knew Liam and Ambrose were outside the locked doors to the children's pediatric department and nothing would get past them two.

"Tell me," she demanded of the doctor, a bit harshly. Skye was surprised to see the doctor smiling widely.

"We have Noah's blood results," he didn't make her wait. "His blood shows no irregularities at all. All the counts are within the normal range and there are no cancerous blood cells at all. As you can imagine, we were shocked. We double-checked the results and they are accurate. Noah is perfectly healthy."

Sky's hand flew to her mouth, tears making her eyes blurry. Her hands shook as she looked at the doctor, trying to take in his words.

"Hhhe…he's okay? No cancer?" she asked shakily, her voice struggling to form the words.

"No cancer. He is perfectly fine." With those words she threw herself into Nate's arms, burying her face in his neck, and sobbed tears of pure joy.

She felt Nate's strong arms come around her and hold her tight.

He stroked her neck, bending to her ear, he whispered soft words–she wasn't, exactly, sure what he said–but the soft murmuring calmed her until she managed to pull herself together.

Dr. Azzabi offered her a tissue and she wiped her eyes and tried to get her head round the fact that her beautiful boy was healthy. She looked up at Nate, who was still holding her tightly to his side. She offered a smile and he tilted his head, briefly touching his mouth to hers.

"Better, *mi amor*?" he asked, as he touched his knuckles to her cheek in a soft caress. Skye nodded and turned her eyes to the kind doctor.

"Sorry," she stated, slightly embarrassed.

"Don't be," he said, "I have never, in all my years, seen anything like this. The change is nothing short of miraculous. We can only attribute it to the drug he was given. As you know, we know nothing about it. We would ask that if you do come by any more of it, you submit it to the relevant authority for testing," he turned to Nate as he said this. "This kind of development could be revolutionary for medicine."

Nate tipped his head in a nod, "Of course," he stated.

"So, what now?" Skye asked.

"Well, we will need to keep an eye on Noah and check regularly that things are remaining stable. I will arrange for blood tests in three months. Other than that, go home, play rugby, let him be a boy."

Skye squeezed Nate's hand and grinned at the doctor.

"Okay." Dr. Azzabi rose from his desk and rounded it as Skye and Nate followed. The doctor shook Nate's hand firmly, "Look after her, young man, she is a very special woman." Skye was shocked at Dr. Azzabi's words, and deeply touched.

"I will," Nate said firmly.

He came to Skye and folded her into his arms in a rare show of unprofessional familiarity. "Look after yourself, Skye, and enjoy life. It's time." Skye felt her throat tighten and her eyes get wet with his words and the fatherly hug. "I will," she mumbled, "And thank you for everything you have done for us. I'll never forget it." The doctor nodded and released her.

She followed as Nate led her to the door. She felt slightly unsteady and very emotional. It was shock and happiness. She clutched Nate's arm and he wrapped his arm around her.

Looking at Noah while he sat, talking to the receptionist and organizing the stickers, she stumbled as her heel caught on a dip in the linoleum and Nate caught her up against him.

"I got you, *mi cielo*, I got you," he said in her ear. And in that moment, she knew he did–he totally did. She walked to Noah with her arm tucked around Nate's waist.

"Hey, champ! You ready to go?"

"Yep. Just finished doing the stickers." Noah said goodbye and Skye confirmed the follow up appointment for three months' time.

The ride home was filled with a contentment that Skye couldn't ever remember feeling. Nate had her hand in his, and was resting it on her thigh as he drove, only letting it to change gears. Her son was healthy. Even thinking that in her head made her want to giggle with unsuppressed joy.

Liam met them as they got out of the car. He had just finished a perimeter check. He had a quick word with Nate and then smiled at Skye and gave Noah a fist bump.

"Hey dude! How goes it?" Liam asked Noah.

"It goes great! Guess what?" he asked, the excitement showing on his face.

"What?" Liam asked as he studied Noah's contagious excitement.

"I kicked cancer's butt!" Liam looked at Nate and Skye who nodded.

"Wow, man that is excellent news! You must be, like, a superhero or something."

Noah nodded in agreement and then his face went serious. "I'm going to need a costume," turning to his mum, he asked, "You can make me one, right?" Skye looked at him and wondered at kids' ability to just keep on going and moving forward.

"Sure can, sweetie," she replied.

"Come on, let's go inside," said Nate, looking around, clearly not happy with being outside.

They went inside and since it was special occasion, decided it was definitely a celebration tonight, so it was Noah's turn to pick dinner, and he chose hotdogs and his favourite toffee, banana sponge pudding. Skye felt her hips widen as she ate, but couldn't care less. Her baby had, in his words, 'kicked cancers butt.' And, anyway, she could think of one or two ways to burn some calories later, she thought, her gaze sliding to Nate.

He was on the floor in the living room, his arms resting lightly over his knees, an Xbox controller in his hands. He had changed into dark running shorts and a pale grey t-shirt after his shower. He'd let

Noah watch him train in his weight room while she made dinner and did the obligatory round of phone calls.

Lizzie had burst into tears, which had made her do the same. They had talked for a while and agreed that when things settled, they would have a girl's night out. Skye got off the phone feeling like Lizzie sounded better, she was still determined to get to the bottom what was bothering her friend though.

Looking over at Nate, again, she marveled at the bond he and Noah had formed in such a short time. They sat side by side, in exactly the same pose, and for all intents and purposes, could be father and son. She thought about what Nate had told her about having kids of his own and knew it would be a crying shame for his genes not to be passed on. Her stomach clenched in the best way at the thought of how they could go about, trying to make that happen.

She'd changed into yoga pants and a thin, long-sleeved t-shirt and felt her nipples bead against her top as her mind went into overdrive as she watched Nate. She wondered if it would always be like this–this need for him. She'd never been overly sexed, she liked it well enough, but she didn't understand when Lauren went on about Dane and how she couldn't keep her hands off him, but she felt the same with Nate. It was as if he had woken some thirst in her she couldn't quench.

He must have felt her looking, because he looked up at her–the smile on his face froze and then turned into something, altogether, different that made her wriggle in her seat. His beautiful, dark eyes went almost black and his eyelids dropped to half-mast, his shoulders flexed.

"Noah, buddy, I'm all tired out. I reckon it's time to hit the hay," he directed his eyes to Skye, but spoke to Noah.

Skye knew she had woken something in him as he looked at her.

She heard her son groan, "Aww, I was having fun." She immediately snapped into mum mode.

"I know, sweetie, but it's already late and you need your sleep if you're going to be a superhero."

"Okay, mum. Nate, will you tuck me in?"

"Sure, buddy. I'll be up soon." Noah, being the good kid he was, went straight upstairs to get ready for bed.

Skye went to step past Nate, but he grabbed her arm and tugged her down so she fell onto his lap. He grasped her hips and lifted her so she straddled him. Threading one hand into her hair, he lifted it from her neck and kissed the pulse that hammered.

Her body, already primed from her visual exploration, shot straight to tingly.

"When you go upstairs, I want you to take a nice, relaxing bath. And when you get out, lie on the bed in nothing but a smile. I want you to do exactly as I say. Do you understand?" The deep command in his voice almost made her climax on the spot. She nodded and he rewarded her with a toe-curling kiss. "Go, baby. Say goodnight to Noah. I'll make sure everything is secure down here and be up soon."

There he was, totally commanding and sexy as fuck, and in the next breath, he made her melt with his constant desire to look out for them like the protector he was. God, she loved him.

Skye went upstairs, said goodnight to her son, and made sure he was tucked in. She read him his stories, but at his request, left the last one for Nate. She left the door open a smidge so that she could hear him if he needed her, not that he ever did. He seemed to have settled well at Nate's house. She wondered if, like her, he felt the innate protection that cloaked them like a shroud.

Climbing the stairs to the room she currently shared with Nate, her blood started to hum and she felt the all-consuming anticipation of Nate's words and the way in which he'd uttered them. Something felt different, he was more commanding, and she found it HOT.

He told her to take a relaxing bath and then lie on the bed naked. Something about lying there, naked, waiting for him, felt deliciously naughty. She ran the bath, adding some of her favourite cranberry bubble bath. She'd pinned her hair to the top of her head and sunk into the hot water up to her shoulders.

It had been years since she felt relaxed enough, or had the time, to just relax in a bath and know that someone else was there to see to Noah. She could let go of the worries that had felt like a dead weight to her.

Granted, they still had the threat of Felicity and the Watchers hanging over them, but she didn't feel the constant nausea and fear that Noah's illness made her feel. She knew Nate would protect them. She trusted him and everyone at Fortis, implicitly.

Maybe that was stupid, and perhaps she was being over-generous about their ability. Nevertheless, that was how she felt, and for now, she would enjoy the moment.

Thinking of the moment made her think of Nate, and she could hear his deep rumbling voice as he read to Noah. She snapped out of her dreamy, relaxed state when she no longer heard him reading. He must be finished. She knew Noah would be out like a light after such a busy day. Finished with her bath, she got out and wrapped the large, fluffy towel around her body.

She chose her favourite orange blossom body lotion and carefully smoothed it all over her skin. Her stomach was full of butterflies as she went to the bed, discarding the towel as she lay down to wait for Nate.

Skye didn't know if it was the anticipation or the nerves fluttering in her tummy, but her skin felt electric–like the slightest touch and she would go up in flames. She turned her head as she heard Nate come in. He didn't say a word as he entered but the look on his face made her tingle in all the right places.

His eyes were hooded and the look of desire in them was so intense, she thought he wouldn't even need to touch her at this rate before she went up in flames. He crossed to the bed and sat on the edge by her hip.

Still looking at her, he ran his hand down her cheek, over her neck and through the middle of her breasts, down to her navel. He stopped as she arched her body towards him.

"I want to blind fold you, *mi amor*." He watched as her breath hitched and she nodded. Somehow, she thought the hypnotic spell would be broken if she spoke. Nate didn't speak again, but leaned in and kissed her. His soft lips teasing until she opened to him, and then he tasted her with a fervor that had her writhing and reaching her hands up through his hair.

He pulled away, though. "Thank you, *mi amor*, for trusting me." He reached into the drawer by his side of the bed and withdrew a black piece of silk. He lifted her head, reverently, and tied it tight– not enough to hurt, but enough that it wouldn't move.

She felt him move, then his weight left the bed. She was amazed that her other senses kicked in so quickly. She could hear rustling as he stripped his clothes and then could hear a tinkling sound, like glass touching glass. Her sense of smell was improved, and she could smell Nate's aftershave and the smell of arousal, which she'd never noticed before. It was intoxicating.

Her tummy started to flutter, and her heart started to race, as she felt him approach. The bed dipped at her feet and she flinched when she felt something cold being dragged up the arch of her foot. She hissed as the feeling was followed by the heat of Nate's tongue. He slid the ice up her leg all the way to her most intimate places, then stopped and did the same to the other leg.

By the time he got to the apex of her legs the second time, she was wriggling and clutching the sheet. Instead of touching her, though, he moved and she wanted to scream in frustration but all that came out of her mouth was a whimper. He came back and she heard the smile in his voice.

"You look so beautiful, Skye. I've never seen anything more beautiful than you, right at this second." She felt her skin flush at his compliment and turned to the sound of his voice. He straddled her hips, then, and she felt his hard erection against her stomach. He grasped her wrists and lifted them above her head. "Leave your hands here or I will have to cuff you," He said in a heady voice. The thought of him cuffing her had a flood of heat flushing her body. That sounded so hot.

He then set about twirling an ice-cube over breasts, but never touched the place she wanted most. Her nipples were hard and aching as she arched, again, trying to force him to give her some relief from the delicious achy feeling.

Finally, after what felt like hours of torture, he fastened his lips around her nipple and sucked, deep and hard. She cried out and arched of the bed, the feeling zipped from her breast straight to her clit. Nate let her nipple go and repeated the treatment on the other side.

Instead of moving down towards, her ignored clit, he moved away, again, coming back seconds later, getting back in the same position–only lower down, so he was straddling her hips.

She felt his erection bob against her clit as he bent forward and they both hissed out a breath. Skye was elated to know he felt the same as she did.

"Open your mouth, *mi cielo*," he said softly. Without thought, she slowly opened her mouth. She was tentative, not knowing what to expect. She jumped when she felt the juicy sweetness of strawberry juice on her tongue. Nate rubbed the soft fruit over her lips and then licked the sweetness from them before taking her mouth in a heady kiss.

Skye itched to run her fingers over his body, and it was only through sheer, stubborn willpower that she kept her hands up above her head. Nate released her mouth, putting the fruit back to her lips and fed her the fruit.

She chewed and the sweetness exploded on her tongue. The blindfold making the taste seem more pure and sweeter. He trailed kisses down her neck and the then did the same with the strawberries he'd done with the ice, driving her to the brink of madness with wanting some sort of release.

Thank god he carried on, tracing the sweet strawberries over her stomach, kissing and licking the juice as he went. He stopped when he got to her navel and dropped soft kisses on the marks from her pregnancy. She let out a soft cry as he did. Part desire and part pure emotion.

Finally…finally he must have felt sorry for her, as her whimpers became louder and her hands scrunched the sheet into knots above her head.

He traced the strawberries over her outer lips then sucked the juice from them. Her body came off the bed and she arched as tiny electrical currents flowed through her body. He twirled the fruit over her clit and she bucked and writhed as he then sucked her clit into his mouth and proceeded to blow her mind. He added his fingers and she lost control as a climax started to crash over her in giant waves, almost drowning her in feelings. She gripped her hands in his hair and rode the wave of bliss as she writhed. Nate slowed and gentled as she came down from her climax–the best, most intense, climax of her life.

She felt him crawl up her body, dropping kisses along the way, causing her to shiver.

"I lied," he said. She frowned. "*That*, was the most beautiful thing I have ever seen," he amended as he slipped the blind fold from her eyes. She blinked several times as her eyes adjusted to the light.

"That was amazing," she breathed. "I never knew being blindfolded would be like that."

"So, you like?" he asked with a sinful smile that said he already knew the answer.

"No," she paused trying to get him back for earlier and he frowned. "I don't *like*, I *love*."

They laughed and he leaned in and kissed her. She thought she was done after the intensity of that climax, but she was wrong. As he slid into her heat a little while later, she marveled at his ability to make her feel so sated–so safe and so loved. As she drifted off to sleep in his arms, her legs tangled with his, she wanted this moment to last forever and prayed that it would.

~~~

Skye woke to the sound of screaming. She shot up in bed, but before she could move any further, Nate was up and running down the stairs. She hurried out of bed and followed the terrified sounds of her son's screams.

Her first thought was the dreams about Kanan were back. He'd been fine for weeks; surely, they hadn't started up again. Noah had predictive dreams since he could cogitate, but it was only when he was three and could properly describe them that she had thought there was more to it than night terrors.

She had been extremely reluctant to admit that her son had a gift. She'd seen the way people treated Uncle Reg, and she didn't want that for her son. It was only meeting Lauren that made her realize she could not deny what it was.

She needed to accept it so that she could support her son properly and not make him afraid, or embarrassed, of who he was.

Entering his room, she found Nate on his knees beside Noah, his big hand gently brushing his hair off his head. Noah was awake, but, as always, after one of these dreams, he looked groggy and confused.

Some dreams he'd have and not awaken. He would just happily recount it in the morning as if it was nothing. Some were more vivid and sometimes he awoke upset or fearful for the person he had dreamt of, as with the dream with Kanan, until all of a sudden, Noah told them it was fine now.

Tonight must have been a bad one. She crawled onto the bed and wrapped her son in her arms, easing him back against her, his little head next to her heart. It always calmed him listening to her heartbeat, even as a baby.

She waited until he was breathing more peacefully. Nate went to get up and leave, but Noah reached for his hand.

"Will you stay, please, Nate?" her son said in a small voice. The sound revealing how much the dream had upset him.

"Of course, buddy," Nate said, catching her eye and easing onto the bed with them. She could see it meant a lot to Nate that Noah wanted him close. His dark eyes were so expressive and warm when he looked at Noah.

They sat like that for about five minutes until Noah started to speak. Skye always found it was better to just let Noah get it all out before speaking. What he said, though, turned her stomach to lead.

"The bad people who tried to steal my dreams, they have Sly and his friend. They were trying to help the girl but it was a trap and now they have them. They have them in a hospital bed like I was in and they are hurting them." Skye felt Nate go rigid at her side and her eyes slid to him. His face had turned to stone, his eyes cold.

She hugged her son tight and realized he'd finished.

"Do you know where, honey?" she asked, "Or when?"

"It was yesterday. I don't know where, exactly, but it is close. I can see writing and it is all funny. I can't read it."

"Is it in this country, buddy?" Nate asked him softly, despite the anger brewing in his eyes.

"I think so. They all speak English and sound funny like, Pop."

"You mean Welsh?"

"Yes, like that."

Nate got up and then lent down to kiss Noah's head and then Skye's. "I'm going to call Zack. I will be back soon. Don't worry, buddy. I'll find out what is going on and we'll sort it out." Noah looked up at Nate, "I know you will, Nate, you're a superhero." Skye watched as Nate smiled and ruffled Noah's hair, "You bet I am, buddy."

Skye watched Nate leave and marvelled at his calm manner. If what Noah said was right, Sly was in big trouble. She prayed it wasn't true, but she also knew her son hadn't been wrong so far.

Poor, Lucy–she'd be devastated if anything happened to Sly. She'd loved him for half her life and they hadn't had chance to do anything about it yet. Skye sent up a prayer to the big man that Sly and his friend would be safe.

Snuggling down next to her son, she held him and sang his favourite rhyme. *"Hush little baby don't say a word, momma's going to buy you a mocking bird…"*

Chapter Twenty-Five

Nate was wired. He paced the room while he rang Zack. The man never slept, so he had no worries about waking him. He wondered if the dream was accurate and hoped like hell it wasn't. These were nasty bastards and god only knew what they would do to Sly and whoever else was with him.

Zack answered with a terse, "Yes."

"Zack. Do you know where Sly and his unit are?" There was a pause and Nate knew, then, that Zack knew something.

"That is classified, but, yes, I do know. Why?"

"Because Noah just had a dream," Nate heard Zack sigh, "And he says the people who took him have Sly and his friend."

"Fucking, fuck, fuck," Zack swore savagely. "Let me make some calls and I will get straight back to you."

Zack hung up and Nate felt coldness seep into his bones. Something bad was going to happen, or was happening. The feeling had abated for the last few weeks, but now it was back with vengeance. Knowing he would not sleep anymore tonight, he got dressed and went to the kitchen, stopping by Noah's room on the way.

Skye was curled up with her son, he thought she was asleep, but when he got closer, she opened her eyes and gave him a small smile. She put her finger to her lips and edged her body out from under Noah's.

She tucked him back under the covers, pulling them up to his chin, and walked to the door with him. Slipping her hand in his, she eased the door shut and they walked downstairs to the kitchen.

Nate grabbed one of his hoodies that was slung over the chair and pulled it over her head. It hung to her knees, and she had to roll the sleeves up four times, but she looked sexy as hell in it, as usual. He immediately decided that he liked her in his clothes. It was primitive, but he liked the thought of her wearing something that had touched his skin.

"What did Zack say?" Skye asked as she busied herself making coffee.

"He's going to check it out and get back to me. He knows something, though." Nate's voice held and edge to it that made Skye turn.

"What?" she asked him as she slipped her arms around his waist and snuggled into his chest.

"I just don't like Zack not giving us the full picture. We are a team and that should mean we have the same information, not have him decide when to tell us what."

Skye tilted her head back and he knew she could see the frustration etched on his face. She nodded, "I can understand that, but…" she paused before going on, "Zack has a lot of confidences to keep and a lot of lives to protect. I get the feeling Zack doesn't always see you as his team, but sometimes as family, and he has definitely taken on the dad role in that family." Nate laughed, then, a big belly laugh. "I would pay money to see you tell Zack that."

"Zack doesn't scare me. I pushed a watermelon through a ten-centimetre hole with only gas and air. He does not know the meaning of the word pain." Nate winced at her description but continued to laugh at her, pleased she was here with him. He had an awful feeling things were about to get ugly.

Nate sobered and tilted her chin up to him with the tip of his finger. "Nobody should scare you, *mi amor*. I will hunt down and hurt anyone who scares you or Noah, and that's a promise." He knew he shouldn't say such violent things, but the heat in her eyes told him she found it sexy, and he couldn't resist that look.

Nate feathered a kiss across her mouth, his hands gripping her ass. He lifted her onto the counter and stepped between her legs. He wondered if he would ever be bored of touching her and making slow, sweet love to her. and decided he definitely wouldn't get bored of that.

Her just being here now was making a shitty situation so much better. He kissed his way across her face and down her neck. He loved the way she tilted her head and the soft little noises she made.

Nate ran his hands over the soft skin of her thighs and she clenched her legs around his waist and crossed them behind his ass. His hands where on her rib cage, under the hoodie and he couldn't help but flick his thumbs over her nipples, causing a loud whimper to escape her.

"God, Nate, I can't get enough of you," she cried as he tweaked her nipples and he thought he would explode when she involuntarily pumped her hips against him, her body telling him what she wanted.

"What do you want?" he asked in a gruff voice.

"You. I want you," she said in a sexy as fuck, husky voice. It nearly undid him. Reaching between them, he slipped his hand into her pajama shorts and found her center. He was overjoyed to find her hot and soaking for him.

"Fuck, you're soaked for me," he ground out. He freed himself from his jeans, pushing the shorts to one side and lined his rock hard erection up with her core.

"I want you, Skye–so fucking much. I don't want anything between us. I'm clean, but I can get something if you want."

"No, I want to feel you and I'm clean, too." As she finished her last word, he pushed into her, hard and fast. The feeling of her tight heat gripping him, with nothing in-between, was the most amazing feeling ever.

It made him lose control as he pounded into her harder than ever. He should slow down and go easier on her. He did, but she gripped him and pulled his head to hers.

"Harder, Nate. Fuck me harder." Those words coming from her sweet mouth drove him over the edge, and in no time at all, they were both crying out as their climaxes hit them. Nate buried his head in her neck as he came down form the most intense climax of his life.

"Sorry, *mi cielo*."

"Why are you sorry? That was amazing. Can we do it again?" He could feel the smile against his cheek. God, she was something. How did he get so lucky?

"You really are perfect, you know," he eased out of her and she whimpered. "Stay here. I'll get a cloth for you." He jogged to the toilet and grabbed a wash cloth from the cupboard, soaking it in warm water.

He returned to Skye, who was still sprawled on his kitchen counter. He felt his gut tighten at the perfectly wonderful sight she made. Crossing to her, he helped her clean up. Just as she was hopping down, his phone rang.

Snatching it up he saw Zack's name flash across the screen.

"Yes," He answered.

"You need to come in. Sly's unit is missing. I need to brief you all."

"I'll be there in ten minutes." He hung up and his gut sank. Sly was in trouble. He turned to Skye, who was standing next to him, and he could tell by the distraught expression on her face that she'd heard.

"I need to go."

"Of course you do. Let me get you some coffee to take with you. That stuff Zack makes is like poison." He pulled her to him by her arm and held her as she hugged him tight. He could tell she was upset, but like the trooper she was, she wasn't showing it. He seemed to fall more in love with her every second.

He pulled away, and she went to grab a travel mug from his cupboard. He raced to his room and geared up for a battle–his favourite weapons all going into a bag or in holsters on his person. He texted Ambrose, who was outside, and asked him to come meet him downstairs in five minutes. He needed to give him the heads up. The Lockwoods could use this distraction to make a move on Noah, and he wasn't risking them.

Moving back into the kitchen, with his bag thrown over his shoulder, he saw Skye had set his mug on the side and had wrapped up a load of brownies for him. It gave him a nice feeling going off to work with coffee and homemade brownies.

This wasn't just another job, though. This was personal. He dropped a kiss on her upturned lips and walked with her to the door. "Lock up, and don't go out today. Only let in Ambrose or one of the team. I will call you when I know something." Skye nodded and kissed him, again, quickly.

He stopped on the other side of the door and listened to her lock up. Satisfied, he went downstairs and briefed Ambrose, who had, incidentally, already been briefed by Jack.

At 4:30 am, he was on the road, headed for Fortis, with no idea that by the evening, his world would be rocked to its core.

Chapter Twenty-Six

Nate walked through the door at Fortis and automatically turned to the reception desk. He had gotten used to Celeste and Samson greeting him. She seemed like a nice girl. A bit quirky, but nice. Samson was big brute of dog. However, a softer animal he had not met, although, he was fiercely protective of Celeste. He didn't seem to like Zin much, either, come to think of it.

He walked into the back and found Zack in his office, a rolled up blanket on the edge of the sofa, indicating Zack was sleeping here again. Zack was on the phone, but beckoned Nate through the door.

He took a seat opposite him and blatantly listened as Zack told, whomever he was talking to, that he would rip his head off and shit down his neck if he didn't call him back. *Nice.* Zack hung up and swiped his hand down his face.

His eyes were blood shot and he had suitcases under his eyes, but his shirt was pristine and perfectly pressed, just like the man. His eyes came to Nate.

"Before you start, I know that you are probably pissed, and believe me, I know I'm going to get it in the neck from everyone else, but this was highly classified. Only Jack and I knew about this, outside of the team, going in. The reason will become clear when I explain it all in a moment. Before I do that, I need to talk to Lucy and Dane in private. This is going to hit her hard. She thinks I don't know shit, but I know about her and Sly and the feelings they have for each other."

"Furthermore, what I have to tell them will rock them badly. I won't say more right now, but I need to know I have my team behind me on this."

"Jesus, Zack. That is, and never will be, in question. I'm just disappointed you felt the need to hide shit from us. If you feel it was the right thing, then fine. You're the boss and I trust you." Nate watched as Zack visibly relaxed, his shoulders slumping a little. It surprised Nate to see Zack was worried about the repercussions of this. He followed Zack as he went into the conference room to wait for the team to arrive.

Will was already there, and a few minutes later, Daniel and Zin walked in. Both seemed tense and wired. The thought of one of their own in danger not sitting well with either of them. Drew followed a few minutes later, then Dane, Lucy, and–what the hell? Lizzie?

What was she doing here? Nate didn't get chance to ask because Zack stood and ushered the three of them into his office. Leaving the others to only guess what was happening. Was Zack worried that Lucy would go off the deep end? Had he brought Lizzie in to comfort her? That didn't sound like Zack, or Lucy, to be honest. Nate got up and went to chat with Daniel and the others. He couldn't shake this feeling of impending doom and he didn't like it one bit.

~~~

Zack led a confused looking trio into his office and shut the door. He knew he had to do this quickly, like ripping off a plaster. He sat behind his desk and looked at Lucy and Lizzie and then at Dane.

They had no idea he was about to shatter everything they thought they knew.

"This morning, at around 3:30 am, I had a call from Nate. Noah had had a dream," he felt the room go tense. Everyone knew about Noah's dreams. "Noah dreamt that Sly," he heard Lucy's slight intake of breath and saw Lizzie and Dane both reach for her hand, "And a friend had been taken by The Divine Watchers."

He stopped to let that sink in for a second before continuing, "He described a hospital-type place and said the people had Welsh accents. He believed it to be in the UK. I can confirm that Sly and his team were, indeed, on a highly classified mission in the UK to extract someone from a facility known to be owned by Pure Living. They are currently classed as missing."

"What the fuck? How did you know about this mission?" Dane demanded.

"Because of our involvement with The Watchers, Jack and I were asked to assist with intel." Dane nodded as if this made sense. "As you know, I couldn't tell you all because it could have compromised the mission."

"So, who was the target?" Lucy asked. Her face a mask of composure. Zack took a deep breath and let it out slowly, knowing this might be the last he made before Dane rammed his teeth down his throat.

"Let me start by saying that Jack had intel that one of the facilities in Gloucester was manufacturing embryos with special gifts. He received this after you made contact with Pure Living about the fertility side of the operation. The Intel is sketchy, and we were unsure of the validity of it." He kept watching Dane to gauge how he was taking this.

"They received video from inside one of the labs. It shows a young woman being drugged and then her eggs are harvested. The video later shows the woman's body being dumped. The body was recovered, and a post mortem confirms the egg harvesting procedure took place."

"Sorry, I don't understand why I am here?" Lizzie said, looking confused. She was an attractive woman, and Zack wondered if she knew her pencil dicked husband was a serial cheat. Not his problem.

"You are here because the name of the person feeding Eidolon info is Megan Bennett." He watched as all their faces went slack with shock. Lizzie looked like she had seen a ghost, Lucy looked ready to puke, and Dane well he looked ready to kill someone.

Dane jumped up and came at Zack across the desk. Lucy, who was impressively fast, shoved herself between them.

"No, Dane. Now is not the time. We need to get to Sly." She made no mention of her sister, who they all thought dead, or disappeared for good. *Interesting*, thought Zack absently.

"She's right, Dane. Sit down, please." Lizzie asked quietly. "How do we know it's her?"

Zack could see the cautious excitement on Lizzie's face as she asked the question.

Dane sat down, but his demeanour did not change. He was beyond pissed and Zack didn't blame him. He would have reacted the same way.

"We don't know for sure, which is another reason I didn't tell you, but we did get a picture of her from when she made the drop of the USB. It is not a great picture, and we couldn't find prints or DNA."

"Do you have the picture?" Lizzie asked, again.

Zack nodded, "Yes." He opened his draw and laid the picture in front of them all. Lizzie gasped, and an intense pain passed over Dane's face. Lucy barely looked at it.

"My god, she looks just like you, Lucy, only she has mum's curly hair." Lucy didn't respond and averted her eyes.

"When do we get Sly back?' she asked instead.

"Let's go back out to the team and I will brief everyone and we can form a plan," Zack answered. Glad to have everything out in the open.

~~~

Nate was floored by the news of Megan Bennett being an informant on the Watchers. Dane, Lucy, and Lizzie all looked shell-shocked. But it was Lucy who had shocked him the most. Everyone was used to her sunny, jokey disposition. That person was not the Lucy sat before him. She had shut down completely.

She had not engaged in any discussion about Megan Bennett and had only been interested in forming a plan to rescue Sly.

When Daniel had mentioned Megan being vulnerable, and maybe being caught in the crossfire of any rescue, she had shrugged her shoulders like it didn't matter. Nate had never seen her like this and he could tell by the worried looks Dane and Lizzie kept giving her that they hadn't either.

They decided, since Lucy's cover was still in place, that she would carry on trying to get a lock on the manufactured baby lab. She had objected, angrily–she was all set to go in guns blazing, but even in her anger and despair, sense had won out and she'd seen that it was the best bet for the mission.

Zack promised she would be kept in the loop about all the leads on Sly and his team. She would, also, be involved in the rescue if Zack thought she was safe to do so. Nate highly doubted she would be.

Jack and his team would work closely with Fortis, and Jack was sending his best analyst over to work with Will. The others had all been given differing assignments of intel gathering.

They were all still aware of the danger to Noah and he was still a priority. Ambrose would continue with that job in the day and Nate would be there at night. Liam had been pulled back to Eidolon. Dane and Daniel would work to try to locate Felicity. She had to be a fountain of information. Zin was tracking Usov. Drew was going to work alongside Lucy, brave boy that he was.

He was on the hunt for Hugo, the bastard. He was going to spend today chasing up his contacts and see if anyone had seen him. Nate, reluctantly, shared his brownies with everyone, and seeing Lucy stood on her own over by the laptops went over to her.

He didn't say anything, just pulled her into a hug and kissed her head. He decided against mentioning her long lost sister and instead said, "We'll get him back, sweetheart." She nodded and sniffed, but quickly pulled herself together.

"Get off me, big guy. I don't want Skye kicking my ass for touching her man." She chuckled then, and Nate could tell it was forced, but went along with it.

"Yeah, she is mean, jealous," he laughed, "And apparently not scared of Zack, either."

"I knew I liked her," Lucy said before making excuses and getting the hell out of there.

Nate sat at the desk in the now empty conference room and called Skye. He wanted to hear her voice. It was after eight now, so he knew she would be up. He spent a few minutes explaining the situation to her and then letting her know how today would go.

He hung up a few minutes later, and despite the dire situation, he had a smile on his face. He was sitting and smiling when Ava came in, armed with another box of reference books.

"Hi, Nate."

"Hey, Ava. How's it going?"

"Okay, I think. I'm getting somewhere. It's just slow. Hardly anything is known about Thracian, so it's a constant back and forth."

"Will you be going home for Christmas?" he asked, making conversation.

"Yes, or my son will come here. I can't bear to be away from him–" She stopped suddenly, as if she hadn't meant to say that.

"I didn't know you had a son." She didn't answer, just nodded her head and started to empty the boxes.

Nate thought it was time to leave, "See you later."

"Yeah, see you, Nate."

Well, that was odd.

Nate finally got a lead at 11a m when he managed to corner Ceecee Camden-Jones. She was a known fuck buddy of Hugo's. He'd seen her coming out of her private gym and followed her. He wasn't normally one to corner women, but these were extenuating circumstances.

"Hello, Ceecee."

"Fuck off, Nathan."

"Well, that's not very nice is it? Have you seen Hugo?"

"No," she said indignantly, "And if you do, tell him I said fuck off, too."

"Wow. For a jewellery dynasty princess, you sure have a sewer for a mouth."

"Do you fancy trying my sewer mouth Nate?" she tried to purr, and to his horror, ran her blood red fingernail down his chest. He grasped her hand, halting its progress, and threw her hand away.

"Ouch, you pig, that hurt."

"Don't touch me," he said angrily. God, he hated women like her. Time to cut the crap, "Tell me if you have seen Hugo, Ceecee, or I will make sure that little sex-tape you made with Katie Phillips in that club's toilets makes it to the internet."

He gave a satisfied smile as she paled. "You wouldn't–"

"Oh, but I would." He saw her shoulders slump and knew he'd won.

"Fine. Last I heard, he was heading to Lockwood Manor."

"See, that wasn't so hard was it?"

"Fuck you, Nathan."

"Not in this lifetime, sweetheart," he replied as he jumped in his car. He quickly called Zack and filled him in. The one thing that came out of the meeting about Sly was that regular two hourly check-ins were now required from all team members in the field.

Chapter Twenty-Seven

Skye looked at the intercom screen as Ambrose buzzed.

"Hey, chicken, I have a Lizzie, Mimi, and a Pop here to see you." He must have recognized them from the hospital, when they had been visiting over the last few days of Noah's stay. She was impressed by his professionalism though.

"Okay. Send them up," she was glad of the company and she'd been worried about Lizzie since she heard the news about her long-lost sister.

She opened the door and they trouped in. Mimi was holding a wicked looking Welsh cake griddle. It was made of solid iron and looked heavy as hell.

She kissed them all, holding Lizzie for just that fraction longer.

"Noah," she called, and seconds later, heard him running down the stairs.

He had grown very close to Mimi and David these last few weeks, and had even started showing David how to play Xbox.

"Aubela! Pop!" he exclaimed, and dove at them both for a hug, which they heartily returned.

"Oh, mind your head on the griddle pan," Mimi warned him.

"What is that for?" Noah asked eagerly.

"It's for making welsh cakes. I thought you and I could make some if mummy doesn't mind."

"Of course not," Skye laughed, "I love welsh cakes and someone else making them sounds great."

"Well, then, why don't Noah, Pop, and I go into the kitchen and you girls have a nice catch up." Mimi caught Skye's eye and Skye knew she had been told.

"Sounds great." She linked her arm through Lizzie's and towed her towards the living room.

Sitting her friend down, she settled next to her and asked her the sixty-four-thousand-dollar question.

"How you feeling?" Lizzie looked at her and burst out laughing. Skye wondered, for a minute, if she had cracked up under the pressure. Lizzie laughed until she cried and Skye wrapped her arms around her.

"I'm not crying because I'm sad–well, I kind of am–but not about Megan," Lizzie sniffed and wiped her eyes with the back of her sleeve.

"I'm thrilled to know she's alive. Gosh, you should see her, Skye. She looks just like Lucy. But she has mum's hair. I'm so excited about meeting her. I know it might be hard for her, and it will be an adjustment, but, oh my god. How wonderful to have her after all these years. Dane was furious, but that was because he felt left out of the loop."

"What about Lucy?" Skye asked, and watched as her friend's face fell.

"She seemed indifferent and kind of annoyed by it. I guess she was just worried about Sly. Poor Sly. I hope he's okay." Lizzie was wringing her hands together now.

"They'll find him, Liz," Skye assured her.

"I know they will. I'm just worried about Lucy and Dane and Sly."

"What about you, Liz? Who is looking out for you?" Liz brushed it off, "Oh, I'm fine. Just a little tired, that's all."

Skye was about to reply when the door buzzer went again. She went to the unit on the wall and answered.

"Girl, this man says I have to ask if I can come up and see you. Will you, please, tell him to let me up?" She smiled, hearing Uncle Reg's voice.

"Ambrose, you can let Reg up." She buzzed, letting him up and stood by the door for him.

"Hey, Uncle Reg," she said as she kissed his cheek. Today his beard was green. It was a mystery to her how he did that without getting it all over his face–she kept meaning to ask him.

"Hey, pretty girl." His face went soft, then. "Best news I've ever had was hearing that Noah was cured. I'm so happy for you and so is Tilly. Oh, there she goes again, butting into my conversations. *'I will tell her, now shush your nagging, wife.'* She says she is happy, too, and she always knew she wouldn't be seeing him for a good many decades, yet."

Skye swallowed past the lump in her throat, "Good. I'm glad. I love you, Uncle Reg and, I'm so sorry about your house." He waved it away.

"Forget it. It's done and it won't your fault. Anyhow, I struck me a deal with that Zack character. I bought all the surrounding acreage and buildings next to Fortis and deeded them over to him. All I wanted was one building and a 1% share in the business. Boy is sharp, he almost bit my hand off.

"I'm going to sign the deal after Christmas and start me up a woodworking business." Skye was, floored. When, what, how. "Don't look like a fish, girl. I ain't always been a weirdo, freak I used to be–quite the tycoon in my day. It's a good, solid investment and, I like them and it means I can be closer to my family."

She hugged him tight then, "Girl, you are going to strangle me."

"Don't care. I love you, Uncle Reg, and we're lucky to have you."

"Well, I reckon I'm the lucky one, sweetheart. Now enough with this mush. I'm a bearded biker. It ain't good for me image, being all mushy. Now do I smell Welsh cakes?"

They went into the kitchen and Lizzie had joined Mimi, Pop, and Noah, who was having a whale of a time. And by the looks of him, he'd eaten more mixture than he cooked.

"Mimi, Pop, have you met my Uncle Reg?" Pop stepped forward and thrust out his hand.

"Pleasure to meet you. Skye and Noah are an absolute delight." Skye blushed at the compliment from Nate`s, normally quiet, father.

"Thank you, and you sure are right. They are the lights of my life." Reg still had his arm around Skye, but she was shoved aside when Noah wheedled his way in for a hug from Reg.

"How is my favourite superhero today?" Reg asked Noah playfully.

"I'm great, Uncle Reg, we're making Welsh cakes," he picked one up to show Reg.

"I thought I could smell them. Can I try one?" Noah looked to Mimi, who had been watching the exchange with a soft look on her face. She stepped up to Reg, "Nice to meet you, Reg, and please, let us know your verdict," she said, indicating the plateful of welsh cakes. Reg took a bite and closed his eyes in bliss. "Heavenly!" he stated with a smile.

Skye went to Lizzie, who was brewing tea, and the others carried on chatting. She could hear Pop and Reg talking about woodworking and how not enough true craftsman were left in the world.

Reg had always loved working with wood. She still had the doll's house he had made her when she was five. It was in her roof space. She, Lizzie, and Mimi carried on chatting about normal, mundane things. They included Noah, who was giving them a rundown of his Christmas list already.

"Do you ladies mind if I steal David away to see my new space for my workshop?" Reg asked them as a group.

"Of course not," Mimi waved her hand, "You boys go play. We have a world to set to rights." David kissed his wife, and Skye got a happy, content feeling in her tummy. You could see the love those two shared even after so many years together. She knew in her heart that she and Nate would be like that.

Smiling to herself, she missed the wistful look Lizzie gave her and the look of approval Mimi gave her. Noah had decided he'd had enough hanging with the girls for now, and went to his room to play Legos.

The three of them went into the living room with mugs of tea and a plate of Welsh cakes. They settled on the sofa and Skye saw Mimi watching Lizzie. Her lips pursed as if unsure about something. She must have decided *to hell with it*, though, because she addressed Lizzie when she asked, "What did he do to put that look in your eyes, *chiquita*?" Lizzie's head shot up and she blushed before trying to hide it.

"Nothing," she replied, shaking her head.

"Please. I have raised a fine daughter and she is happy and in love. But do not think I don't know when I see a broken heart. Tell me, let me help you." And just like that, Lizzie caved.

It all came out about how she had caught her despicable husband cheating on her with his younger, thinner, blonde secretary. How he begged for her forgiveness, and like a fool, she had believed him, only to find out he'd done it again with the girl who ran the local pub.

She explained how stupid and humiliated she felt. Mimi wrapped her in a motherly hug and murmured soothing words while she rocked Lizzie like a baby as she cried. Skye held her friend's hand, offering what comfort she could. She felt a little hurt her friend hadn't confided in her.

"I'm sorry I didn't say anything," Lizzie sniffed as if sensing Skye's thoughts. "I didn't want to bring you down with my problems."

"Oh, honey, you would never do that. I'm your friend and I always want to be there for you. Please don't shut me out."

Lizzie nodded, "Okay."

She explained how she and Mateo were staying with her dad until she could find somewhere of their own. They agreed to try to keep things amicable for the sake of their son, with Mateo spending every other weekend with his father.

Skye felt bad that her friend was going through this alone. Dane and Lucy didn't even know. Lizzie was worried they would try to beat her soon-to-be ex-husband to a pulp. She, for one, thought that sounded like a good plan, but refrained from sharing that.

"We have many lessons to learn in this life," Mimi started, "One of those is forgiveness. You must forgive yourself for being human and trusting in love. The one who holds the other half of your soul is out there. I know you won't believe me, but it is true. You have kissed a frog who turned out to be a toad, but you got something very precious from it. A love so pure it breaks your heart the same time it fills it to bursting. That is something to be proud of. When you are ready to open your heart again your prince will come. You mark my words."

Mimi's words made Skye's heart swell with emotion and she could see they had the same effect on Lizzie.

"Now, it's time for more tea. Come, Lizzie, help an old woman." Lizzie smiled a true, beautiful smile that reached her eyes, and snorted just like her sister.

"Old my ass," she laughed.

"I'm going to go check on Noah," Skye said suddenly, wanting to kiss her son's soft cheek. She climbed the stairs and found him playing happily with his Legos. That was the last thing she thought before all hell broke loose.

A loud crash sounded from downstairs followed by the sound of gunfire. Her heart stopped then continued to beat double-time. Oh my god! They were here for Noah! With no time to think, she grabbed Noah and dragged him up to Nate's room. Her son was silent with fear. She had no time to think of that now–she needed to hide him.

She heard more gunfire from downstairs and prayed Mimi and Lizzie were okay. She knelt to Noah, "Sweetheart, listen to me. I need you to hide in here." She opened the door to Nate's weapon store. He'd made her memorize the number in case this very thing happened. He'd shown her a compartment in the back of the room, just big enough for two adults.

Noah nodded and she thrust her phone at him. "When it goes quiet downstairs, call Nate, but do not come out of that room. This is very important, Noah, no matter what you hear you stay in here. Got it?"

"Yes, mummy," he said in a small voice. She kissed him then pushed him inside the room.

"Love you, baby boy," she whispered as she shut the door and ran back to the third floor.

As she ran to the stairs, a shadow came at her and grabbed her– one arm round her waist, the other around her face.

"*Cyka!*" the man in the black balaclava shouted when she bit the hand that grabbed her. She realized it was Russian. He was speaking Russian. That was her last thought as the man backhanded her so hard she fell to the ground and blacked out.

Chapter Twenty-Eight

Mimi and Lizzie clutched each other's hands as the two men yelled at them in Russian. They herded them into the corner of the kitchen and tied them, back to back, with thick rope. Lizzie felt sick as she saw the third man walk down the stairs with Skye thrown over his shoulder.

She had blood dripping from a cut near her eye and she was out cold. Mimi saw her and let out a tirade of Spanish. Mostly promises that her son would tear out their innards with his bare hands for this. She was sure some curse words were thrown in, too but A level Spanish was a long time ago and she was a bit rusty.

She glared at the two men who were now shouting at the man who had Skye. He turned back to them, and in broken English, demanded they tell them where Noah was. Lizzie didn't get time to answer because Mimi did.

"He is with his grandfather you, *hijo de puta*," she spat on the floor next to him. Lizzie was sure that was a bad idea. But Mimi had lost her cool now and was railing at them in Spanish. She questioned their parentage, their manhood, and promised retribution that Lizzie was sure she must have misunderstood, it was so gruesome.

The tallest man was looking at Mimi with a look of complete bewilderment. Like he'd never met a woman who looked like a sweet motherly type and spoke like a sailor. He must have decided he'd had enough because he lifted his gun to hit her, when gunfire exploded from downstairs.

The men looked at one another and decided it was time to leave. They ran for the door, more gunfire erupting from the ground floor.

"Quickly *mi hija*, help me work these ropes. We have to get to Noah and tell Nate what's happened," Mimi said in a strong, confident manner that belied their situation.

Lizzie felt Mimi tugging at her ties and in no time had them undone. Lizzie untied Mimi and got up, racing for the door. Geez, where did this woman get her energy? Mimi stopped short as a large, dishevelled man stepped through. He looked scary as shit and the fact he had a gun in each hand did not help.

Mimi backed up, keeping Lizzie behind her.

"Who are you?" Mimi asked indignantly. He didn't answer but asked a question of his own, "Where is Noah?"

Mimi kept backing her up towards the stove.

This man seemed more formidable than the others, and his cool demeanor did nothing to make her feel better In fact, it scared her more. It was a shame, really, she thought. He was hot in a scary assassin kind of way.

God, she had finally lost the plot. He was speaking English, though, and his voice had a strong, almost lyrical, quality. English was good though, wasn't it? Lizzie felt Mimi groping around behind her when they came to stop with her wedged up against the stove. What the hell was she doing now? The woman was going to get them killed.

The man in front of them must have thought they weren't a threat because he turned towards the stairs, and when he did, Mimi struck.

Grabbing the iron griddle, she swung with all her might, nearly taking Lizzie's head off in the process, clonking Mr. Scary on the head. He went down like a lead balloon.

Liz didn't know whether to be proud or terrified. What if she had killed him? Liz knelt down and checked the man's neck for a pulse. It was strong and steady. That made her feel better.

"Quick help me tie him up," Mimi said. Lizzie knew where Nate got his badass moves from now. They quickly found some brown packaging tape and wound it around his hands and feet. Thank god, he was still breathing. She didn't think she would survive prison. The thought made Lizzie laugh and she wondered if hysteria was setting in.

She wasn't like Lucy–she had never been one for adventure and intrigue. She owned a bloody antique shop for, Christ's sake. And yet, despite that, she couldn't stop the tiny bit of excitement from unfurling in her belly.

"Come on, let's find Noah," Mimi said and headed for the stairs. They hunted high and low but couldn't find him. Mimi decided it was time to call her son. No, this wasn't for her, she decided hours later when the adrenalin wore off.

~~~

Nate was in his car, pondering his next stop. It was 4 pm and he had struck out with his last lead. Despite Ceecee telling him that Hugo was at Lockwood manor, he wanted to try his other haunts, again, first. Eidolon had sent people to Lockwood Manor earlier today and he would have heard if Hugo was there. He was thinking maybe it was worth a shot trying Lockwood Manor when his phone rang. He swiped the screen, a smile on his face, "Hey Ma, what's up?" His smile froze and bile filled his mouth while she told him what had happened. "I'm on my way," he said stiltedly.

He had never felt fear like this. He felt a coldness come over him and fear that he had never felt before invaded him. Skye had been taken away unconscious and bleeding by some scum Rusky and Noah was missing. His Skye and Noah were gone and someone hurt his mum. A rage started to boil in his belly. He tried to control it so he could do his job.

He cued up his phone and hit dial. The call going straight through to Will in the tech room. They only used this in dire emergency, and this was one. Will came on the line in seconds.

"Go," he said calmly.

Nate explained what his mother had told him and Will soon had emergency services on route to his house. The team would be called in immediately, this being the new protocol Zack put in place.

His hands gripped the steering wheel so hard his knuckles turned white and started to go numb. His brain stubbornly refused to think they wouldn't get them back. He instead thought of all the ways he planned to torture the men who had taken them.

He pulled up to his house just in front of the ambulance. Abandoning his car, he ran for the door. Ambrose was just inside. He had a gunshot wound to his collarbone, but it looked like the real problem was the blood coming from a head wound.

It was likely caused when he fell and hit his head off the step, if the blood he'd seen there was any indication. Nate bent to him, checking for a pulse and found a weak one. The fact that he was still unconscious after over thirty minutes didn't bode well. Nate ran for the stairs as the paramedics came in and started to work on Ambrose. He found his mother and Lizzie sitting at the kitchen table.

They raced to him and he enveloped his mother in his arms. He noticed a man, with his hands tied up in his front, sitting behind her. He released his mother and went to the man, he turned his head back to her his eyes asking his mother what had happened.

Nate lifted the man's slumped head, he had a massive goose egg on his temple and blood dribbling down his face. He blinked in surprise as he stared down at Kanan. Who had opened his eyes and was now glaring up at him, the tape over his mouth stopped him from speaking.

"What happened, ma?" he asked gently as he stepped away from Kanan and towards his ma.

Mimi calmly explained what had happened, including all the bits he didn't need, like welsh cakes, cheating ex-husbands, and woodwork.

"Ma, just the short version."

"Okay. Yes, sorry. So after they left, this guy came in asking about Noah, looking all scary, so I hit him with the griddle pan." Nate winced. Fuck. That was going to hurt. Kanan would be lucky to come away with all his brain cells in tact after that. He felt an immense amount of pride in his mother, though.

"Well done, ma, you did good," he turned to Lizzie then. "And you, sweetheart."

"Hey, it was all your mother. I'm team Mimi all the way from now on." She grinned then before her lip started to tremble a bit. Nate was sure she was going to cry but she held it together, and for the first time, he saw a lot of Lucy in Lizzie.

The paramedics came in and swarmed around Kanan, but Nate wasn't interested because just then, Lucy and Dane walked through the door. Seeing Lizzie, they raced for her enveloping her in their arms.

The next few hours were spent with Mimi and Lizzie answering questions from the police and Zack and Jack Granger, who had arrived just after Dane and Lucy. Will was going over all the CCTV. He'd picked up the van that took Skye and Nate's stomach clenched and pitched when he saw her limp body thrown in the van.

He needed a minute to get himself together. Kanan needed to be sedated in the ambulance after he'd apparently thrown a hissy fit and tried to get up. He was going for a CT scan to see if Mimi had done any permanent damage.

Nate sat on his bed and idly picked up Skye's sleep shorts. They were a pale gold colour with burgundy lace running down the sides. He could smell her everywhere and his heart ached with a physical pain as he thought of her scared and hurting.

He was deep in thought when his phone rang. He took it out of his pocket and looked at the screen. His heart danced with hope when he saw it was Skye calling. He quickly swiped to answer,

"Skye!"

"Nnnate, is that you?" a small voice whispered.

"Noah? Oh my god, where are you, buddy?" he asked as he got up and started to pace his room.

"I'm in a secret place in your room."

Nates eyes shot to the weapons door and dove for it. Throwing open the door, he went to the back and pushed open the panel that led to the tiny space. Opening it, he found a very frightened Noah.

Dropping his phone, he swept Noah into his arms and held him tight, tucking his head into Noah's little neck. Noah held on just as tight, sobs shaking his little body.

"Okay, buddy. I got you, you're safe now. Nobody is going to get you."

"Is mummy okay?" Nate looked at the boy who'd stolen his heart and couldn't lie.

"They took her, Noah. But we're going to get her back."

"Kanan–he knows!" Noah said resolutely.

"What do you mean?"

"I fell asleep and dreamed that Kanan was here and he knew where they would take us." Nate felt his muscles go tight and had to fight to control his temper. The last thing he wanted to do was scare Noah any more than he already was. Kanan knew! He fucking knew and never said anything.

Nate walked downstairs with Noah still clinging to him like a vine, straight into a room full of shocked people. Everyone started talking at once and he held up a hand to shush everyone.

"Noah was hiding in a secret place, weren't you buddy?"

"Yes. Mummy told me not to come out, so I didn't and then I fell asleep." He seemed better now that he was surrounded by people he loved."

"You did great." Nate said as set Noah down on a chair at the kitchen table. "He had a dream, didn't you buddy. Tell Zack and everyone about your dream," He said gently to Noah.

"I dreamt that Kanan was here and he knew where they were going to take mummy."

Zack let out a foul word and punched the door, which was very un-Zack like. Nate passed Noah over to Lizzie and his ma, who were sitting at the table with his Pop and Uncle Reg, both looking ill at the thought that they hadn't been here to keep the women safe. Although, if you asked him, his Ma did a bang-up job.

Mimi and Lizzie showered Noah with hugs and kisses. Noah turned his face to Nate, doing a typical boy eye roll and giggle. Thank God, he was okay. At least now he could concentrate on getting Skye back.

Chapter Twenty-Nine

Skye could feel a blinding pain shoot through her head and wondered if she had one of her migraines. She hadn't had one in ages. She blinked her eyes a few times and looked around. She was on the floor in what looked like a church.

She was confused for a minute, then it all came back to her. The house. Noah. Lizzie and Mimi–oh my god, were they dead? She remembered gunfire and hiding Noah. Had they found him?

She felt her nape prickle and turned to see the two men who had come into her home and taken her. She fought to push down the anger and think rationally. The men were watching her as they played cards.

The one she had bitten got up and came over to her. He crouched down and she tried scooting back, but her hands were tied behind her back and her movements were clumsy. Her head hurt like a bitch and she thought she might puke.

The man grabbed her hair and pulled her face up to him. The pain made her see stars and she fought nausea as he hissed hateful words at her in Russian. He palmed her breast and pulled hard on her hair and she lost the battle with her stomach.

Bile rushed into her mouth and she puked all over him. He threw her away from him yelling at her, as his mate laughed so hard he nearly knocked over the table. The man walked away, still yelling, and she managed to get control of her stomach.

If puking on him was the only way to keep him away, so be it. She slowly sat up and looked at the other man. He seemed to be ignoring her. Now she was no longer entertaining.

A few minutes later, vomit man returned and glared at her before sitting down opposite the man dealing the cards out. She wondered why anyone would use a church as a place to keep hostages.

She looked around at the beautiful stained glass windows depicting Jesus on the cross. The ornate wall hangings that graced the far end of the church looked to be hundreds of years old. Brass candleholders and a brass cross were in front of her, near the font. The pews were all made of oak wood, the carvings on them beautiful.

Skye could tell by the waning light coming in through the stained glass that it was dusk, which put the time at about four-thirty in the afternoon. She wondered if Nate was coming for her and wished she had access to a phone.

Her heart sank when she cast her eyes to the end of the first pew and noticed the carving. It was the Lockwood family crest. She knew it because Hugo had a pinky ring with the same crest. He'd said it was his father's and every Lockwood man passed it to his first born son. She remembered feeling sad that he would not do that for Noah.

As if thinking of him conjured him up, Hugo appeared at the side door. She watched as he arrogantly walked into the room and up to the two Russians.

"Why is she here? Where is my grandmother?" The two men looked at each other and seemed unsure what to do. Hugo walked over to her and roughly pulled her to a sitting position.

"Where is Noah?" he asked, seeming anxious.

"Somewhere you will never get to him," she spat. She was sure she saw relief cross his features before he hauled her up to stand and sat her in a pew that was just behind her. He sat next to her, roughly turning her to face him.

"Don't talk to me like that you little bitch," he hissed, but bizarrely, he winked at her. Then he freaked her even more by slipping his hand behind her and loosening her ties. Was he…he was trying to help! He tucked something into her back waistband and she tried not to flinch as he touched her skin seemingly accidentally. It felt like a card or square of paper.

It sure as hell wasn't back maintenance for his son that would a whole lot bigger. She wondered for a second if the bump on the head had given her an aneurysm and that was why weird shit was happening.

She sobered as Hugo squeezed her hand and she was sure he muttered *I'm sorry*. She had no time to think about it, though, as Felicity Lockwood walked in. With…oh my god. Why was he here? Moreover, why was he with her? The feeling of betrayal scorched her throat.

She cast him her a glare and he just looked back at her as if she wasn't there or he didn't know who she was. What the fuck was going on?

Fortis, 5 pm

Nate paced the room, waiting for Zack to get back. He had insisted on going to get Kanan by himself and bring him back here. Dane and Daniel were in the conference room with Zin, planning a rescue op for as soon as they got the green light and co-ordinates.

Nate had stayed in the tech room with Will, Drew, and Lucy. Noah was sleeping in one of the rest rooms with Lizzie. Reg and his parents had commandeered the reception area.

The building was in lock down. Zack had locked the front doors and activated the electromagnetic wave transformer in the reinforced glass. Will had developed a wire that ran around the edge of the glass, allowing radio waves and signals through, but at the touch of a button on Zack's desk, could also conceal the entire building in a cone of silence.

The technology allowed sunlight through but was invisible to the naked eye. The glass was, to some degree, bombproof and after the attack on them a few weeks ago, that had proved a wise move. Nate had no clue how it worked and didn't care to, either. He was glad Will worked for them. That technology could net him billions on the open market. But Will had no use for money and was happy to let Fortis and Eidolon spend it on things they needed. At least he was smart enough patent it, though.

Will was a geek and was happiest when he had a computer, an energy drink, and a large bag of beef monster munch. For a pale, skinny, tatted up, uber geek, he sure had his pick of women and those women were hot.

Will had picked up the Van on the A40 moving towards Symonds Yat. Nate was sure that they were headed for Lockwood Manor but Zack wanted confirmation before sending then in.

Nate left the tech room and walked to the conference room. He'd changed into his black BDU trousers and black, long-sleeve top. He'd brought all his favourite weapons from his personal stash. His Browning handgun, his best and most trusted sniper rifle, and a spare that was nearly as good but not as smooth.

He even brought some charges and Imx-101. It was used by the military and was brilliant in firefight situations since it was a lot more stable than TNT. A RPG was also brought along. Liam had proved that there was always a need for an RPG and if that sentence made him crazy then so be it.

Thinking of Liam, he wondered where he was. They had pulled him back to Eidolon and it had all been very secretive. Nate wondered why. It seemed odd that when the threat level went up, Jack had assigned him to something else.

Cleaning his gun, he watched Ava and Celeste going through paperwork at the far end of the table. Both women had refused to leave when they found out Skye was missing. Neither knew her well, but both obviously liked her. They had taken coffee out to his parents, Reg, and Lizzie and just mucked in and helped with whatever needed doing.

The two women seemed to have grown close in the few weeks they'd known each other. He watched as Celeste kept casting sideways glances at Zin, who had just walked in and was helping himself to coffee. It was funny because Zin kept looking at her, too, but he wore scowls. And Celeste? Well, he wasn't sure really what her's said. Mild attraction, maybe? Samson, who still growled at Zin when he got close, clearly didn't share the feeling.

Nate's mind went to Skye and he wondered if she was okay–if she knew in her heart he would come for her. Maybe she hated him for failing her so badly. He hoped she knew he would move heaven and earth to get to her. The thought of her hurt, or worse, dead, made him break out in a cold sweat.

He couldn't comprehend of a world with no Skye in it. She was his heart. He thought Nikki hurt him, but that paled in comparison to the pain he would feel if anything happened to the woman he loved.

Nate rose as the door opened and Zack walked in, followed by Kanan, who pointed at Nate and said, "You keep your crazy mother away from me."

Nate almost laughed. Kanan had an ugly bruise forming over his right eye and down his temple. "I think we should bring her in here and give her the griddle pan back," Nate said standing, and getting in his face. Nate had called a reluctant peace with Kanan after he brought Noah back. That didn't mean he liked him and it certainly didn't mean he could talk shit about his Ma.

"Okay, okay. Settle down," Zack said, waving everyone to chairs. The men eyeballed each other for another second then sat.

Zack took his place at the top of the table, buzzed the tech room, and asked everyone to join them.

Nate watched Kanan as he watched Celeste. He felt a twinge of sadness when he saw grief and regret cross Kanan's face when he looked at his sister. For her part, she watched Kanan from her place next to Ava. Her face had a look of silent question. Nate felt that that particular secret would not stay a secret if Kanan continued to be a regular at Fortis.

He concentrated on the people in the room. If he thought about Skye, he knew he would lose his shit. So he closed his thoughts down.

When everyone had come into the conference room and were settled, Zack began.

"Kanan has been tracking Hugo since we lost him after rescuing Noah. He finally caught up with him entering Lockwood Manor a few days ago. K, would you like to continue?"

Kanan sat forward, "Hugo was alone when he entered and has remained in the house for that time. I had hoped he would lead me to Felicity."

"Why didn't you tell us?" demanded Dane.

"I don't work in a team and I don't owe anyone, except maybe Noah." Kanan glanced at Nate who was giving him daggers.

"I know I fucked up and I wanted to make sure he was safe. I won't explain myself to you or anyone else."

"Wow. How not to make friends and influence people," Ava snorted and Zack gave her a look that would freeze hell. She put her hands up in a placating gesture, bringing her hand up, pretending as if she was zipping her lips.

Kanan continued, "Earlier this morning, Felicity and ten men arrived at Lockwood Manor and started unloading dozens of wooden crates from their vehicles. The crates were then taken to the church that is on the estate. Shortly after, three men left, and for whatever reason, I decided to follow. I was too late to save Skye from being taken." He hung his head. "And then I was obviously attacked by the blue rinse mafia."

"Why were you asking about Noah?" Nate asked K.

"I told you, I feel bad for what I put him through. He didn't deserve that he's a good kid."

As he said that, the door pushed open and Noah ran in. He stopped when he saw everyone. His eyes landed on Kanan and he ran to him and hugged his neck. The gesture threw the big man and he froze, then very slowly put his arms around the boy and awkwardly patted his back.

"K, you're okay! I was so worried about you. I had a dream. You need to stop looking. It's making her sad. She's worried about you." Kanan seemed to go preternaturally still at Noah's words. He pulled back and Nate fought the urge to go to Noah and drag him away from Kanan.

For whatever reason, Noah had no fear of the man and even seemed to have some weird bond. Noah let go and came round the table to Nate. He pushed his little body in beside Nate and put his scrawny arms around his thick neck. Nate hugged him and made sure he was okay.

"We need to make a plan now to get your mum home. Can you go sit with Aubela and Pop while we be prepared?

"Sure, Nate. Don't forget, you promised me a re-match later, so don't get too tired." Nate shook his head with a small smirk. Ava came over and took Noah's hand, guiding him out while he talked ten to the dozen about Lego Batman.

Nate looked at Kanan, who looked pale and shaken.

"Is he...." Kanan trailed off. Nate remembered the last time the man had seen Noah, he'd been at deaths door.

"He's fine," Nate said, not going into detail. They weren't his to give. Kanan just nodded and a small smile twitched his lips.

"Can we plan this fucking op now, please?" Zin growled angrily.

Thirty minutes later, they were geared up and on their way. Eidolon was sending men to guard the perimeter of Fortis. Zack didn't want anyone else inside except Will, Drew, and the civilians.

Nate was traveling with Lucy, Zin, and Zack. Dane was with Daniel and Kanan. Zack had said he wanted Nate where he could see him and Nate conceded. He didn't like the idea of not being close enough to keep an eye on Kanan, but also knew if Kanan wanted Noah or Skye hurt, they would be, of that he had no doubt. Kanan was a lethal operator who got caught out by his Ma. Nate would be a fool to underestimate him or fully trust him and Nate was no fool.

Chapter Thirty

Skye watched as Felicity had at least nine or ten men with her and her companion. The men carried box after box into the back of the church. Felicity ignored her after that first glance. The satisfied smile she had given her when she registered Skye's shock at seeing *him*–she refused to say his name–made her want to pull the woman's hair out by the roots.

Hugo had gone running to her and been given a withering look. They had exchanged a few words, which she couldn't hear, and then he'd left with another man.

Felicity was, as always, primped and preened. She looked like the perfect Lady of the Manor. Her pearls were round her neck, her cream tweed suit was immaculate, and her pink, wool coat must have cost a small fortune.

Shame it was wasted on a cheap whore like her. Nate had told her of Felicity's history, and honestly, it didn't surprise her one bit. Class was bred, not learned, and she had none.

Yes, Skye wore high-street jeans and jumpers, but she had bluer blood than the Lockwoods would ever hope for. Her family were snobs and didn't do well with people who were different. Their loss, she mused as she watched the coming and goings.

Hugo came back in and came over to her. She watched as he knelt before her and offered her some water.

"Here you need to drink." He undid the sealed water bottle and she drank as he tipped it to her lips.

It was smacked out of her mouth and flung to the ground as Felicity cuffed her grandson across the head.

"What are you doing, boy?" she hissed.

"She needs some water. We're not animals. And please, don't treat me like it, either. I am Lord Lockwood and you will treat me with respect." Skye wanted to applaud him for finally growing a pair.

Felicity looked down at Skye and suddenly bent towards her lashing out with a vicious slap to Skye's face. Hugo went to intervene but Felicity pulled a gun on him. She held it to his forehead and everything seemed to move in slow motion.

Hugo stood and faced Felicity.

"Now, my young boy. I want to tell you a story," she said coldly as she looked at her grandson. "Many years ago there was a whore. She was a good whore and had many high profile clients, including Jack the Hat, Reggie Kray, and many other well-known gangsters. But this whore wanted more, she wanted it all."

"One day, she met a man. He fell in love with her and didn't care about her background. He just wanted to make her happy. The whore fell in love with him and they married." Felicity turned and looked at Skye. She tilted her head to the side slightly and inquired,

"Have you heard this story?" Skye and she wisely shook her head.

"Well, keep listening." Felicity turned back to look at Hugo, "One day after a few years of marriage, the whore found her beloved husband with his face buried in the cunt of a maid." Felicity's face went blank. She looked like she was deep in her head.

"The whore," she continued as if telling a bedtime story, "wanted to kill the girl, but alas, she was pregnant and the husband begged her not to. The child was born, a bouncing baby boy, and the whore and the husband raised the child as their own. Unfortunately, the maid met a very sad end," Felicity smirked and Skye realized she was barking mad.

"The whore tried to love the child and was a good mother to him and even forgave the husband. Over time, the boy married and produced a son of his own." Hugo had gone as white as a ghost. "Unfortunately he found out, through vicious gossip, what had happened to his birth mother and threatened the whore with the police.

"He didn't know the whore still had very powerful friends in the east end. He and his wife met a sad end, too–a nasty car crash into a river where they drowned. So sad, don't you think?" She caressed Skye's cheek while still pointing the gun to Hugo's forehead.

"Well, the husband was so sad over the loss of his son, he had a heart attack and died. That left the whore and the grandson. Except he isn't her grandson, is he? He's the grandson of the maid slag that stole the whore's love. So, the whore will have no compunction about killing the boy, will she Hugo?"

"You killed them all," Hugo said in shocked confusion.

"I'm afraid so. You see, I, the whore, if you will, liked the title and power that goes with being Lady Lockwood, and with

Armageddon coming, I will rise to the highest rank. I will help our one true leader rule when all of the lower beings perish. You producing an heir with such exciting abilities was brilliant and probably the best thing you have done in your miserable life. Now all I need is for Nate to bring Noah to me in exchange for Skye's life and you can all die."

"Actually, you can die now." Felicity faced Hugo and sent a bullet straight into his forehead. Skye screamed as she saw Hugo fall at her feet, his blood covering her face. Skye shook, her breathing became shallow as she tried to keep herself from fainting.

Felicity calmly walked away. "Clean that up," she said to the traitor and flicked her wrist at Hugo's body. The woman felt nothing after killing Hugo in cold blood. Skye needed to get out of here. Fear clawed at her as she sat there, not knowing what to do. She felt her heart thudding against her chest and forced herself to slow her breathing and calm down.

She flinched as the traitor came close to her and picked up Hugo's body. He glanced at her out of the corner of his eye and she thought she saw a brief flash of something in his eyes. But he said nothing and left, taking Hugo with him.

~~~

Nate and the team assembled in the same spot as last time and hoofed it to the house. They were in grouped in two's, each in the same pair as last time. They rounded the hedge that bordered the large pond and were about to go on to the house when they heard a weapon discharge. The sound came from the church. The two from

Eidolon motioned that they'd take the back. Nate was on sniper duty and the others would go in hot using the smoke flares Nate had brought.

Nate slipped into the bell tower and on silent feet, climbed to the top. Zack and Kanan were covering his six and heard grunts as they took care of the perimeter guards. Zin and Lucy would go in through the front door. Dane, Daniel, and Eidolon's men would go in through the vestry.

Nate skirted the massive bell and lying flat on his belly set up his rifle and checked the scope. He looked into the church. His stomach lurched when he saw Skye sitting in a pew, her hands tied behind her back, blood all over her face. She was shaking like a leaf, but otherwise seemed unharmed.

He saw a man dragging a body but didn't get a good look at him before he went out of sight. He clicked his mic on his wristwatch twice to relay that he had eyes on the target. Then he clicked eight times to say how many hostiles where inside.

Nate knew Zack would work with Jack, who was securing the main house with the rest of Eidolon. Jack had taken it pretty badly about Sly, and he knew Jack would do anything to get blood from these bastards.

Zack whispered into his comm, "We go in on your signal, Nate."

Nate lined up his shot and was about to say go when he had the shock of his life.

Walking into shot was the man who had dragged the body out. He was dressed in the same uniform as the Russian bastards. He walked straight up to Felicity and took her flank like he was some guard dog.

He watched as Skye threw him an evil glare. He was so proud of her for being so brave. But he was also confused how this happened and why.

He slid back from his position and keyed his comm, "We have a problem," he whispered. "We have a potential friendly, but he could also be a hostile. He is dressed in the Watcher Uniform of black with an insignia on the pocket."

He didn't know how to say this, he switched to a private channel for only Zack's ears.

"Zack come in," he whispered.

"Come in," Zack replied.

"You need to lock Lucy down. Sly's in there and he seems to be working with them."

Zack went silent and then swore softly. "Copy that," he said.

Nate crawled back to his position and watched, for maybe ten minutes, trying to assess the situation. He couldn't believe Sly would have turned–no way, he didn't buy it. Sly must have sensed something, because he looked up to the bell tower and winked.

Nate felt the air leave his lungs in relief.

He quickly accessed his comm and relayed things to Zack.

"We go on my count." He watched as Sly got into position next to a seething Skye, then gave the signal.

"Go!" he shouted.

Nate didn't take out Felicity–they needed her alive. Instead, he took out the most credible threat to Skye, the hulking Russian who he'd noticed kept casting disgusting looks at her. His shot was true as always and the man went down with a perfect shot to the forehead right between the eyes.

Then all hell broke loose. A charge on the door blew it in, and through the smoke came Lucy and Zin. Dane was taking care of a man by the vestry door and easily subdued him with a couple of well-placed elbow strikes.

The plan was to keep as many alive as possible, but everyone knew that in a combat situation, that meant jack shit. Nate took out a man who was skulking down the side of the pews towards the exit. Zack and Kanan were dealing with the men near the side door. He couldn't hear any weapons going off, but that meant nothing with those crazy bastards.

Nate saw Felicity turn and issue an instruction to Sly, who, for a second, looked as if he might obey, but then lifted and held a gun to Felicity. Daniel dragged a zip tied man towards the front pew and left him to go help Dane out.

The smoke and gunfire towards the front was clearing now and Nate spotted the second Lucy noticed Sly. Her concentration went for a second, and a guy they hadn't seen, came from behind a curtain and got the jump on her.

He grabbed her in a headlock and she went to her knee, executing a perfect half shoulder throw. The man jumped to his feet and came at her again. He threw a couple of punches, which she blocked, and in her signature move, threw an uppercut to the man's stomach, wrapped her arm around his neck, and threw herself backwards so they rolled end-over-end with her ending up astride him. The rice bale was perfect for a smaller person, and deadly since it snapped the neck if you didn't let go during the roll–Lucy hadn't let go.

Nate winced. Lucy was awesome and any other time he could watch her do this all day, but he needed to get to Skye. Sly, and now Zack and Kanan, flanked Skye. She looked up towards the bell tower.

Nate was about to move when he saw Felicity shift her stance, turning towards Skye, leveling her gun at her chest. In a split-second decision, Nate pulled the trigger, putting a bullet in Felicity Lockwood's shoulder. She fell to the ground and Zack and Sly were on her.

Nate didn't wait to see if she was secure, he needed to feel Skye in his arms. Grabbing his gear, he raced down the steps in time to see Lucy throw herself at Sly. Her legs went round his waist and her mouth collided with his. Sly palmed her ass as he kissed the life out of her. It was clear to see how those two felt.

He raced to Skye and grabbed her up in his arms. He buried his face in her hair, breathing her in. He kissed her all over her face, all the fear he felt was poured into it as he ran his hands over her checking for injury.

A door slammed and they pulled apart. Jack walked in and stopped dead. He looked awful. The relief that washed over his face when he saw Sly was palpable. He cleared his expression, though, and nodded at Sly.

Sly had put Lucy down but was holding her close to his side. Dane was scowling and Daniel was openly smiling.

"Get that bitch to Eidolon. I want a full team on her." Said Jack angrily. Felicity flinched but didn't look scared as she was roughly pulled up by Liam who'd come in with Jack.

"You won't stop us, you know," she said haughtily. "You're too late. We have everything in place. You're all going to die," she laughed like a deranged woman.

"Well, so are you, bitch. And you can bet your ass it will be slow and painful if I have anything to do with it," said Lucy coldly.

Skye caught Lucy's eye, "Don't forget, Felicity, I heard your little speech before you murdered Hugo. You have nothing. The Lockwood money and title is not yours. The estate passes to the oldest living male as per tradition of an aristocratic title. You only had control because Hugo was weak. But it will pass to his heir now, and that would be my son. Therefore, as his guardian until he is of age, that means me. So get your scrawny ass off my property." Skye took a step towards Felicity and Nate tensed. She reached out and snatched the pearls from Felicity's neck, "I believe these belong to my son now."

Felicity was opening her mouth like a fish and had gone deathly pale. It was dawning on her that she was fucked, and without money, the Watchers would let her swing in the wind.

She was a cold bitch, though. Felicity stiffened her spine and glared at them everyone as she was dragged out.

Skye sagged into Nate then. "Who has Noah?" she asked.

"He's back at Fortis with my parents, Ava, Celeste, Drew, Will, and of course, Samson."

She nodded and huddled into him. It was freezing in here and she only had on a thin jumper and yoga bottoms.

"Come on. Let's get you to him."

Zack, Daniel, Dane, and Zin stayed to investigate what was being kept there. Eidolon was taking care of clean up. Nate watched as Lucy and Sly walked towards the gate and the vehicles hidden there. Nate was so relieved that Sly was okay, but beyond curious as to what happened.

How had he and his team been taken? Where was the rest of the team—and why did Felicity think she had some sort of control over him? Moreover, if she thought she did have control over Sly, why didn't she? His arm tightened around Skye as he lifted her into the vehicle. Sly and Luce were taking the other one.

"Are you okay, *mi amor*?" he asked, as he buckled her in.

"Yes, I am. It was so much worse when it was Noah. I was scared, but I knew you'd come. I don't understand why Sly was acting that way, though. When he came in, he looked like he didn't even know me. He was following Felicity like some lackey." She shook her head as if in confusion. "It was weird."

Nate kissed her gently, "We can get that figured out later. As long as you are okay, that's all that matters right now."

"I'm fine, Nate, honestly. I might get scared later when the adrenalin wears off, but I have a strong, handsome man to hold me tight and look after me." She smiled at him, then, and his heart melted.

"You will always have me, Skye. You and Noah. I was so scared when they had you, I could hardly breathe." She sucked in a breath and he saw tears in her eyes.

"I love you, so much, Nate. I never thought I would have this– this once in a lifetime thing that you read about."

"Believe it," he whispered and dropped a brief kiss on her upturned mouth before pulling away.

"Let's go get our boy and go home." Skye said tiredly.

On the drive back, Nate filled her in on what happened after she was taken. She found the bit about Kanan hilarious. Her eyes welled with emotion when she heard Noah had dreamt about her abduction.

Four long hours later, they were finally home. Noah was asleep as Nate carried him up to bed. He and Skye tucked him in and left a small nightlight on in his room in case he woke up scared. He'd been ecstatic to see his mum safe and sound and talked non-stop the majority of the way home.

They had hung around briefly, but Zack had called and told everyone to go home and they would have a briefing in the morning. He demanded that all civilians be there so he could debrief them about today's events.

His mum hadn't taken kindly to being bossed around, and it had taken his father a good, long while to calm her enough to get her to agree. Then he'd had to use underhanded tactics and promised her a new griddle pan. She was having the other hung in the living room over the fireplace.

Nate turned and picked Skye up as she turned to leave Noah's room. She squeaked then settled against his chest, tucking her head into this neck as she rubbed his chest. She seemed to hit a wall. She stifled a yawn against his neck, tickling him.

All the blood in his body rushed to his groin at her softness nestled against him. He didn't intend to act on the impulse, though. She was exhausted and needed comfort and some TLC, not him and his raging erection bothering her.

He gently placed her on the bed and walked to his bathroom to run her a bath. She had a vicious bruise on her jaw where that scum had hit her. He wished he could go back and kill the bastard slower, but had to be okay with the fact that he was dead.

Skye explained how she'd puked on him and he was weirdly happy about it. Not that she was hurt, obviously, but the fact that she gotten a little revenge on the prick.

He came back to the bed and Skye was watching him with hooded eyes, gone dark with desire. No…no. He would not do this. She was exhausted. He lifted her top half as he eased her shirt over her head. She winced when his fingers accidentally grazed her jaw.

Pulling her to stand, he stripped her of her bottoms and underwear then lifted her into his arms, again. Her soft, plush breasts pushed against his arm and pebbled into hard points. He groaned feeling his dick twitch as if trying to fight its way out of his trousers.

He bent and tested the water and decided it was perfect and eased her in. She groaned when the hot water flowed over her body. He stripped and eased himself in behind her.

Taking the body wash, he soaped up the sponge, and with upmost care, washed her body. When he was done, he washed her hair, combing the long strands with his fingers. As much as this was killing his poor cock, he loved just taking care of her.

Everything done, he climbed from the water and tucked a towel round his waist. He caught the blatant look of arousal in her eyes as she looked at his erection and she licked her lips.

"Skye, if you carry on looking at me like that, all my good intentions are going to fly out the window." She didn't answer but turned and knelt in the bath. Water pouring over her beautiful, sinful body. She reached for him and grabbed the towel, tugging it until it fell away.

Leaning forward, she grabbed his erection and licked the tip. *Oh, fuck.* He was so done. Her tongue licked from the root to the tip and swirled around the head. Cupping his balls in her hand, she took him into her mouth. Her eyes came to his and he thought he was going to lose it.

Such an erotic sight, Skye on her knees in front of him, his cock filling her mouth. He put his hand on her head and pumped his hips as she did unspeakable things to him. She moaned and he knew she was as turned on as him.

Deciding he couldn't take any more, he pulled out of her mouth and lifted her under her arm pits. In one smooth move, he lifted her where they stood and she straddled his hips, her legs wrapping round him. He filled her with one stroke and she cried out his name.

God, she was so wet and her muscles held him so tight. He walked to the bed and laid her down, never once losing connection. He made love to her slowly, showing her with every stroke and every climax that he loved her and she was his world.

They finally fell asleep around 3 am, both knackered after the last few days.

Noah knocking lightly on the door woke him around eight in the morning.

"What's up, buddy?" he whispered loudly.

"Umm, can I get some breakfast?"

"I'll be right down. Go get dressed and I'll meet you in a few minutes."

"Okay, Nate," Noah replied. He was such a little star. He'd been through so much and bounced back every time.

He kissed an obviously still exhausted Skye if her sleeping through that was any indication and eased out of bed. Pulling on gym shorts and a T-shirt, he went downstairs.

He made him and Noah bacon and eggs; he had coffee while Noah had milk. He wondered if now would be a good time to approach Noah about his mum. Based on previous conversations, he thought it was a good time so he went for it.

The debrief had been tricky. Zack explained what he could to the civilians and made them promise not to breathe a word of it to anyone. They'd all agreed when they realised the seriousness of the situation.

Celeste had been allowed in on the team brief since she was a Fortis employee. Kanan had also been there. It was interesting to observe Kanan watch Celeste–and definitely intriguing to watch him noticing Celeste snatch glances at Zin.

He had almost laughed as Kanan's jaw tightened. The resemblance was obvious to see, but Celeste seemed none the wiser. In fact, she seemed to studiously ignore him. Samson, who sat at her feet, had decided he didn't like either Zin or Kanan and growled at them both.

He'd greeted and licked everyone else as if they were long-lost friends, even Zack who was very standoffish with the animal.

The biggest thing to come from the Skye`s kidnapping was that Felicity was a fraud who murdered anyone who got in her way, even the boy she had raised as her son and then her supposed grandson.

Skye had been correct–by default, Noah was the rightful heir to the Lockwood title and fortune. Hugo Lockwood`s, Grandfather had left everything to Felicity but in trust for Hugo until he reached 30yrs of age. As Hugo was 32yrs old it was all his and he had in fact made a will and left everything to Noah. Finally in death he had done what he hadn't in life and looked out for his son. That, however, would be locked up in probate for a while, then Skye could decide what she wanted to do.

The drug that Sly had been given brought out latent gifts in people. Sly was now able to read minds. They had been blown away by that particular news and very sceptical until he had proven it. He had gone round the table and started shouting out what each person was thinking.

After he read the first three's minds, Zack had shut it down.

Luckily, the SAS had granted Sly immediate release from his duty on medical grounds. They didn't want someone who'd been given mind-altering drugs anywhere near them. Nate assumed Zack and Jack had pulled some strings. Sly would need to undergo a battery of tests now, but physically he was fine.

Kanan was leaving for pastures unknown but had promised to stay in touch with Zack. He'd left a gift with Skye for Noah for Christmas.

Noah had changed that man's life–not that he was surprised– Noah did that to everyone he met. He had also left a new griddle pan for Nate's mother.

Nate chuckled at the thought of his ma's reaction to that. She'd promptly put it out back to use as a doorstop. Said her David would buy her griddle, not another man.

~~~

It was week before Christmas and Skye and Noah were showing him how they decorated the tree.

They were still living with him, and if he had his way, it would be permanent arrangement. His parents and Reg were coming for dinner on Christmas Day. He was excited and slightly nervous.

This holiday seemed so important. He'd purchased all the gifts he wanted for Noah and Skye and wrapped and hidden them. He'd been delighted when he managed to get Noah's favourite Rugby player to sign his knew shirt for him. He hoped Noah liked it.

He and Skye had spent loads of money buying Noah Legos, Xbox games, toy cars, Star Wars figures and costumes. They'd probably gone a bit overboard, but after the year they had, they both felt he deserved to be spoiled a little.

Skye walked into the living room with bags of decorations they had picked up and brought over from her house earlier. The tree was set up in the corner, cheesy songs were playing and hot chocolate was made. They were ready to decorate.

The three of them sang and drank hot chocolate until they thought they would be sick while decorating the tree and the rest of the house. They'd even decorated Noah's room. They decorated his home until it looked like Christmas had thrown up everywhere. He couldn't have been happier.

Every night, they tucked Noah into bed then Nate made love to his woman as if she was the most precious being on the planet. They'd enjoyed a few more nights with more exotic things and Nate had been thrilled when she let him tie her up.

The sex got better and better, the variety was amazing. He loved it all and loved her. He couldn't wait for Christmas.

Chapter Thirty-One

Lucy was worried. Ever since Jace, Sly to everyone but her, had returned, he'd been holding something back from her. He was overjoyed when he saw her at the church, kissing her as if she was the air he breathed. But since then, he hadn't touched her.

She thought he was upset over Smithy and the team members who were still prisoners of the Divine Watchers. They had raided the place where he was kept and the place was clean. Nobody was there and no evidence they were ever there, either.

Then she wondered if it was his new ability. It was pretty intense and would upset anyone. He seemed to be grasping the new ability, though, and had told her he could block it at will. It was her he seemed off with and it worried her.

He never mentioned what she was thinking and she wondered if he was upset by something she might have thought, inadvertently. She needed to talk to him, so she got in her car and drove to his house.

The lights were on when she got there and she ran up the stairs to the second floor. Her heart was banging in her chest, her stomach had butterflies. This was stupid. This was Jace, whom she'd known and loved for half her life. Walking up to the door, she stopped when she heard raised voices.

She didn't mean to listen, honestly she didn't, but when she heard him say her name, she couldn't stop herself.

"Seriously, Zack. I can't be around her. I have no idea what she is thinking, because as luck would fucking have it, she's the one person I can't fucking read."

There was a pause as she listened and her heart began beating faster. He must have been on the phone.

"No, Zack, I can't. How can I, when every time I look at her I want to throw up? It makes me sick and I can't hurt her. She's too good. She would try to stand by me and Dane would rip my heart out. How can I be with one sister when the other could be carrying my baby?"

Epilogue

Skye had warned Nate how early Noah was likely to wake up on Christmas morning, but she wasn't certain he really understood how early.

It had been lovely last night going through all the Christmas Eve rituals with him. Putting out the milk and mince pie for Father Christmas. Sprinkling the magic reindeer food on the lawn and leaving a thank you letter for Father Christmas.

Nate had been as excited as Noah to find a Christmas Eve box from the elves. She had filled it with a movie, hot chocolate mix, popcorn, a small toy, a book, and new pajamas. They had spent the day together watching movies, playing games, just being together.

That night they put Noah to bed together and Nate and Noah had been whispering. She didn't know what it was about, but every time she walked in, they looked guilty and shut up. It was adorable, really. Nate had such a cute guilty face.

Nate was like a kid. He kept checking on Noah, who predictably couldn't sleep, even though he tried to go to bed earlier than normal. Noah eventually fell asleep around 10 pm and Nate promptly decided it was time for bed. She gently remind him there was not, in fact, a Father Christmas and they had to put the presents out, drink the milk, eat the mince pie and fill Noah's stocking.

He'd carried all the presents down from the hiding place and put them round the tree. She tip-toed into Noah's room and stole the stocking, only to replace it with a filled replica. The milk was drunk, the mince pie eaten, then it was time for bed.

Nate had made love to her as if she was the most precious person on earth. Every kiss, every touch, was filled with so much love she thought she might cry. He'd held her tucked into his side, her head on his chest, and they had fallen asleep with their legs tangled, bodies sated.

She woke up the next morning around 5 o'clock. For some reason, she always woke up early on Christmas morning. She liked to be awake to watch Noah open his stocking. She let her hand trail over Nate's chest, traveling towards his toned stomach.

She stopped as he rolled into and over her so she was underneath him. He looked at her with his dark, soulful eyes and then his mouth descended and he kissed her. The kiss was long, heated, and full of promise. He broke the kiss and smiled a heart-stopping smile.

"Morning, beautiful," he said. "Merry Christmas, *mi amor*."

"Merry Christmas, baby," she replied.

They heard the sound of a thousand baby elephants running up the stairs and Noah ran through the door.

"Mummy, Nate look!" he beamed. Noah was dragging his stocking with him. He dragged it to the bed and climb up onto it then proceeded to pull every item out of the stocking one-by-one.

Before long, pencils, pens, colouring books, sweets, chocolate, and so many small toys her vacuum would be blocked for months, surrounded them.

Skye got up and handed a stocking to Nate, who seemed surprised. She and Noah watched as he delved in with the same enthusiasm as Noah. His had fewer toys, though. But she did think he liked the I.O.U gift certificate for any favour he wanted.

She was last and she loved how much trouble Nate had gone to and wondered who had helped him. She especially loved the l'octaine bubble bath and body cream.

She sent Noah off to get dressed, while she and Nate threw on some clothes. Nate finished first and went down to wait with Noah. They were under strict instructions not to go into the living room until she came down. She always tried to capture the awe and joy on Noah's face as he walked in a saw the presents.

Finally, she got downstairs where Nate handed her a cup of coffee. He was taking care of the camera today. He went in first and she followed. Noah was last, and as usual, the joy and happiness of seeing all the gifts laid out stole her breath.

She didn't think it would ever get old–that look of wonder on his little face. She sat on the sofa, Nate and Noah sat on the floor for present access obviously. They watched as Noah started opening presents.

He loved his Lego Millennium Falcon, he loved his signed shirt from Nate. Nate loved the Tag Heuer watch she'd bought him and the Xbox controller with his name on it from Noah.

Then Nate got up and reached on to the tree and took down a bauble she hadn't seen before and offered it to her. It had a picture of the three of them on it and underneath it said *Jones family* and the date.

She looked at Nate in slight confusion. The round bauble had a hinge and she realized then he had a big grin on his face and so did Noah. She lifted the hinge and inside the bauble was a platinum, princess cut, diamond engagement ring.

Her hand flew to her mouth and she lifted her head to see Nate down on one knee in front of her. Her eyes instantly filled with tears, her throat clogging with emotion.

"Skye. Since the moment I walked into that hospital room, my heart has belonged to you and this guy," he said indicating a giggling Noah. "Will you do me the greatest honour of becoming my wife, my partner, and my happily ever after?"

Instead of answering, she threw herself into his arms, toppling him over. He caught her as they fell backwards.

"Yes, I'll marry you!" Her tears were flowing now and she kissed him hard. She pulled back, her heart was so full of love and happiness she thought she would explode. Noah jumped up and shouted, "Yes! Now you can have my other present Nate."

Skye was momentarily taken aback since he hadn't bought Nate any other present that she knew of. Noah raced to his room and came back quickly, thrusting a package at Nate.

"Open it! Open it!" Noah said excitedly, jumping form one foot to the other. Nate carefully opened it and drew out a blue t-shirt. He held it up and Skye heard his breath hitch. He lowered the t-shirt and held out his arms for Noah. Noah jumped into Nate's arms and wound his little arms round Nate. She took the shirt and looked at what had made him so emotional.

It said *World's best Daddy*. Her eyes went blurry and she moved in to embrace both her boys.

"So, can I Nate? Can I call you Daddy now?"

Nate looked at Skye who nodded, too overwhelmed with joy to enunciate anything.

"Yes, buddy. You sure can."

They stood, the three of them huddled together. Their first Christmas as a family

"I love you, *mi amor*."

"I love you, too, baby, so much."

"I love you Mummy and Daddy! Can we finish opening presents now?"

"Yeah, buddy."

"Thanks, Dad!"

Skye and Nate looked at each other and saw the love, and hope in each other's eyes. This would be the first Happy Christmas of many for the Jones family.

The End

Sneak Peek

Lucy felt the walls around her start to close in as she listened to Jace's tortured words. How had this happened? She thought he loved her and yet Lizzie might be carrying his baby. *What the fuck*! Was she in some fucked up parallel universe where everything was going to shit? Her vision started to tunnel and she felt faint.

Dragging in a deep lungful is of air, she tried to steady her breathing. What was she going to do? She couldn't go home, tomorrow was Christmas day and that meant she was supposed to go to Lauren and Dane's for lunch. She couldn't do it, though–how could she sit there opposite her sister and her dad when her world had fallen apart? Dane would know something was up straight away. She was never able to hide anything from him. Where would she go?

She teared up as she thought of her big sister. How could this happen? When had this happened–why would she do this? She would never get over this betrayal.

Who else would know if Zack knew? Maybe everyone knew and it was just poor, sap Lucy who didn't know. Maybe that was why Lizzie was living at her dad's?

Feeling steady on her feet now. She ran down the stairs and jumped in her car. She put the car in gear and did the only thing she felt she could and ran to her happy place.

~~~

Jace hung up with Zack and ran his hand through his hair. He walked to the balcony to get some air. He looked down just in time to see Lucy run from his door to her car. She looked like the hounds of hell were after her.

His breathing almost stopped when he realized what she overheard. She'd think he'd betrayed her and didn't want her. The truth, though, was even more heinous than that. He had never betrayed her. He loved her with every fibre of his being, which is why he couldn't do this to her.

He couldn't tell her what had happened at the facility and what the possible outcome could be. But god, he couldn't let her believe he didn't love her. He should go after her and explain. Zack seemed to think she was made of sterner stuff, but he knew Lucy and knew she was vulnerable, especially where her family was concerned.

He should follow her to make sure she was okay. He grabbed his keys and headed out. What a shitty Christmas Eve.

Thank you for reading this book. You have no idea how much your support means to me and I love each and every one of you. When I started writing, I never believed I would get such a warm response. The readers who reach out to me to let me know they love what I do always make my day.

If you've enjoyed this story, please consider leaving a review on Amazon or Goodreads.

If you haven't read Healing Danger here is the link for Amazon.
https://www.amazon.co.uk/dp/B01GVC5WUS

If you would like to stay in touch, join my mailing list. I only send out emails when new releases or giveaways are running, so you will never be flooded with emails from me.

http://maddiewadeauthor.co.uk/newsletter/

Follow me of Facebook:

https://www.facebook.com/maddieuk/

Join my Maddie in the UK group, to talk all things Fortis once you have read the book:

https://www.facebook.com/groups/546325035557882/

Follow me on Twitter:

https://twitter.com/mwadeauthor

Check out my Pinterest boards–every team member has one!

https://uk.pinterest.com/maddie_wade/

Check out my Instagram:

https://www.instagram.com/mwadeauthor/

CPSIA information can be obtained
at www.ICGtesting.com
Printed in the USA
BVHW041830150121
597966BV00028B/334